Praise for Jaso

"*What the Hell Did I Just Read* is remin[...]
stuffed with layers of absurd pastic[...]

"Like Jonathan Swift for the internet age. His newest [...]
proof that he will be remembered as one of today's great satirists."
—*Nerdist* on *Futuristic Violence and Fancy Suits*

"While the story gleefully wallows in absurdity, thoughtful themes of addiction, perception, and the drive to do the right thing quickly emerge beneath the vivid and convoluted imagery. The plot's rapid pace holds the reader's attention to the truly bitter end."
—*Publishers Weekly* (starred review) on *What the Hell Did I Just Read*

"If you want a poignant, laugh-out-loud funny, disturbing, ridiculous, self-aware, socially relevant horror novel, then *This Book Is Full of Spiders: Seriously, Dude, Don't Touch It* is the one and only book for you."
—*SF Signal*

"Reads as if Bill Murray's world-weary *Ghostbusters* and sassy *Buffy the Vampire Slayer* spawned a slacker child–like *Clerks* with monsters . . . surprising, disturbing. and inventive."
—*Herald Sun* (Australia) on *John Dies at the End*

"*John Dies at the End* . . . [is] a case of the author trying to depict actual soul-sucking lunacy, and succeeding with flying colors."   —*Fangoria*

"[Pargin] once again achieves the perfect balance between sardonic humor and satirical digs at the digital age." —*Library Journal* (starred review) on *Zoey Punches the Future in the Dick*

"[Pargin] sneaks a nuanced examination of the surrealist nature of the digital age into the nonstop action, whipping technological, philosophical, and ethical questions into a wild romp that satirizes everything from the men's rights movement to gaming culture to the cult of celebrity. This is a brilliant modern parable disguised as pop fiction."   —*Publishers Weekly* on *Zoey Punches the Future in the Dick*

"It's his grounded sense of humanity that elevates this work."
—*Booklist* on *Zoey Punches the Future in the Dick*

ALSO BY JASON PARGIN

Zoey Punches the Future in the Dick
Futuristic Violence and Fancy Suits
What the Hell Did I Just Read
This Book Is Full of Spiders
John Dies at the End

IF THIS BOOK EXISTS, YOU'RE IN THE WRONG UNIVERSE

A NOVEL

JASON PARGIN

ST. MARTIN'S GRIFFIN
NEW YORK

Published in the United States by St. Martin's Griffin, an imprint of St. Martin's Publishing Group

www.stmartins.com

Designed by Steven Seighman

The Library of Congress has cataloged the hardcover edition as follows:

Names: Pargin, Jason, 1975– author.
Title: If this book exists, you're in the wrong universe : a novel / Jason Pargin.
Other titles: If this book exists, you are in the wrong universe
Description: First edition. | New York, NY : St. Martin's Press, 2022. | Series: John dies at the end ; 4
Identifiers: LCCN 2022019288 | ISBN 9781250195821 (hardcover) | ISBN 9781250195845 (ebook)
Subjects: LCGFT: Novels.
Classification: LCC PS3623.O5975 I34 2022 | DDC 813/.6—dc23/eng/ 20220425
LC record available at https://lccn.loc.gov/2022019288

ISBN 978-1-250-19583-8 (trade paperback)

First St. Martin's Griffin Edition: 2023

10 9 8 7 6 5 4 3

For Ginger the Dog, who is now barking at the garbage trucks in Heaven

BEFORE WE BEGIN THE STORY, PLEASE CONTACT THE AUTHOR IF YOU ARE INTERESTED IN PURCHASING ANY OF THE FOLLOWING ITEMS:

* A Haunted and/or Cursed Glass Patio Table

In good condition, the haunting/curse can be mitigated with any common tablecloth. It doesn't make a noise or anything, but the reflection in the glass is delayed by exactly twenty-four hours. For example, this morning I sat and ate cereal while staring at my phone, but in the reflection, I saw myself as I was at that time yesterday (eating cereal and staring at my phone while wearing a slightly cleaner version of this shirt). This can have unexpected consequences; the previous owner was a woman whose brunch was once disrupted by the sight of another woman's ass pressed against the surface from the other side. Specifically, it was the ass of the owner's young housekeeper, rocking back and forth in the act of lovemaking. The sex partner, the reflection revealed, was the table owner's husband. The glass is very strong; the previous owner tried to shatter it with a baseball bat, a brick, and a Range Rover, none of which left a scratch. One leg is a little shorter than the rest, so it does wobble, but you can stick a matchbook down there or something.

   PRICE: $75 OBO

* An Autobiography of Ernest Hemingway Entitled *A Congenital Liar* That Appears to Be from an Alternate Dimension

Copyrighted 1973, twelve years after the man died in our universe. WARNING: It's kind of boring and also makes the author sound like a real dick.

   PRICE: $5 OBO

* A DVD Box Set of a Ken Burns Documentary About a 1978 Mission to the Moon to Recover the Corpses of the Apollo 11 Astronauts

Also from an alternate dimension, I guess; also boring. Disc 4 has some scratches and may not play in your machine.

   PRICE: $10 OBO

* A Growing Chinchilla Coat

As in, the fur continues to grow. My friend John wore it for a while, says it is very warm, but he got tired of having to trim it every week.

   PRICE: $50 OBO

* A Rare (?) Copy of *Purity Warrior Magazine*

The June 2011 issue, again appears to be from another reality or whatever. The cover depicts victims being crucified in front of a strip club under the headline, "The Consecration of New Orleans"; includes articles on how to detect and report sins committed by your neighbor ("Fornicators will frequently refuse eye contact and wear dark clothing") and a list of ways to punish a child who has befriended a heretic ("#4. Simulate the fires of Hell by pressing a heated clothes iron against their most sensitive patch of skin!"). It's all pretty gross, but the ads are hilarious.

   PRICE: $3 OBO

* A "Cursed" PlayStation 2 Console

Causes all characters in all games to appear nude aside from their shoes and socks. Includes copies of *Madden NFL 2005*, *Wild Arms 4*, and *Summer Heat Beach Volleyball*. NOTE: Has not been tested with any games other than those, so I guess it's possible the console is normal and only those three games are cursed.

PRICE: $25 OBO, games included. No memory card.

* 62 Supposedly Haunted/Possessed/Cursed Dolls of Various Types and Sizes

Call for pricing and details.

* A "Cursed" Camera

An early-2000s Canon Rebel. Does not function as a regular camera. The previous owner claimed when she used it to photograph her home, the house in the photos was much larger, with new siding and neat hedges. When her husband used it to photograph his Toyota Corolla, the photo displayed it as a cocaine-white 1980s-era Lamborghini Countach. When I tried to test the camera by taking a mirror selfie with it, I saw only a normal photo of myself, but with a much larger penis. That must have broken the curse, because the camera now only produces that exact photo no matter who is using it (my girlfriend, Amy, and my friend John both tried it).

PRICE: $5 OBO
[Contact info redacted]

And now, we begin our tale . . .
Wait, one more thing:

A NOTE TO THE ROSSMAN FAMILY REGARDING REIMBURSEMENT FOR THEIR COOLER

"This is really about my wife," said the man with the parasite gnawing on his skull. "I'll let her explain."

He nodded to the chair next to him, where absolutely no one was sitting, then waited in silence like he was letting his "wife" speak. John, Amy, and I exchanged glances, none of us quite sure what to do.

The man appeared to be in his early fifties and had the kind of sad, droopy features that made him look like God hadn't finished inflating him. He had shown up at my apartment two minutes ago saying he'd been dropped off by the police, who apparently hadn't stuck around to explain. He was now sitting at my kitchen table with me, Amy, and the empty chair, John leaning on the counter and fidgeting with the red, white, and blue novelty cowboy hat in his hands.

The guy was now looking at us expectantly, like he was waiting for us to reply to whatever his invisible wife had just said. The parasite made soft grinding noises like an inmate surreptitiously sawing through prison bars. It was chewing away more of his skull, I guess—it had already made quite a hole up there. The parasite, or whatever word you'd use to describe the creature attached to the dude's head, had a body about the size of two fists, its sleek carapace a vivid purple. It had six long, black segmented legs, covered in bristles. It kind of looked like somebody had glued half a dozen fat centipedes to one of Prince's codpieces. The creature's legs were wrapped tightly around the man's face, one running under his nose like a mustache. Around its purple body was a ring of several eyes that twitched back and forth as if scanning the room, each moving and blinking at different intervals. Under the creature, I could see a sliver of the man's exposed, pink brain, surrounded by blood-matted hair. The victim seemed to not feel this at all and in general was clearly unaware of the creature's presence.

Amy finally broke the silence, bless her. "I'm sorry, can you explain why the police brought you here, again?"

The "here" she referred to was our apartment, which was small enough that the table we were sitting around overlapped the borders of the kitchenette, dining room, and living room. In general, I'm not sure either we or the apartment made for a reassuring first impression. Only two of the four kitchen chairs matched. Behind me, a window air conditioner was making a noise like it was being dragged down a gravel road. John was in the process of placing his garish American flag cowboy hat back atop his head; his outfit included a T-shirt featuring a photo of himself in which he was wearing the same hat and T-shirt he wore in real life. So the John in the photo was wearing a shirt featuring John wearing the photo of John wearing that shirt created a recursion that presumably continued for infinity. Below it was a pair of denim shorts that were too small. Much too small.

"Weren't you listening?" said the guy, suddenly exasperated. "Why does nobody listen? Eve and I went out to eat lunch at Loew's Steaks. The place was packed, because of the Fourth. We waited for an hour for a table. I sit down, we both order, the waitress brings my food but nothing for Eve. We ask *politely* what's going on with her order, and the bitch talks to me and just ignores Eve completely. I demanded to talk to a manager. He comes over and does the same, won't even look at her. Right, honey?"

He glanced to the empty chair, then nodded in confirmation.

"Right," he continued. "So, at this point, I'll admit I got a little agitated. Some words were exchanged. Long story short, the cops come, smirking at us while we try to tell the story. Like they think it's funny. They take us to the hospital for some damned reason; that was a total waste of time. I talk to a doctor and the doctor turns around and calls the cops again. Nobody will give me a straight answer, like everybody's in on the joke but us. The cops finally bring me here and tell me to do whatever you say. They actually giggled as they drove off. I thought they were taking me to the loony bin . . . ."

He trailed off as he glanced around at the apartment, scrutinizing it, now doing the exact same thing the purple creature on his head had seemingly done a moment ago: sizing us up. The man noted the centerpiece on the kitchen table, a glass sphere in a brass frame with a floating severed finger inside it. The finger was pointed right back at him, wobbling slightly as it hovered in the center. He then looked toward the counter, where there was a rusty iron box about the size of a human head, with a ragged hole where something had clawed its way out. Next to it was an oversize glass jar, half-full of crinkled dollar bills with a masking tape label that said:

"I'VE GOT A BAD FEELING ABOUT THIS" JAR

"Who are you people?"

I said, "Oh, that's John. This is Amy. My name is David. We, uh . . ."

"We work with the police sometimes," finished Amy. Well, that was definitely one way to put it.

The man seemed skeptical. It probably didn't help that I was wearing a T-shirt bearing a crudely drawn Stars and Stripes behind the words THIS FLAG NEVER FLAGS in a bombastic font (John had found it at a garage sale). Amy was holding a white straw hat and pink sunglasses in her lap, securing them with her right hand. She wasn't holding anything in her left because it didn't exist—that arm ended in a stump at the wrist. Old car accident. She was wearing so much sunscreen that the sweet chemical coconut stink was giving me a headache. When this guy had arrived, we had been on the way out to get a spot for the fireworks at the lake, and Amy knew she had to go in prepared, having descended from a tribe of freckled redheads in some sunless part of the world.

The parasite squeezed its legs around our visitor's head, digging furrows into his cheeks. I knew from experience that none of the parties involved in this incident—this guy, the cops, the doctors, the steak house waitstaff—had been able to see the little purple monster.

John lifted his patriotic Stetson and ran his hand through his hair, which at the moment was long enough to tickle his shoulders. "Let's back up," he said, replacing the hat. "Now, your name is . . ."

"Lou. This is Eve, like I said."

John glanced at the empty chair. "Sure. Uh, can I get you something to drink? Dave, what do we have?"

"Hmm, well, we have the beers out in the cooler in the van. In here we have, uh, tap water that kind of tastes like it came out of a squirt gun, some warm cans of the Walmart Dr. Pepper knockoff, Dr. Thunder, a bottle of 1985 vintage Austrian wine, and two cases of that Dan Aykroyd Crystal Head vodka—"

"Am I free to go?" asked Lou, somehow ignoring this amazing offer. "Why is everybody treating me like I got caught with a damned dirty bomb at the Vatican? It was a ruckus at a restaurant. Who cares? No punches got thrown. Or none that connected, anyhow. I don't know what's happening here."

"Is it okay if we ask a few questions?" asked Amy. "How long have you and Eve been together?"

"Why do you need to know *that*?"

"Please, this will only take a minute. We are actually here to help."

I was sure Amy believed that, but it seemed clear to me that regardless of what we did, this dude was already dead.

"Been with her about five months. Married for two. It's not official; got somebody local to do the ceremony back in May. So what?"

"And this problem, people acting like they don't want to acknowledge Eve, is this the first time it's happened? And if not, when did it start?"

Instead of answering, the man deferred to the empty chair, like his wife was answering instead.

When she'd apparently finished, he said, "I'll take her word for it. My memory's not so good these days. Chemo messes with your brain cells. But like she said, she doesn't go out much. Got the agoraphobia, on top of her disability. Doesn't like crowds. But I told her weeks ago, we're going out for the Fourth, so get yourself right in the head. Do whatever you've got to do, because we're going out in public and we're gonna enjoy the holiday. That's no way for somebody to live, cooped up like that."

I asked, "What was her response?"

"Just what I'd expected. She pitched a fit. I waited for it to blow over and told her this was what we were doing, if I had to carry her out of the house." He smiled at the empty chair. "She eventually came around."

I found myself staring at the parasite and realized it was making eye contact with me with about three of its eyes. It's entirely possible that up to that moment, it thought it was as invisible to me as it was to everyone else, and now knew otherwise.

What is your game here? I thought to myself, not entirely sure the parasite couldn't hear it.

I've been calling the creature a "parasite" because 1) half of all known living creatures are parasites, so that's always a fairly safe guess, and 2) it was allowing this guy to continue walking around and functioning as normal while it fed on him. That's what parasites do: climb on and leave the host healthy enough to do the hunting and gathering and fighting. It's a sound strategy if you can pull it off. As for why it would make him hallucinate a wife, I wasn't sure but also didn't particularly care.

I glanced down at my phone to check the time. We needed to get going; the good sitting spots around the lake would fill up fast (under the trees, where Amy wouldn't get roasted alive). I'm sorry if this seems cold, but it's not like this guy is the only one walking around with an interdimensional parasite leaching off his system. You've probably met somebody in that very situation in the last month. Hell, some of the people reading this are in that situation. Have you ever found yourself obsessively watching a TV show you don't actually enjoy? That probably means you're just watching your parasite's favorite show.

John said, "I want to try something, if that's okay." He dug into his front pocket and pulled out a quarter. He addressed the empty chair where "Eve" was supposedly sitting and said, "I'm going to toss this quarter to you. I want you to catch it and toss it back to me."

Lou immediately looked outraged. "I'm sorry, is that some kind of sick joke?"

"It's just a test. It will only take a moment."

"How do you expect her to catch it?" shouted Lou. "Look at her. You can clearly see that her arms don't work. Got the nerve damage, on account of her disorder."

John dropped the coin to the table and sighed, defeated. He glanced at me with a look that said it all: *This is one of the few days of the year when this town's collective day drinking isn't considered a tragedy, and we're missing it.*

To Lou, I said, "This may seem like another odd question, but do you get headaches?"

"No," he replied over the gravelly rasp of the parasite munching on his cranium. "Why would I get headaches?"

John suddenly got that alarming look he gets when he thinks he has an idea, then positioned himself behind the empty chair and said, "All right, let me try this. Just stay where you are, Eve. Are you ready? Here we go."

John pulled the chair away from the table, then picked up and lifted it above his head.

"Whoa!" said John. "Look at that. I'm the world's strongest man, apparently, because I just lifted your wife above my head like it was nothing."

"Are you out of your mind?" barked Lou. "She's standing right there. What's going on here? Am I being filmed? Is this a prank?"

I said, "I'm sorry. You've caught us at a bad time. We were just about to head to the lake to do that thing where we celebrate America's birthday by terrifying all of its dogs, so we've not been able to go through our normal meticulous process for evaluating a situation like yours. We're not trying to be rude, we're really not, but we have a narrow window in which I can get just drunk enough to not care that nobody has invented any new fireworks for the last thousand years."

"Then let us go," said Lou. "Hell, that's where we were headed. We were going to head out after we'd eaten. So why are we here?"

I looked pleadingly toward Amy and then John, silently soliciting ideas. Normally, the ideas were Amy's department, but she likely couldn't see the parasite and so probably didn't understand what exactly we were dealing with. John probably could see it, but I think he was out of ideas after the chair thing.

I sighed and said, "Look, I'm just going to rip off the Band-Aid. What if I told you that the reason people aren't interacting with your wife is because she doesn't exist?"

Amy recoiled. Usually we would try to use a little more finesse with this kind of thing, but, hey, you get what you pay for.

Lou smirked. "Now I know there are cameras recording this. Where are they? Is this for YouTube or TV? What, you get everybody together to work out some elaborate prank, and then I win a Hooters gift card at the end?"

Amy said, "He's telling you the truth. There are exactly four people in this room. Well, let me clarify—David said that Eve doesn't exist; I should say that none of us can perceive her. She's real to you, that's clear, but it appears she's *only* real to you."

"How—"

"You have a, uh, condition," I said. "There's no easy way to explain it, but it appears, from where I sit, that it's eventually going to kill you. Though none of us here are doctors, obviously. If you want to leave, we won't stop you. But something will have to be done about it at some point."

John said, "There's a chance you could become a danger to other people."

Lou scoffed, then grabbed a patch of air and held it, like he'd put his hand on his invisible wife's forearm.

"You hear that, babe? You don't exist! I'll have to remember that at tax time."

John said, "I don't know how to explain your, uh, condition because I don't know what you're ready to believe. So let me just put it like this: There's an invisible parasitic creature, probably from another dimension, chewing on your skull. It is apparently making you hallucinate Eve in order to manipulate you. Dave and I can see it, but no one else can, for reasons that would take forever to explain. But any parasite's strategy is going to start with going undetected. The exact way it's hiding itself and preventing you from feeling the huge hole in your skull isn't really important in the long run, is it? Oh, right, it has also chewed a huge hole in your skull."

Lou stood, forcing a laugh. "You people are nuts. Come on, honey." He turned as if to go, then stopped and looked down at the empty chair. "What do you mean? That doesn't even—"

He became still, then sat down again.

"But," he began, then stopped as if he'd been sharply told to shut up and listen for once in his damned life.

After a couple of minutes of this, he said, "Can you three step outside? We need to talk in private."

It was my home, so it didn't seem right that we had to go stand in the sun while he had his private conversation, but now didn't seem like the time to press the issue. We went out onto the landing of the rusty exterior stairway/bird toilet that led up to my second-floor apartment. When we closed the door behind us, Lou and "Eve" were already having a passionate heart-to-heart.

I raised my hand and said, "Who else votes that we just leave and go watch the fireworks?"

Ignoring this, Amy asked, "Exactly what are you guys seeing?"

"He's got a creature on his head, sucking on his brain."

John added, "It kind of looks like a robot crab wearing a purple bicycle helmet."

Amy closed her eyes and let out a breath. We'd seen people in similar situations before, and if there's a cure, we never came close to finding it. You pull the parasite off and the guy's brain comes out with it. A team of a dozen of the world's best neurosurgeons could maybe do something if they actually possessed the ability to see the creature or the wound, which they almost certainly wouldn't. There was no need for the three of us to say any of that out loud.

"You don't see it at all?"

Amy shook her head. "I can sense something is there but can't make it out."

If given enough time, she probably could. It was a skill one could acquire with practice, the way mechanics can tell what repairs your car needs just by looking at how expensive your shoes are. Seeing these entities had nothing to do with the anatomy of the human eye and everything to do with how the mind chooses to store memories—you might see it, but won't remember seeing it, even while you're actively looking at it. If you find that hard to grasp, keep in mind you've forgotten 99.99 percent of your life up to this point. Can you remember the face of a single cashier you've ever interacted with?

"So," I said, "which of the three options do we want to go with here?"

Again, I didn't need to state the three options, because they never changed: We could A) let the guy go, B) painlessly kill him and then try to somehow kill the parasite (and these creatures could be *very* hard to kill), or C) make some token effort to remove the thing and see if, by some miracle, Lou survived. If that last one is your knee-jerk answer, that just means you're new to this. Knowing that there's a near-zero chance he survives, wouldn't it be better to sneak up from behind and quickly put him out of his misery, instead of making the poor bastard spend his final hours strapped to my bed while we tried to wrestle an invisible monster off his face? And please note that when threatened, these creatures can do very nasty things to a human body and even nastier things to the mind, if not the soul.

Amy said, "He seems to be physically healthy at the moment, so we have some time to figure out what we can do for him. We could get an expert on the phone. Maybe Dr. Marconi is around, maybe he knows somebody . . . I don't know. As long as there's life, there's a chance."

"She's right," I said. "We should tell this guy to go home and stay by the phone until we can figure out what's going on. In the mean-time, we can go get drunk and watch fireworks, blow some shit up, eat some hot dogs. When we get up tomorrow afternoon, Amy can find some kind of freaky doctor or veterinarian who knows how to work on patients like this, and if not, we can always kill him then."

John shook his head, oscillating his patriotic hat in the process. "Nah, we can't let the guy run around free with that thing control-ling him. Did you see its eyes? It was listening the whole time; it knows we're onto it. Hell, it may be able to hear us out here, for all we know. What if we send him home and 'Eve' instructs him to go on a shooting spree? Or makes him build a little catapult to fling his own turds at a crowded playground?"

"Right," said Amy. "We have to keep him here, or somewhere, and keep an eye on him. You know what? You guys go watch the fireworks; I'll stay here and babysit Lou and try to contact somebody. It's fine, the Fourth always stops being fun once I'm the only non-drunk adult around anyway."

"I'm obviously not leaving you here," I replied. "If you're staying, I'm staying."

John said, "You're both assuming this guy's just going to hang out while you try to get on the phone with a . . . surgical exorcist, I guess? One who's working on the Fourth of July? So a surgical exorcist who hates America. The guy is going to demand you let him go, and at that point, you'll either have to let him become a public health hazard or shoot him."

"I don't want you shooting anybody today," said Amy, "even if solving a complicated problem by shooting it is just about the most American thing I can imagine. We have to get the guy to stay willingly."

"And since the parasite is controlling him," I said, "you mean we have to get the guy to stay willingly in a way that somehow won't alert the parasite that we're just stalling until we can get somebody to remove it."

John considered this, then said, "I wish we had a tranquilizer dart, something like that. Just knock the guy out."

"There's actually no such thing as a human tranquilizer dart," said Amy. "Same with knockout gas. It's only in movies; otherwise, police would use it all the time. What we could do is—"

There was a noise from inside the apartment, something falling hard to the floor. Then an interior door slammed shut. All our eyes snapped in that direction.

I muttered, "Get the shotgun."

We'd taken it out to the van earlier (we have a Fourth of July tradition where we soak bags of flour in gasoline, light them, and then blow them apart with buckshot). John ran down and returned with the shotgun a moment later, checking that there was a shell loaded into each of its five barrels. It was a custom item he'd just bought off the internet, and it had, to our knowledge, never been fired. But it had to have been of good quality; otherwise, the maker wouldn't have charged a whole forty-seven dollars for it.

If I leaned out over the landing, I could peer into the nearest window a little and get a look inside. I saw one chair knocked over at the kitchen table, but no sign of Lou. I scanned the floor to see if

Eve had detached and was maybe skittering around in there, looking for another brain to munch. I could detect no movement, but noticed the bedroom door was closed.

I made a hand signal to John to try to convey all of this, and he nodded as if he understood me. He readied the shotgun, checking that both bayonets were firmly attached. I threw the door open and then stepped aside. John went in, scanning the room with the five laser pointers that had been duct-taped to the barrels. Amy and I followed him in and, finding the kitchen/dining room/living room empty, the three of us advanced to the closed bedroom door. There was a thump, and the floor shook, like something heavy slammed against the wall. From behind the door came the sounds of rustling and a low, animalistic grunt, like someone or something struggling against their own body.

I held up three fingers to signal a countdown.

Three. Two. One.

I threw the bedroom door open. We all jumped inside, then froze.

Lou was completely nude, lying on our bed and frantically stabbing the air with his erection. His hands were groping the air above him, squeezing breasts that weren't there. Making passionate love to a woman only he could see.

The three of us stood in the doorway in silence—it was clear Lou either did not know we had entered or was too distracted to care—then we slowly backed out and closed the door. We all sat down at the kitchen table without saying a word. We stayed there for the next thirty minutes, occasional howls of ecstasy filling the tiny apartment.

Finally, Lou emerged, looking sheepish, now clothed but still wearing the purple parasite like a jaunty hat. "I'm so sorry about that," he said. "We got to talking and realized that we may never get another chance. We, uh, cleaned up as best we could."

Well, I thought, *at least I won't feel bad about killing him now.*

He sat down at the table and started to pull out a chair for Eve, then silently slid it back into place. "She, well, she explained everything to me."

I made eye contact with the parasite. "She, as in, your wife?"

"Yeah. Eve, or the thing that created her in my head . . . whatever or whoever is speaking through her, we talked it out. I know Eve isn't real. Or she isn't real in the way you would think of it. I know the chair is empty, I guess is what I mean. She said you guys spotted her, and she doesn't want to keep up the charade."

"So," I began, having been truly thrown for a loop by this, "you know you have a creature sucking on your brain? A purple thing with six legs?"

"Don't describe it to me. I'd rather not know. She—or it—offered to let me go look in a mirror, saying she would allow me to see her for real. I declined. I'm trying to keep my wits about me, and I don't think that would happen if I saw the situation as it really was."

I thought, *That's probably how a lot of marriages are maintained,* but didn't say it.

Amy asked, "Did she explain why she's doing this? Or what her purpose is?"

"She's lost," said Lou. "She wound up in this world but doesn't know how. She needed a host, so she picked me, because she detected that I wouldn't resist, not in my state. So she latched on and created this imaginary woman, my dream girl, to keep me pacified. To keep me mostly at home. It must have dug around in my thoughts, figured out what I needed." He shrugged.

"It was nice of her to come clean about it," said John. "You don't usually get that kind of honesty from parasites."

Lou scoffed. "She said that once she got to know me, she felt guilty about it. And it didn't work anyway. She's dying. She can't survive here. And when she dies, I'll die. We won't make it through the night, no matter what anybody does. That's why she agreed to go out with me today, even though there was no chance it wasn't going to be a calamity. It's our last day. Our bodies will shut down, and it's probably going to be very, very painful, she says. For both of us."

Amy said, "I'm sorry."

"Will you help me?" Lou asked Amy, having already identified which of us was likely to give him a yes.

"You just said nothing could be done," I said, kind of annoyed that this guy couldn't have had this epiphany on his own, before he screwed up our holiday.

Lou paused in a manner that I now recognized was him letting Eve talk, then said, "We want you to do it for us. If you don't mind."

"Do . . . what?" asked Amy. But she already knew.

"We would like this one last evening together. Then we want you to kill us. As painlessly as possible. Maybe a bullet through my head and her . . . it . . . at the same time. You guys have experience with this sort of thing, yes? That's why the cops brought me here? Afterward, put the gun in my dead hand and leave me wherever. Let everyone think I did it to myself. Everyone already thinks I went crazy, so . . ." He shrugged and wiped a tear from his left eye. The creature scooted one of its segmented legs aside so that he could do it.

I deferred to Amy because this seemed like the kind of plan she would object to.

She said, "I don't think I can do that," which I noted wasn't the same as saying it shouldn't be done.

John said, "I can do it, if I get a couple of drinks in me."

"We could do it at the lake," suggested Lou. "In the woods, out away from the people, where we can still see the fireworks. Do it at the finale, when everything is going off at once, to hide the noise. Eve and I will sit there and hold hands, and we'll go out together. Or it'll seem like we're holding hands, to us. You know what I mean."

I said, "You don't have any family or friends around here?"

He shook his head.

I realized it probably sounded like I was asking if he had loved ones who could help guide him through this difficult time, but what I was actually asking was if there was anyone who might raise a stink about the cops not looking too closely into his "suicide" (and they wouldn't). I didn't want to do it and then find out the guy's brother was our congressman or some shit.

Amy asked, "If Eve feels so bad about this, why can't she just detach herself? It's obvious that you're healthy enough to walk and talk, so why not go to the hospital, say goodbye to Eve, and tell the doctors you need them to rebuild that side of your skull? Without her camouflage, the wound will be visible, won't it?"

"She can't detach. Her body is merged with my brain and nerves, all that stuff in there. It was the only way she could interact with our world, using my eyes and ears. There's no separating—we're one thing now. I'd end it myself, but I don't think I can bring myself to pull the trigger. Too scared. And I know I sound nuttier with every word I say, but with what I've had with her over the last few months . . . I really don't mind. I haven't made much of my life, spent most of it high, getting fired from shit jobs. I said earlier that she detected I was too weak to resist the attachment, and what she meant was that I didn't have much time left regardless. Got cancer, pancreas. But me and her have had such a good time together . . . it's been a gift, to spend my final months like this. I'm telling you guys, I'm okay with it."

Amy asked Lou to excuse us and led John and me back out to the landing.

I closed the door behind me and whispered, "This feels like a trap."

Amy glanced toward the kitchen and said, "How?"

"Maybe this parasite wants us to kill this dude. Maybe that was the whole point. Maybe it spawned a hallucination purely to lead him to this."

"Why would she need us to do it?" asked John. "Eve can turn the dude's brain into Sloppy Joe anytime she wants just by doing this." He twirled his finger around.

"Maybe it's toying with us. Wants to make us do it, just for the fun of it."

Amy asked, "So what do you suggest?"

I lowered my voice even more. "Well, for one, it's irresponsible to take that creature out to the crowded lake. Maybe we get him out there and it jumps off this guy and latches onto somebody else's head. Maybe *that's* its plan."

"But he's been living among the public for months. She could have done that at the restaurant, the hospital, the cop car on the way over, anywhere."

John asked, "You think she's just telling the truth?"

"Why not? Not everything is an evil scheme."

I said, "Hold on. Are you now in favor of us taking him to the lake and shooting him in the head?"

"No. I don't know. How about we take him to the fireworks and let him eat a funnel cake and enjoy the night. While we're there, we try to talk him out of it. Maybe Eve is wrong, maybe there's a way to live on. Maybe we can find some kind of solution. I don't know."

John said, "I'm fine with that." He looked at me. "You want to make it unanimous?"

I shrugged. "I'm outvoted either way."

"The way I figure it, when you're given multiple choices with no way of knowing which one is right, you just do the easiest—that's called 'efficiency.' In this case, we pick the choice that lets us also go drink and watch fireworks."

Amy said, "Well, if at the end of the night we may have to, uh, cure this guy, then you probably shouldn't drink beforehand."

John adjusted his Stetson and said, "Oh, I'm gonna get drunk *as hell*."

We live in a part of the world where everyday citizens can still get genuine "blow your fingers off" fireworks from roadside stands starting around May. The professional fireworks show at the lake would kick off at around 9:00 p.m., but prior to that point, the gathering would feature plenty of increasingly inebriated spectators setting off all sorts of irresponsible explosives that may or may not have been made in a garage. Some didn't even buy their fireworks; they just got creative with what they had on hand. Last year, a guy filled giant balloons from tanks of oxygen and acetylene from a blowtorch and then detonated them, birthing a huge flash of orange and a deep *boom* that rolled across the water and echoed off the hills. The year before, an old guy brought a box of white chunks of rock that Amy said must have been pure sodium; he would chuck them into the lake, where they would fizzle and then explode, sending up a geyser like a cannon shot from a pirate ship. Mass gatherings in this town always made for great people-watching, especially if you liked seeing people get loaded into an ambulance.

John parked along a gravel road near the lake, and the four of us hauled lawn chairs and a cooler toward the sound of music and minor explosions. Once we got close enough that the crowd came into view, Lou stopped.

"If it's okay, we wanna go off on our own," he said, "maybe deeper into the woods, away from the people."

Before I could answer, Amy replied, "Okay, we'll come to check on you," and kept walking.

John and I stayed where we were. It was bad enough that we were bringing this creature near a crowd of potential victims, but now this guy—if he was even in control of his own brain at all—was wandering off to where he wouldn't be observed.

I said, "I'm not sure that's such a great idea."

Lou said, "I want to be able to talk to Eve. My wife. For the last time. Out there, around the people, I'll just look like I'm crazy. I'll scare the kids. We'll stay close to the lake, I promise. I'm not looking to get lost out there and eaten by a coyote."

We still didn't move.

He said, "*Please.* Give me this."

Amy said, "Come on, guys. We have to get a spot."

We followed her, as always, and Lou veered off and disappeared into the trees. I was pretty sure that Eve was making eye contact with me the whole way.

The Independence Day revelers were spread out in a grassy field between the lake and the woods, a constellation of picnic blankets and lawn chairs around a huddle of decrepit food stands and carnival games under faded tents. The good shady spots we were hoping for back at the edge of the woods were, in fact, all occupied. We eventually found a couple of John's friends—Vinnie and his boyfriend, Other Vinnie—who had set up their own shade under a blue tarp and poles. They let us squeeze ourselves in with them in exchange for John sharing some of his weed. Then, within an hour, the couple got into a fistfight over one of the carnival games (it was one of those punch-the-bag-and-measure-your-strength games, and Other Vinnie insisted on clowning Vinnie about getting a lower score), and after they were both hauled off by the cops, we had their tarp to ourselves.

Some part of my brain kept reminding me that we were probably going to have to explode a dude's head at the end of the night, but, as usual, a few beers helped me get proper perspective on the whole thing. If you think about it, anxiety is also a kind of parasite. And isn't it unpatriotic to spend America's birthday distracted by nonsense? Sometimes when life's Warning Light won't stop flashing, the best thing you can do is just put some electrician's tape over it. Every now and then, Amy would get up and go check on Lou and his passenger, each time returning to say that their situation was unchanged.

Once the sun went down and it was clearly getting to be time for the professional fireworks, John leaned over to us and said, "Are we still doing this?"

"I want to talk to them one more time," said Amy. "I want David to come with me; maybe we can tag-team it."

"To accomplish what?" I asked. "To try to convince the guy that it's better to die horribly than to get quickly snuffed out while cuddling his imaginary wife? I don't think I'm going to be much help, even though I don't particularly want to do the shooting."

Instead of replying, Amy gave me a hard look that yanked me to my feet. I followed her to a poorly maintained trail through the woods, a path booby-trapped with dangling branches and broken beer bottles. It was just getting dark around the lake, but in the dense woods, it was already midnight. Amy plunged ahead like she knew the path, so I followed, though neither of us had flashlights and the drunken ground was tilting beneath my feet. I stomped through dead leaves and nearly tripped over exposed roots. Bugs buzzed around my ears. I lost all sense of direction. The pops and thuds from the lake behind me made me feel like we were fleeing a war zone.

The wilderness is stupid and should be burned to the ground.

There was a moment when I wasn't sure if I was even on the trail anymore, and I imagined my emaciated corpse getting found out here weeks from now, wild animals having chewed out my eyes and genitals. Then everything lit up red around me. It was the first of the main fireworks going off, a burst of hellfire in the sky followed by the thump of detonation a moment later, the sound trailing the light. In that moment of illumination, I saw movement up ahead.

Amy, on the ground.

Flailing limbs. Grunts. Heavy breathing.

The firework faded, and I rushed ahead blindly, the flash having robbed me of my night vision. A dangling branch raked across my forehead, drawing blood. There was another sunburst, a white light that illuminated a clearing in the woods. I saw Amy kneeling over Lou, who was thrashing around in the leaves.

"Hey!" I yelled. "Are you okay?"

"He's having a seizure!"

As I arrived at the spot, another explosion in the sky revealed the man's rolled-back eyes and foam oozing from his mouth.

"Do we, like, shove a wallet or something between his teeth?"

"No, no. You don't do anything for a seizure except make sure they don't hurt themselves. He landed on top of a beer bottle, but I got it out from under him. You just have to let it run its course."

This was fortunate, because I happen to have an advanced certificate in hanging back and letting things run their course. After about a minute of thrashing, Lou went still. I thought he was dead for a blissful moment, but then he blinked and sat up, like he was surprised to be there. A prolonged burst overhead like the explosion of the Death Star illuminated the clearing, and I got a glimpse of the parasite. Eve appeared *dried out,* somehow. There were little cracks on its carapace, one of its eyes had closed, and one of its segmented legs was dangling free, like it no longer had the strength to hang on. It seemed like Eve had been telling the truth: It was dying.

Lou caught his breath and finally noted our presence. "I'm okay," he grunted. "Well, I'm not okay; I can't stand up. Whatever part of my brain kept my balance has checked out for good. My left arm's gone numb. Eve says she's holding on as long as she can, but time is running out. She tells me it's like a person trying to survive on a planet where the atmosphere is poison. She keeps apologizing. She's crying right now, seeing what she's done to me." He waved his hand in front of his right eye. "Think I'm starting to go blind, too. She said that would happen. It's okay, honey. It really is. We're in this together."

Amy said, "Let us take you to a hospital. There may be experts in this kind of thing, maybe somebody knows how to—"

"If I'd wanted that," he interrupted with a dismissive wave, "I'd have asked you to take me there myself. What's the best that could happen? They turn me into a vegetable to run up a million bucks in medical debt until the cancer eats me alive? Look, if you don't wanna do it, leave me the gun. I'll try to do it myself. I'd just ask that if I mess it up, you finish the job. On both of us. Eve is suffering, too. More than me, I think, though she tries not to let on."

I said, "No, we'll do it."

A fresh flash of orange lit up the scene, the pop arriving a second later. That delay always freaked me out as a kid, like time was broken, the signal of reality out of sync.

"Wait until the finale, like I said—" Lou stopped to attend to something Eve was saying, then grinned broadly. "She's never seen fireworks before. She's loving it, even through the pain."

I dug out my phone and texted John.

hey get the shotgun we need to shoot this dude

After a minute he replied,

k be there in a sec

About ten minutes later, a flashlight beam stabbed its way through the trees, and then John stepped into the clearing with the shotgun. I asked Amy if she wanted to stay for this part. She didn't answer, but also didn't leave. I mean, she'd definitely seen people die before.

Lou glanced at John, noted the gun, then turned back to watch the fireworks.

He took a deep breath and let it out slowly, as if to savor his final air. "This world, it really is beautiful sometimes. Eve said that just now. I agree. I wish I'd stopped to appreciate it more. But that's okay. It's all okay. We're gonna sit here and watch the fireworks, and you do it whenever you're ready."

He drew his knees up to his chest. The finale began, the ground crew launching all their remaining arsenal, filling the sky with blooms of magnesium. Amy turned away from Lou. I stepped back. Then John did what I had already suspected he would do: He aimed the shotgun at the parasite, but not directly into Lou's skull like the man had requested. He angled it exactly how you would if you were trying to blow the parasite free, maybe scraping the guy's skull with pellets in the process. I know that probably sounds ridiculous, since blowing away the parasite would surely kill the man just as quickly, the thing's tentacles yanking out brain parts as it flew. But there was a difference between this man dying from our projectiles and dying as a side effect of us killing the creature who'd hijacked him. If you don't see the difference because the outcome is the same either way, well, see if you feel the same when it's your finger on the trigger.

John hesitated only for the amount of time it took him to get the aim just right. He fired, and the parasite went flying, leaving a wound in Lou's skull the size of a grapefruit. The man continued to sit upright for just a moment, before his brains came tumbling out of his skull. His purple, bulbous brains, spilling out and rolling away . . .

Hmm. That doesn't seem right.

What was falling out of Lou's skull was a stream of what looked like purple golf balls. Dozens of them, more than what could be contained in a human cranium. His body sank to the ground, but he wasn't slumping over—he was *deflating*. Within seconds, Lou's entire head just went flat, then his chest and arms and torso followed suit. It was like he contained no bones or musculature, just a sack of skin full of hundreds of those little balls.

No, not balls.

Eggs.

The eruption of fireworks illuminated the spheres rolling past my shoes. They were translucent, and inside each ball was a black, squirming shadow.

Amy jumped back at the sight of them. "Wha—*how was he even walking?*"

I started to say something to John, but he wasn't there anymore. I found him stomping off into the woods, toward the lake.

He said, "She's getting away!"

"What?"

"Eve's still alive! She landed and took off through the woods! She's heading toward the people!"

Looking for a new goddamned host.

Amy and I took off in that direction, blindly trusting that John was even going the right way. I looked back at the spot where Lou had been. He was now just a popped skin balloon, completely flat. It even seemed like his remains were oozing and melting, his clothes deteriorating right along with the rest, like they'd always been a part of him.

What the—?

I wasn't sure about leaving the eggs behind (if they hatched, who knew when we'd have another normal holiday?), and I was about to ask if I should go back and stomp on them or something. But at that moment, a gunshot rang out, a noise closer and sharper than any of the fireworks. I turned and plunged into the woods toward John—we were not on any kind of trail—and found him aiming at the ground. He apparently hadn't hit his target, because he took off running again, dodging around tree trunks and leaping over protruding roots. The idiot was going to trip and blow his own head off. I tried to follow, but I was watching him instead of my own feet, and then I was the one who tripped, landing hard and scraping up my hands.

Amy raced past me and said, "Come on!" like I was down there taking a nap. I struggled to my feet and kind of got lost again, but eventually, the lake came into view.

The grand finale of the fireworks was still raging across the sky like an interstellar battle that the combatants intended to win purely on style points. I saw the silhouette of John holding the shotgun, Amy behind him. They were standing right among the seated crowd, a family on one side of them and a row of college-age kids on the other. All eyes were turned upward. Somewhere, a terrified baby was crying, the poor kid probably thinking the world was coming to an end.

I caught up to them and scoured the ground until—

"There!"

Amy was pointing. Eve was up ahead, skittering between a couple of old women in lawn chairs. The fireworks died out overhead, and darkness claimed the lake. I heard drunken applause. John sprinted up with his flashlight and found Eve with the beam—

It was dragging something.

A severed human arm.

Wait, no. It was *growing* an arm, like it was birthing a fully grown man, one limb at a time. The fingers were wiggling around like they were testing their range of motion, the arm clothed in a dark shirt-sleeve. A moment later came a shoulder and a neck, then a bubble of skin appeared, grew hair, and formed itself into a head. The parasite had stopped moving because it was now dragging about 20 percent of a fully grown and fully dressed human and was rapidly trying to birth the rest of it.

The face it had created, its features still only partially formed, turned to look at us and said, "Haha! Your fireworks suck shit!"

Eve, the head, arm, and now part of another arm tried to run away from us, the limbs clumsily slapping the ground along with Eve's six spindly legs. John waited for the monstrosity to get clear of the nearest group of revelers and then ran up and held the shotgun just inches away from the face Eve had secreted from its underbelly.

He fired. The new head immediately deflated, splattering dark fluid and sputtering like a released balloon. Spectators nearby jumped and turned but mostly seemed annoyed, probably thinking somebody had tossed a cherry bomb among them as a prank. John aimed again, but Eve tore itself free from the partial body it'd tried to spawn and took off through the crowd once more. I pursued the creature, intending to, I guess, punch it to death? I didn't even have a weapon.

When I had drawn near enough, I dove, snatching Eve with both hands. The parasite thrashed in my grip, the weird hairs on its legs scraping my skin. One leg reached out and wrapped itself around a full can of beer that had rolled into the grass, and then started repeatedly smacking me in the face with it.

"Ow! Fuck!"

From behind me, I heard Amy say, "Excuse me!"

She had grabbed a nearby cooler, dumping its contents onto the grass over the protests of the family sitting nearby. She ran over and held the cooler open. I threw the creature inside. Amy slammed the lid and flung her body on top to hold it shut.

I was aware of people standing all around us now, the owners of the cooler yelling at Amy. Some of the people recognized us, and that did nothing to alleviate their annoyance.

John arrived then, the shotgun resting against his shoulder. "It's all right. It was a rattlesnake. We're with animal control. There's a whole bunch of 'em back there, in the woods. A little kid got bit and had to go to the hospital. We need to commandeer this cooler."

"Fuck off!" suggested the father of the cooler family. "You're not with animal control. You're gonna clean all this up and give me my cooler back."

"Okay, but there is actually a snake in here," said Amy. "We'll bring it right back, I promise. The cooler, not the snake."

As usual, the bystanders accepted Amy's reassurances after refusing ours. Pushing the blatant sexism out of my mind, I picked up the cooler and held it against my body, hugging it closed while Eve thrashed around inside. We all headed toward the gravel road, in the direction of where we'd parked the van. We passed the two Vinnies, themselves heading toward where they'd parked their giant pickup, carrying their rolled-up tarp between them. John asked them how they got out of jail so fast, and Other Vinnie said he didn't know what the hell John was talking about. I didn't think anything of it at the time. We'd had other things going on.

I shouted ahead to John, "Hey, we have to see about those eggs."

"I didn't forget."

When he reached the van, he retrieved a red plastic gasoline can and found some duct tape to hold the cooler closed. Obviously, we didn't know if that would be enough to keep Eve contained, so we brought the cooler with us as we headed to the spot where Lou had deflated. There was now no sign of the man himself. All that remained was the pile of eggs, dozens of them. John uncapped the gas can.

Amy said, "Kick them into a pile. And don't let the fire spread. Everything is pretty dry out here."

"Don't you worry," said John as he soaked the eggs. "Fire and I are old lovers. You treat her with respect, give her room to breathe, and everything will be juuuuust fine."

Four hours later, we watched from afar as the city mobilized to put out the massive forest fire we'd started. The three of us were in the van, Amy and John up front, me in the back, perched on top of the cooler. The parasite had gone quiet a while ago. Maybe it had suffocated?

John was now leaning out of the driver's-side window, talking to a cop.

"Everybody saw you go into the woods," said the policeman. "A minute later, it's going up like the devil's shithouse. Were you shootin' flaming bags of flour back there?"

"You wanna know the truth?" asked John. I leaned forward a little, actually eager to hear what he told the guy. "That dude you dropped off at Dave's place? The guy having the hallucinations? He asks us to take him with us to the fireworks, then he goes back to the woods. One thing led to another, and we had to deal with him with gasoline and a lighter. It could have gone way worse than it did."

"What guy?"

"Lou something? Went nuts at Loew's? I don't know who dropped him off at our place, but somebody did."

"Loew's shut down two weeks ago. Nobody took anybody to your house. Why would we even do that?"

"He said you'd dropped him off."

"Did you see a squad car?"

"No, but he had to get there somehow. Unless . . ."

John turned back to me.

"There was no guy, was there? That parasite probably turned up at your place and inflated 'Lou' just to trick us into giving it a ride to the fireworks. He was just a walking egg sac. I bet those babies need to feed after they hatch, and Momma was just trying to get to the crowd."

The cop rubbed his forehead and said, "Have you people ever thought about moving away? I think the whole town would chip in for a U-Haul. Get the hell out of here."

We wound up walking home because John and I had both been drinking and Amy doesn't have a driver's license or any capacity for compromise. We went back to John's house because it was closer, spending much of the walk discussing what we were going to do with Eve. John noted that the point-blank shotgun blast hadn't even left a smudge on her shell (unlike the eggs, which had instantly popped and vaporized in contact with the fire).

I'm not going to go into details, because what occurred next doesn't cast us in a good light as professionals. I'll just say that over the next few hours, we discovered that Eve's carapace could not be penetrated or even damaged by a drill, nail gun, blowtorch, chain saw, sledgehammer, or bolt cutters. The creature could not be boiled like a lobster or repulsed with crosses or holy water. It was extremely annoyed by certain music but showed no signs of permanent damage even after prolonged exposure to John's guitar.

The next morning, John announced that he had one last thing he wanted to try. He dug around in his garage until he found a couple of five-gallon buckets of clear resin he'd been saving for a craft project (he'd wanted to make a clear, double-necked electric guitar with a bunch of child-size plastic hands positioned inside as if they were clawing to get out). We mixed the thick liquid and dumped it into the cooler, submerging Eve. It took a few days to fully cure, at which point the parasite was suspended in a solid, clear block, like it had been frozen in ice. We'd had to destroy the cooler with crowbars to get it free, but the result actually made for a pretty cool piece of art.

So anyway, Mr. and Mrs. Rossman, that's what happened to your cooler. This model (the 30 Qt. X-Treme Arctic Tundra Icebox) sells for $24.99 at Walmart. Accounting for depreciation, we are including a check for $13 as reimbursement.

—Amy, David, and John

Okay, now here's the story. It picks up about seven weeks later. Thanks for your patience:

SATURDAY, AUGUST 20, 3:33 A.M.
MARSHMALLOWS
HUNGER AT 41%

BLOOD EVERYWHERE GUY CHOPPED UP IN MY WALL GET HERE
ASAP I THINK I LEFT MY PHONE CHARGER THERE

I had been staring silently at that text message for several minutes. John had sent it, which I had known the moment the phone had dinged. No one else would text me at this hour. Or any other hour, really.

The phone hadn't woken me up. I'd gone to bed at 1:00 a.m., but had just tossed and turned, tormented by two slices of days-old pizza I'd left uneaten in a box on the counter, knowing I would be unable to sleep until I got up to finish the job. I'd then had a moment of doubt as to whether it was safe to eat sausage pizza that had been sitting at room temperature for that long, so I looked up that information on my phone while standing at the kitchen counter, then wound up tumbling down a rabbit hole of Wikipedia links about the history of food preservation. So now I was sitting on my kitchen floor, eating rubbery room-temperature pizza and reading about how, in Ireland, they routinely find four-thousand-year-old containers of butter that ancient tribes had sunk into the bog for preservation.

It's still edible; people have actually tried it. Surprisingly, they say it tastes like shit.

A second messaged dinged in:

I THINK ITS BY THE TOASTER

I was going to have to get dressed and go, I knew that. John would just keep messaging me until I did. And yet, my body didn't move. In my current state of mind, it felt like I was being asked to lie facedown and drag myself across town with my eyelids. Depression means expending all your energy to avoid having to expend energy. I wish someone would invent a pill that would give me the motivation to go pick up my Lexapro refill.

My phone dinged again. This time, an image. It appeared to be a pile of meat cut into slabs a few inches thick, with human body parts sprinkled around as a garnish. I saw fingers and half of a foot and a dead face attached to a skull that looked like it had been bisected by a laser, brains oozing out the back. It was all intertwined with scraps of clothing soaked black with blood.

I tore off a bite of pizza and chewed. It was like a slab of pizza-flavored gum that had been scraped off a schoolboy's desk. There was nothing here to do or watch; there was no one to talk to. I was miserable where I was, and I would fight anyone who tried to make me leave. I realized this was madness, that I was stuck in a self-pity loop that was turning me into a zombie. I visualized myself throwing away the remaining pizza, getting dressed, brushing my hair, and then driving to see what crisis John had encountered or, more likely, created. Then I congratulated myself for having successfully visualized this and, having not moved an inch, gnawed off another hunk of a substance that tasted like pizza in the way that getting splashed by a toilet feels like a waterslide. It tasted like the final entry in an experiment to see what, if anything, Americans won't eat. It tasted like a meal that was prepared sarcastically.

A fourth message dinged in. It was another image, this one of

John's hand holding a thin black cable attached to a plug. With it came the caption:

LIKE THIS ONLY WHITE

I stuffed the rest of the pizza in my mouth and managed to shuffle my way into the apartment's only bedroom. I had developed a habit of glancing over to the bed every time I passed, as if I'd magically find Amy there again, the lump under the blankets and the mess of copper hair spilling out, taking her half of the bed out of the middle. I didn't bother this time. That void could be felt from outer space.

I tried to think of what clothes would be most appropriate for dealing with a sliced-up corpse, and while I was thinking of that, I robotically pulled on the first T-shirt and pair of cargo shorts I came across on the floor. I went to the fridge, grabbed a can of a locally produced red energy drink called Fight Piss, and headed out, feeling like I had done all of this before.

I stepped out onto the rusty metal stairway to find the August night air had been pre-sweated for my convenience. My apartment sits at the second floor of a brick building that looks like it was painted with mayonnaise, the first floor of which used to be an establishment called the Venus Flytrap Sex Shop. The dead neon sign bearing that name still hung over the darkened store entrance, though the big pink cursive X in the third word was missing because somebody had smashed it with a thrown chunk of pavement. That somebody had been me.

The couple who had owned the store had taken an insurance buyout after the place got damaged in a flood last year. They'd quickly left town, either forgetting to evict us from the apartment above or deciding they just didn't care. The good news was that the utilities had stayed on, and I had no idea who was paying for them, if anyone. I had been running the little window air conditioner day and night for several weeks, seeing how much free juice I could extract before somebody finally noticed and cut it off. The bad news was that they had also left that neon sign on, apparently intending for it to forever buzz pinkly outside my window. It had only taken twelve throws to break it.

I slid into my cherry-red 1967 Chevy Impala, a car that had been given to me by a former client, and by "given," I mean the guy who had owned it is now a vaporized corpse, and his wife left town without saying anything about the car. I keep getting stopped at red lights by bros yelling compliments at me and asking what's under the hood. I have no idea, I don't know anything about cars, and right now, this Impala's defining feature is that it doesn't have AC and the upholstery gets so sticky that you'd think a toddler had been eating waffles in it. Also, it's hard to steer, and every pothole rattles my teeth. I could probably pick up a lot of girls in it, though, if I was interested in that.

Without a glance into the back seat, I said, "I wondered when you'd show up."

I checked the back seat, but it was empty. It usually was, but I have been ambushed by bad guys waiting in a dark back seat before, so every time I get in, I try to say something to mess with them, just in case. I'm thinking about switching it to, "I'm surprised you came alone." Plant some doubt in their mind.

I turned out of the parking lot, the streets mostly deserted at this hour. I passed by a construction site next door. The shop that had burned a while back was being replaced by another payday loan operation. Some kid had spray-painted a swastika on the unfinished plywood followed by a slur, then some kind soul had come in with their own can of paint and turned the swastika into a cartoon stick figure in a running pose, then had painted over two letters in the scrawl below it so that it now read NO JOGGERS. The racist had never come back to paint a rebuttal, so I took that as progress. Next door was a convenience store called Open 24-7-365, with a slogan below it proclaiming, "We Are Always Here For You!" It was closed.

You know how you'll see a department store go out of business, and then that fall, a sad Halloween supply store will set up in its place? Well, imagine if that happened to an entire city. As always, the actual name of this place will remain undisclosed as to prevent any further tourist deaths. "Undisclosed" was supposedly nice in the 1980s, but it was trash when I was in high school a little over a decade ago and, since then, we've gone from four McDonald's locations to one (two burned down; another was closed after a local news investigation detected horse DNA in their milkshakes). The high school basketball team only has four players, and one of them is thirty-six years old. The number one industry is multilevel marketing schemes, with meth manufacturing coming in a close second. There's a citywide ordinance that all corpses must have their legs and arms severed before burial.

If that doesn't sound like a tourist trap to you, well, you're imagining the wrong kind of tourist. On any given day, you can find multiple squads of college kids with cameras looking for an abandoned warehouse or factory to spelunk, hoping to capture some phenomenon or other for their YouTube channel. Once, inside the infamous abandoned shopping mall, a group of ghost hunters pursued noises and voices in the darkness only to discover they'd been tracking another group of ghost hunters filming for their own channel. These people rarely turned up anything real (that they or their viewers were able to see anyway), but sometimes a group will step into a darkened structure and simply never come back out. Which, of course, only ensures more will follow. Meanwhile, just in the last week, John and I had met with:

- A woman who claimed her dead son was texting her photos of his torture chamber in Hell;
- A man who said his dog had been replaced by another, identical dog that instead of barking would melodically sing the phrase, "Kiss my shit!";

- A young woman who discovered a hole in her bedroom wall in which a twitching, lecherous eye would sometimes appear, despite the fact that on the other side of the wall was her own living room and she lived alone.

Our solutions to those problems had been, in order, to take the woman's phone and block her son's number, to laugh at the dog until the owner made us leave, and to sloppily spackle over the hole. Only one of the three paid us anything. These days we mostly get by on—

Hold on, as I get closer to the Open 24-7-365, it looks like it is in fact open for business; the lights just weren't very bright inside. That's too bad; it would have been really poignant if they'd been closed.

What was I talking about? Eh, it doesn't matter. It's all routine for me, like how the people who live in Pisa probably don't get the fascination with their shitty leaning tower. John keeps up with that stuff more than I do. He says the town's lore among ghost chasers changes every six months or so. Last year, all the YouTubers were saying they had proof that Undisclosed is a testing facility for military PSYOPS warfare, seeing how far reality can be warped via hallucinogens and holograms before a society descends into chaos. Before that, they all insisted the town was full of doppelgängers that can transform into horrific monsters via nanobots that rearrange cells on the fly (which is, at best, a half-truth). An amateur astronomer messaged us around Christmas claiming that he spotted a large geosynchronous satellite parked overhead that doesn't turn up on any records and is almost the size of the International Space Station. Maybe that'll be the new thing. I haven't heard a theory about it, but I've no doubt somebody will cook one up, say it's beaming reality-bending microwaves at us or something. Humans will twist themselves into knots rather than admit that the unknown might be unknowable.

A few minutes and a couple of lazily blinking stoplights later, I arrived in what was considered a pretty good neighborhood in this moldy bathroom carpet of a town. John's place came into view, a two-story house that was mostly painted yellow, aside from a band of the prior black paint at the top that we couldn't reach because his ladder got stolen during the job and he never got around to replacing it. The house was surrounded by a chain-link fence bearing multiple painted signs that said:

DO NOT ENTER
YOU WILL BE SHOT BY ROBOTS
THROW DELIVERIES ONTO PORCH

Then with a scrawled addition at the bottom:

EXCEPT PIZZA (YELL FROM YARD)

John met me at his back gate (his alarm system screeched anytime someone pulled into the driveway or drove past, or if it just got bored and felt like screeching).

He was tying his long hair back into a ponytail as if preparing for some hard labor and, with some urgency, asked, "Did you bring the charger?"

"No, sorry. I forgot to look. Things have been really hectic tonight. What's happened?"

He was already walking away. I followed him into his kitchen. His cabinets were painted black and had labels written in yellow stencil ("Baking Shit," "Here's Where the Plates Live" "Drug Paraphernalia"). Next to his refrigerator was a cabinet the size of a second refrigerator and on it was an easily missed label that said, "DO NOT OPEN!"

He said, "God, you can already smell it down here."

"The pic you sent looked a lot like slices of a dead guy on your bedroom floor. Is that a real thing that occurred?"

"It's actually worse than the pictures."

"Who is it?"

"No idea."

"Why did you do that to him? Actually, from what I saw, I think I'm more interested in *how* you did it."

"I didn't do it," he said matter-of-factly. He wasn't being defensive, he was just letting me know. If he'd had to slice up a dude, he'd have said so. "What happened was I woke up and saw, well, it was like a ghostly figure, I guess, coming out of the wall right next to my bed. Like most of him was standing within the wall and only the front bit of him was showing, kind of like when they froze Han Solo in carbonite. So I assumed it was a dream, but I felt my teeth and they were all pretty solid in my mouth. I sit up and, yeah, he's still there, standing in my wall. So I'm wide awake now, and I say, 'What is your name, spirit?'"

"You did not say that."

"But he didn't act like he heard me. He says, 'You will not remember me, but I have granted you a second chance.' And as he's talking, he's kind of becoming more solid. I can't see through him as well, like he's phasing into the room, like he's beaming down from *Star Trek* and the guy operating the beamer didn't know the wall was there. So I ask, 'What second chance do you speak of, spirit?'"

"Why, in your retelling of the story, are you making yourself sound like Ebenezer Scrooge?"

"And then he says, 'Your friend purchased this opportunity for you, at tremendous cost, so that you may undo your mistake.'"

"What friend? And what mistake?"

"I started to ask him that, but he says, 'Listen carefully, you must—' and then he just starts screaming and screaming. Then he fell to the floor in chunks."

"Because . . . ?"

"Well, he had fully solidified, but he was still standing right in the wall. Sliced him right up. Come look."

The entity that had visited John was definitely human, or at least it had human guts. Here's a piece of advice from me to you: If you ever have the chance to smell the inside of a person, don't. Especially the liver.

What lay on John's bedroom floor looked like somebody had run an adult man lengthwise through a band saw at a slaughterhouse. The front third of him was piled onto the floor like discarded laundry, complete with a sliced-off rib cage, a shocked-looking face, and a pair of bisected feet connected to slivers of shin. The white wall above was a pink splotch in the vague shape of a body. Judging from the wet scraps of cloth, he'd been wearing a suit and tie.

I asked, "So where's the rest of him?" because sometimes I ask questions even when I desperately don't want to know the answer.

"Well, there's another thin slice on the other side of this wall—that's Joy's room, and this is where her closet is. She has her shoes in there; his thigh and butt meat is all over them. But the rest is embedded in the wall. See this hole I drilled here? You can see his lungs mixed with the insulation. And see the patch of tan down here? That's intestine stuff, his last meals just merged with the plaster and wood and everything. Man, I hope no wires go through here . . ."

"How in the hell are you going to clean this up?"

"I think we'll have to do it in steps," he said, recruiting me into his cleanup operation with the insertion of a single word, "and the second step, after we scoop up as much of his entrails as we can, will be knocking out this wall. Studs included, this whole section has to go, all that embedded tissue. Sledgehammer and Sawzall. And it can't wait, either. That stink is going to embed itself in the whole house if we don't move fast. Joy is gonna kick my ass if she walks in the door and gets greeted by that smell. Also, if the cops come, it's going to be hard to explain it, so probably best to dispose of all this before the sun comes up."

"Oh, and look at that, you've already got the tools out."

"And those buckets over there are to haul out debris."

"I definitely need to start asking for more information before I just race over to your house like this. All right, we need to back up. I take it you didn't recognize this guy? If he even was a guy?"

"No. Do you?" He nudged the sliced-off face with his toe.

"Not in this state, no. What did he look like before he was bi-sected?"

"Wearing just a dark suit, white shirt. The guy himself seemed muscular, like he had that kind of face, you know? Skin real tight around his jaw? And you see the long blond hair there. You remem-ber Kelly, used to be in the band? I'd say he looked like how Kelly *thought* he looked."

"And he didn't say anything else?"

"No, what I told you was the whole thing. It all happened over like thirty seconds."

"But he said he was doing this, whatever this is, at someone's request."

"That's definitely what he said. A 'friend.' I figured he meant you."

"No, this is the first I'm hearing of it. And it was to undo some mistake that you made?"

"Yeah, to give us a second chance."

"My point is, if he was telling the truth, what are we supposed to do in response to that? I mean, right now, what do we do? How do we know what mistake we made?"

John lit a cigarette while he considered it. "It's tough, because I'd previously assumed we'd done everything in our lives perfectly up to now. Don't tell Joy I smoked in the house." John picked up a snow shovel that had been leaning in the corner. "So we shovel this up and dump it all in the incinerator. Then we bust out this whole tainted section of wall and burn all the chunks of that, too."

John had an incinerator installed in his garage a few weeks ago, after the Eve incident. We'd since found there aren't many objects, living or nonliving, that won't break down at fifteen hun-dred degrees Fahrenheit. Only once had we had to use it on some-thing that was still alive at the moment of insertion, and after twenty minutes in the oven, all that was left of it was a few scales, claws, and its tiara.

He continued, "We've got a few hours before it gets light out, so if we have it all done by then, nobody will see the smoke and get curious. Then we'll go to Waffle House and have breakfast, *on me,* then we'll stop by Ace to rent a carpet shampooer. And maybe one of those ozone machines to get the stink out. Boom, done, good as new. Except for the hole in the wall, but as far as I'm concerned, it just turns that into a shared closet. I'll explain it to Joy when she gets back. She'll understand."

Joy was John's roommate, I guess? I mean, I know who she is, I just don't know how to describe their relationship. She'll probably turn up later. I'll just explain it then.

I said, "All right. Put on some music that'll get me motivated. And light a scented candle or something. Let's do this."

Well, we weren't done by sunrise. We weren't done by lunchtime, either. All told, the cleanup took thirteen fucking hours. I'm not going to detail the process, because I don't feel like it. It turned out that a lot of the wall material wouldn't turn all the way to ash, so we had to scoop it out of the incinerator and bury it in the yard. The cops actually showed up twice because of complaints about the stench (there is a reason there are no air fresheners that smell like charred insulation and hair), but John's solution to this was to just tell them exactly what was going on. They walked away before he could even finish the story, telling us to wrap it up and stop stinking up the neighborhood.

By the time the project was finished, we were both so tired, sick, and pissed off that we didn't go to Waffle House and, in fact, were barely speaking to each other. It was late afternoon by the time I left, and the day had grown as hot as the dashboards in Hell's parking lot. As soon as I stepped through my door of my apartment, I got a text from John that said,

i forgot to tell you we have a client appointment at 7

I closed my eyes and groaned.

Fuuuuuuuuuuuuuuuuuuuuuuuuuuuuuuuuuuuuuuuuuuuuuuuuuuuuuuuu uuuuuuuuuuuuuuuuuuuuuuuuuuuuuuuuuuuuuuuuuuuuuuuuuuuuuuuuuu uuuuuuuuuuuuuuuuuuuuuuuuuuuuuuuuuuuuuuuuuuuuuuuuuuuuuuuuuu uuuuuuuuuuuuuuuuuuuuuiuuuuuuuuuuuuuuuuuuuuuck.

I threw my keys on the counter and went and sat on the edge of the bed. I do that sometimes, just sit there and stare at the wall. Alone. I grabbed my phone and began sorting through my old pictures.

Nobody tells you that when someone is suddenly gone from your life, you lose their face almost immediately, like you can't perfectly bring them to mind without a photo for reference. Amy had only been gone for thirteen days, and already she was fading. I scrolled to a pic from a couple of years ago, of Amy and a friend from her old job standing in a public bathroom. There was a huge, angry sign on the wall behind them that said, "DO NOT FLUSH FOREIGN OBJECTS DOWN TOILET." Amy, whose red hair was having a frizz day, was smiling and giving a thumbs-up with her right/only hand. Her friend was holding a store-bought apple pie, still in the box, making like she was about to tip it into the toilet nearby. Amy's face was a constellation of freckles around green eyes and a smile that said she thought what was happening was literally the funniest thing anyone had ever done. Looking at her drove a hot blade through my sternum.

I wanted to cancel John's client appointment but, deep down, knew that was a bad idea. What would I do instead? Sit here, on the bed, in silence? A man can drown in silence like this. My life these last thirteen days has been a chain of distractions, like continual gasps for air above the surface of that terrible, waiting stillness. But how long can a man live like that?

Get up. Get some coffee. Take a shower. Get ready for the job. That's what Amy would want you to do.

So I did just that. I stood up to head for the bathroom, only mildly surprised to find two hours had passed.

John showed up in his van that evening, clanged his way up the stairs, barged through my door, and said, "You gotta get dressed. It's time to go."

"I am dressed."

I was in mostly clean jeans and a pink T-shirt that didn't have any logos on it or anything.

"No, these are fancy people," said John. "We need to look business." His hair had been heavily gelled and tied back. He was wearing black pants, a black shirt, a black vest, black cowboy boots, and a white belt. The belt had a golden buckle with a pentagram on it.

"And what's their thing, again?" I asked as I rummaged in my drawer for a shirt that had some kind of a collar or buttons.

"It's their daughter. There's unusual activity with one of her . . . things she owns."

I froze. I slowly turned on him.

"John, does this object happen to be a *toy*, by chance?"

"I would have to double-check my notes. It's not a doll, if that's what you're thinking."

We'd eventually had to rent a storage locker to keep all the haunted/possessed/cursed dolls we'd accumulated, thanks to a series of enormously popular movies on the subject. We were constantly being inundated with emails like, *I woke up one morning to find the doll, which is normally sitting on a low shelf, lying on the floor! And next to it lay my dog, which was dead! Also the dog was nineteen years old, and the doll had chew marks on it.*

I said, "But it is a spooky toy of some kind, right? I can tell by the look on your face."

"Maybe."

I went back to fishing for an acceptable shirt. "Look," I said, "I'm not mad. I know what you're doing. You're trying to get me out of the house, to take my mind off things. But if I have to stand there while you pretend to purify somebody's haunted SpongeBob, I'm going to start laughing, and that's going to ruin the whole bit."

"First, did you hear me say that these are fancy people? They're going *to pay us.* I know, because I asked. Second, check this out."

John stepped over to the kitchen area, pulled out a Ziploc bag, and dumped twenty bloody human teeth onto the table. "The mom thinks the daughter is into Satan worship or some other kind of occult thing. Yesterday, she found those in her room."

I approached the table, pulling on a shirt that was, at best, a lateral move from the last one. "Are those real teeth? You could have just told me what she had. You didn't have to dump them on the table for dramatic effect. We eat here. And what does this have to do with the haunted toy? And whose teeth are these?"

"You want the answer to those questions, go put on some business pants and get in the van."

John's van, like my car, didn't have air-conditioning. The air that blew in from the windows felt like we were driving through a forest fire.

As soon as we were on the road, he said, "Hey, I want to say thank-you for coming over and helping me clean up that mess. I know it's been a bad couple of weeks." He shook his head. "I wouldn't have wanted to deal with that alone, that whole situation was *da filthy.*"

I whipped my head around to face him. "It was *what?*"

"It was crazy. The whole thing, I mean, I woke up and—"

"No. No. You didn't say 'crazy.' Tell me what you said."

"Oh yeah, I said it was *da filthy*. It's what people say now, like when a party gets out of control and stuff gets broken, the kids are like, 'Man, that shindig was hella *da filthy*, hog-swingers.'"

"Pull over. Let me out of the fucking van."

"What?"

"No one has ever said that phrase in the history of language, and they're not going to start."

"Language evolves, Dave."

"Not like this it doesn't. New slang doesn't come from straight white dudes, and it definitely doesn't come from you. If you say it again, I will grab the wheel and run this van into a utility pole. So help me God, John, I will kill us both."

"I feel like this is misdirected anger that doesn't really have anything to do with me. I know this hasn't been easy without Amy, I do. You don't do well alone. You're not a lone wolf. You're a wolf that needs other wolves. A team wolf. Like that Michael J. Fox movie."

"And I know you're intentionally saying wrong things because you think it's funny to make me correct you. Like yesterday, when I told you that good Italian place had closed and you texted back, 'The restaurant business is a doggy-dog world.' There is no way you think that's how that saying goes. *No way.*"

"Yeah, well, if you don't have something to yell at, you just turn the rage on yourself."

I stared out at the passing scenery for a bit, letting August blow its hot breath in my face. "At the risk of in any way implying that I agree with you, the thing I can't handle is just the *emptiness*. The apartment, I mean. It's empty in a way I can't even describe. And also . . . weightless? I don't know how else to say it, like sometimes I'll be there by myself and think, 'There are no rules now. There's nobody to have to explain myself to, no expectations to meet.' One day, I got up at nine and just went back to bed at eleven. Slept until four. Ate a tube of Pringles and then went back to bed. Got up and stayed awake for the next twenty-two hours. I'll be like, 'I could just piss in the sink right now or climb up and sleep on the roof. Go get in the car and pick a direction and just drive until I run out of gas money. Grow a huge goatee and wax it so it stands out horizontally like a beak. There's nobody to stop me.' When I was a kid, I'd have thought being on my own like this was freedom. But this is 'freedom' in the sense that a severed limb is 'free' to slide down the throat of a shark."

We stopped at a traffic light. In the yard next to us was a kiddie pool with two large, wet dogs sitting in it. An enraged little boy in swim trunks was yelling at them to get out. They were ignoring him.

John lit a cigarette and said, "I know you're going to take this the wrong way, but I do kind of feel like you're being a little over-dramatic at this point."

"*How can you even say that to me?* The two of us were one person, and she was most of it. It's like losing three limbs and one eye in a battle and everybody just expects me to keep fighting. For what? For how long?"

"Well—"

"Well, what? What else is there to say?"

"Doesn't her plane get in tonight?"

I sighed. "Yeah, but it'll be really late. Like midnight or something. And that's even if none of their flights get delayed, which they will."

Amy had been in Tokyo, along with John's aforementioned roommate, Joy, at some Japanese nerd convention called Comiket. We couldn't have even thought about affording those plane tickets, but a group of their internet gaming friends pooled money to go and meet there. I wouldn't have gone along even if somehow there'd been enough for my ticket. Just thinking about the entire day spent on various plane rides almost gave me a panic attack. And once you're there, how do you function if everybody's speaking Japanese? Like how do you order food? Or tell a cab driver where you need to go? Do they even have those?

"And that's assuming she comes back at all," I said, "and that she hasn't met some fellow anime enthusiast and fallen in love."

"If so, I'm sure she'll bring him back here so you can all live together as a throuple. In the meantime, we just have to do our jobs. I mean, how badly can we screw this up without her?"

We were approaching a new housing development featuring rows of brand-new McMansions that, at one time, I'd have thought no one in Undisclosed could afford. When they'd started bulldozing that land a couple of years ago, I'd speculated to Amy that it was probably somebody's money-laundering scheme, maybe taking advantage of some government grant to renew the swaths of rural America that had been amputated from the economy like gangrenous flesh. I told her that I didn't care, because I'd take whatever gentrification we could get. From her reaction, that was apparently an offensive thing to say?

As for the appointment tonight, John was explaining in his haphazard way that we were meeting with a woman who'd said her nine-year-old daughter had bought a toy that was brainwashing her, or possessing her, or something? John was hazy on the details, because he has extremely poor retention when it comes to verbal instructions and never takes readable notes. The mother's name, he'd said, was Vageena Galvatron, which seemed incredibly unlikely. In theory, she could have come to meet us at John's place, but he didn't exactly have an office space that would reassure someone used to dealing with actual professionals. John's living room didn't have enough rugs to cover the stains on his carpet, and those rugs also had stains on them.

Then again, meeting at the client's home meant we'd be arriving in John's flesh-tone, windowless van. It still had John's old band name airbrushed on the side, which was:

"DOCTOR" ENRIQUE'S MOBILE ANAL MASSAGE

Also, there was a thermos glued to the roof above the driver's seat, as if the driver had set his coffee up there and driven off.

About twice a day, somebody at an intersection would yell over to try to warn John about it. As for what all he had stored in the back, John liked to describe the collection of instruments and contraband as, "Just band shit and banned shit," which was only clever if you saw it written out.

The housing development wasn't gated, but its designers had other ways of making the situation clear to the rest of us peasants. For example, no through-roads in town would accidentally land you there; instead, there was exactly one easily missed turn that took you to a road that wound around the neat, new homes like a snake until it circled right back around to poop you out the same way you came in. We took that turn (John did, in fact, miss it on his first attempt) and soon passed through a pair of decorative stone pillars that announced we were entering a different, better world, one where the lawns were like Astroturf and all the windows were clean and unbroken. Cars were tucked neatly away in garages. The trash cans along the sidewalks weren't overflowing. The whole area reminded me of a perfect birthday cake in the middle of a party full of toddlers poised to just go wild on it.

John said, "These houses are so similar that I wonder if people ever come home drunk and pull into the wrong one."

"I think that's it over there, with the landscaping. You said three-oh-three, right?"

"Yeah. Gonna park in the street. Don't wanna drip oil on that driveway."

The woman who met us at the door probably had a kind face under normal circumstances. Or, rather, the sort of face we associate with kindness: no frown lines around her mouth, skin free of sun damage, eyes that haven't been hardened by despair or trauma. She seemed like the type who'd never describe her own life as easy, but only because she didn't know what a harder one looked like. She was dressed in leggings and a sweat-wicking workout shirt, like she'd just crawled out of a yogurt commercial. She had a hairstyle I'd seen on a thousand sitcom mothers, straight up top turning into loose curls at the ends. It was intended to look casual, but there was some money in that hair.

Ms. Galvatron glanced around nervously as if worried her neighbors would see, then invited us inside with a gesture. A huge TV over a fireplace played what looked like a horror movie about a creepy pair of identical twins who go around renovating houses. There were no cables draped from the set, so they'd had someone embed them in the wall, I guess? The sofa was real leather and was placed perpendicular to the TV, like you'd have to look across your shoulder to watch anything. Not a speck of dust anywhere in the room; whoever they paid to clean their house did the job like they knew they'd be fired the moment they left a single strand of lint behind. There was a big framed photo on one wall of the whole family when everybody was younger, mom and dad and three kids—two girls and a boy.

John, who was trying to not look intimidated by the fancy house, said, "Hi, uh, just to make sure I have your name right—"

"Regina."

"Regina, I'm John. This is Dave. So I understand your daughter is worshipping a little too much Satan?"

"You have thirty minutes," said Regina as if we were imposing by providing the service she'd ordered. "My husband doesn't know you're here, and we're going to keep it that way. If I find out you're running a scam, I'll go right to the police. Am I clear?"

Without acknowledging that he'd heard, John said, "If you don't mind, could you turn the television off? In fact, any television in the house, they all need to be off. Just for now."

This, as far as I knew, would have no effect on anything. This was something he'd been doing recently, issuing odd instructions, asserting himself as an expert. If the client was wearing a gold chain, he'd ask them to put it in their pocket, or instruct them to take off their shoes and socks. One time, he asked for a glass of water, then just set it by a window and stared at it for a couple of minutes, like he was checking the surface for vibrations.

While Regina turned off the TV, I glanced around the room and asked, "So what do you do? For a living, I mean?"

"My husband is a life coach; I worked in public relations but took time away to raise the kids. We moved here a year ago."

"You moved *here*? On purpose?"

Like, did you lose a bet, or . . .

John said, "So this is about a toy?"

"Yes. Come with me. We took it to the garage."

The garage, like the driveway, had no oil stains on the floor. Everything was neatly placed on shelves, with free floor space to actually park two whole cars in it. The husband's vehicle was missing, the wife's silver BMW SUV was there, and it was as clean as those cars they park in the middle of shopping malls. Even the tires were spotless. Where the hell do people like this come from?

Ms. Galvatron kneeled over a blue plastic storage tub on the floor. "We wanted to get it away from Gracie. Thought it might be, I don't know, evidence or something. We didn't know."

She popped off the lid. Inside was a kids' play set, a white plastic egg about the size of a football that was covered in green polka dots, surrounded by a brown plastic nest. Judging by the festive lettering at the bottom, the egg, or the thing inside the egg, was called "Magpie."

"It makes a noise," she said, "and that's when you're supposed to 'feed' it. After a few weeks, it hatches, and a toy pops out, a little stuffed bird. If you're lucky, you get one of the rare editions; they sell for thousands on eBay. Gracie's had four of these eggs before now. None of them were a problem."

John made a show of studying the totally normal toy, even pulling out his phone and taking video as if there was an actual phenomenon to observe and not just a cheap hunk of plastic from some foreign sweatshop. The bulk of our income these days was from charging people to watch clips of our investigations online, and if there's one thing we'd learned, it's that the videos didn't actually need to show anything. If you keep the lighting and resolution poor and prime the viewers with the right backstory and eerie music, they'll see whatever they want to see.

John asked, "What do you feed it?"

"There's an app for your phone," said Regina, "a game, where you make treats for it. You hit a little feed button on the app, and the toy makes yummy sounds. Then it resets for the next time it gets hungry."

I said, "Let me guess. If she doesn't have time to play the game, she can pay a dollar or two through the app and it will make the candy automatically. Jesus, that is diabolical."

"Yes, you pay to get the toy you already paid for. And then after it's 'born,' you have to feed it like a pet the same way, until it 'grows up' or something. But that's not the problem. We caught Gracie feeding the toy for real. Fingernail clippings, then her own hair. Maybe other things, dropping them into the egg somehow. She's constantly playing with the app, so I don't know if the game was telling her to do it, or something else. She won't talk about it."

John said, "That's when you caught her with the teeth?"

"Found them in her room, under her mattress. God knows where she got them."

I said, "We should probably find out, right? They still had blood on them. Nothing turned up in the local news about somebody having all their teeth ripped out?"

"She's a nine-year-old girl. Someone gave them to her. She just wouldn't say who."

"Still, if there is an older boy out there doing it for her or whatever, it's probably good to let the police know—"

"There's no evidence she asked for it to be done."

Oh, I thought. *So it's like that.*

Now, if you've been paying attention, you may have noticed that nothing supernatural in nature has been posited here. Either this little girl took an innocent toy and an app with a shady revenue model and turned it into something macabre on her own, or some joker altered the app to start demanding kids feed their toy human teeth just to see if they were gullible enough to do it. Either way, it wouldn't be a situation that required our services, but I sure wasn't going to say that out loud. If this woman had money and was willing to pay, we'd give her what she wanted, which was for this problem to quickly and quietly go away before the neighbors started whispering about it. That meant she needed someone to *appear* to solve her problem, and John, Amy, and I have actually gotten pretty good at that.

Before I could reply, John said, "From what I'm hearing so far, it's not clear why you need us. If it's the app doing it, why not just complain to the manufacturer or make a big stink about it on social media until they address it?"

Goddamn it, John.

"Other things have been happening. After we found Gracie with the teeth, I took her phone away. Locked it in our wall safe in the bedroom. The safe is top of the line, can only be opened by fingerprint. It's where we keep private items, Dalton's gun. I put the phone in there at bedtime, get up in the morning, Gracie's in her bed with the phone. There's no way she could have gotten it out. Also, Gracie had a pet mouse. It went crazy as soon as she took the toy out of the box, scratching at the glass wall of its cage. The next day, the mouse disappeared. No way it could have gotten out. How do you explain that? But the main thing is the dreams. Everyone is having them, the same ones, over and over."

I tried not to let my face convey that I didn't find any of that particularly convincing. I'm not a parent myself, but I'm fairly confident that wherever you find grown-ups with a secret safe where they keep the dangerous stuff, you will find kids who figured out how to open that safe within days of its installation. I'm also confident that mice have been finding their way in and out of mouse-proof containers since before humans ever thought to keep them as pets. If my skepticism seems strange in light of everything I've told you about us, I really can't emphasize enough the incredibly high ratio of cases we take that turn out to be bullshit. There's a reason we have all those "haunted" dolls crammed onto shelves in a storage locker: If they were actually possessed, we'd have been able to sell them for quite a bit of money.

I said, "Can you describe the dreams?" because I knew she was dying for someone to ask.

"It's dark. Not nighttime, but permanently dark, like the sky is blotted out. And no one is allowed to use light, like everyone is hiding. Everyone is starving. Everyone is sick. We can hear these noises echoing from somewhere. High-pitched, a mocking noise, like inhuman laughter. And in between, you catch the pleas and cries from people somewhere in the distance, people we were sure were dead. But they're out there, begging to die. And in the dream, I've gotten separated from my children and I'm crying out for them, but I can't find them in all that dark. And suddenly, out of nowhere appear these black figures, totally featureless, walking and floating toward us. They have these red, glowing eyes. And as they close in, people start disappearing. Or, worse, they start *changing*. Everyone in the house has had these dreams, and they keep getting worse."

John and I exchanged glances.

Regina caught it and said, "What?"

I said, "Maybe nothing. Some dreams are just dreams. But if you should ever, uh, see something like that in real life—the walking shadows with the eyes—you'll want to get as far away as possible, as quickly as possible. And by 'far away,' I mean if you have the means to leave the continent, do that. But again, maybe just a dream."

What I didn't say was that I wasn't totally sure she was safe from the Shadow People even when encountering them across a dream. Hell, I'm not even sure it's safe for you to read about them.

John asked, "Can we talk to Gracie? Is she here?"

"She's up in her room. But I want to warn you right now, she stinks."

Gracie's hair was a disaster. It was blond and flowed down her shoulders, but had two obvious gaps where chunks had been roughly hacked off near the scalp, presumably by Gracie herself. I could only imagine how much her mom hated having to explain that to friends at the organic produce section of the grocery store. The girl was staring at her phone and seemed to be watching someone else play a video game. Her screen was cracked.

"Gracie, pay attention," said Momma Galvatron. "These men are here to help. Please answer their questions." Then to us, she said, "She's stopped bathing. I'm really sorry about that." I honestly couldn't smell anything myself, but I could tell Regina liked calling out Gracie in front of company.

"Hey, Gracie," said John. "Your mom here says you've got a toy that eats teeth. My friend Dave and I look into things like that, objects that behave in a way that's not normal or may be hurting people. We just want to make sure you're okay."

Gracie let out a theatrical sigh. She didn't take her eyes off the screen.

"Hi, Gracie," I said, unsure of how to calibrate my voice for a modern nine-year-old. "My name is David. I'm going to tell you something that you might not know, being a child and all. But *you don't actually have to do every single thing your phone tells you to.* These apps, they're made by shitty companies so they can steal your money and personal data all in one shot."

"Please don't curse in front of my daughter," said Regina.

John decided to try again. "Can you tell us where you got the toy from? The Magpie egg thing?"

Gracie mumbled, "Amazon."

"Her big brother got it for her," said Regina. "Birthday gift. But you can get them anywhere. All her friends have them. Those birds on the shelf up there, they all hatched from one of these."

There were four of the little stuffed birds, each a different color or maybe species. They didn't appear haunted. I also took note of the fact that it was Gracie's older brother who'd purchased the toy. A nine-year-old girl might not be capable of yanking the teeth out of some poor bastard, but her big brother?

"So, the thing with the teeth," I asked, "was it the app that told you to get those for it?"

"No," said Gracie impatiently. "I don't know anything about that."

"How did you get them?"

"I don't know. Somebody put them in my backpack at school."

"So you're saying your toy didn't ask for them? Or your phone?"

She just shrugged.

John turned to Ms. Galvatron. "Would you mind if we spoke to Gracie alone?"

She pursed her lips. "I would mind that very much, thank you."

I sighed and rubbed my eyes. I mean, it's not like I could blame her. I sure as hell wouldn't leave us alone with my kids. But I knew what John wanted to ask Gracie in private: Was her older brother an occult-monster-summoning enthusiast?

"All right," I said. "Gracie, we'll get out of your room now. We're going to leave our contact info with your mom. If you think of anything you want to share with us, she can get us on the phone, or if she's okay with it, you can text us directly. This toy, if it is the kind of thing we deal with, this could get real bad. So before we go, I just want to say, if something is talking to you, through your phone or through your dreams or by whatever means—it's lying. Whatever it's saying, it's not true. All right?"

She mumbled something like, "Whatever."

John said, "Good to meet you."

We stepped out, and the mother closed the door behind us. We headed back downstairs to get out of earshot.

I said, "I assume you want the toy out of your house?"

"Yes. Please. You need to take it before Bas gets back."

"Who?" It sounded like she'd said "Bass," like the fish.

"Her brother, Bas, short for Sebastian. He'll throw a fit. Like I said, it was a gift from him. Anytime I've talked about getting rid of it, he's started yelling. He's at the pool. He'll be back any minute."

John said, "We'll take the toy and run some tests on it." Note: I have no idea what "tests" he had in mind. "But if you can get Gracie to open up about it, that would help a lot. If something inside this thing is asking for flesh, we want to know its name. If the dreams continue, or if anything else happens around the house, let us know immediately." He pulled out a business card. When did he have those made? "We're available at all hours."

I nodded as if that were true, then headed for the garage.

John climbed in through the rear doors of the van and shoved aside an inflatable raft, an armored suitcase, two chain saws, a set of bongo drums, a bullet-riddled guitar amp, and several haunted dolls to reach the special artifact containment box he'd built. It was a box of thick glass, large enough for a pig to sleep in, the interior etched with various symbols from the world's religions and, according to John, some religions from other worlds. It had an opening at one end with a vertical sliding panel that could be held shut with a padlock, but I had no idea if it would actually hold any kind of serious creature. John insisted the glass was bulletproof, but I think actual bulletproof glass is like $1,500 per sheet, and he just got this stuff from some guy in town in exchange for a hundred Adderall. We'd never tested it. I'm sure it's fine; if a monster were to pop out of the egg, it wasn't going to come out brandishing a pistol. To be honest, the box was mainly for effect. It meant a lot to clients to see us taking their supposed haunted item seriously. We locked up the polka-dotted Magpie egg inside and said goodbye to Ms. Galvatron.

As we pulled away, I happened to look up at a second-floor window and saw Gracie staring back at me, terrified. All her feigned disinterest was gone—she clearly hadn't known we were going to take the toy. Then her gaze shifted to the driveway we'd been afraid to park in earlier. A sedan had just pulled in, and a teenage boy had gotten out, wearing swim trunks and a gray sweat-drenched T-shirt bearing the name of the high school football team.

I said, "The brother's home."

Gracie was yelling something from her window. The brother listened, then took off running after the van.

"He's, uh, chasing us."

He moved like he was sprinting to defuse a bomb before its timer hit zero, arms pumping like the T-1000. The kid could run. He absolutely looked like he could rip a person's teeth out if he really wanted to, or even mildly wanted to.

"John, I think he's gonna catch us."

He glanced into the rearview. "Are we going to have to get out and beat his ass?"

"I think we'd wind up losing the mom as a client," I said, though I was actually pretty sure this kid could thrash both of us. "Speed up."

John did, though the kid managed to keep up for a surprisingly long time. We turned a corner and eventually stopped at a light. We both checked to make sure he wasn't going to come flying into view behind us.

John said, "I don't like this. Not at all. I want to take the egg back to the lab, wait for the next mealtime, see what happens."

"We're calling your garage 'the lab' now?"

"A room is whatever you call it."

"Why not just toss the toy into your incinerator?"

"Well, it's not a rare antique, right? It's off the shelf. They could just buy another one and start over."

"Whatever you do, keep track of your hours so we can bill the mother. Did you ever find out anything else about the guy in your wall?"

"No, and I'm not sure how I would. Somebody, somewhere is missing a muscular dude in a suit. Maybe they'll come asking. Otherwise . . ." He shrugged, then yawned. "Man, what a weird day."

SATURDAY, AUGUST 20. 8:28 P.M.
MARSHMALLOWS
HUNGER AT 68%

I was back at my place, picking out the laundry from my floor that smelled like it could pass for clean and folding it to be put away. Amy was due back in a matter of hours, and I had set to frantically cleaning the place so that it would look roughly the way it had when she'd left. After the laundry, the dishes were next. Fortunately, I hadn't cooked even once and had just been reusing the same red Solo cup for two weeks. I tossed it in the trash. Dishes done. I then went to carry a stack of six pizza boxes to the dumpster in the parking lot next door. It was surrounded by a tall, locked wooden fence bearing a sign that said:

DO NOT DUMP HERE—PROPERTY OF CORAL ROCK MOTEL

I was climbing over that fence when I heard the soft patter of bare feet on pavement, somewhere in the darkness behind me. I quickly chucked the boxes in on top of the thirty-six bottles of Natty Light I'd tossed in earlier and jumped down.

"Hey, the, uh, wind blew those boxes out of the dumpster and into my side of the lot so I was just putting them ba—"

No one was there.

No. That wasn't right. Someone was there, I just couldn't see them. That's a feeling that would have chilled me ten years ago, but I've kind of gotten used to it. I tried to focus my eyes. Or, rather, I tried to focus my perceptions in that particular way that reveals things my brain is trying to ignore.

"Hello?"

I heard the footsteps again, soles slapping ground at a hurried pace. I spun in time to see a figure dash past me, spindly limbs flailing, too thin to be human. I jumped back. An impossibly pale man of skin and bone scrambled up the fence and leaned into the dumpster, frantically grabbing at the cardboard, ripping open pizza boxes. It snatched a handful of pizza crusts and jammed them into its mouth, breathing hard through its nose as it ate, moaning and grunting as if it hadn't tasted food in a year.

I took a few steps back. The thing heard me.

It turned its head. Its face was just a skull shrink-wrapped in sallow skin. Embedded within was a pair of very familiar eyes. It pivoted toward me, jumped in my direction, and—

It was gone.

I stayed there for several seconds, braced with my hands in front of my face, breathing heavily.

That's one of the five weirdest things I've ever seen in this parking lot.

I scanned my surroundings but sensed I was now alone. I got out my phone and turned on the flashlight, then I climbed back onto the fence and scanned the dumpster. The top pizza box had been yanked open; the discarded crusts I'd left behind were gone. I aimed the light at the ground below me and saw a half-eaten crust lying there.

Hmm.

I went back up to the apartment and did a room-by-room search. Nope, still alone. Then I happened to look down at the open top drawer of laundry and froze.

The shirts I'd folded were now rolled up, like a row of burritos. I absolutely had not done it that way. Sure, I'd done it that way before, because I once saw a YouTube video saying it would prevent wrinkles, but it made it harder to stack everything in the drawer, and I'd abandoned the method months ago.

Did the thing I saw in the parking lot come up here and . . . roll my shirts?

I tried to make sense of it. Now, in a horror movie, this is where the character decides it was all in their imagination, at which point we'd immediately cut to some other character having an inexplicable sighting of their own, then neither character ever shares what they know with the other until like eighty minutes into the movie, after six other people have died horribly. John, Amy, and I have thus made it a formal rule that anything weird is to be shared with the rest of the group immediately, if at all possible. Granted, we had just made that rule a couple of months ago, after almost a decade of fucking around to increasingly disastrous results, but better late than never.

I dialed John, who quickly answered with, "You wanna tell me your thing, or do you want me to tell you mine?"

"I'll go. I just saw a starving man, like starving on a level that he shouldn't have been alive, like a Holocaust victim, in the parking lot next door. I saw him go eat out of the motel dumpster, and then poof, he was gone. Before he disappeared, he turned to me, and I'm pretty sure it was your eyes looking back."

"You said he was eating out of the dumpster?"

"Yeah, I was out there throwing out pizza boxes. He jumps up and starts eating the leftover crusts. And get this: After he disappeared, the crusts were gone, like he'd really eaten them. Did you hear me say that he looked like a starving version of you?"

"It doesn't sound like me. I don't like the crusts."

"What's your thing?"

"We brought the egg back here, right? In the plastic tub Ms. Galvatron had kept it in? But I go out there to transfer it to the containment box, and the egg is already in there, sitting by itself. The tub is nowhere to be found."

"No, you're remembering wrong. We took it out of the tub and put it in the containment box back in the van. We left the tub in the Galvatrons' garage."

"Man, I am one hundred percent sure that tub was here at my place when you left. We had a whole argument about—"

"I believe you remember it like that. I'm just saying that's not what happened. No, listen—I was folding my laundry, I went outside, came back in, then everything was arranged different in the drawer."

John took a moment to think.

"So," he said, "whatever is messing with us, is it messing with the events, or is it messing with our memory of the events?"

"'Whatever' is messing with us? I'm gonna take a wild guess and say that it's your goddamned haunted toy. And if it's messing with the actual fabric of reality, I now *really* do not want that egg to 'hatch' or do whatever it's going to do if people keep feeding it teeth."

"It also means we can restrict the feed to Platinum." Note: We only had five reliable purchasers of Platinum content on our site, and I'm pretty sure at least one of them was jerking off to it.

"Well, that's good," I said. "Let me know if it glitches you out of existence."

I hung up and sat on the bed to think about what needed to be done next, in terms of cleaning. I was asleep before I could even finish the thought.

I dreamed I was flying.

I was pushing myself through moist night air on leathery wings, flinching because bugs kept smacking into my face. I was over one of the residential neighborhoods in town, scanning the ground for movement, though in the dream, I didn't consciously know what I was hunting or what I intended to do when I found it. Then my whole system jolted at the sight of a raccoon, a fat one, nosing around some trash cans. Hunger roared through my system, blowing all other thoughts aside. I swept down toward the animal, intending to snatch it with my feet and swoop back up into the sky in one seamless motion. At the last minute, the raccoon took off toward the trash cans, moving faster than I'd anticipated. I instinctively changed my trajectory, but this threw me off, and before I knew it, I was crashing into the trash cans, scattering take-out boxes and diapers. Now porch lights were coming on all around me, and someone was shouting. I limped away, crossing a lawn, vaguely aware that I had a burger wrapper stuck to my face, trying to take flight but struggling to get one of my bat-like wings working. I heard someone shout, and then there was a gunshot—

I woke up. I was facing the wall of my bedroom and heard a light shuffling somewhere in the darkness behind me.

I held my breath.

I heard the creak of floorboards. Coming closer.

I felt a light weight on the sheets behind me. I rolled over.

Perched on the edge of the bed was a creature with bright yellow eyes, brown fur, and with six stumpy legs on each side. It was grinning at me.

Fear drove its fist deep into my butthole.

A figure moved in the shadows behind it. Thin, but not like the starving thing in the parking lot. It was wearing glasses.

Amy said, "I was trying not to wake you!"

I turned on the lamp on the nightstand.

"What the hell is this thing?" The twelve-legged stuffed horror on the bed was even weirder in the light.

"Catbus? From *Totoro*? I didn't want to come back without a souvenir, and this seemed like you."

"Oh, did you go to Japan already? When did you leave?"

She picked up the cat monster and smacked me in the face with it. "Twenty hours, from door to door! I have no idea what day it even is here. I'm kind of surprised it's night. Did you miss me? I missed you."

"You must be exhausted. Come to bed. You can unload your Japan anecdotes on me in the morning."

She unbuttoned her jeans and stepped out of them. "Yeah, I'm really sleepy." She pulled off her T-shirt. "I'll just put on my pajamas and go right to sleep." A moment later, her underwear was on the floor, and she was crawling naked toward me. "Yep, just going to go riiiiight to sleep." She pulled off my shirt.

Note: I will never include a detailed description of our lovemaking in these books, at Amy's request. If you want to imagine it, just picture a walrus attacking a rose garden with a jackhammer.

Soon, we were lying there, Amy spraying Japan stories into my ear. She had chipped a tooth on her first day there. It didn't hurt, but she'd have to get it fixed soon. She ate squid. They have a million flavors of Kit Kat candy bars, for some reason, including baked potato, rum raisin, and cherry blossom. They went to a pachinko parlor. When she walked in, they were actually playing the theme from *Evangelion,* which she thought was so stereotypical that she almost burst out laughing, but then wondered if they just do that for tourists. She got lost in the city at one point, and a group of guys had to help her get back. They were enthralled by her red hair; they all took pictures with her. She and the rest of her gaming friends took a trip to the mountains. Not Mount Fuji, but Takao. They did the easiest hike possible, but she could still barely walk the next day. Comiket was a little disappointing. The crowds were insane. Joy had the best costume there. Joy got tons of attention wherever they went. Amy wished she'd dressed up. She definitely wanted to go back.

"You have to come next time," she said, tapping my bare chest with a finger to drive the point home. "Every five seconds, I saw something you'd have thought was hilarious, and I wanted to point at it and elbow you in the ribs. But I couldn't, and I hated it. How did you do while I was gone?"

"Oh, uh, great. I started a new diet. Just . . . salads mostly. Some steamed . . . roots."

"How are you doing on the medication?"

"Oh, fine," I said, shoving aside the thought that the physical act I'd just performed had made her suspicious that I'd stopped taking it.

"Did anything happen while I was away?"

"Yeah," I said, thrilled to change the subject. "A few things."

Twenty minutes and a lot of questions later, Amy was pacing around the room in an old T-shirt she'd dug out of her suitcase, her mind going a million miles an hour, her thumb dancing around the screen of her phone.

"Okay," she said, "all right. Let's rewind. Before the guy got walled to death, he didn't say anything helpful about who he was or how he got there?"

"No, he didn't get the chance. He kind of fell apart in mid-sentence."

"And he mentioned giving us a second chance, but neither of you recognized him as anyone we'd ever dealt with? Nobody we've wronged or failed in some way? Even tangentially?"

"I was kind of hoping you'd know, based on the description. You know I don't remember faces."

"And you didn't keep any parts of the guy? You didn't keep his hands? Or his head?"

"No, we burned it all. It was stinking up the place. Why would we keep it?"

"Maybe we could have gotten someone in the police department to run the prints and figure out who he was. Or get dental records? Even if he didn't come up on anybody's database, that alone would have told us something."

"Hmm. Yeah. You know, I think I brought that up to John about keeping something for ID, and he was like, 'No, you're dumb for suggesting that. Amy wouldn't do that.'"

"Can I see the video? Or does John have it? We need to get it up on the site."

"What video?"

"You guys recorded the whole thing, right? The aftermath, the cleanup?"

"Oh. No, I guess we should have. We were too focused on the job itself. The stench was terrible, and John was worried about the cops—" I stopped talking.

Amy and I have one thing in common, which was that we both have what can politely be called anger issues, only we express them in very different ways. I tend to take some kind of rash action that will ruin my life for months or years after. Amy, on the other hand, tends to shut down, or cry, or otherwise remove herself from the situation. Or, as she did here, simply release air out of her nose and press her lips together so hard that they were probably bleeding a little. She had a bunch of things she wanted to say in that moment and was biting it all back because she'd just gotten home and didn't want a fight. Still, in those few seconds, I could sense everything she was thinking, and it crushed me.

Amy had spent dozens of hours coding a website to stream our videos to people, had set up a payment processing system, and had blown a tax refund on fees to create an LLC (she'd gotten help from John for that, the man having created several limited liability corporations over the years). The payment tiers she'd set up for viewers had been ruthless: Fifty dollars per clip for Platinum-level content—videos of some kind of real paranormal action occurring on-screen, coded so that it could be streamed but not saved or copied unless you really knew what you were doing. Twenty-five dollars got you time-based access to a variety of Gold content, like a live feed watching our storage locker full of creepy dolls (so you could be the first to see if one of them moved or spoke or something—you never know!). There were no Silver or Bronze tiers and no videos were free, aside from extremely brief previews.

Amy's goal had been to make enough money that she could quit her day job, and within a couple of months, she'd achieved that goal

(I mean, it helped that we lived in a place that charged neither rent nor utilities, but still). She had worked just as hard on her rationalizations: If voyeurs wanted to watch, fine, make them pay. No one had a need that was being exploited here. Their entertainment budgets would either go to this or video games, and none of her medications were free. Amy hadn't come off like a ruthless capitalist when I'd met her, but I suppose the system has a way of shaping us into whatever will sustain it.

The point of all this being, of course, that video of a teleporting man sliced up like a roast beef and embedded in a wall—a phenomenon that was presumably visible to everyone who watched—could have been our first clip to get maybe thousands of paid downloads instead of the normal ten or twenty. That'd have been real money, the kind that could have turned around our whole situation, and the opportunity hadn't even registered with me. I watched as her face transitioned from rage to mere disappointment, and it made me want to fling myself into a trash can.

I said, "I'm sorry, Amy. I wasn't thinking—"

"All right," she said. "Well, let's keep an eye out for anybody who gets reported missing with that description. For all we know, there's some science lab in Sweden trying to figure out where their first artificial wormhole test subject went. So the toy. You didn't destroy it, and that's good. I definitely want to know more about it. I'm downloading the app. You have to scan a thing on the bottom of the egg to pair the game with it. The toy is only twenty bucks on Amazon. I bet they make all their money off the app. Average customer rating is four and a half stars, so it doesn't seem like that many people have gotten weirdness from it before now, unless they're just being really forgiving with the scores."

"Maybe that's what the toy does: It possesses its owners and forces them to leave good feedback."

"Did you try searching for news articles about it? To see if there are similar stories out there?"

"No. I mean, I was about to do that—"

"A group of kids in Florida got in trouble a few days ago," she said, scrolling through news on her phone. "Ooh, they pulled a homeless man's teeth out. Said this toy's app told them to do it."

"Really? Jesus. Also I'm just now realizing that, as a team, we'd be more effective if it was just you, working alone."

"Ugh, they've got photos of the incident. They're *da filthy.*"

"They're *what?*"

"Ha. When I landed, the first text message waiting on my phone was John telling me to use that in conversation; he said you get really mad. So the family's name obviously isn't Galvatron. What are their first names?"

"Uh, the girl is named Gracie, brother is Sebastian; they call him Bas. The dad, I don't think I got his name, but he's a therapist or motivational speaker or something? They moved here a year ago, the mom said. She's Regina."

Amy's thumb drummed the screen. "Galveston. That's the family name. Ooh, this is interesting. Regina's husband is Dalton Galveston."

"Who?"

"He's a self-help guy, writes books and does speaking tours, that kind of thing. He had a viral video about bullying a while back. What did the brother have to say about all this? You said he bought the toy for his sister, right? Maybe this is more about him."

"We thought about that, but he wasn't there. We just talked to the girl. He showed up at the end, but we didn't get to speak to him. It, uh, didn't feel right."

"Did Regina say anything about their other daughter?"

"There isn't one. Just the boy and the girl."

"There was. Another sister, named Silva."

"Nobody mentioned her."

"That's because she died last year. Suicide. Under weird circumstances."

She met my eyes.

I said, "Oh. Oh, shit."

John texted at around six the next morning, explaining across several messages that he'd downloaded the app and played with it, but it didn't give the user a specific feeding time for the Magpie. Instead, there was a meter in the shape of a green cartoon stomach that slowly filled with red to represent hunger. The app clearly intended for the toy's owner to continually check it, rather than just giving set mealtimes. They wanted it to always be at the back of your mind, almost as if some forms of modern entertainment are really about creating a continuous sense of low-level anxiety. Anyway, John had said that meant we had a few hours to come up with an approach, which was good. We'd need time to experiment and to prepare for however the toy might respond if we fed it or, more importantly, if we didn't.

Unfortunately, I'd silenced my phone, and Amy's was still in airplane mode from the trip, so we slept right through those messages and all of John's subsequent attempts to call. It wasn't until after nine that we bobbed back up into consciousness and saw all the missed notifications. Then Amy couldn't find her toothbrush, meaning it was presumably still on the other side of the planet, then there was a long line at the convenience store to get coffee—you've had mornings like this at your job; I won't bore you with the details. The point is, by the time we actually made it to John's back gate, he had just sent a text saying the stomach meter was pretty much entirely red.

Looking back, it's almost grotesque how casual we were about it, but, hey, hindsight makes assholes out of everybody.

SUNDAY, AUGUST 21, 9:49 A.M.
MARSHMALLOWS
HUNGER AT 98%

John greeted me at the gate with, "Is this one Amy?" Then, to her, said, "Sorry, you've been gone so long, and Dave has gotten so much poontang these last two weeks, I wasn't sure which one you were. The Impala is like catnip. Been a lot of redheads."

"No time for your wonderful jokes," Amy replied. "We've got a potentially serious haunted toy situation here."

I said, "It appears this may already be a Category H situation."

John's eyes went wide. "Oh. Oh, shit. Who?"

Note: The *H* in "Category H" stood for: *Holy Shit Someone Has Actually Died from This, Are We Absolutely Sure Nobody Else Can Handle It?* A Category H, as you can imagine, can go from curiosity to crisis real fast.

Amy said, "They had another daughter, died last year. We'll circle back to it later. Has the toy done anything unusual?"

"Not that I can detect." John whipped out his phone. "The mobile game says we're supposed to feed it twenty marshmallows."

Amy peered over and said, "Look at the marshmallow icon. See how the shadow at the bottom—"

"Yeah, it makes it look like a tooth," said John. "I noticed that."

He showed me the phone. I squinted at it and said, "I guess? Kind of?"

We passed through John's kitchen and into the garage. The plastic egg was on the floor, inside John's supposedly bulletproof glass case. About ten feet away was a camera on a tripod; I assume he had invited Gold-tier viewers to sit through the night and see if the haunted object did anything interesting.

Amy asked, "Can I pair my phone with the toy? Like can we co-parent the Magpie, so I can monitor its hunger, too?"

"Yeah, I just have to send you an invite. Here . . ."

He was interrupted by a tinny speaker on the toy making a sound like a mewling baby or animal. Begging to be fed.

Jesus, does it just do that until the kid finally gives in? How is that legal?

I said, "Okay, I can't handle that noise. Do you have twenty imaginary marshmallows to feed the thing?"

John messed with his phone. "There's a little puzzle game you play to earn them, I tinkered with it last night, and I have . . . let me see . . . eight hundred and forty marshmallows."

"But that's not what it really wants, right? Do you have the teeth?"

"They're in the house, but this is decision time, isn't it? Whether or not we really feed this thing human tissue?"

"Well," said Amy, thinking it over, "I assume feeding it the marshmallows in the app won't affect anything. We can at least make that terrible noise stop."

John tapped the screen, and the toy played a sound clip of an obnoxious baby voice saying, "YUMMY! THANK YOU, MOMMY, I WUV YOUUUU!!!"

Man, the stuff kids like today is just absolute trash.

We studied the egg, which showed no change. There were zigzag slits along the sides, where one day it would crack itself open and let the offspring out. If I'd gotten one of these as a kid, I'd have just pried it open with a screwdriver.

Amy said, "So I think the next step is to try feeding it one tooth. Observe what it does."

"Well, how close does that bring us to the end?" I asked. "Does the app imply the Magpie is on the verge of hatching? Are the teeth the final step?"

"No," said John, "there's a bunch of feedings and other stuff still to go. They don't make it that easy."

Amy nodded. "So there shouldn't be much risk in giving it one—"

She was cut off by a howl that split the air. All three of us clutched our ears. It was a noise like a beast the size of a planet had accidentally stuck its dick into the sun.

The Magpie, it was clear, was still hungry.

Amy, yelling to be heard, said, "Where are the teeth?!?"

"Locked in my gun safe, in my bedroom!" shouted John. "I didn't know if something was going to come to life and crawl out of there, looking for a snack. Want me to go get them?"

"No!" I shouted as the noise drilled through my skull. "Let's fucking destroy it!"

Amy said, "Wait! I think we should—"

And then she blinked across the room.

She hadn't actually taken any steps or moved her body in any way. In mid-word, she had just suddenly vanished and reappeared about eight feet away, now standing near the door to the kitchen. John had also moved, though not as much—he was a few feet closer to the glass cube than he had been. I was in roughly the same spot, but I was now holding an empty plastic bag, the interior smeared with dried blood.

The garage was dead silent. The shrieking from the egg, or the Magpie inside it, had stopped.

SUNDAY, AUGUST 21, 10:01 A.M.
STRAWBERRY POPSICLES
HUNGER AT 0%

I shouted, "What the fuck?" in a tone that was earnestly pleading for an answer.

John held out his hands like he was trying to catch his balance. His eyes darted around the room. "Uh, are you missing some time?"

"Yes!"

Amy said, "Look in your hand. Would that be the bag the teeth were in?"

John said, "That is . . . less than ideal."

The egg was still sitting smugly in the glass case. It hadn't moved or changed in appearance at all, but the padlock on the hatch at the end had been opened and removed—it was lying nearby, the key still inserted.

I tossed the bloody bag to the floor. "Well, great. The haunted toy can apparently mind-control us? Or something? Now that I think of it, we should probably have considered that as one of the potential dangers before we began. And we all agree that it made us feed it the teeth, right? We didn't, like, shove them up each other's asses?"

Amy said, "Either way, let's make sure that never happens again. How can we prevent it?"

I said, "Distance? Maybe? It never mind-controlled us before we got in the same room with it. Or maybe we could bury it in the yard?"

"You think its powers will be blocked by dirt?"

John said, "Whoa, I just had déjà vu."

"That's not déjà vu," I spat. "That's the fact that we have this same damned conversation every time we bring a dangerous artifact home with us. *Why don't we have a set process for this?*"

"We do! I built this box! Did I tell you that glass is bulletproof?"

"Guys, guys. Listen." Amy was looking at her phone. "We got a notification from the app. We've leveled up, apparently."

I said, "Oh, wonderful. What does that mean?"

"You know how in these games, if you collect enough stuff you win a thing that then helps you collect more stuff, so that you feel like you're actually accomplishing something? Well, we've just earned a minion to help us collect the next batch of treats. Its name is Swallow the Gumball Swiper. It'll arrive after the next feeding."

A couple of hours later, we were gathered in John's kitchen, watching him deep-fry several Hot Pockets for lunch. Amy was telling John about the third Galvatron sibling, the sister who'd passed away.

"They say she jumped, did it while they were on vacation in Mexico. The father went public with it, talking about how she'd been driven to it by bullying at school. He did speaking engagements about it in high schools around California. Using his kid's death to teach other kids not to be mean."

Amy seemed strangely offended by this.

I said, "That's a good cause, isn't it? Seems like the kind of thing you'd be on board with."

She shrugged. "He probably thought it was. When you make martyrs out of suicides, it can spread the message that it's a great way to give meaning to your life. It's also kind of specious to say someone was 'driven' to suicide. It's never that simple, and you're kind of saying, 'Hey, here's a good way to get revenge on your bullies. Just kill yourself and the whole world will rally to your cause.'"

John said, "You think the suicide was connected to this Magpie situation somehow?"

"We don't have any reason to think that, but, well, they moved *here,* right after her death. They could have moved anywhere, but they picked the most haunted spot in North America? Maybe something wanted them here, wanted a chain of events that would lead to, well, whatever is happening right now."

"If there's a lead there," I said, "we need to get to the bottom of it fast. This might be controversial, but I personally don't want this minion thing, this Swallow or whatever it was called, to show up. I feel like there's no way that's going to be a positive development in our lives."

John said, "But if we try to just not feed it, we now know that the toy might just force the issue, take over our brains. So how long do we have until it gets hungry?"

Amy studied the screen. "I can tell you the meter is running faster than last time. It's already showing a sliver of red. It's definitely not going to last the rest of the day."

I said, "Even if we wanted to feed it, and we definitely don't, we don't even know how to, right? I mean, we can feed it in the software, but we don't know what it wants in real life."

"The game says spawning Swallow the Gumball Swiper requires four strawberry Popsicles. There's a little puzzle where you have to find the hidden strawberries and then I guess move them through a maze thing to get them to the 'freezer.' There's a bunch of steps here. Where do kids get time to do all this?"

"So if the marshmallows looked like teeth, what does a strawberry Popsicle look like?"

John leaned over Amy's screen. "See how it's kind of got that line going down the middle? Tell me that doesn't look like a tongue."

"Oh, god," said Amy.

"There's a menu down the side with the upcoming feedings," said John. "After the Popsicles, it's going to want gumballs, then gingerbread men, then once the Magpie hatches from the egg, it'll demand pies. So I guess our goal is to never have to find out what the rest of those actually are, in the real world."

John fished a Hot Pocket out of the oil and set it on a plate covered in paper towels.

Amy said, "I want to talk to the brother, Bas. If we can, I want to talk to the little girl, too."

I said, "We already did that."

"No, *I* want to talk to the little girl. You guys probably scared her."

"We needed to go back there anyway, to hit the mom up for payment. We need to include all the stuff we've done since leaving their house. Just need to make sure we go when the dad isn't home; she hired us on the down-low."

John pointed to the Hot Pocket on the plate and said, "You had the Philly cheesesteak, right? If we all go to the Galvatrons, do you think it'll be okay to leave the Magpie here unattended? Joy has to work."

"No," said Amy. "David and I will go. You can stay here and look into the company that makes this thing. Talk to someone there if you can. You're good at piercing layers of customer service defenses."

I let out a howl of pain. "AUGH! SHIT!"

John said, "Man, you should have let that cool a bit before biting into it. It just came out of the fryer."

I forced the hunk of lava down my throat and said, "Don't tell me what to do," then took another bite.

NOTE: PREVIOUS ACCOUNTS SUBMITTED BY JOHN HAVE OFTEN NOT CONFORMED TO THE KNOWN FACTS OF THE EVENTS AS DESCRIBED BY OTHER PARTICIPANTS. AS SUCH, THE FOLLOWING IS BEING INCLUDED PURELY OUT OF A DEDICATION TO COMPLETENESS. WISE READERS WILL SKIP THESE SECTIONS ENTIRELY.

John

John squinted against the sun as Dave squealed out of the driveway in his Impala, tearing down the street like he had just spotted Satan in his rearview mirror sporting a lustful look and a white-hot erection. John stripped off his shirt and felt waves of heat waft across his chest, like puffs of Lucifer's horny, trembling breath. John closed his eyes and tilted his face to the sun, mentally steeling himself. He sensed something big was coming, massive and dangerous but concealed, like the smoldering bulge in the devil's leather pants that promised the arrival of his forked, fiery boner.

John strode back into his living room and slammed the front door behind him. He powered on his computer. His monitor was one entire wall of the room, the image emitting from a projector mounted on the ceiling. He had rigged it to respond to voice and gesture commands, all with parts he'd found on Craigslist. He stood in the middle of the floor and spread his arms.

"COMPUTER! ON!"

He went to work, making his cursor fly across the screen by swooping his hands like a symphony conductor. The company that made the Magpie egg was called ChuckleCave Entertainment. They'd been in business since the 1980s, selling toys to varying degrees of success, usually stuffed animals enhanced with some kind of technology. An early hit had been a talking dinosaur with a tape recorder inside it that sang songs about the environment. In the early 2000s, they sold a stuffed sheep that told bedtime stories, with new stories that could be downloaded off the internet for a fee. These days, it was all toys with some kind of mobile app tie-in, clearly intended to keep squeezing the kids and their parents for cash for months or years after that initial purchase. John wondered if they sang jolly instructions for how to steal Mommy's credit card number.

He waved his cursor up to the search bar and shouted a series of terms, looking for prior incidents of kids feeding human parts to their Magpies. He found the news story Amy had referenced earlier, the gang of kids in Florida who had taken a homeless man's teeth. The kids actually insisted they had paid the homeless man to pull the teeth out himself, though that was almost worse. Man, Florida seemed like a terrifying place.

Further searching turned up a mortician in Germany who got caught selling teeth from a corpse to some kids for the same purpose. There was another article about a similar incident that was only available in Chinese. Prior to this, there were complaints about kids' hair getting "caught" in the egg, but to John, that seemed like a convenient excuse kids would make up to explain why the chunks were missing. One thing was clear: Not every Magpie was demanding body parts. They sold these toys by the million; if they had all grown carnivorous, there'd scarcely be an undamaged mouth in the country. John also found out that the eggs were released in waves, according to the Zodiac calendar—Magpie was apparently a Virgo— and each release sold out instantly. That meant the feedings and births were synced. Kids would go online and watch livestreams of stuffed birds all being born at the same time, some shrieking with joy if their egg birthed one of the rare collectors' editions (the rarest marked with gold tips on their wings).

John next went looking for articles about what exactly these real-life feedings were supposed to accomplish or how this small group of egg owners had even discovered how to do it. He quickly fell down a rabbit hole of bullshit. Here were the familiar ghost and conspiracy websites, talking about how the toys were secretly alien embryos, or part of a mass Satanic ritual, or something to do with the supposed military satellite hovering overhead (something about it beaming a mind-control signal to the app, or something?). He did notice a group that kept coming up across the articles he skimmed, something called the Simurai. He made a mental note to follow up, but for now, he needed to stay focused on the toy's manufacturer, and his arms were getting tired.

Amy

Amy shifted in the passenger seat of David's Impala, trying to get comfortable. She was so jet-lagged that she felt detached from the world, at that level of fatigue where reality is like a rerun you're half paying attention to while working a sudoku. She had left the Tokyo airport on Saturday afternoon, traveled for an entire day, then landed in the wee hours of Sunday morning, having gone ten hours into the past while in the air. So it was now Sunday afternoon, and the sun was blasting down like it was about to go supernova, but her body was telling her it should be midnight. Meanwhile, her medication told her that she should be splayed out on the sofa, watching *Ace of Cakes* reruns while absently feeding Twizzlers into her maw. She'd been back in town for barely half a day, and already she was falling back into the sluggish rhythms of this place.

David was saying something about the new housing development they were heading toward, saying it was silly for the builders to think commerce would return to Undisclosed after having spent the last fifteen years or so fleeing it like rats from a sewer alligator. On one hand, Amy hoped he was wrong—the town needed jobs. On the other, the rich developers behind these projects were definitely imagining those jobs going to a new class of people. Their ideal version of Undisclosed wouldn't have her or David in it. They also probably wanted to bulldoze all the haunted houses and warehouses and replace them with open-air shopping plazas and Amazon distribution centers. Never mind that this would result in inferior hauntings, which are never as dramatic under the stark glare of fluorescent bulbs.

Amy yawned and tried to force herself to be present in the moment. The windows were down, and the wind was pummeling her ears.

"I mean, even her tires were clean," said David. "Who has the time and energy to keep everything looking perfect all the time?"

"They hire people," mumbled Amy. She shifted in the seat again. Her back was killing her.

Amy thought of these client meetings as invitations to join their secret society. The concept that the world is a series of secret societies had come from a therapist she'd seen years ago, after the car accident that had taken her parents and her left hand. The therapist had said that you've joined one of these groups when you've experienced something that utterly changes your life so thoroughly that you now share a secret language with others who've been through the same, a dialect incomprehensible to anyone on the outside. So, for instance, there's a secret society of people who've been diagnosed with a terminal disease, another made up of assault survivors, or people who've lost a spouse, or been to war. Amy's society—or one of them—was Those Who Live With Chronic Pain.

Hers was the result of damage done by the accident combined with years of bad posture when hunched over her laptop. What she really needed was surgery, but even if they could afford it and the many follow-up costs, there was a strong chance that she'd be right back in the same condition soon after—modern medicine is still frustratingly inept when it comes to the human spine. On good days, the pain was dull enough that she could forget about it entirely. On bad days, it was like she'd been submerged in a vat of molten metal. With back pain, it doesn't matter what position you're in. It hurts to sit, stand, lie down, or hang from the ceiling like a bat. Ice didn't help. Heat didn't help. Over-the-counter pain pills might as well have been candy. Narcotic painkillers could get her through a workday, but, well, they came with their own baggage.

Once, Amy had gotten up in the middle of the night and opened her bottle of prescription pills—the ones her doctor had pushed on her while confidently claiming they were addiction-proof—and accidentally dumped all twelve of them down the drain. She'd collapsed onto the floor, crying into her elbow so as not to wake up David. She didn't tell him about it the next morning; she was too ashamed. Instead, she'd gone to John and asked if he knew where she could get some through, well, unofficial channels. She had said that she just wanted to replace the pills she'd lost, that she knew her doctor wouldn't believe she'd done anything other than taken them all or sold them.

John had said he thought he knew where some could be obtained, but that would be a crime and was she really, really sure? Amy had cried and told him yes, but that he wasn't to put himself at risk, that if he just told her who to talk to, she'd do it herself. John had responded by turning, walking ten feet, and receiving exactly twelve pills from a friend who'd been sitting in his living room and lazily strumming a guitar. She'd hugged John and tried to ignore the expression on his face that said he didn't necessarily believe she'd lost the pills, either.

Amy once heard that about one in five people are living in some kind of chronic pain; about one in twelve are in debilitating pain, so bad they can barely function. You always have to keep that in mind whenever you run into a cranky shopper in line at the checkout or an aggressive driver. There's a good chance that person is in absolute agony, living in a world where the air is razor blades. If you know what that's like, you've joined the secret society, an unseen subculture that was always around you but that you never knew existed because, let's face it, you didn't want to know.

"It's right up here," said David. "Be ready. I don't think people like this forgive bad first impressions. Oh, and don't swear around Gracie. The mom hates it."

Amy sat upright and rolled up her window so she could try to get her hair under control. This could, after all, wind up being the most important day in this client's life. Amy's weekday work routine was the crisis that threatened to shatter Regina Galveston's worldview.

That brought to mind the other thing Amy's therapist had talked about, which was survivor's guilt, the futile attempt to divine why she had lived after everyone else in her household had been so cruelly snatched away. The process of trying to find some grand purpose can be destructive, she'd said, as you spend years beating yourself up for not living up to some impossible standard, thinking you've been designated to cure cancer or become some kind of inspirational role model. Then, when you find out otherwise, you'll say, "If I wasn't spared because God needed me to accomplish something great, maybe it was all just dumb luck?"

But the therapist had been wrong about that, at least in Amy's case. David had shown up at her door a few years after the accident and (inadvertently) invited her to another, much weirder tribe, the one the Galveston family was about to join. And with that, Amy had found that she did have a purpose after all. There was no substitute for that, for feeling special. She wouldn't trade her spot in this secret club for one of the houses in this fancy subdivision or bigger boobs or any number of trips to Japan. She wouldn't even trade it for a pain-free back.

Well, on most days anyway.

SUNDAY, AUGUST 21, 1:31 P.M.
STRAWBERRY POPSICLES
HUNGER AT 21%

Me

A text to the mother, Regina, had confirmed that the father wasn't home and wouldn't be for some time, but that both kids were there. Perfect. I parked along the street, and we found Regina watering some potted plants on her porch. The day was hotter than a nude slide down a chrome volcano.

"Hi," I said as we approached. "This is my girlfriend and associate, Amy. Did anyone have any bad dreams last night?"

Regina, without looking up, said, "Not a one. It's like the whole black cloud got lifted. Can't you feel it?"

"It seems like whatever dark energy was coming off this thing, it followed us home. But we'll be all right, this is what we're trained to do and it's the reason we have a reputation for fixing problems like this," I said, fitting three bald-faced lies into a single sentence. "I know we come off like weirdos, but what normal person would go into this business?"

"Bas got so mad about you taking the toy that I thought he was going to blow a gasket."

"Yeah, I don't think I can do anything about that part. Hey, uh, Amy is going to email you an invoice for the work we've done so far;

that's going to be due upon receipt. But we'd like to talk to Bas and Gracie both. There's really nothing stopping them from going out and buying another one of these eggs and starting the whole thing over again."

"Starting *what* over again? And how did they get wrapped up in something like this?"

"We're not sure yet," said Amy, "but it's not just them feeding these toys with hair and teeth and gross stuff like that; it's something kids are doing in various places. Not just in America, all over."

"Is it like a devil worship kind of thing?"

"Well, the problem is that there can be a really big difference between what they are doing and what they *think* they're doing. They may think it's just an internet fad, kids doing it for shock value, topping each other with who can put the grossest stuff in their egg. You know how kids are. Or they may be getting manipulated into performing a ritual with a goal they're unaware of and that we'll hopefully never get to see. But you're right, they had to get the idea from somewhere. We need to find out."

"But we can't do it for free," I said, saving Amy from the part of the conversation I knew she hated having.

"I pay my bills," said Regina coldly.

Amy asked, "Have you ever seen any odd behavior from your kids in the past? Ever discovered anything strange in their rooms or associating with creepy types? Especially someone older, the type who could try to trick them into doing something they wouldn't normally do?"

"Gracie, no. As for Bas, I can see that you've never raised a teenager. One day your baby is there, the next, they're locked behind their bedroom door and only stick their head out for food, swapping out personalities like they're trying on hats. I try to respect his privacy, but these days, I don't even know the name of his girlfriends until they've been going steady for a month."

I said, "This is going to sound like a weird question, but have you ever seen him in possession of small amounts of a really thick, black liquid? Would look like motor oil but darker. It would probably be in a small but sturdy container, maybe something metal, and probably always cold to the touch."

"No. Is that a drug?"

"Sort of. It's hard to explain. But it's definitely something you don't want inside your house."

"You're free to look in his room if you want."

"We are? He's going to just let us do that?"

As a teenager, this would have been my worst nightmare.

"He's not here. He just left to go to a friend's house. You probably passed him on the way. I told him he had to stay and talk to you. He wouldn't listen, as usual. I'm not going to let you ransack the room, but you can get a look at it. If he has contraband, especially anything that would give the police an excuse to seize the property, then Bas's privacy goes right out the window. That's the rule, and he knows it. No drugs. No cigarettes. If there's pornography, he's grounded."

The substance I was asking about isn't a drug, necessarily. It has many names. The now-incredibly-dead drug dealer who first turned up with it sold the stuff under the street name Soy Sauce, but it has a consistency more like molasses or oil from a badly neglected engine. Oh, and it moves on its own as if alive. We've found various paranormal communities online referring to the substance as "Shadow Jizz," "Demon Semen," "The Grim Reaper's Cum," "The Dark Nut," and several other names that follow that oddly similar pattern. Amy found all those distasteful and suggested we rename the substance "Armus," saying there was an evil, tar-like alien in Star Trek named that. Then John started calling it "Arby's Sauce," either because he misheard or because his mind is deteriorating at a frightening rate.

I don't actually remember what we landed on, and I guess it doesn't matter. In this context, let's just say that I'd let out a huge sigh of relief if instead of this stuff we found several kilos of black tar heroin and three corpses stuffed under Sebastian's mattress.

I said, "Lead the way."

As we passed into the house with its perfect central-air climate control, Amy muttered to me, "I grew up with religious parents, so I'm something of an expert in hiding illicit things in a bedroom. I bet I find his contraband stash within two minutes."

"Oh, please. Have you tried being a teenage boy in a world in which everything a teenage boy wants is considered creepy and wrong? I can probably tell you where he's got the good stuff hidden without even going in the room."

"Uh-huh. Want to make a bet that I find the secret thing before you do?"

"Sure," I replied. "I win, you have to spend an entire day doing a thick Cajun accent. Even if we get into an argument, you have to do the accent the entire time. And I mean so thick that I have to constantly ask you to repeat things. And I choose the day. It could be the day you're giving the eulogy at a funeral. You won't know."

"And if I win," she said, "we *both* have to do the accent."

Once upstairs, Regina unlocked the bedroom door and stepped aside. Bas's room was what I imagined my high school bullies went home to every night. A shelf with trophies. A row of autographed pictures of famous athletes on the wall. A framed news story about a high school football team, presumably his, winning a state championship. A TV positioned so that he could play video games from his bed. Dirty clothes scattered on the floor, mostly T-shirts and shorts. In one corner, there was an altar built out of human bones, topped with a glowing skull that was floating two inches from its stone base, slowing spinning in circles.

I said, "Anything jump out at you?"

"I'm going to go check around the altar."

"Good idea."

It wasn't the worst altar of bones I'd ever seen. You can get plastic ones online that are no more than Halloween decorations, but this seemed to be made out of actual human bones, probably sourced from a medical supply outfit and assembled for sale by some witchy online craft store targeting the upscale poseur market. The bones were held together by barbed wire, everything neat and clean. The hovering skull effect was achieved by a couple of powered magnets. No blood sacrifice offered here would be accepted by any ravenous demigod who had any kind of self-respect. Remember that in a genuine ritual, the bones aren't just an aesthetic, they are the evidence of a price paid, that you have proven that you're willing to violate the most sacred of taboos as a show of devotion. I mean, it's good that the kids just dabbling in this stuff don't understand that; it's not like I'm rooting for their spells to work. But if you offend the wrong entity, one day you're gone and your parents don't miss you because all memory of you is also gone. But maybe you do still exist, or a part of you, as a soul in the jaws of a dark appetite that chews and chews but never swallows.

There was a drawer below the spinning skull, and inside it was a leather-bound book. On its cover was a tangle of thin lines, like a complex maze or a doodle drawn during a very long, boring lecture. Above it were the words *The Book of Xarcrax,* and I was immediately a little embarrassed for both the author of the book and everyone who'd purchased it. They'd named their god like a goddamned miniboss in a video game. Bas had the bedroom of a high school jock, but if the dudes on the football team saw this, he'd be saddled with a permanent and shameful nickname within minutes.

Amy pulled out her phone and took a picture of the cover, probably already wondering how much we could sell the book for if the mother told us to confiscate it.

I said, "New bet. Before we open it, do you think it contains some kind of powerful forbidden knowledge, or has he hollowed it out to hide an object inside? I say it's hollowed out."

"I'm going to say forbidden knowledge. If he was going to hollow out a book, he wouldn't have chosen a creepy-looking one like this. He'd have gotten a copy of *Infinite Jest* or something. Start hollowing it out after, like, page seventy, since you know nobody is going to get that far. I bet this will open right to a bookmarked spell recipe that will supposedly give him mind control over his crush."

Every teenager we've found dabbling in this kind of occult bullshit was either trying to brainwash an object of infatuation or destroy a rival. We had one case of a fourteen-year-old girl trying to do a spell that would spawn a live rat inside the skull of a cheerleader who had made fat jokes about her.

"All right," Amy said. "Here goes."

She opened the book to find a face looking back at us.

Not a picture of a face—a live face, staring out like it was on the other side of a tiny window. The book had in fact been hollowed out, in a way, only the "compartment" was apparently a portal to somewhere. The face, just a few inches from Amy's thumb, gruffly shouted something at her that may or may not have been in another language.

She was so startled that she dropped the book. The cover slapped itself closed when it hit the floor.

Regina immediately popped into the room from the hall. "What did you find?"

I said, "Oh, uh, it's just a book. We'd like to take it back to the, uh, lab. To examine it. In case there's something hidden in there."

"What is it? Drugs? That black stuff you're talking about?"

"I'm . . . not sure."

"Let me see."

I snatched the book off the floor, holding the cover tightly closed. "We really shouldn't—"

"*Open it,*" said Regina in her Stern Mom voice. Amy and I glanced at each other. Amy had seen the portal, apparently. Would Regina? If so, it was hard to predict how people would react to that kind of thing.

I opened the book just enough to peer into it. The face wasn't there, but where there should have been text, there was instead an eight-by-ten window to some other place, or time, or something. It seemed like I could put my arm right through it. The portal seemed to lead to a large, dim space, with filthy concrete floors and high walls with rows of metal grates that I thought might be cages. A faint noise could be heard: human voices, or animals, a chorus of moans and whispers and grunts. Standing some distance away was a figure, a man bathed mostly in shadow. He turned as if he could see me, like the opening of the book was visible from his end somehow, maybe to him just a little square of light hanging in midair.

The man inside the book strode toward us. Then he broke into a run.

At Regina's urging, I turned it around for her to see and held my breath.

She said, "It's just a book." She seemed to scan a few lines. "It reads like nonsense."

"Ah, exactly." I could still hear the guy's rapid, muffled footsteps. I snapped the book shut, wondering if he could reach out and grab one of us by the throat.

"What is it?"

"We don't know," I said, "that's why we want to—"

Regina snatched the book from me and opened it again. "Why are you so nervous? What are you trying to keep me from seeing?"

She was holding it at an angle so that I could still sort of see into it. The man on the other side of the portal had stopped, but seeing the cover opened once again, resumed running toward it. He seemed very pissed off and also very sure that he could do something about it.

Amy, thinking quickly, said, "If you're going to hold it that close, I'd recommend you hold your breath. And if you want to handle it that much, I'd strongly suggest gloves. If Bas was using it for what we think, then the chemical can be transferred any number of ways. Can I take it back?"

Amy reached out and gently tried to close the cover, minimizing skin contact like she was handling something dirty. Regina didn't let go. She didn't like being forced to do anything, it seemed, and she certainly wasn't used to the hired help talking back. The footsteps from the other side of the book portal grew louder. The man shouted gruff demands that I couldn't make out, but it now sounded like he was in the room with us.

Thick, calloused fingers emerged from the book a split second before Regina relented and let Amy close it. Amy took the book and held it against her body. The book thumped in her hand, like the guy was punching at the cover from the other side. Amy flinched and almost dropped it again.

She gathered herself and said, "Sometimes books like this have hallucinogens in the paper fibers. Users tear off bits and put them on their tongue to get high. But if you so much as breathe the particles, you could be tripping for a week."

"Or," I said, in reaction to Regina's look of alarm, "it could be nothing, just a dumb book he got at a New Age store that sells crystals and bumper stickers about coexisting. We're just trying to be extra careful."

Thump.

Regina showed no reaction to the spasming book in Amy's hand.

Amy said, "If you're not comfortable with us doing the tests, you can take it to the police. But as far as I know, they don't know how to test for this. Or maybe I'm wrong. We're trying to help you here. We work for you."

"Let me know what you find. I mean immediately, the moment you get your results."

The book knocked again, then stopped, like the guy had given up.

Amy said, "Absolutely."

I said, "There's an additional fee for the test; Amy will have that all broken down for you in the invoice. Where did the altar of bones come from?"

"Oh, that stupid thing. Bas said he won it in a raffle at school. It was a decoration from a Día de Muertos event, something like that. Wait, do you think it's cursed? Should we get it out of the house?"

"I don't think so," said Amy. "Would you mind very much if we talked to Gracie? Oh, and, uh, do you have a bag or something I can put this book in?"

John

John steeled himself to do battle. He flexed his arms and swiped the ChuckleCave website onto his wall. He steered the cursor onto the Support Chat box and opened a window. He buckled in.

Please be patient while a customer service representative joins the chat.

You are chatting with JEREMY

JEREMY: Hello, how can we help you today?
JOHN: hi i have one of your egg toys, the magpie, and its acting weird
JEREMY: I'm so sorry to hear that! Is your issue with your Feathered Surprise Nest Play Set, or the Feeding Time Fun app?
JOHN: uh i guess both im not sure there have been some stories about people feeding them human parts, not like whole body parts or anything but like hair and teeth and stuff have you heard anything about that
JEREMY: It sounds like you're having problems with both the Feathered Surprise Nest Play Set and the Feeding Time Fun app. I'm so sorry to hear that! We'll do everything we can to get that resolved as soon as possible. What is your ChuckleCave username or email address?
JOHN: email is mrtatemyballs@lycos.com
JEREMY: Thank you so much for that! Unfortunately, I do not show that you are the original owner of the Feathered Surprise Nest Play set. Was it given to you by someone else?

JOHN: uh yeah it was originally bought by a girl named gracie gal-vatron, wait actually her brother got it for her, and they gave it to me. she couldn't handle the responsibility so they gave it to me i took all the steps in the app to transfer ownership

JEREMY: I'm so sorry but unfortunately, since you are not the original owner of the Feathered Surprise Nest Play Set, you are not eligible to receive a refund. Is there anything else I can help you with today?

JOHN: im not looking for a refund

JEREMY has left the chat.

John cursed and closed the window. He clicked the Support Chat link again.

Please be patient while a customer service representative joins the chat.

You are chatting with DOUGLAS

DOUGLAS: Hello, how can we help you today?

JOHN: yeah im a police officer and im investigating a crime involving one of your products, somebody is stealing teeth and i think its because of your egg toys i need to talk to somebody in charge

DOUGLAS: I'm so sorry to hear that! Is your issue with your Feathered Surprise Nest Play Set, or the Feeding Time Fun app?

Me

I was wearing a belt because I'm the kind of fat that makes my old pants too big somehow. I took it off and gave it to Amy so she could wrap it around the book to keep the filthy man from punching the cover open from the inside. We then dropped the belted book inside a cloth Whole Foods grocery bag that Regina gave us (do those stores not give you bags at the checkout line?).

What I wanted to do, more than anything, was leave. Sit down with this book, talk to Amy and John, maybe get in touch with somebody smarter than us to figure out what it all meant. We know from prior experience that, as a supernatural ability, making little holes in reality that let you travel from one spot to another is rare, but not unheard of. There are doors around town that open to spots miles away. For a while, at least—it's always a temporary state and one bestowed by experienced people or groups whom you hopefully will never meet. It's not the kind of thing amateurs can do, is my point, at least not without accidentally sucking themselves out of the universe in the process.

But if this book was opening to another country, or another planet, or timeline, or dimension, that would be the equivalent of finding that Bas had an entire neutron bomb in his closet. That's the kind of thing dark institutions can do with a lot of experts and techniques that are very closely guarded. If the president of the United States put out a request for a book like this, he not only wouldn't get it but would likely die of mysterious causes within weeks. Or, just as likely, wake up the next day to find he now lived in a reality in which he had never been president at all.

We followed Regina out to the backyard. I spotted Gracie some distance away, sitting in the shade of a massive tree near a plastic slide and swing set. She wore a yellow dress that she'd already gotten dirty. She had a pad of paper in her lap, and colored pencils were scattered around her. We stopped out of earshot, and Amy went to work on Regina.

"I know this is all super weird," she began in her Client-Soothing Voice, "but I want you to know that you've done everything exactly right so far. I just got here, and already I can tell that whoever or whatever is messing with your kids is going to get stomped into the dirt, because you won't quit until that happens. Your kids are lucky to have you. I mean that."

"Well . . . thank you."

"That said, it would be good for Gracie to see a counselor. Trauma is trauma no matter what causes it, and—"

"Dalton is taking care of that," said Regina in a tone that slammed the door on that line of inquiry.

"That's good. We have a list of good ones around town if you need—"

"We don't."

"Okay. Now, the stuff we found in Bas's room has us concerned, and we think there's a good chance this is about him, not Gracie. But this isn't about casting blame. If Bas is wrapped up in something bad, I want you to know that it's not his fault or yours. People get sucked into a—I don't want to use the word *cult*—but any kind of weird secret society thing, because what they offer is *real*. I'm not even talking about the supernatural stuff right now. Friends, a sense of purpose, or just the feeling like you're in on a cool secret club that sets you apart from everything else in this dumpy little town. You were a teenager once. You know how it can be."

I watched Regina closely. I don't know if Amy has great people skills or if they're just great compared to mine.

Regina said, "I was friends with a girl in high school who decided she was a devil worshipper, all because she got a crush on a boy in a death metal band. Dyed her hair black and wore a pentagram necklace, looked ridiculous. Her allegiance to the devil ended the day she heard the boy was seen making out with his ex at a party. She's a Christian singer now, has a record deal."

"Exactly," said Amy. "At that age, stuff comes along and you latch onto it. So right now, all David and John and I are trying to do is understand. We're not here to accuse anybody or demand you do this or that. We want to find out who roped your kids into this. Then we go from there."

Regina shook her head. "This is just a nightmare. I can't believe this is real. All the stupid rumors we heard about this town before we moved here, that silly special on cable that claimed it's full of werewolves, that the people all turn into monsters and prowl around at night? Ridiculous. But the moment we arrived here, I could feel it. I told Dalton, when it's sunny here, it feels like nighttime. Like the light isn't real light; it's just a disguise for the dark."

I was only half paying attention. I watched the woman's daughter scribble on her notepad on the other side of the yard, seemingly oblivious to us. The grass was so perfect and soft that I kind of wanted to roll around on it like a dog.

I asked, "How is Bas's relationship with Gracie?"

"She worships him. He protects her."

Amy nodded as if she already knew the contours of that particular relationship, then said, "I'm not going to interrogate her about her brother. I just want to ask her how things have been going. Either she'll open up to me or she won't. Are you all right with that? Obviously, you'd be right here, observing. I know I'm a stranger to you, so I'm not offended by whatever answer you give me."

Regina sighed. "I've asked her and asked her about all this and gotten nothing. You're welcome to try."

Regina and I watched as Amy walked over to where Gracie was doing her art, the mother making no effort to follow. We'd be far

enough away that we probably couldn't hear much of what was being said but were close enough that the mom could monitor the situation, to see if Gracie was getting upset or if Amy pulled a knife
on her or something.

To me, Regina said, "If you run into Dalton, my husband, just say
that I paid you to do a psychic cleansing of the house, because of the
bad dreams we were having. Don't mention anything about Bas or
this mysterious black drug."

"He'll be okay with you spending money on a psychic cleaning
ritual but not this?"

"It's not about the money. It's about what kind of conversation
he'll want to avoid. You mention psychics and, well, that's silly female stuff. You mention drugs, and it's time to start yelling and
grounding everyone. All wives have secrets. All wives learn how to
navigate their husbands' rage."

Regina was watching Amy as she said that. I sensed that she was
expecting me to disagree with her. I didn't.

Amy

Amy made it to where Gracie was sitting. The girl glanced up and then immediately went back to her drawing.

Amy raised a hand to shield her eyes from the blistering sun and said, "Can I sit here with you? That weird guy back there is my boyfriend. He wanted to talk to your mom, so they made me go sit in the yard."

Gracie shrugged.

Amy sat cross-legged next to the slide, then tugged at the neck of her shirt. "I can't believe how hot it is. At least you've got some shade under this tree. Do you think trees get hot? They don't have any shade."

Gracie said, "What happened to your hand?"

Amy held up her stump as if to examine it.

"I was in a car wreck, years ago. It got messed up bad enough that they decided to just lop it off and toss it in the trash. I also have a little piece of metal implanted inside my back, in my spine. Isn't that weird?"

"Does it hurt?"

"My back does. My hand doesn't. Not anymore."

"When you have dreams, do you have your hand back?"

"Sometimes. Sometimes I have bad dreams, where I'm trying to do something that's hard to do with one hand, like a monster is chasing me and I have to try to climb a ladder to get away from it. Other times I have nightmares where something bad happens to my other hand, so then I don't have any hands at all. Then I wake up and I'm thankful that I have a hand, and two feet, and a nose. And both eyes, even if I am blind without my glasses. A lot of people would trade places with me!"

"I know a girl at school who can't hear. She has a lady who helps her. They do sign language."

Amy nodded toward Gracie's drawing. "Is that your dog?"

"Not mine. It's just a dog. His name is Pooper."

"Oh, and there's the poop. Yeah, I see how he got that name. One day, I was out for a walk, and a man came by with a dog and the dog didn't have a nose. So I stopped the guy, and I said, 'Your dog doesn't have a nose? How does he smell?' and the guy says, 'Terrible!'"

Gracie scrunched up her face, then smiled a little. "Was that a joke? Oh my god. You shouldn't tell jokes, you're not good at it."

"I've been told that before."

"What is your boyfriend talking to my mom about?"

"Do you believe in magic?"

She shrugged.

Amy said, "Well, you know how magicians can do a trick to make it look like they're pulling a rabbit out of a hat? Some people can do that for real, making objects disappear and reappear somewhere else, that kind of thing. I think maybe your brother is one of them. Or he has friends who are."

"I'm not supposed to talk about that."

"That's fine. I try to mind my own business. But what David does—that's his name—what he does is go around and help people with weird problems, things having to do with that kind of magic, things that might be dangerous. Usually, it's nothing, but we just try to make sure. You see, this kind of magic isn't free. Doing a trick like this is like asking a favor from a mean friend who makes you do bad things in return. We don't want anyone to get hurt. That's all. We're not here to get anybody into trouble." She pointed at the drawing. "Is that where Pooper's owners live?"

"That's where he lives. His castle."

"David says you and I have something in common. I used to have a little pet mouse, years ago. I didn't have a cage or anything for him. He'd just come out at night and hang out under my bed. I'd give him a little bit of crust to eat and watch him hold it in his little hands. I called him Phil. One day, he just stopped coming around. I figure he probably got a job in another city."

"My mouse was named Penelope. Mom says she got out of her cage and escaped, but Bas says he thinks Dad flushed her down the toilet."

"Why would Bas say that?"

Gracie shrugged.

"Is your brother nice to you?"

"Yeah. I've seen some other brothers that were better, but he's pretty cool."

"I used to have a brother, too," said Amy. "His name was Jim. He was nice. He's gone, though. He's in heaven now."

"Why did he die?"

"Remember how I said magic stuff could be dangerous? That's how I found that out. It was scary. I was sad for a long time. I miss him every day. I miss my parents, too."

"I had a sister who died. Bas says there's no heaven, though. Can you do magic?"

"Uh, kind of. I can only do one thing, but it's pretty cool. But also kind of scary. Do you want to see it? I don't want to scare you."

"Does it take very long?"

"Not at all. I need a piece of paper, though."

John

Please be patient while a customer service representative joins the chat.

You are chatting with BRIAN

BRIAN: Hello, how can we help you today?

JOHN: hi brian are you a bot or a person?

BRIAN: I am here to assist you with whatever issues you may be having with your ChuckleCave product! Can you tell me which product you are contacting us about?

JOHN: you are the fifth person or bot i have talked to today

i am a journalist doing a story about how your toys are killing kids and are about to kill more of them

i was wondering if you'd like to comment before we publish

BRIAN: Please hold for just one moment.

BRIAN: Hello, John, someone from our customer satisfaction team would like to speak to you. What is a good phone number to reach you?

JOHN: what do you know, i found the right combination of words to get through. my number is

hold on, i just heard an alarm go off

something has tripped one of my booby traps i'll be right back.

Amy

"Do you like birds?"

Gracie shrugged.

With one of Gracie's black pencils, Amy drew a bird shape. Then she grabbed another pencil and gave it a red eye.

Amy said, "This is the crow. She's magic. Do you see her?"

Gracie nodded.

"If you listen really close, you can hear her calling to us. Do you hear it?"

Gracie listened. "No."

"That's okay. Just do what I say. And I mean exactly what I say. Okay? The first part of the trick, I'm going to point to different parts of this crow. And you're going to say the part out loud. We're going to try it. What am I pointing at?"

"Her beak."

"Good. Now, I'm not going to say anything, I'm just going to point. And each time, I need you to say the name of the part."

Amy pointed.

"Eye."

She pointed again.

"Feet."

Again.

"Wing."

Amy whispered, "Stop. Say that one again."

"Wing."

"Now I want you to keep that word in your mind."

Amy curled up the drawing into a tube, about an inch in diameter. Then she bent it into a U" shape.

"Make two fists, but hold up both of your thumbs. Like you're giving me a dual thumbs-up, about six inches apart. Like this. Good. Hold them very, very still."

Gracie did. Amy placed the paper tube so that it was sitting atop Gracie's hands, one end on each thumb, forming a paper arch.

"Now," whispered Amy, "I want you to say the name of that last body part."

"Wing."

"Now I want you to say it three times, as loud as you can. And we'll see if the crow calls to us."

"WING! WING! WING!"

Amy grabbed the paper tube off Gracie's thumbs, held it up to her ear, and said, "Hello?" Then she set it back on Gracie's thumbs and said, "It was just a telemarketer."

Then she burst out laughing and collapsed onto the grass.

Gracie said, "I don't get it."

"I turned you into a phone!"

"Oh my god," said Gracie, giggling. "That is so dumb. Why are you like this?"

Me

Amy and Gracie were laughing about something. I glanced down at the belted book in the Whole Foods bag, but it wasn't doing anything unusual at the moment. What I wanted to ask Regina about was her dead daughter, Silva, but I'll admit that I had no idea how to raise the subject. There was no way to do it that wouldn't imply it had something to do with this haunted toy business and, by extension, her son. Once we planted the idea that Bas had possibly used demonic forces to drive her teenage daughter to suicide—or something even worse—that was probably all Regina would want to talk about.

Regina said quietly, "You're not the police. You don't have the power to arrest anyone. So let's say you and your partners find out who or what is behind this. What can you actually do about it?"

I remembered the forest fire we'd started last month and said, "We, uh, adjust to whatever the situation calls for."

"What I'm trying to find out," said Regina, "is what actual abilities or skills do you have to handle this?"

I suddenly realized I was in a job interview and felt a cold sweat coming on.

"Let me put it like this. I think that someday somebody will invent a gadget, like a pair of special glasses or something, that you can look through and just see what's really out there. The things that haunt houses, the part of you that survives after you die, the invisible force that always seems to make all of the exact wrong things happen at once, all of it."

"The things that are inhabiting this town, you mean?"

"Sure. And other places like it. And maybe our lives will suddenly make perfect sense once that happens, the same as the first time somebody peered through a microscope and saw the tiny creatures that were turning their cheese moldy. And then, maybe they'll look back at people like me and John and all the hucksters out there and laugh at us, the same way we laugh about old-timey doctors trying to cure infections with leeches. But until that day, we're all you've got. There are other people who can do this, but not many, and they're very hard to find. Real ones, I mean—the hucksters, well, they're everywhere."

"But what's so special about you?"

"I won't bore you with the story. Basically, I think somebody tried to come up with the thing I described, something that would let a person see through reality, perceive what's really going on. I came in contact with it. So did John. Only it's not a pair of glasses."

"What is it?"

"A thick, black liquid. And the things you see with it, well, they look back at you."

Regina paused to take this in. Amy and Gracie had stopped laughing and were having a friendly conversation. Gracie seemed totally at ease.

"These things, the ones that look back," asked Regina, "are they what I saw in my dream? The walking shadows with the glowing eyes?"

"Don't talk about them. Don't think about them or picture them in your mind. What they can do to you . . . Imagine the whole world is like, let's say, a big painting. A huge mural, depicting all the people and nations and history. Now imagine a little kid snuck in with a pen and scribbled all over it, blotting out whole people or turning them into a crude mockery of what they were. The shadows can do that, somehow, with reality. Vandalize it. And the worst part is, you don't even know, because your mind is just another landscape for them to fuck with."

"That—no, that can't be real. Can it?"

"The way I understand it, under normal circumstances, they're restrained from interfering, locked out of our universe. But when humans start tinkering with time and space, anything that messes with the fabric of reality, the shadows can slip in, start wreaking havoc. But like I said, don't think about—"

I stopped talking. Amy was jogging toward us.

She skidded to a halt and said, "Bas went to retrieve the egg! He went to John's house!"

John

"OW! WHAT THE FUCK?!? OW!"

Sebastian "Bas" Galvatron was lying in the grass clutching his leg, which was caught in a modified bear trap. The rest of him was getting pelted repeatedly by a nearby paintball gun mounted on a tripod.

John approached and said, "Security bot, stand down."

The paintball gun continued firing. After a couple of more attempts at voice commands, John finally walked over and just unplugged it. He had four of them around the exterior of the house, attached to motion sensors. If you don't understand why a paintball gun would be an intruder deterrent, that only means you've never been shot by one. They hurt like hell.

John approached Bas, who was covered in colorful splatters and looked like he'd just come from learning a hard lesson at Willy Wonka's chocolate factory. The kid was now trying to free his leg from the trap. It didn't have the teeth of a bear trap, just a pair of curved bars covered in a roll of foam. It probably wouldn't break a bone, but you'd have to be Superman to free yourself, and you definitely wouldn't enjoy the experience.

Keeping his distance, John said, "Did you not see the signs? When somebody warns you that you'll be shot by robots, what just happened is the *best* outcome."

"I'm telling the police! This is assault!"

"You're going to tell the police you got painted by a robot sentry because you were trying to break into a house to steal back your possessed artifact? Go ahead. It'll be the third call like that the cops have gotten in the last ninety days. Maybe they'll do something this time, who knows?"

"It's mine!"

"Are you the one who gave the teeth to your sister? Where did you get them?"

"I don't know nothin' about that."

"We're not trying to build a case against you, dude. We're not the cops. Do you have any missing time? Like maybe you blacked out and did some things you don't remember doing?"

"Fuck you!"

"Look, you've got a genuine haunted flesh-eating toy, and you and I both know that's cool as hell. But your mom hired us to take care of this, and if we just give you the egg back, she's gonna yell at us and leave all kinds of bad reviews online. Dave and I are specialists at this. We—"

"I know who you are!"

"Then you know we're the real deal, and you know that when we say you're on dangerous ground, you should maybe listen. Who told you how to feed the Magpie? And what did they tell you would come out when it hatches? Or did they even tell you that part?"

"Let me out of this! It's cutting off the circulation in my leg!"

"I will, once I'm confident you're not going to storm in there, steal the egg, and try to summon something nasty. What's supposed to come out of it instead of a stuffed bird? A real bird? A mean one? Or a whole flock of murderous birds like in that old Hitchcock movie *Chicken Run*?"

Bas stopped struggling with the trap. He closed his eyes and began muttering words that John couldn't understand. He was deep in zealous concentration, like he was praying for the recovery of a loved one who was currently flatlining.

John said, "Hey, stop that! If you're trying to fire some kind of hex at me, you need to cut it out. You don't know what you're doing. Hey—"

Bas opened his eyes. With a look of malicious determination, he reached out with his right hand as if grabbing an object directly in front of him that only he could see. His hand disappeared, like he'd stuck it through an invisible hole.

John said, "Goddamn it! Bas, you shouldn't be doing— AAUUNNNGGGHHH!!"

John doubled over in pain. His stomach felt like it was being torn apart from the inside. Acid pushed its way up his throat.

He growled, "What the . . . Bas . . . stop—"

He felt something twisting and turning in his gut, like several objects writhing around in there, pinching and stabbing at the lining of his stomach. John lifted his shirt and saw lumps moving around his abdomen.

Fingers, pushing around from the inside.

John fell to his knees. "Stop that! FUCK! BAS!"

Bas was concentrating again, eyes closed, this time focusing on his trapped leg. His shoe tumbled to the grass, empty. His jeans, from the knee down, deflated as if there was suddenly no limb inside. He pulled the empty pant leg out of the trap, and a moment later, his leg reappeared.

Bas put his shoe back on and walked past John, his hand still missing, the fingers remotely wreaking havoc with John's guts. He went into the house and, a few minutes later, reemerged with the Magpie egg under one arm. As he passed, he kicked John in the face, then climbed onto a motorcycle he'd parked down the street. He made a motion with his right arm, the hand reappeared, and John felt his guts loosen. He collapsed to the grass, moaning as Bas rode away.

Me

We pulled up to John's place, and he met us at the gate. He could barely stand.

He read our expressions and grunted. "You missed him."

I said, "Bas was here?"

"Yeah. Nice kid. Left a while ago. He's got the egg."

"He does? Goddamn it, John, he's probably feeding tongues into the thing right now. You had one job!"

"You gave me like three jobs! I did all of them but that one. I never even had a chance; he showed up, cast a spell, said, 'Man, this shit is *da filthy*,' and took off."

Amy said, "He cast a spell? Are you all right?"

"Yeah. He teleported his hand inside my guts. I didn't like it. Oh, and if you're wondering how he got the egg out of the locked containment box, I'm going to assume it was the same way. It's still locked, but empty. Come inside before the sun makes the products in our hair spontaneously combust."

We entered his kitchen, the air-conditioning freezing the sweat on my skin. John immediately sat down, wincing.

I said, "He had an altar in his room, made of human bones but clearly store-bought. Amy has a picture on her phone. Oh, and that book she's carrying? There's a portal embedded in it. An angry dude from the other side tried to reach through. I guess that's weirder than the altar; maybe I should have led with that. I need caffeine. Do you have any Fight Piss?"

John said, "Bottom shelf of the fridge. Let me see the book."

Amy took the belt off the book and opened it for John. The angry man wasn't anywhere that we could see him, but otherwise the view was the same.

John leaned close and said, "The place it opens to, it looks like a slaughterhouse or something. And you hear that? It sounds like people and . . . whoa, do you *smell* that?"

I hadn't, but I also hadn't put my face that close to the book.

He said, "It smells like boiled sewage. Come smell it."

"I'll take your word for it."

John tentatively poked his hand through the portal, then drew it out again. "It's warm on the other side. Whatever the place is, it definitely doesn't have AC."

Amy said, "I can *almost* see it. When I opened it, I could sense the face there, could feel the guy breathing on me, but if you asked me if I could *see* him, not really? It'd be like if you were in a completely dark room and somebody came right up to you. But"—she leaned closer—"I can hear that place and, *ew,* I can smell it. Oh, god."

She backed away. John grabbed an empty paper coffee cup from the counter and tossed it through the book. We watched as it landed on the filthy concrete floor on the other side of the portal, then rolled to a stop. Nothing else happened, so we closed the book and re-belted it.

Amy said, "That confirms something that we already knew or should have known. From now on, you definitely don't want to put your face right in front of the book when you open it."

I said, "Because of the smell?"

"Because that guy on the other side might throw a rock and smash your face in."

"Ah, right."

John shook his head. "If that's opening to an entire other world, that's some industrial-grade wizarding. *We* can't even do that. Well, not on purpose anyway. Who the hell gave this to a teenager? You think he stole it?"

I said, "If so, the owners are gonna want it back. I guess it's bad news no matter how he got it."

Amy asked, "Did you get to talk to anyone at the company who makes the toy?"

"Yes, thank you for asking. It was a dead end at first, but I finally told them I was a reporter and wound up on the phone with a PR lady. Actually just got off the call. She insisted there was an internet hoax about their toys being possessed. Said some trolls started posting videos of themselves feeding them blood and hair, just as a prank. She said that if the story I wrote implied that they were complicit or liable in any way, I'd be hearing from all their many attorneys. We talked for three minutes, total."

I said, "If they're secretly in the carnivorous toy business, we'll be hearing from them, all right. And probably not their legal team, either."

"I hope they like bear traps. Did you get anything out of the girl?"

"I got confirmation that the toy is Bas's deal," said Amy. "He bought it, told her how to feed it. It's been his project from the start. Which, again, makes me want to find out what happened with the sister who killed herself. Gracie didn't want to talk about what exactly happened there. Not at *all*."

I said, "You think Bas caused that? Or even hexed her to death and the suicide was just a cover story?"

"We don't know anything like that yet. Even if he was involved, it could have been an accident. He could have summoned something he couldn't control. We should find out." She glanced at her phone. "Right now, we've got, I'd say, a little more than half of a hunger meter until the egg demands to be fed and, if all goes badly, this minion thing emerges. We have no idea where Bas took the egg. We know he wouldn't take it back home; his mom would see. Maybe a friend's house?"

"I was getting to that," said John. "There's an organization that kept coming up in my google searches, called the Simurai. That's spelled S-I-M—"

"Got it," said Amy, already tapping it into her phone. "They've got a local chapter and, yep, here's their Facebook page. And there's Bas Galveston, right there in their header image. There's like a dozen members."

"So do they have a secret clubhouse or temple or something?" I asked. "If so, finding the egg is probably as simple as figuring out where—"

"Doll Enema!" screamed John, pointing at the screen over Amy's shoulder. "Makes sense, it's been closed ever since the flood."

He was pointing at a picture of a pack of pale nerds dressed in black in front of a boarded-up movie theater. The actual name of the place had been the Undisclosed Dollar Cinema, but several of the letters had been stolen from the sign out front, and it now just said:

DOLL

INEMA

As John had said, it was one of a bunch of businesses around town that had closed after the flood and never reopened, same as the sex shop under my apartment. That flood was the kind of disaster that gets maybe one minute on the national news, probably with some helicopter footage of submerged cornfields and the washed-out bridge, maybe ending with a quick shot of a distraught family sloshing around what had been their living room. Then the anchor moves on to some celebrity scandal, and the audience never thinks about it again. Meanwhile, there are hundreds of people here still waiting on insurance payouts, every wall of their old homes now black with mold. Not many deaths in a disaster like this, but plenty of anguish.

I said, "Yeah, we definitely have to pay that theater a visit. Obviously, we don't know that's where they've taken the egg, but—"

Amy said, "Here we go."

The most recent update on the page was from just minutes ago: a pic of a few members of the group, including Bas, posing in front of a large box made of chain-link fence—a kennel designed for a couple of big dogs. Inside the fencing was the plastic Magpie egg, and behind the kennel was a silvery-white wall.

Damn, social media makes investigating people a breeze.

"That's a movie screen behind them," said Amy. "They have the kennel up on the stage. They probably plan to all gather tonight and watch it hatch this minion thing. Swallow the Gumball Swiper."

John said, "But that means the place may be full of people who can teleport their hands, just slap us from across town. We need to be prepared. We have the white magick dolls. Maybe we could tape them all over our bodies, create a field of protection."

I said, "Don't be ridiculous. We may still need to sell those."

Of the supposedly haunted dolls we'd accumulated, twenty or so were said to have "positive energy" or "white magick" (you could just hear the *k* John was adding to the end). Their powers mostly consisted of lending a vague peaceful vibe to the household and/or warding off bad dreams. John kept those in the back of his van for "emergencies" and because he worried that if we put them in the storage locker, they may start fighting with the dark energy dolls.

John said, "My point is, we can't just charge in with chain saws buzzing. If all these guys have actual power, we probably wouldn't have a chance to saw off their spell-casting hands before they teleported their entire bodies into our urethras."

"Right. And if everyone but Bas is just a poseur, then we'd just be dismembering a bunch of nerds and we'd all go to jail after the world's most baffling trial."

He thought for a moment. "I have an idea. This is going to sound crazy, but—"

John vanished from in front of me. So did the room.

AN EXCERPT FROM
PROJECTIONS INTO THE VOID,
BY DR. ALBERT MARCONI

Before I proceed, allow me to address the proverbial elephant in the room: How can an educated man like myself believe in powerful, cruel entities that exist in the void of the unknown? In fact, does that belief not just as egregiously conflict with my identity as a man of faith? To answer this, I am afraid I must introduce you to Tlaloc. Here, I should warn you that what I am about to share is only for those with strong stomachs and an exceptional tolerance for reading about the suffering of innocents. The rest of you may wish to skip to the next chapter.

First, allow me to establish some context. In the Chinese province of Shaanxi, a dig site revealed an ancient city dating back more than four thousand years. Under one stone wall was found eighty skulls of young girls, the remains of a mass human sacrifice intended to imbue the foundation with supernatural protection. In the town of Huanchaco, Peru, experts unearthed the five-hundred-year-old remains of more than two hundred sacrificial victims, all children between the ages of five and fourteen. Engineers laying a water line in Oxfordshire, England, dug up two dozen butchered skeletons dating back nearly three thousand years, including a woman who'd had her arms bound and feet severed. These grisly discoveries lay bare for us a harsh but undeniable truth, which is that our frivolous modern lifestyle was purchased with oceans of blood. The god I am about to discuss, Tlaloc, is the cruelest known to me, but that means little considering how much of human history was not documented at all. No doubt, some were worse. If so, I myself am satisfied to never know their names, just as a few moments from now, you may find yourself wishing you had never heard of Tlaloc.

Under modern Mexico City, you will find the centuries-old remnants of Tenochtitlan. There, archaeologists have recovered thousands of skulls of human sacrifice victims, many of which would have had their chests hacked open by Aztec priests and their still-beating hearts ripped out, before their heads were removed and impaled on a rack for public display. Here, I offer my second warning about the subject matter: The paragraph you just read is tame compared to what is coming.

Tlaloc, you see, was one of the deities the Aztecs were attempting to please with their brutality, a god of fertility and water who was worshipped for more than fifteen centuries (his reign may date back even further; reach back in time and you will often find familiar gods reigning under older, now-forgotten names). Tlaloc was believed to grant the rains that nourished the crops, as well as the hailstorms that ruined them, depending on his fickle mood. If Tlaloc was displeased, he could withhold the rain entirely, dooming the local population to a slow death via starvation. And what pleased Tlaloc, the Aztecs believed, was the tears of children.

Thus, in one recent find, the skeletons of forty-two children were discovered among the sacrificial offerings at the Great Pyramid of Tenochtitlan, mostly males of an age when a modern child would be attending kindergarten. Here is where we must remember that the children's blood was not sufficient for Tlaloc—the tears were his prize. This is why every single tiny skeleton bore signs of intentionally inflicted dental cavities and abscesses, as well as broken and infected bones. These were wounds specifically intended to impose constant, unthinkable suffering over the course of weeks or months prior to sacrifice. If a child's weeping were to cease in the course of the final ceremony, their hands and feet would be burned, their fingernails ripped out, lest Tlaloc be enraged by the insufficient wailing. These sacrifices were performed en masse before, during, and after the growing season. Children were tortured to thank Tlaloc for rains provided in the past, children were tortured to atone for sins committed in the present, children were tortured to ensure productive rains in the future. This went on for century, after century, after century.

Now, please, ask me again why I believe in the existence of dark gods.

Understanding why this occurred in so many places and for so long seems paramount to understanding humanity, society, and (in my opinion) the nature of the universe we inhabit. Volumes have been written about how these practices came about, but in my view, they had to have occurred for only one of two reasons:

1. A cruel, possibly deranged deity made contact with primitive peoples and deceived them into mutilating their own children for reasons incomprehensible to a sane mortal mind;
2. These peoples peered into the void and, finding nothing, *chose to believe* that it contained powerful, undying beings who demanded the anguish of their innocent children as a form of tribute, nourishment, or both.

My friends, if I am mistaken in my belief that the truth lies in something like option #1, please see it as a form of wishful thinking, an old man who prefers not to believe that such a call is coming, as they say, from inside the house. This brutal method of worship is the oldest known to us; it is even theorized by some scholars that human sacrifice actually predates both religion and written language. This would mean that, long before humans were capable of complex thought or mythology, tribes from all over the globe looked to the sky and sensed that it hid a chorus of sadistic, ravenous faces.

As for how I can reconcile this with my Christianity, I would note that the Old Testament does not assert that the bloodthirsty gods of rival nations, such as Ba'al or Moloch, were imaginary, only that they were cruel and unworthy of worship. Of course, my atheist friends are fond of reminding me that Yahweh Himself ordered His followers to punish rival tribes with total annihilation, specifying that, yes, not even their children were to be spared. I can assure you, I have spent more time pondering this than you know. I am also aware that when the Spanish were forcibly converting the indigenous peoples of Mexico to Christianity five centuries ago, they told worshippers of Tlaloc the story of God demanding Abraham sacrifice his son Isaac.

For you see, this was how they reassured them that their gods were not so different after all.

SUNDAY. AUGUST 21. 8:58 P.M.
STRAWBERRY POPSICLES
HUNGER AT 98%

Me

A man was talking. It wasn't John. I felt like I was going to fall, and I put my hands down to catch myself, only to find I was sitting in the lotus position on a dirty floor. I found myself in a large, dim, musty room, a chain-link fence just a couple of feet from my face. Beyond the fence in the darkness were rows of moldy seats. I whipped my head around and found Amy sitting next to me, John next to her. Amy met my eyes, and her startled expression said that she had experienced the same jump forward in time I had, unless by sheer coincidence she was being startled by something unrelated. She immediately reached up to her face and stuck her fingers in her mouth. It only occurred to me later that she was making sure her tongue was still there.

We were inside the kennel we had just(?) been looking at in the photo on Facebook. I was unsurprised, yet still alarmed, to find the Magpie egg on the floor right behind us, on our side of the chain link. The fucking thing had mind-controlled us right into its pen.

Standing directly in front of the kennel was Sebastian Galvatron, closing a padlock on the kennel gate, tugging on it a couple of times to double-check. He wasn't the one talking, though. There was a college-age man in a black overcoat nearby on the stage, finishing a sentence.

"—they certainly won't be laughing then."

He was putting on some kind of an accent. He was pale, and his hair was a mop of greasy curls. I think he'd modeled his look after Sherlock Holmes as he appeared in the BBC series starring a British actor whose name at the moment was coming up in my mind as Benito Krimblesnatch. That's the look he was going for anyway; he actually looked like the kind of guy who'd stay up late flirting with girls on social media, then switch accounts and spam them with rape threats if they rejected him. He looked like the kind of guy who soothed himself to sleep at night with fantasies of peeling the skin off his high school bullies. He looked like the kind of guy who, in middle age, would get a job with some modicum of power over others and make their lives hell.

There was movement to my left, inside the kennel—John was frantically brushing something off his shirt. His cigarette had fallen out of his mouth because, from his point of view, it had suddenly appeared between his lips, and it had presumably tumbled out when he'd opened his mouth to ask what the fuck was going on. Amy pulled out her phone, I thought to check the time, but she instead went right into the Magpie's feeding app. She showed me the hunger meter—the stomach symbol had been almost entirely taken over by ravenous red. Within minutes, the egg was due to start howling for its meal of tongues and, once it got it, the assistant body parts collector known as Swallow would presumably emerge. It's hard to say which of those two events would be worse for us.

Under my breath, I asked her, "How long has it been?"

"It's almost nine. So about six hours?"

Jesus Christ. A whole quarter of the day gone, more if you only count the part you're awake. What in the hell had this thing been making us do? For all I knew, we'd committed multiple shooting rampages. Somewhere on the stage could be a garbage bag full of tongues we'd collected. We could have gone on camera and done a six-hour-long Christian rap concert. Nothing was off the table.

Benito said, "This won't get us all the way there, obviously, but it's a start. Of course, if you're right and we're wrong, you have nothing to worry about. But if we're right, it will give you an opportunity to see hard proof. And them as well."

Benito gestured, not to the theater seats (where I could make out several black-clad members scattered in the darkness) but to a camera on a tripod that was recording us and the toy. I was even more confused now, because he was talking to us in a casual tone that implied he was continuing a friendly conversation we'd been having. I made eye contact with Bas, and more than anything, he just seemed curious and excited. Eager to witness something he'd waited a long time to see.

What in the hell had the Magpie been making us say and/or do?

"I'm sorry," I said to Benito, "I got distracted for a moment. Can you please quickly repeat who you are, why we're here, and what's about to happen?"

He seemed genuinely taken aback by this request.

Amy said, "Yeah, like for viewers who are just joining the stream? People always tune in late."

"We are the Simurai," he began, suddenly invigorated. "We are the emissaries of Xarcrax. We are here to break the simulation."

He turned toward the camera and adapted a manner like he was a Bond villain explaining how the deviousness of his master plan was exceeded only by the righteousness of his cause.

"For you see," he began, "all of the world's greatest experts agree that our universe is an artificial creation. The logic is very simple: It is a certainty that human technology will evolve to the point that it can perfectly simulate reality, and once that occurs, it is also a certainty that humans will run countless simulations simultaneously, just as how on any given day we are simulating tens of millions of fictional worlds in our video games . . ."

I immediately got bored with what he was saying and studied the kennel instead. It was maybe ten feet long, six feet wide, and not quite tall enough for me to stand up. On one hand, it was clearly built to withstand the assault from multiple muscular dogs who badly wanted out; the frame the chain link was anchored to was metal, and the whole apparatus was bolted to the floor. The padlock Bas had placed on the gate opened with a combination. But surely a cage intended to hold two or three demoted wolves could not hold three humans who, combined, had the intelligence of two humans.

"—therefore, statistically, we can conclude that we ourselves are living in a simulation," said Benito, who was apparently still talking. "This was known to be true even before physicists discovered that high-energy particles reveal space-time to be arranged in a neat, artificial grid. But we don't need to get into the messy details. All of you have observed evidence of the simulation, in the form of its glitches. Have you ever lost a small object, maybe a tool or a piece of jewelry, in a way that shouldn't have been possible? In my experience, virtually everyone has that story."

It sounded like a rhetorical question for the camera, but the guy paused as if waiting for an answer from us.

Amy said, "Sure," while glancing at her phone. It had been nice of the Magpie to let us bring our phones along. We sat in silence again until the three of us realized Benito wasn't going to move on until she elaborated.

"Uh, when I was in third grade," said Amy, "I was riding my bicycle down the sidewalk. I had a Barbie in my hand and dropped it in the grass. I immediately stopped, but the doll was just gone. I searched for an hour; it was broad daylight. My dad came by, and we both looked for it, even checking places it couldn't possibly have gone. Never turned up."

"Exactly," said Benito. "That is a glitch; small objects routinely just fall out of the world. Have you ever actually finished a stick of lip balm before it disappeared? Or an ink pen? The system eventually just deletes them, either on accident or maybe just to free up memory."

John said, "One could almost call this simulated world a kind of . . . *matrix*."

Amy muttered, "Oh, god." She glanced back at the Magpie, waiting for it to start howling.

"Our group," said Benito, "has mapped the parameters of the simulation and found ways to manipulate it. That is, in fact, the entire purpose of the simulation—to develop entities who can become aware and break free from the NPCs who've been planted here to challenge us."

"The what?" I asked, before I could stop myself.

"Non-player characters," said Amy. "Like the computer-controlled characters in a game. Right?"

"We call them the Empties," said Benito. "The 'people' who clearly do not have any kind of internal life, no self-reflection, no ability to perceive their place in the world, nothing like what you would call a 'soul.' It is the duty of us—the real, living persons—to break the simulation, so that we can be freed from it."

"Like in *The Matrix*," I said. "Thank you. We now know one hundred percent of what we need to know about your belief system. We will all live by *Matrix* rules from now on if that will end this conversation. John already has the PVC clothes. He dressed like that all through high school. We mainly are waiting for you to get to the part where you explain how your belief system ties into this egg toy thing."

"The toy in the hands of an Empty is just a toy. The toy in the hands of a human is a key. Or part of a key that will manifest Xarcrax and crash the system."

Amy said, "Ah, there it is."

It was going to be a real struggle to keep from laughing at this guy. If I died getting eaten by a "Xarcrax," I'd spend my last breath giggling at its name. I imagined something with tentacles and a flashing weak point in the center that you have to shoot exactly three times.

"The feeding ritual requires us to collect tissue from Empties, to prove that we accept that they are not real and cannot feel pain. The act of collection proves we have seen through the simulation."

Amy said, "Yes, that all sounds great. So who's in charge of your group here? Is it you?"

I said, "Trust me, it's not him."

Benito shot a meaningful look toward Sebastian and said, "Your mind is not yet capable of grasping the answer to that question."

Amy turned to Bas. "Do you think your sister is an NPC, Bas? She seemed real to me when I talked to her."

Benito burst out laughing, then faced the camera. "So, as we have said, two of the three in this cage are human. One of them is not. I would hope that it would be apparent by now which one I'm talking about." He then turned back and stared directly at me.

There's always this awkward moment when people say they've heard of me, because it's always going to come down to *what* they've heard. And, more importantly, what they chose to believe. I worked under a pseudonym for years, but by this point, both my real name and fake name can be found in books, articles, videos, at least one song. Lots of the biographical details you find out there are bullshit, but some are not. Those particular details tend to bias people's opinions against me, and by that, I mean they start actively rooting for my home to be targeted by a cruise missile.

John, Amy, and I exchanged glances, then John said, "Ah, we actually knew that already. We feel like every friend group should have at least one nonhuman in it. It's not even a sensitive subject for us anymore."

"That's certainly not what you were saying an hour ago," replied Benito through a smirk.

Wait, this guy didn't know we were being mind-controlled? Was the Magpie doing it without him knowing? Why? What the fuck is going on here?

I said, "Look, we aaaalllll remember what was said an hour ago. But now that we're all on the same page, why not leave me in here and let them go? Tongues can only be collected from nonhumans, so . . ."

Benito was confused. "What good would that do?"

He checked his watch and then held out a hand to Bas, who

responded by wordlessly handing him the portal book, which we'd apparently brought with us?

Benito peered into the book and said, "Hello? Are you there?"

There was a muffled answer from the other side, presumably the man who'd yelled at us when we'd tried to look through it earlier today. Bas then tore open a case of bottled water that was on the floor nearby and handed the bottles to Benito one at a time, who in turn fed them into the book, making a kind of ceremony out of it.

"The irony," said Benito as he handed a bottle through, "is that the app and the 'actual' feeding are really the same, once you know the truth. Cells from an Empty are just pixels, like you see on the screen of your phone."

He fed the last bottle into the book, and a moment later, something metal was handed back through from the other side. It was a dirty, dented elongated bowl, like something you'd see on the mess kit in a World War I trench. Benito set the bowl on the floor, then was in the process of closing the book when the voice from the portal yelled angrily at him. Benito grabbed the bowl, dumped its contents onto the floor at his feet, then handed the empty bowl back through the book before closing it.

I guess I shouldn't have been surprised by the contents of the bowl: four pink human tongues, each ending in a ragged mess of bright red where they'd recently been hacked out of a mouth. I heard Amy suck in a breath, but I was secretly relieved that they'd met their quota without having to slice anything out of us.

"So one weird thing we've noticed about our, uh, simulation over the years," said Amy, trying to keep her voice steady, "is that if you kill or mutilate someone, *you still go to jail*." She stared down Bas, whom I noticed had quietly backed away from the stage. "Even if it's just simulated jail, it feels very real, and the people who go there seem to hate it."

I said, "Actually, I'm kind of done with this. Bas! Hey! Open the cage. Right now."

"Oh, so you're losing confidence in your friend's little experiment?"

said Benito, looking at John. "Sounds like they disagree with your point of view."

I glanced at John, who of course had no idea what this guy was referring to but seemed to also be done playing along.

John said, "Bas, if you don't let us out of here, I'm telling your mom."

Bas looked more confused than ever, and I remembered that, for all we knew, his mother was tied up in the next room or dead at our hands—we'd been acting as puppets all evening. Hell, maybe we were the ones who'd given Bas a ride here.

With that, the toy unleashed its obnoxious crying sound effect. Benito pulled out his phone, did the "feeding" through the app, and received the thanks from the electronic voice ("YUMMY! THANK YOU, MOMMY, I WUV YOUUUU!!!"). He then grabbed two of the tongues, one in each hand, and approached the kennel. I felt around my pants to see if maybe I'd wound up with some kind of weapon in my pockets during the time I wasn't in control of myself. No such luck.

I said, "Buddy, I'm telling you, you don't want to feed that thing, and we're not going to let you. We'll be doing you a favor. Nothing that is summoned into our world is going to obey you. The entities that lurk out there, they are very good at manipulating people like you and Bas to do what they want. That's because for the most part, they have no power here unless *you give it to them*."

"The more fear you show, the more we know we're right. All who are locked in the simulation are programmed to fear any disruption, just as an infant fears leaving the womb. As with the infant, your liberation will come with screams."

He moved to the rear of the kennel, so that he would be near the toy. The plastic egg opened just a little, maybe a quarter of an inch. I couldn't make out what was inside. Benito held a tongue above the cage and dropped it in. I reached up to try to catch it before it fell to the egg, but the pink chunk of meat was snatched from the air and yanked downward in a blur. A hair-thin appendage had whipped up from the crack in the egg and pulled the meat down into the gap, leaving a red smear on the white plastic.

All three of us recoiled. I noticed that Bas did, too.

A smirking Benito said, "This thing will take your fingers right off if you try that again."

Amy said, "Okay, on some level, you guys—all you guys—have to know this is a bad idea. Just mentally take a step back and think about what you're doing right now."

Benito smirked and addressed the camera. "Spoken like a true Empty. A noise designed to test my resolve. Look, guys, the simulation even gave her freckles, as if playing to my fetish would make me weak in the knees. A character manufactured in a blink, for this exact moment in time."

I said, "Wait, you think *she's* the nonhuman?"

Benito dropped in another tongue. The egg snatched it out of the air before it fell halfway down. Growing impatient for its meal. I admit I didn't try very hard to interfere that time.

"All right," I said, "I need you to listen to me very carefully, because I can absolutely get this cage open if you force me to. But I don't want this Swallow thing to get out into the world, and I'm not totally sure that it won't just go grab the remaining tongues off the floor regardless of what you do next. So, what you need to do is take the two tongues that are left and, if you can, *get very far away from here.* Let us deal with this."

Benito bent over and picked up the two remaining tongues, one in each hand. "It is in moments like these when humans like you and I can get distracted from the obvious truth of our humanity. But haven't you ever noticed that things seem to just kind of work out for you? That the disasters and mass deaths only target other people? That everything that happens seems intended to teach you, personally, a lesson? Like all of these background characters and movie extras"—he gestured at Amy with a severed tongue—"are just here to help you get context for yourself, for your own actions, your own nature? I assure you, when she's out of the view of humans, she ceases to exist."

He turned to his right fist, which was clutching a severed tongue, and said, "Isn't that right?"

He wiggled the tongue to make it flap and in a high-pitched voice said, "That's right, Jonas!"

He dropped the third tongue into the cage. The egg snatched it before it had even fallen all the way through the chain link. Benito yanked his hand back, counting his fingers.

Addressing the camera, Amy said, "For anyone out there watching this, if Mr. Swallow hatches and murders all three of us and gets out of this building, please call Dr. Albert Marconi. He's the guy who used to have all those ghost hunting shows on cable? Show him this video. If there's a chance this can still be fixed, he's the guy who can fix it. And please don't blame this kid here; he's being manipulated. Oh and, uh, please buy merchandise from our site; somebody's going to get stuck paying for our funerals, and hopefully that will help offset the costs."

John said, "I agree with all of that, aside from the part about not blaming this guy. There's one tongue left, he can make a choice right now to stop whatever's about to happen. So I'm telling you, if he lets this Swallow thing out and it wreaks havoc to, god forbid, let some much bigger and worse monster into the world, find this dude and give him the ass-beating he deserves."

Benito reached over us with the fourth and final tongue. The egg snatched it out of his fingers as they hovered above the chain link. He recoiled and then shook off flecks of blood. The Magpie had sliced open his palm.

We had all positioned ourselves to face the plastic egg, which was still just barely open. I thought I saw something moving in there. Knots of hair, tangles of white globs, human teeth, a licking tongue.

I twisted around to grab at the door of the kennel, shaking it. "Hey! HEY!" I kicked at the jamb, growling, doing more damage to my foot than the metal. "BAS! ONE OF YOU! OPEN THIS FUCKING THING!"

John

Dave sat back and nodded, now satisfied that the kennel just might hold.

"All right," he said, addressing the pale man in the overcoat wiping blood and tongue juice off his hands, whom John had been mentally referring to as Benjamin Cumbadger. "Pay attention. Whatever happens, *do not open this cage*. Because of your foolishness, it's now up to us three to destroy Mr. Swallow before it can get out there and hurt anybody. Amy, remind me, what's the next food the egg says it needs? Because that's what this little monster is going to try to collect from us when it hops out."

Barely taking her eyes off the egg, Amy tapped at her phone and said, "It was gumballs. Eight of them, it says. Vanilla. See?"

The man outside the cage was studying his own phone. More to the camera than anyone, he said, "That one seems pretty obvious, wouldn't you say?"

Amy showed John her screen. The pixelated "gumballs" were round and white, with a smaller shadow in the middle, tinted blue. There was a hint of pink pixels around the edges that could almost suggest tiny threadlike veins.

"All right," said John. "This thing is coming for our testicles. It needs eight, between the three of us, we only have five." John stripped off his shirt. "One of us needs to act as bait. The other needs to trap this Swallow thing, whatever it is, in my shirt."

Amy, who was always one step ahead, said, "I have deterrent

music on my phone. We can control it with that—that is, assuming Swallow isn't going to turn out to be the size of a skyscraper. Remember, that egg is probably a portal, like that book. The creature doesn't necessarily have to fit in there."

"The music should work regardless of size. But let's hope it's not a kaiju-scale entity, because I don't want to have to pay for the damage its corpse causes when it goes down."

Something was stirring inside the egg. Pink flesh pushed through the crack—one of the disembodied tongues, now operating on its own.

Amy readied her phone, ready to tap a Play button.

The three of them had no clear idea as to why unholy entities are repelled by, if not completely incapacitated by, beautiful music. One theory is that uplifting melodies are connected to the holy vibrations that emanate from the golden light at the center of all things and that no creature that feeds on suffering can bear to be in its presence, kind of like how it's hard to eat a steak if a cow is staring at you from across the table. Others say that what repels the darkness is not the music but the effect that music has in strengthening the human spirit—there is a reason why victorious battle scenes in films are accompanied by the sounds of a triumphant orchestra. But in moments like this, all that matters is that it almost always works if you have chosen the right music. It must be a piece that instills the same joyous thrum of the soul in any human who hears it, one that transcends time, culture, and language. The particular track Amy had locked and loaded on her phone was "Regulate" by Warren G, featuring Nate Dogg.

The plastic polka-dotted egg was pried partially open from within. What birthed itself into the kennel was a knot of hair, teeth, and tongues in the shape of a starfish, like a sculpture from a serial killer's Etsy shop. It hopped out onto the floor, and the egg snapped closed behind it. The newborn horror was closest to Amy, and she quickly scooted backward, only having a couple of feet to go until her back banged into the chain link behind her.

Then the creature simply wasn't there anymore. Or, rather, John could no longer see it.

The floor was covered with a thin layer of silt, the dusty film that had been left behind by the flood and still remained on every neglected surface in town. Where the testicle-hungry creature had been, there were now only four moist spots where it stood on its tongue appendages.

Dave said, "Shit! I can't see it! Can you?!?"

John and Amy both yelled that they couldn't, then Amy said, "Track its little footprints!"

As she said it, those four moist tongue-prints became six, then eight—tracks left behind as the creature moved.

John held his shirt at the ready and said, "NOW!"

Amy hit Play. There was a synth track and a whistle, followed by a voice urging the regulators to mount up. In response, there was a terrible shriek, and the tiny, moist tongue-prints in the dust took off . . . in the wrong direction, toward Dave. He recoiled and screamed like a man who was feeling a ravenous tongue monster on his chest. He reached up and appeared to be fighting to keep the invisible Swallow away from his face.

"AAUGH!" he reported. "Get it off me!"

Damn it, thought John. Whatever the Magpie had forced them to do during their period under its control, they now knew one thing for certain: Dave's face had ended up smelling like balls. Dave was gritting his teeth, feeling the slimy creature crawling its way up onto his cheeks. Then he opened his mouth and bit something near his face that he could feel but not see.

The creature shrieked, and Dave said, "Catch!"

He chucked a squirming ball of nothing at John, who had his shirt ready like a net. He caught the thrashing monster and pulled the shirt around it like a bindle. John didn't know how long it would hold; the shirt was just a normal T-shirt, made of patches of crimson leather and golden chain mail. He raised it above his head and slammed it to the floor. Then he did it again with all his strength, intending to repeat the process until the tiny monster stopped thrashing. On Amy's phone, Warren G was being robbed of his Rolex after a dice game gone wrong. Would Nate Dogg arrive in time to regulate?

"AMY!" shouted John as he slammed the Swallow monster to the floor. "Bring your phone closer! Warren is about to say the part about how he wishes he had wings so he could fly away!"

Amy did as asked. The creature spasmed and shrieked. Outside the kennel, Benjamin moved closer, fascinated and more than a little nervous. John got the sense that this was the first time he'd actually seen a manifestation from the other side, and nothing about it was what he'd been imagining. Bas, on the other hand, was utterly awestruck, like he was witnessing an uncertain miracle, the long-lost lover who has returned from the grave but may still turn out to be a zombie.

Amy brought her phone to bear on the thrashing little beast. John held the bundled shirt firmly to the floor. He reached into his boot for the ivory-handled dagger with the obsidian blade that he had just now noticed was in there. He had no idea if this creature could be killed by such a weapon, but its health was almost certainly not going to be improved by it. John raised the blade, and at the same moment, Benjamin made the fateful decision to run up to the kennel and yell, "Stop!"

He put his fingers on the chain link, his face pressed against it. John swung the blade down, and the invisible creature burst through the shirt to avoid the blow, ripping open a hole in the direction of Benjamin's face. The man backed away from the kennel, startled but unsure of what was happening—he apparently could not see the creature any better than the three prisoners could. What he did see were strands of chain-link fencing first bending, then snapping and curling inward, the creature tearing its way out, proving that its kennel-escaping capabilities were beyond both dogs and humans. *This*, thought John, *is why you use bulletproof glass instead.*

John yelled to Benjamin, "Fly, you fool!"

The man did not move. Maybe it wouldn't have mattered if he had.

The hole in the fencing opened enough for the creature to slip through, and in a blink, Benjamin's face was contorting in a way that John had never seen before, aside from one other time: When Arnold Schwarzenegger was exposed to the vacuum of Mars near the end of *Total Recall*. Benjamin's left eye was wide open, bulging unnaturally. He grabbed at his face, but his hands stopped an inch away, blocked by the body of the unseen creature that had latched onto him.

"Damn it!" shouted John. "All of us were wrong. It's going for our *eyes!*"

The man's eyeball bugged out farther and farther, the creature sucking it out of the socket. Benjamin screamed in a way that would ruin slasher films for you if you ever heard it. No actor can imitate it; it's the sound of an adult human reduced to infancy, the universe suddenly such a terrifying and treacherous place that the only reaction is to utterly abandon dignity and howl at it with all your mind, body, and air. When you encounter that awful noise for real, actor screams seem like a halfhearted mockery in comparison.

John, Amy, and Dave watched as the man's eyeball pulled itself out of the socket, then with a *snap* was severed from the muscles and optic nerve. The eye fell off his face, but was in the clutches of the invisible creature—it never hit the floor, jiggling to a stop an inch above the four wet prints in the dust. Then the eyeball bounced and twitched, the creature swallowing it. Once it came to rest in Swallow's belly, the severed eye stopped moving but remained visible.

John saw a shape moving in the darkness of the theater. It was one of the nerds in the audience, making for the exit like he was being launched off the deck of an aircraft carrier. He was leading a pack, several of the dudes who'd come to watch having abruptly lost their enthusiasm for the project. Sebastian Galvatron chased after them, yelling at them to come back, to man up, to have faith.

This prompted Dave to let out a howl of rage and grab the ragged hole in the chain link, ripping it open using the superhuman strength that Dave could summon from time to time but that the authors of this account may have failed to mention prior to this moment. On the floor outside, the hovering severed eyeball that marked the location of Swallow moved toward the screaming Benjamin. There was still another eye left to claim. The guy fell to his knees, and Swallow, marked only by the severed eyeball inside it, jumped up onto his upper arm.

Seeing that Dave clearly wasn't going to get the fencing open in time to save the man, Amy yelled, "Get on the floor! Facedown! Guard your face with your arms! We're coming!"

Amazingly, Benjamin apparently heard this advice and still had enough of his wits about him to act on it. He threw himself to the floor, sealing off his face with his forearms. The floating eyeball and invisible tongue-feet of Mr. Swallow danced around the floor at the perimeter of the prone man's defenses, leaving an arc of those little moist prints.

Dave, trying to climb through the wound in the fencing, shouted to the few remaining guys out among the theater seats hidden in shadows, the ones who hadn't lost their nerve. They were standing now, but weren't moving.

"HELP HIM! HEY!"

They were muttering to each other, but none came to their friend's rescue. The creature crawled up Benjamin's forearm and pawed through his curly hair. Swallow apparently decided on its approach, and suddenly there was a spray of blood, bone, and dark curls as it drilled its way through the back of Benjamin's skull, the wound erupting like a shaken-up can of meat soda. Benjamin screamed right up until the part of his brain that controlled that function was shredded and ejected from the back of his cranium. His head thrashed around as the creature inside mined for its prize. A moment later, it emerged, invisible body covered in bits of brain and with now two human eyeballs floating in its gut.

Amy slapped her hand over her mouth and was trying to blink

tears out of her eyes. The creature hopped off the stage and disappeared into the vast, darkened theater.

Dave had squirmed his way through the gash in the fence and tumbled to the dusty stage, right next to Benjamin's corpse.

"You!" screamed David toward the men in the seats. "Dipshits! Seal every exit, every window, every little hole that leads to the outside. Do *not* let this thing escape! And protect your eyes!"

The dipshits didn't act like they heard him. They were freaking out now, looking at their dead friend and having a hushed and panicked conversation with each other. It really seemed like a pack of dudes watching everything fall apart and deciding that job #1 is to figure out who is going to get blamed. Dave cursed and ran past the man who was now lying facedown in a pool of his old personality. He jumped off the stage, down among the rows of moldy seats, scanning the floor for the monster.

"Why can't we see this thing?!?" he yelled, knowing damned well that nobody had the answer. "Fuck!"

Amy crawled through the hole in the kennel that was now twice as big as it needed to be for her frame. She called after David and held out the phone, Nate Dogg announcing that it was the G-Funk era and that you don't want to step to it. She made like she was going to toss it to him.

"No!" he yelled back. "Keep it! Don't let this thing get near you!"

Dave carried no weapon, but from the expression on his face, John thought that if the creature launched itself at him, he would just open his mouth and eat it out of the air in a single bite of rage. John climbed out of the kennel, pulled on his ripped shirt, and joined Dave among the filth-encrusted seats, his dagger at the ready. Amy was behind them, the song winding down. John figured that all three of them had to be thinking the same thing: Even if the creature had been five times bigger and wearing a flashing novelty Cinco de Mayo sombrero, it could hide forever in this big, dimly lit building packed with seats it could crouch under. As it was, the little monster was only visible by the contents of its guts and, for all they knew, could climb walls or slip under doors.

Dave said, "Look! There's the trail!"

In the dusty floor was a track of smears the creature's tongues had left in the layer of silt. The tracks, sure enough, led directly under the seats, and soon Dave was climbing across the rows, trying to follow them. John heard a commotion behind him. The dipshits had made their way to the stage and were now messing with their magic portal book, arguing with each other, realizing all their grand plans were now just splatters on the floor. John was very familiar with that scene. Fuck 'em.

Amy

Amy forced herself to look away from the dead man. She had seen a ridiculous number of corpses in her short life and always imagined the ripple of notifications that ensued, a chain of gut-punch grief passed from parents to siblings to grandparents to friends to coworkers, the news crashing through unsuspecting lives like a tsunami. God, what if the guy had a baby at home? She could hear the dead man's friends back there, arguing. Not a hint of grief in those voices. She tried to find Bas, but he seemed to have left, maybe to make sure the members who'd bailed out weren't going right to the police.

Meanwhile, there was David, straddling two rows of theater seats and using the light on his phone to scan the floor, seemingly oblivious to the idea that the little monster could ambush him at any moment. The song had ended, and her phone went silent. She pulled it up to start it over.

David made a motion as if to stop her. "We want to catch it. The music's going to drive it away."

"It's going to eat your eyeballs!"

"I'd rather it try that than have it escape into the neighborhood. The trail veers over toward the wall. See anything over there?"

John and Amy hustled over to the narrow aisle along the wall that led to the fire exit by the stage. This was apparently a high-traffic path, though, as the dust had been smeared aside by hundreds of footprints. John swept his phone light around, looking for a reflection off a tiny pair of bouncing, human eyes.

John muttered, "You see anything?"

"No," said Amy, thinking that if she spotted the monster, everyone in the building would immediately know from the sound she made.

From behind her, David said, "All right. We've gotta block every possible exit point. But that means we have to recruit those morons to help. That could be a problem." He shot a glance at the stage, where the morons were kneeling around the corpse. "They may still *want* this thing to get out. See if you can talk to them. I'll keep looking. If I go up there myself, I'm liable to just start smashing their faces in."

Amy thought it was a sign of progress that David recognized in advance a situation that he would likely have just made worse. The guys on the stage seemed to be in the process of feeding their dead friend's leg into the portal book, apparently trying to get rid of the corpse (at the moment, she didn't see how he'd possibly fit). All the men seemed fairly young, all wearing almost entirely black clothes, way too many layers for this heat. One of them had a bucket and sponge and was cleaning up brains from the floor.

"Listen up!" she said as she approached. "You guys have seen what that Swallow monster is capable of. We have to do two things, and we have to do them right now. We have to keep it from getting out, and we have to separate it from the egg. If, god forbid, it collects the eyes from the people in this room, it *can't* be allowed to feed them to the Magpie and start the next cycle. That means that first, we need to seal off the building, and then we need to corral Swallow into some kind of container that will hold it until we figure out what will kill it. Hey, stop doing that—"

One guy briefly glanced her way, then went back to work cramming the dead man's leg into the book as if he'd heard a noise that turned out to be wind. The other four hadn't even done that. The book had already swallowed the corpse's right leg up to the knee.

"Hey!" shouted Amy, waving her arms. "Are you listening? You guys get that this is a problem now, right? If we don't get on top of this, there will be between three and six more people either dead or in really bad shape before morning. At least."

None of the five would even look at her now.

One of them spoke to the man next to him. "All the stream shows is Jonas reacting to something happening to his face. He backs up, and at that point, he's out of the shot. I cut the feed right after that. They'll have nothing. Remember, there are no humans in jail. Doesn't work like that."

They resumed shoving their friend into the book, now having gotten his other leg in. Amy swore the book had grown bigger to accommodate the task, somehow.

Amy said, "Guys, what if the creature goes after somebody's baby? Are you picturing that? Crawling into a crib, sucking its eyeballs out?"

One of the men who hadn't spoken yet said, "You hear something?"

Another said, "Nope."

Humans, David had once told Amy, find nothing more enthralling than the act of exclusion. Starting a club and locking out new members, basking in the cruel joy of seeing a sad nose pressed to the window. If the members grew up as outcasts themselves, they'd sooner die than give up their chance to finally be the only ones on the warm side of the door. Amy had no idea how to get through to them.

"Hey, dipshits!" yelled David from behind her. His face had gone hard and cold, the way it does. His decision to not make things worse had held out less than a minute. "You still agree that I'm a human being, right?"

"As far as we know," said one of the men.

"Great. As a real human living in this simulation, I am hereby declaring that all of you are dipshits. This little monster you've got running around? We catch and kill pests like it all the time. So I'm really sorry that your whole worldview has fallen apart, but, you know, welcome to adulthood."

The guy holding the book that had now eaten their friend up to the crotch said, "Nothing has changed. Jonas was an Empty. We know that now. He was sent to tempt us—"

"Shut your idiocy hole. If you want to help contain this thing, do what she said and help us block off these exits. If you don't help and Swallow gets out, I'm telling you right now that I'm personally coming for you."

Amy said, "Forget these guys. We need to go into the kennel and get the—"

She stopped.

The kennel, she now saw, was empty.

"Where'd it go? Hey, where'd you take the egg?"

The five still wouldn't even look at her. This triggered David's rage, and he started yelling, demanding they give the toy back. Amy didn't want to stick around for that argument; she already knew where it was headed. She turned and immediately ran into John, who had also apparently given up looking for the creature. It could already be outside, for all they knew.

She said, "They're useless to us."

John nodded. "Don't worry, I have a better idea."

He pulled out his phone and dialed.

"Joy? It's me. I need you to get everyone together. Owen, Crystal, Munch, Head, Kelly—everybody. Tell them to each bring their vehicle to the Doll Enema theater and park in a circle around the building. I need you to come, too. Take my van. The keys are on the hook in the living room next to the halberd. Then all of you will turn on your stereos at full volume and play 'Set Adrift on Memory Bliss' by P.M. Dawn. We're creating a containment perimeter around the building. There's a creature on the loose, and if we're lucky, the musical energy will be so beautiful that it just paralyzes the beast where it stands."

He paused.

"That's right," he said. "Uh-huh. Gotcha."

He hung up and nodded to Amy.

"She said no."

"They wouldn't have gotten here in time anyway."

"But Joy did say that my van isn't there, which means the Magpie made us drive it here and . . . yeah, I've got my keys with me, so that makes sense. It's probably in the parking lot right out front. I've got three thousand watts of sound system. I say I go out there and crank it. Unleash positive waves so powerful that it pulverizes Mr. Swallow, and then everyone in the neighborhood just spontaneously starts fuckin'."

"If you go out," said Amy, "you'd better be darned sure Swallow doesn't slip out with you. Oh, and don't let those guys leave, or if they do, don't let them take the portal book. We need to know exactly who's on the other side of it and whose tongues got chopped out."

He was already running toward the back of the theater, to the exit that led to the lobby. Amy went the opposite direction and made her way to the fire exit door next to the stage, which she knew led to the alley out back. She could at least get some deterrent tunes playing at that door and cut off one route of escape. To be honest, she really didn't know what else to do.

Amy pushed through the door and then pulled up like she'd smacked into an invisible wall.

She was facing a dim hallway packed with strange, shadowy figures. Her eyes soon adjusted to the dark, and she realized she was just seeing a bunch of old cardboard standees for movies, faded and warped with water damage. She pulled out her phone and activated the light, flinging deformed shadows across the walls. She shoved aside a standee for *Legend of the Guardians: The Owls of Ga'Hoole*. She scooted past another for *Cats & Dogs: The Revenge of Kitty Galore* and knocked over *The Imaginarium of Doctor Parnassus*, only to find the hallway was blocked entirely just ahead; cardboard boxes of toilet paper and cases of bottled water had been stacked up next to a greasy old popcorn machine. There wasn't room to scoot around it without doing some heavy lifting—

She heard a rustling nearby.

One of the cardboard displays falling over, maybe?

She heard it again. Mr. Swallow was here.

Maybe.

Amy slowly backed away. She considered yelling for David, but worried it would only attract the creature. She backed up some more, listening for any hint of movement around her, still hearing David and the guys barking at each other back in the theater. There was grunting and scuffling, like the argument had descended into a fist-fight.

She could hear nothing in the hallway around her now. Her only weapon was the music, but if Swallow was in the hall with her, playing it could just as easily force the creature toward the exit on the other side of the blockage. If so, could it get the door open and leave the building? She couldn't chance it.

She took another silent step back, scanning all around her, listening.

Still nothing. The silence was worse than literally anything else. She imagined the creature jumping on her face and sucking out her eye, and that was all it took—she was doing the music, dang it. She still had her phone in her hand and brought it up to start a new tune, and when she did so, she found two severed eyeballs hovering over her thumb. She felt four human tongues squeeze around her fingers. A circle of human teeth pinched her skin.

Amy screamed.

Then those two hovering eyeballs jumped up off her hand, and now she was staring right at them, a bloody optic nerve wrapped around one like a ribbon. She felt tongues and teeth on her cheeks and forehead.

She screamed again and stumbled backward, and the world went blurry.

Her eyes were being sucked out of her head.

Wait. No. It was her glasses.

They were being pulled away from her face, the creature apparently trying to figure out what had gotten between it and its prize. Then the frames snapped and the lenses shattered, bits of glass bouncing off Amy's cheeks.

The creature shrieked, having pierced itself with glass, then tumbled to the floor, the glasses frames still in its clutches. Amy backed away, wanting to turn and run but also terrified of losing sight of the thing. Wait, what was she saying? She'd already lost sight of it. The world had turned into a blurry mess.

She had miraculously not dropped her phone. With shaking fingers, she pulled up the music app and—

The monster leaped at her again. Amy squealed and spun, but it was now clinging to her shirt, the fabric being wrenched and pulled by invisible tongues.

She dropped her phone.

It landed faceup, and with the monster still clinging to her, Amy dropped to her knees and managed to hit the Play button.

"Sweet Freedom" by Michael McDonald filled the hall.

The creature froze, then jumped away and took off like a shot.

It was heading toward the boxes of toilet paper and the popcorn machine, which meant it was also heading toward the exit door and the alley. It skittered through the cardboard standees and slipped between two of the boxes blocking the path, vanishing from sight. Amy got up and stupidly tried to gather up her broken glasses as if they could somehow be fixed, the dozens of little shards glued together.

"Amy!"

It was David, from behind her, barreling up the hall like a freight train.

She said, "I'm fine! It went that way! Through those boxes!"

David lowered his shoulder and knocked the boxes over, clearing enough of the path that he could climb over. The exit came into view.

The door to the outside was standing wide open.

It had been propped open by a brick, presumably by whoever had been hauling in the toilet paper and water. David skidded to a stop, eyes darting around the hall, then ran out and kicked the brick aside, pulling the door shut. He turned and met Amy's eyes. Neither of them said a word, because what they both knew didn't need to be said: There was no way the creature hadn't gone out that door and into the night, into a town full of unwitting citizens getting ready for bed. Amy's phone was still playing the song.

"I forced it out," she hissed. "I-I didn't know the door was open. I got scared and played the music and forced it out into the world. Oh my god, I'm so stupid, oh my god."

"Calm down," said David. "It could still be right here. Look around."

He searched around the hall, muttering something about how this was still where Swallow could most easily shop for eyeballs. He was making a show of it, trying to make Amy feel better. She stared at the broken glasses in her palms and tried to hold herself together. Then she thought of her own admonishment from a minute ago, telling the *Matrix* nerds that, if allowed to escape, the Swallow could go after somebody's baby.

She thought she was going to be sick.

A minute later, John's van blasted some hippie rap song, and the man himself turned up in the hallway soon after. He joined the hunt, scouring the building for any sign of the little monster, desperate to find it for the town's sake, and for Amy's.

They found nothing.

Me

Out of desperation, we decided the only remaining option was to search around the exterior of the building, thinking the creature might have stuck around to ambush us. Or, even better, maybe it had been killed by the sheer magnitude of the music from the van. We had a debate about whether or not to keep the tunes playing. Was it more likely to paralyze the creature or drive it farther out of our search area? We finally decided to shut it down, since the neighbors would otherwise call in the cops on a noise complaint (despite John's insistence that he only had the thing at 40 percent volume, you could still feel the bass through your shoes). John then rooted around in the back of the vehicle, finally emerging with three enormous black, metal flashlights.

He held one up and said, "Just got them. On this end it's a flashlight, bright enough to summon Batman." He flipped it around to show us a quarter-size hole in the back, where you'd expect the cap for the batteries to be. "On this end, it's loaded with a single shotgun shell. Buckshot. Push the button forward for light, pull it back for the shotgun."

Amy said, "So when you're aiming the flashlight, the shotgun part is aimed back at you?"

"Yeah, you want to hold it up over your shoulder, like a cop. Just in case."

"Can you just unload mine before you hand it to me?"

We heard voices and car doors on the other side of the building. That was presumably the last of the Xarcrax-worshipping *Matrix* nerds getting the hell out of there. Amy spun that direction, threw up her hands, and made an exasperated noise like she'd just dropped her phone in the toilet.

She turned back to John. "I don't suppose you got the Xarcrax book from them before they left?"

"Oh, no, sorry. As soon as I turned on the music, I ran back here because—"

"Because I let the monster out. Yeah." She pressed her palms against her forehead and grunted, like she was frustrated by her own brain not living up to her expectations. "We have to get that book back after we take care of this thing. As soon as possible."

I said, "Why?"

"David, we just watched them put a whole dead person into that book. If people can go in, people can come out. Do you *want* that guy we saw in there to come climbing into our world? Or something worse?"

She didn't have to articulate what she meant by "something worse." Walking shadows, glowing eyes.

"Well, we'll add that to the to-do list."

"Speaking of which," said Amy, "who wants to contact Regina Galveston?"

"Why do we need to do that?"

"*In case the little eye-stealing monster comes for Gracie.* For all we know, it thinks of her as its mommy and will be coming to feed."

"Jesus Christ, Amy. But they already know what happened here, or at least one member of the family does."

"Sebastian is a teenager. He's going to sneak back into the house and pretend nothing happened."

John said, "I'll text her."

"You're going to give her that news over text?"

"Have to. She's keeping all of this from her husband. We don't want to call while he's there and then she has to do that thing where she pretends she's talking to someone else. It's always so awkward . . ."

He trailed off because an unmarked cop car was pulling up.

I felt my shoulders slump. "Ah, here we go."

We already knew who was driving it: Detective Coiffure. That was probably not his real name; we'd all been calling him that because he was a fairly young guy, and his hair was always gelled to wavy perfection. He seemed to catch a lot of Undisclosed's impossible disappearance cases these days, which must mean he'd pissed somebody off—none of these things ever got solved. The last guy who handled them had eventually retired and was now presumably hunched over a bar somewhere, slurring his way through a series of incredibly implausible tales. If nothing else, I hope the stories were getting him laid.

Coiffure's sedan rolled to a stop, and the man himself emerged. His hair was impeccable.

John sighed, lit a cigarette, and said, "You're a tad bit late."

"Jonas Cashdollar," replied Coiffure in the tone of a man calling out the winner of a raffle. "He was here, now he's dead, according to an anonymous tip we just got. Parents confirm he never came home tonight. What do you know about it?"

I said, "That's what they're calling the guy? What was his real name?"

"That is his real name, fucko. Lives with his mother, Dana Cashdollar. Owns the beauty shop downtown? The Cashdollar Salon?"

"Huh. I thought that was just the name of the place. I assumed it was named for the, you know, urban market."

Amy sighed and said, "It's German." To the detective, she said,

"And he got his eyes and brain eaten by a little monster that his friends summoned in a ritual. They disposed of his body in a way that you'll almost definitely never find it. You'd have detected his blood and DNA on the stage in there, but his gang has had time to scrub it down, so who knows."

John said, "And, before you ask, yes, the thing that ate him is still out there, somewhere."

The detective's facial expression didn't so much as twitch. "And just for my own morbid curiosity, can you tell me what it looks like?"

"It's invisible. Or at least, it can turn itself invisible. The good news is that it eats eyeballs, and the contents of its guts are not invisible, so you can see the clump of eyeballs waddling around."

"That's great news."

I said, "Look, from a cop perspective, here's what you can put in your report. A bunch of crazy people have decided that they need human parts for a ritual. The nature of the stuff they're collecting is escalating; it started with hair, and now they're up to eyeballs. A few hours ago, we saw one of them in possession of four human tongues, but we have no idea where they found them. It needs six more eyes, and after that, who knows. Maybe they'll decide they need twelve buttholes. We're trying to stop them, but—"

"Shut the fuck up," rebutted Detective Coiffure, pushing past me.

He was heading for the theater. Fifteen minutes later, he re-emerged, strode right past us, and said, "Call me if he turns up or if you have any information at all. If I don't come up with anything on my end, I'm just arresting you people again."

John nodded. "Fair enough."

Amy said, "There's also a cursed toy, looks like a little plastic egg. If you see it, confiscate it. And a big, leather-bound book."

Without looking back, the detective replied, "I'll be sure to not keep an eye out for that."

We watched his taillights shrink into the night. Amy powered up her flashlight. It was so bright I was surprised it didn't hum like a lightsaber.

"All right," she said, "this thing doesn't move very fast, unless it has some teleportation ability, in which case we're wasting our time regardless. So it's got to be nearby, probably within earshot of where we're standing. We keep going until we find it or until somebody else finds it."

And by that, we all knew that she meant we keep going until we heard someone in one of the surrounding businesses or residences scream that they were having their eyeballs torn out of their skull.

I said, "You both seem to have forgotten that we have an equally pressing issue right now. The thing we're hunting? It was controlling our bodies for the entire evening. For all we know, we've built an altar for it back at the house, made from the severed genitals of an entire church choir. We need to find out what the hell we were doing during that missing time."

John said, "We'll catch up with that as soon as we find the monster."

"John, for about six hours, *we were the monster*. Do you get that? We were collectively acting as the monster, doing its bidding, and for all we know, that detective is about to stumble across an orgy of evidence that will point right back to us and be national news by morning. One of us has to go find out while the rest look for Mr. Swallow."

"If we committed atrocities, then the cops will have an easy investigation if we did them at the house. It'll be on camera and, for all we know, has already been streamed out to the Gold Subscribers."

"We need to check those feeds."

"*I* need to check those feeds," said John, already dialing his phone. "I'm the only one who knows the setup. You'll never find the files. I'll have Joy pick me up. You can keep the van; you'll need the containment box when you catch Swallow. There's a green ammo box behind the passenger seat. There are some Little Debbie cakes in there if you get hungry."

I turned on my flashlight and surveyed the area around us, trying to think of where I'd hide if I were a monster. Well, a smaller monster. To the right of the theater was the Waffle House, where seven or eight people were eating, but no one was running and screaming. To the left was Pizza Circus, a clown-themed pizza restaurant that had burned and then closed down years ago. Beyond that was a car wash, and then everything else was residential, houses and apartments full of vulnerable, sleepy people. Amy and I headed down the sidewalk, sweeping the lawns for the reflection of at least two eyeballs, both of us listening for screams in the night.

John

John watched Amy walk away, saw her slumped posture, and knew that she felt responsible for all of this, as if there weren't a hundred other ways the little monster could have slipped out of the building regardless of what she'd done. That's what she did, tried to carry it all on her narrow shoulders, to eat the whole world's pain. John wished, for the hundredth time, that Amy possessed the ability to forgive herself as easily as she forgave others. If you can't do that, every mistake just sets up camp in your memory, gnawing on your happiness like a tumor.

He shouted to Amy to get her attention. When she turned, he looked her square in the eye and tried to put all of that into words.

"Hey," he said, "I promise you that before the sun rises, the three of us are gonna punch this mother right in his fucker."

John shined his flashlight around, figuring he'd make the most of the few minutes he had until his ride arrived. He found nothing, aside from a single shoe. If the universe were a simulation, the constant appearance of random shoes along the road seemed like a good example of a glitch that never got patched out.

Headlights approached. Dave's Impala pulled up, and sitting behind the wheel was something inhuman: John's roommate, Joy.

Dave, John had noticed, conspicuously left Joy out of every anecdote. Sometimes you have a person in your life whose nature and relationship doesn't fit any standard template, so it's easier to just not say anything. Joy, for example, *appeared* to be a woman somewhere between the ages of nineteen and thirty-nine, had straight black hair and, due to how her body was shaped, probably did not know what normal eye contact looked like. Over the years, John had encountered quite a few creatures from outside his own universe, but of all of them, Joy was only the second or third to move in afterward. Dave had warned him about letting her stick around, said to always keep a close eye for signs of odd behavior or betrayal. It really hadn't been necessary; John knew you could never be too careful. But she was also paying rent and was never late with it.

John approached the driver's side and said, "Scoot over. I'm driving." He put his hand on the door handle.

"No," replied Joy, slapping his hand away. "I never get to drive the Impala!"

"Do you even have a license?"

"Sure I do."

"Where did you get it?"

"Where did you get *your* license? Clown college?"

"*What?*"

"Are you getting in or not?"

John relented. Sometimes it was better to let Joy think she had the advantage, to think he had let his guard down.

He circled to the passenger seat and said, "The creature got away," in a somewhat accusing tone.

"Sorry to hear that," replied Joy. "Eunice fell. They had to take her to the hospital. Probably a stroke; I don't think she made it. We were dealing with that when you called."

Joy worked in a nursing home. She had apparently passed their hiring process and background check, even though she shouldn't have existed in anyone's records.

"Speaking of which," said John, "has anything weird happened to you today?"

"Yes! When I came back from Japan, I opened my closet door and all my shoes were missing, and I could see directly into the other bedroom, where you were practicing tai chi in the nude.

Also, you insist you don't smoke in the house, but when I got home, the place stank so strongly of cigarettes that I could smell it from the driveway."

"I was fully clothed doing the tai chi."

"I'm adding nudity when I tell the story as a punishment. I told everyone at work. It was the last thing poor Eunice heard before she died."

"Dave, Amy, and I are all missing some time, several hours today, starting in the afternoon. We were sitting and talking, and suddenly, it was nighttime and we were in another place. Did you drop by the house at any point from the afternoon forward? Or call or anything like that? And if so, were we acting weird?"

"No. I just got off a little while ago. The house seemed normal. I found a huge rat in the garage when I was taking out the trash. Does that count?"

"No," said John. He was fairly confident that he did not have rats in his house, but Joy liked to exaggerate her every complaint, for some reason that normal humans could presumably never understand.

"Oh, I brought home some leftover German chocolate cake. We had a staff birthday, and we can't leave stuff in the break room overnight. It's really good."

John eyed her suspiciously and said, "Thank you."

Joy took a sip from a giant iced coffee she'd apparently gotten at a convenience store on the way. It was odd that Joy was eating or drinking anything, since she was not a person but rather a hive of interdimensional insects that could camouflage themselves as one. John wondered if the cake thing was another of her subtle mind games. For example, when John brought home takeout, Joy would never order fries but would always, *always* eat some of his. When John started just getting a second order of fries for her, she'd refuse them and act insulted, like he was calling her fat. When John cooked something for both of them, she'd always *say* she liked it but then, without fail, would add some little note like, "You know what this needs? A little cream in the sauce. Smooth it out a bit."

John said, "You don't have any further questions about the 'creature' I just referred to? Not curious about that at all?"

"Oh, yeah, I always like to hear about your work. Then I can tell you about mine. Henry—the ninety-year-old in the wheelchair?—tried to pinch my butt again. But, no, tell me your thing first."

"Somebody—we don't know who—is using kids' toys to collect human tissue, all over the world. We just talked to a bunch of nerds who think it's a ritual to summon something that will crash the software that runs the universe. And, even worse, we think we may have helped it along during a period of missing time when it possessed our bodies, maybe."

"That's crazy. Did I tell you Jolene got fired? Failed her drug test."

John pulled his cigarettes out of his pocket, and Joy said, "Don't smoke in here."

"It's Dave's car. He said I could."

"It's not about the car, it's about me. I can't handle it. Put it away."

John obeyed. No reason to rock the boat. Better to just hang back and observe, like Dave said. Joy presumably did not have lungs or a need to breathe at all, yet she was constantly complaining about his smoking, even if it happened hours before she entered the room. When John and Joy had taken a road trip to a water park back in June, the subject of smoking in the van had been a constant source of conflict, for whatever reason she'd cooked up in her diabolical alien mind. He'd had to keep pulling off at gas stations just so he could get a smoke in.

She said, "You look tired. Do you want me to stop and get coffee?"

"No, I'll make some at home."

"Are we going to record tonight?"

"No, I'm busy. You know, with the monster stuff I was just talking about?"

John and Joy hosted a relationship advice podcast called *Fucking Stupid* that was getting pretty popular. They actually made a fair amount of money off it, thanks to sales of T-shirts bearing the show's catchphrase, "LISTEN WITH YOUR EARS, NOT YOUR DICK."

"Then why are you having me take you home?"

"If this entity controlled us like puppets, it's entirely possible we did things while we were out. Bad things. And for all we know, we did it on camera. I have to find out. Joy, this could be a rough one."

"So you're saying you may need me to help you cover up a crime? All right, I'm in. But in exchange, you have to fix my closet."

Me

Amy and I had completed a circuit around the theater and found nothing. We were now about to expand the perimeter, but I honestly wasn't sure how long we were supposed to keep this up. Until morning? Forever? Did we just keep drawing bigger and bigger concentric circles until we hit the ocean? Mr. Swallow could be hiding in the sewer, or a rooftop, or ten feet away behind one of these shrubs. It was dark, and we hadn't been able to catch the thing even when it was in the same room with us.

I said, "Maybe we should put out a public call for people to keep a lookout."

"I think if somebody spots a bundle of floating human eyeballs bopping down the sidewalk, they already know who to call." Amy hesitated for a moment like she was practicing her next sentence in her head, then said, "So . . . I don't know what's the best time to bring this up without seeming cold or tasteless, but we have to talk about it because I don't know what we're gonna do."

"About . . . ?"

"My glasses. They're totally destroyed, both lenses, the frames. I'm also overdue for an exam. That means we're talking four hundred dollars."

"We'll figure something out."

"David. I do our budget. I'm telling you we don't have it, and *I can't see.* Do you have any idea how bad my vision is? I mean, I'm squinting, hoping to see my flashlight reflecting off tiny eyeballs in the distance, but the reality is that if I look down, I can't even see if my shoes are tied."

"We got five hundred bucks coming from the Galvatrons, if it hasn't come through already."

"That money is already spent. The cell phone bill is due, and we have to get groceries. The refrigerator is empty and you bought all of those salads while I was gone. And no, don't ask if we can get it from John. He's in deep with a payday loan thing; he's already struggling to get out from under that. If anything, *we* should be helping *him*."

I was actually taken aback by that. John had always had an ability to just summon money when he needed it, usually without even breaking the law. He'd book shows for his band every now and then for a few hundred bucks a pop. He played a ton of poker online and won more than he lost. Last year, he got five grand in a settlement after he was kicked and then repeatedly bitten by a horse during a visit to Colonial Williamsburg. He also liked to cash in on his Undisclosed fame in ways he knew Amy and I didn't really approve of, including charging for guided "ghost tours" through desolate neighborhoods that weren't so much haunted as neglected—basically charging people to come look at our poverty. The idea that his "something will come along" financial strategy maybe wasn't sustainable forever hadn't really occurred to me before.

"Then I'm going to say the same thing I say every time this comes up," I said. "There's a way to get the money instantly, anytime you want. You turn on a camera, press Record, and say to the fans, 'This is Amy, a monster ate my glasses, and we need four hundred bucks for new ones. Here's how you can donate.'"

"Oh, god. I think I'd rather be blind."

"Would you really?"

"I don't know. Let me think about it."

Don't get me wrong, I understood her hesitation. The relationship with the stream viewers was weird, and I don't think either of us fully understood it. Half the messages we got in the site's general inbox weren't about the monsters, it was our "fans" wanting to know more about us. Details of our lives, our relationships. Our most-downloaded video was an unremarkable clip of a doll that levitated about an eighth of an inch off the table, and it took us a while to realize it was because the preview thumbnail made it look like Amy wasn't wearing pants. This, in a world swimming in free internet porn. There was an intimacy hole these people were trying to fill, a fierce and acute desire that I found every bit as creepy as the thing made of human tongues. Still, money is money.

"And hey," I said, "those glasses saved your eyeballs. That's a small price to pay."

"I know."

"See, times like this, I think, 'What would Amy say?' and that was an example of it. If the roles were reversed, you'd try to see the positive."

"I know. I know."

We turned down a street that on one side featured a few businesses that were closed for the night—a law office, a psychic, a florist—and on the other was an apartment building. Three stories, maybe twenty units, and probably fifty waiting eyeballs.

If Mr. Swallow gets in there . . .

I stopped and shined a light in that direction. I saw no monster, but multiple open windows it could effortlessly crawl into.

From behind me, Amy said, "I just wish we could get some breathing room. On the money stuff, I mean. Just so we wouldn't have to constantly worry about it."

I suddenly found myself wishing Swallow would jump out and attack my face. Otherwise, this conversation would keep dancing us closer and closer toward the precipice of Things We Don't Talk About. If I lean out over the edge, I can see the anxieties lumbering around down there in the darkness: the fact that Amy needs back surgery and we can't afford it, that she also mentioned needing dental work and we can't afford that, either. That my résumé is nothing but a few years managing a video store among a whole lot of inexplicable self-employment and empty space, that we could get kicked out of our apartment at any moment . . .

At the level of poverty where we exist—not starving but hopelessly locked out of the middle class—it feels like flying over an active volcano on the back of a winged creature that is friendly but also very drunk. America is, after all, full of dirt-cheap comforts. My T-shirts are five bucks at Walmart. The most amazing fast food costs less than what you'd pay to make it yourself. A good coffeemaker will beat anything you get in a fancy café. Cheap alcohol gets you drunk faster than the expensive stuff. So you can chill in a lawn chair on a nice autumn day with a beverage in your hand and say, "This isn't so bad." But if one of us gets a toothache or breaks our glasses or, god forbid, *both?* Well, now our whole world is threatening to come apart.

The fact that, at any moment, your drunk Pegasus could dump you into the lava lurks behind every moment of joy. I'll hear about a friend getting pregnant, and the happiness lasts about ten seconds before I think, *How is she going to afford maternity leave and diapers, considering she's a waitress and the father is a dumbass?* I'm not good friends with any rich people, but I've known plenty on the level of the Galvatrons, the ones who probably don't think of themselves as rich because they don't have a yacht. Their true wealth is invisible to them because it comes in the form of what they're missing: that constant hum of anxiety that sucks the energy from the rest of us. If their refrigerator craps out, they can fix it. If they fall down the stairs, their insurance will cover the hospital bill. If the breadwinner loses his job, he'll have his pick of landing spots. When I daydream about having money, it's not about jewelry and Jacuzzis and Jet Skis. I dream about having that unseen cushion, that margin of error I can just take for granted.

I don't doubt that if they were here, the professionals out in the Galvatrons' housing development would say they have plenty of anxiety, that they spend sleepless nights worried about their retirement and investments and if their kids' extracurriculars are good enough to get them into a top school. But I'd kill to have that, the luxury of worrying about the future. At our level, you don't get to think beyond this month's bills. Looking too far ahead is dangerous, like trying to read a map while you're driving. So we get locked into a loop where the best possible future is one that looks exactly like our present.

Amy squinted and shined her light at the apartment along with me, pretending she'd actually be able to see the creature if it was up there crawling across the red brick.

"I know what you're thinking," she said. "We could have covered this if I hadn't taken the trip to Japan. I ate at restaurants, bought souvenirs."

"I wasn't thinking that."

"I was off having fun and you were stuck here, and that was selfish of me."

"I wasn't thinking that, either."

"I've lectured you about money stuff for the last year, and here I've screwed everything up. I fuss at you and John about not taking safety and containment seriously and then I let the monster get away, and now all these people are in danger."

"Would it make you feel better if I agreed with you? If I got mad? I can if you want. I'm here to help."

"I'm just trying not to cry, because you freak out when I cry."

"Go ahead, and then you can appreciate that you have two intact eyes you can cry out of."

"LOOK!"

I spun in the direction she was pointing. "Where? Do you see it?"

"No. But there's a bus stop."

It took me a few moments to understand what she meant. Just down the sidewalk from the apartments was a group of several weary people standing at said bus stop, the bus rolling down the block from the other direction. If Mr. Swallow was looking for prey, here was a whole pack of them, out in the open, unarmed and unaware.

We jogged toward the group. The bus's brakes hissed to a halt, and the doors flipped open. The people shuffled on board, and I shined my light at them, seeing nothing, until . . .

The last girl climbed into the bus with a pair of gleaming eyeballs clinging to her backpack.

I ran.

John

As he booted up his computer, John had to admit that he was nervous.

He was quite familiar with being confronted with behavior he didn't remember, something said or done on a night when all memories had been deleted after hearing the phrase, "You have to try this. Ricky learned to brew it in prison!" Somebody would share videos from the night in question, and John would watch the loose, uninhibited party-time version of himself, cringing but also envying him a little. But what he was about to do now was different. Running back video of the missing time today would mean watching himself be the victim of the most intimate kind of violation, a domination of his will, knowing control had only been handed back after he was safely in a cage. It was like the puppeteer wanted them to know what had been done to them, to fully feel what had been taken. Cars must feel like this when you drive them to the dealership to shop for their replacement.

Waving his arms, John clicked around the folders where the various cameras stored their files. It wasn't their habit to film every minute of their lives. John thought something that profane yet erotic would surely be banned from the internet within days. But aside from the security cameras watching the yard (one of which was blocked because some birds had built a nest in front of it) and the camera in the garage that had been pointed at the containment box, John had two motion-activated cameras watching the front and back doors from the inside. That meant anything they did or said in those parts of the kitchen and living room should have been recorded for posterity, as long as someone had triggered the camera by moving across that part of the room.

So, for example, the first clip he found was the back door camera kicking in when Amy and Dave returned from the Galvatron house, with John recovering from his assault at the hands of Bas. That one, of course, played out exactly as John remembered it. The camera captured the first part of their conversation and then went back to sleep a minute after they walked out of frame. John noticed how terrible his posture was in the clip and involuntarily straightened while watching.

John next found a clip that, from its time stamp, would be from later in the day, during the lost period. He braced himself and brought it up on-screen.

There was the partial view of the living room, seen from the grainy camera aimed at the door from the opposite corner. John had activated it by walking toward the front door, pulling out his cigarettes and lighter. He seemed completely normal and was doing something he did a dozen times a day: going out onto the porch to smoke. A muffled conversation was happening off-screen, Dave and Amy talking in the kitchen. Or was it the puppet master entity speaking through them?

John cranked the audio and listened closely:

DAVE: . . . *if they're recruiting nerds, they surely have at least one pretty girl to draw in new members.*
AMY: *This doesn't look like a sex cult to me.*
DAVE: *You think male recruits have to be offered sex? She just has to pay them a single compliment. Boys are so starved for compliments that if you give them just one, they're your slave forever. In fifth grade, a cute girl told me I looked "tough," and I still remember it to this day.*
AMY: *That's depressing. When I was in Japan, I told a guy I liked*

his dye job. He had this electric blue hair. Do you think he obsessed over that for the rest of the day?
DAVE: I'm surprised you didn't find him clinging to the bottom of your plane when you landed.

At that point of the video, John had burst back into the living room from the porch, eyes wild with excitement.

JOHN: Holy shit. Come take a look at this!
AMY: What is it?
JOHN: Three squirrels are porking on the fence! It's a threesome. They're switching positions, up there around the barbed wire. These guys are freaks. Bring your phone! Look, I think a fourth is joining in! Haha! What the fuck?

The clip ended at the point that the camera went back to sleep due to lack of motion. Everyone had stayed on the porch for quite a while, it seemed. John closed the file. He continued his search, but the next three clips captured just seconds of unremarkable conversation. Joy walked up to him as he watched, having wrapped herself in a sweater. Joy was always either too cold or too hot. There was no adjusting the climate control to suit her. He'd tried.

Joy said, *"Brrr.* So what did you discover? Did you commit crimes?"

John shook his head, but said nothing. He needed to think. He went to the kitchen and got out his coffee-making supplies, which included a stick of butter. John went through a lot of butter. The only reason restaurant food tastes better than what you can make at home is they use so much butter that if you tried to buy that amount for yourself, the grocery store would call the cops—

"What's wrong?"

Joy had followed him in.

"I think the entity we're fighting," he said solemnly, "possessed us and then made us act like a bunch of useless assholes."

Me

I made it to the bus and stuck my arm in the door just as it was closing.

The bus driver, a grizzled old guy who looked like he'd been pulled off the cover of a 1940s blues album, said, "You gettin' on?"

"This is an emergency!" I shouted, while trying to catch my breath. "Something dangerous got on the bus! Everyone needs to get off!"

From behind me, Amy was running up saying, "It's a bomb!"

The bus driver showed no alarm at this. "Says who?"

Instead of answering, I pulled myself up into the bus and took in the few passengers. There was a teenage boy sitting with a black case shaped like a giant lollipop, an old woman leaning on her window who may possibly have been dead, a drunk young couple in the back making out and ignoring the commotion entirely, and the girl who'd had the eyeball swallower on her backpack. She was tall with cornrows, wearing a T-shirt that marked her as an Ace Hardware employee, unless she was wearing it ironically.

I said, "You! It's attached to you! It was on your backpack!"

"What? It's on my—"

She stood up, then reached down to where she'd apparently stashed the backpack on the floor. Amy and I ran up to her.

Nothing on the backpack. Nothing on the floor. Nothing on the girl.

I checked the floor, the ceiling, the back of my own shirt. "Shit! It's gone!"

The Ace Hardware girl turned to me, and a horrible look of recognition hit her face. Her eyes went wide.

I thought she was about to say I had a clump of eyeballs clinging to my chin, but instead she said, "Oh no! You're . . . you're that guy! The monster guy! Oh my god! It's not a bomb, is it? IS IT?!?"

"Don't panic!" I screeched. "It's a small creature, nearly invisible."

Ace Hardware reacted to this by panicking, even though I'd *just* asked her not to.

"People, there's a monster in here! This is that monster guy! And look, this is his girlfriend with the missing hand! Everybody run!"

The driver, who sounded like he was very familiar with nighttime freak-outs on his bus, said, "Now, everybody settle down. We're already behind schedule, so what I need everyone to do is AAAAU-UUGHHH! OH, LORD, WHAT IS IT!"

The driver was clawing at his face. Mr. Swallow was trying to latch onto his right eye socket.

Amy and I both started to run back that direction, but just then, the bus lurched forward, and I grabbed a rail to keep from falling. Amy failed to do that and tumbled to the floor. The driver had lost control of his body, and apparently his foot had landed hard on the accelerator. The bus rumbled down the street, picking up speed much faster than I'd have thought the vehicle was capable of. Passengers were screaming. The bus driver was punching himself in the face, the two extra eyeballs hovering there bouncing with the impact. The bus veered off the street, bumped up over a curb, and headed directly toward a house.

Amy yelled, "STOP! HIT THE BRAKE!" but the bus driver had seemingly lost all awareness of his surroundings, pummeling the invisible horror on his face and screaming for the Lord to banish this demon from his presence. The bus flew across the lawn, closing the distance with the house in three seconds. In that time, I caught just a glimpse of a living room lit by a lamp and a flickering television before everything became a roar of cracking wood and tinkling glass.

The bus slammed to a halt, and everyone was flung forward. I landed right on top of Amy and immediately worried I'd flattened her.

I stumbled to my feet to find the front of the bus was now in a living room—the front tires were parked on top of a coffee table we'd crushed, the rest of the bus still out on the lawn. The windshield in front of me had been turned into a scatter of glass jewels on the floor.

I turned to ask if Amy was okay, but she was already up, waving me off. I then found the driver, who was feeling his right eye with his hand and looking dazed. The creature was no longer clinging to him, apparently having been flung free on impact. The man now had a ring of red indentations around the eye socket where Swallow had latched on with its borrowed human teeth.

Amy scanned the area. "Everybody okay back there? Keep an eye out for, well, eyes. A pair of floating human eyeballs."

"Did that thing *attack the driver's face?*" asked Ace Hardware. "Oh my god. Nobody's going to believe this. Where's my phone?"

It seemed likely that Swallow had been flung out of the windshield and into the house we'd just plowed into. After several attempts, I figured out the bus's door-opening mechanism and stepped out into the living room, trying not to trip over a scatter of boards, drywall, and vinyl siding. I had no idea where my flashlight/shotgun went. Back in the bus somewhere.

I heard a noise. I turned to find an elderly couple, both wearing T-shirts, both completely nude from the waist down. They were sweaty, like they'd been interrupted in the act of oldfucking.

Amy jumped down from the bus and said, "Go back into your room! It's dangerous!"

They did not do that. The bus driver then ambled up behind us, looking very much like he considered this his jurisdiction, as if the house were now an extension of the bus.

He said, "There's been an accident. There's something in here. Something demonic."

I'd personally have gone with "wild animal," because you never

know who does or doesn't believe in demons. But the driver had
made the right call. Upon hearing this news, the old woman gasped,
and the old man first gasped and then covered his penis with his
hands, figuring a demon or wild animal would both be tempted to
make a beeline right for it.

Amy said, "The creature is small. And like I said, all you'll see
are its eyes."

Everyone looked down at a spray of shadowy debris that could
hide a dozen creatures that size.

I said, "We need lights! And a container to trap it in! Something
that stays shut."

A voice behind me said, "Will this work?"

It was the kid with the giant black lollipop case, which he had
opened to reveal contained a banjo. The case had those little metal
clips on the side, which was probably better than nothing.

I said, "Sure, open it and put it on the floor. Now we need to—"

"AAAAAIIIIEEE! WHAT THE FUCK? OH, GOD—"

The half-nude man was clutching at his face. His right eye was
already being yanked out, with a noise like a dead possum getting
slowly crushed by a steamroller. Somewhere in the room, Ace Hardware was shrieking.

Amy yelled, "THE BANJO!"

I turned toward the kid with the banjo case, who was now holding the instrument itself in his hands, the open case on the floor. I
yanked the banjo from him and squared up to face the screaming
man, who had fallen to his knees. His right eye was now a bloody
socket. Mr. Swallow had already hopped over to his left eye and was
going to work on it.

I grabbed the banjo by the neck and held it up like a baseball bat.
I had to judge the distance to the inch if my goal was to swat the
thing off the guy's face and not knock him unconscious, which, to
be fair, would actually be a blessing for him.

I swung with everything I had.

It was perfect.

The creature hadn't quite latched onto the other eye at the moment the banjo impacted it square in the body. It was smacked clean off the half-naked man's face and went sailing across the room.

I tracked its path to where it landed:

Right onto the bus driver's face.

"OH, LORD! IT'S BACK! OH, GOD!"

Amy grabbed the banjo from me and said, "I meant have him play music with it!"

The driver clutched at his face, then ran with determination toward the bedroom the elderly couple had just vacated.

He pointed at me and said, "YOU! Bring the case!"

I snatched the empty banjo case from the floor and followed him in.

He said, "SHUT THE DOOR!" but I was already doing it and knew why he'd commanded it: He didn't want any more bystanders getting hurt. His passengers were out there, damn it, and they were still counting on him to keep them safe.

I said, "Over here! Put your back to the door!"

The bus driver shuffled over, clutching Swallow like he was trying to keep it on his face instead of tearing it off, like for now he just wanted to control it, using his own damned eyeball as bait. He put his back to the door, and I positioned myself on the opposite side of the room.

From outside the door came the tentative pluckings of the banjo, presumably played by the instrument's owner, though I wouldn't have put it past Amy to figure out how to play on the fly. The notes became a tune, the fingers gaining confidence until the melody rolled over the ears like a cool, gentle stream flowing around dangling bare feet. I imagine it's like what a choir of angels would sound like, if they were all collaboratively playing a single banjo.

The bus driver screamed. His right eye was torn out of his head. Mr. Swallow now had four, halfway to its goal.

But the music was getting to it. The creature jumped off the bus driver's face, landed on the floor, and sought to get distance from the country melody oozing out from behind the door like a cloud of noxious gas. That meant it was heading toward me, which meant this was, so far, going exactly according to plan. I crouched, grabbed the open banjo case, and got ready to spring the trap. The four twitching severed eyeballs that marked the location of Swallow took a few steps in my direction, paused as if noticing me, then did exactly what I knew it would do: It launched itself at my face.

I quickly raised the banjo case and snapped it closed in front of me, calculating the exact spot where I would be snatching the creature out of the air.

I missed.

Swallow wrapped its tongue-feet around my face and pressed its circle of human teeth around my left eyeball. It felt like the entire contents of my skull were being sucked outward. Something dripped down my cheek.

Then it stopped.

The creature recoiled as if it had tasted something unexpected and toxic, like if you bit into what you thought was a chocolate chip cookie only to find out it was oatmeal raisin. It jumped off my face and I caught it with both hands, stuffed it into the banjo case, and trapped it inside.

John

All told, John watched nine clips from their span of missing time, some more than once. The longest sustained piece of video was the three of them in the kitchen, eating dinner. John had made tuna salad sandwiches that they ate with chips, and for the most part, everyone ate in silence, looking at their phones. At one point Amy looked over at the can of Fight Piss Dave was drinking, and this exchange ensued:

Amy: I don't know how you can drink that stuff with meals. Actually, I don't know how you can drink it at all.
Dave: Well, it's better this way. The food dulls the taste of the Fight Piss. And I need it because it actually keeps me awake; Red Bull has eighty milligrams of caffeine, that's like a third of a cup of coffee. If you ever think you're bouncing off the walls with that stuff, it's either a placebo effect or you drank five of them. Which would equal one of these.
Amy: You sound like their spokesperson.
John: We should reach out and see if they want to sponsor us. See if we can get paid every time we mention Fight Piss in the after-action report.

It was all painfully, stupidly normal, from the outside impossible to distinguish from their regular behavior. Their possessor, John thought, was either deviously subtle or very lazy.

But then there was the final clip, one recorded as they were preparing to depart for the theater. He'd watched it over and over again, unable to make sense of it. He needed Dave and Amy to see it. He'd texted both of them, but had not gotten an answer. He wasn't sure how worried he should be yet. He would have hit the road to try to go join them, but who knew where the hunt had taken them by this point—

The gate alarm sounded.

John checked the camera feed on his laptop, expecting it would be Dave standing there with Mr. Swallow impaled on a spear. Instead, it was a beefy guy with his arms crossed, like he was ready to give somebody a stern talking-to. He was wearing a suit.

Joy leaned over John's shoulder. "Who is that? He looks mad."

"I'm thinking that's Dalton Galvatron. The dad of the wizard child who assaulted me this afternoon? Maybe he's here to apologize about that."

"He doesn't look like he's going to apologize."

John had to agree. The man looked like he was ready to administer a medical-grade ass-beating. He looked like the kind of guy who didn't *like* having to yell at a waiter about getting his order wrong, but he didn't *not* like it, either. He looked like the guy who, back in high school, was the type of well-rounded superman you never see in teen movies: a star on the wrestling team who also was valedictorian, a kid who could bench-press more than anybody else but was also smarter and handsomer, too. A genetic lottery winner who would spend his life getting frustrated by the losers who couldn't keep up.

"Actually," John said, "I think he's going to demand we give back the money his wife paid us. Do you want to come with me, for backup?"

"Nope."

John went out to meet the man at the gate and said, "How can I help you?"

"I'm Dalton Galveston," grumbled the man, apparently so angry that he mispronounced his own name. "Regina's husband."

"Of course. You want to come in? I've got coffee brewing."

"No, I don't want coffee," he growled. "I need to get home and get some sleep, because unlike you, I work for a living. But I can't do that, because a short time ago, I was informed that one of my son's friends has disappeared and that people are saying my family is involved, because it turns out that the missing boy was part of some goth club that my son is into. I hear all of this from my crying wife, who admits that she paid you people to handle it, saying you were sending her weird text messages all evening. Then I find out you were at the theater when this kid disappeared, but when I talk to the cops, they don't seem to show the least bit of interest in even talking to you about it. So I sat down and searched for you people online, trying to figure out what in the blue blazes is going on here. I learned a lot."

"My friend, if we had a dollar for every time we got accused of killing somebody just because we showed up at the scene of their death-by-monster, we'd have, like, four dollars by now. Which I guess is not a lot of money unless you're making it in this exact way."

"Did I say I thought you killed him? Would I have driven over here alone if I thought that? Or if I thought your best friend turns into a winged monster at night and feeds on vagrants, like a whole lot of people around here seem to think? No, you and your friends are social parasites, making money off the squalid ruin that is this town. I think you took my wife for five hundred dollars. I think you sell snake oil to scared people, and I think sales spike every time somebody turns up dead."

"Yeah, we get accused of that one a lot, too. What do you want? A refund?"

"The only part I don't understand is how you get the police to cooperate. There's clips online, you know. Cops escorting you guys right through yellow tape."

John lit a cigarette and said, "If we're cooperating with the police, what does that tell you?"

"I don't know, but I intend to find out. Are you cutting them in? Is the whole town corrupt? See, I'm used to the grifters. They see a grieving family and swoop right in. What did you tell my wife? That you'd help her talk to our dead daughter? Is that what this nonsense Bas's into is all about, trying to contact her? Oldest magic trick in the books, right there: turning anguish into profit."

"Your wife came to us because Bas was into something, and she was worried that he and Gracie were in danger. But she was afraid you wouldn't understand, so she asked us to look into it and keep it quiet. We were all hoping it was nothing, some internet bandwagon nonsense. You grew up in the eighties, right? You had friends who drew pentagrams on their denim jackets? Most of the time, this kind of thing is just that, kids playing with devil stuff to freak out their parents. This time, it was something else. If you're willing to listen, I will explain every weird little detail to you. But I have a feeling you won't believe me."

"I know all I need to know. It's a town where no matter what crime is committed, the locals will blame it on dark forces from beyond. I bet this place attracts more predators than a child beauty pageant."

"This situation would be way easier to solve if it were just that."

"You're not to come to my home, or speak to any member of my family, ever again."

John sighed and shook his head in resignation. "We tried to make you and your family safer tonight. I know you don't want to hear it, but we do real work here."

The man was already opening the door of his Audi sedan, having declared the useful part of the conversation over.

"You're a snake in a town full of pigs," said Dalton across the roof of his car. "The culture of this place is so toxic that I swear I can smell it on my clothes when I get home. All your ominous phrases and smoke and mirrors, it's about as mysterious to me as a toddler saying he's got my nose. I say somebody needs to come in and bulldoze all this degeneracy and start fresh. In the meantime, you're going to stay away from me and mine, and if you don't, I will break you over my knee. Have a good night."

Only when the man was driving away did John realize his phone had been vibrating. He pulled it out to find it had been Dave, calling over and over.

Me

It was midnight. Amy and I were in the van, parked in a muddy field next to a huge, dark building that had been a turkey farm not too many years ago. The two of us were in the back, positioned on opposite sides of the glass containment box, inside of which was the banjo case that contained Swallow. Taped to the top of the box, above a patch of small holes that I guess were breathing holes John had added, was a Zune music player we'd attached with electrician's tape. It was currently playing "Crossroads" by Bone Thugs-N-Harmony. We could still faintly hear the fleshy creature scratching around in there, tones of tongues and teeth we'd catch in between songs. For the first time, I really looked at the markings scrawled in the glass, the religious symbols that were supposedly the containment hex that would keep anything from escaping. One of the symbols was the *V* and *H* of the Van Halen logo; another was a human dick with wings.

When I had finally gotten through to John, he'd told us to meet him here. That had been more than an hour ago.

"There he is," said Amy, sounding relieved.

Headlights were turning down the lane, hopefully belonging to my Impala and not Detective Coiffure's unmarked sedan or a pair of teen wizards on motorcycles.

"Sorry it took so long," said John a couple of minutes later as he rooted around in the Impala's trunk. "Munch had to show me how to hook this up. I got blasting rope."

He pulled out a reel of thick yellow cable with black stripes that he handed to me before fishing out some switches and wiring.

I said, "You got *what?*"

"Det cord. I think we'll have to sacrifice my box; I don't want to risk opening it. We wrap this around, hook up the detonator, put some sandbags on top to press the shock wave downward, the force should pulverize the little monster into a wet stain."

I heard a "Woo!" and just then realized that Joy had come along and was bouncing on her feet in excitement. I assumed she'd demanded to come after she heard it would involve an explosion. Hopefully, John has already explained Joy to you; I really wouldn't know where to start.

I asked, "Where are we going to get the sandbags?"

"I've got canvas bags in here. We'll have to fill them ourselves. Got shovels in the back seat."

"Goddamn it."

"The bus crash and the people with the missing eyes are all over the news. Reporters are blaming it on some kind of brutal sadist who's still on the loose. They're calling him 'the Marquis da Filthy.'"

"Man, just give me a shovel."

It was another ninety minutes of setup. John had to stop twice to call for further instructions on rigging the blasting caps, and on at least three occasions, I resigned myself to being accidentally exploded due to a random surge of static electricity through the wires. I'm still kind of surprised that it didn't happen. Finally, we drove about a quarter of a mile away, out to a gravel road in view of the field. We plugged our ears, John detonated the box, and a thunderclap bounced off the hills and rumbled toward the horizon. Dozens of dogs started barking in the distance, probably terrified that the Fourth of July had somehow come back around.

Joy groaned and said, "Where's the fireball? That didn't even look like anything!"

John said, "I tried to tell you! Explosions are never as good as what you think. The ones in movies are slowed way down."

We cautiously approached the blast crater, half expecting to find Mr. Swallow was either totally unharmed or even granted superpowers by the blast. But when we arrived at the scene, John with his shotgun at the ready, we found nothing but bits of glass and debris twisted and pounded into the dirt. Nothing moved, nothing came for us. I was so relieved that I thought I was going to shit myself.

At worst, we'd bought ourselves some time. At best, the ordeal was over entirely. The Magpie would be back to square one with building a new minion, and I had no idea if it was even capable of doing that. The Xarcrax nerds were scattered to the wind and were probably taking a hard look at their lives after seeing the gruesome death of their compatriot (this world, simulated or not, does not go soft on its reality checks). We could get some sleep, then go after whatever evil mastermind started all of this once we were up and around tomorrow. Or maybe the next day.

"So," said Amy as we loaded our gear into the van, "here's the thing. If the Magpie was going to take us over, that'd have been the time to do it, right? When we were about to destroy it? Both times it happened, everything we did while we were out wound up serving its purpose. It got its full meal both times."

I said, "Maybe it couldn't. Maybe we're too far away from the egg, or maybe the music protected us."

John said, "Ah, about that. You need to watch the video from the house cameras. From the blackout period, I mean."

"Why? What's in it?"

"You have to watch it. I'm not trying to build the suspense, I just don't want to bias your opinion in advance. We'll go back to my place."

I said, "Man, I was really hoping to sleep in my own bed tonight, while there's still some darkness left."

"It won't take long. Besides, like you just said, it's over for now. It sucks that it stole four eyeballs, but its eyeball-stealing days are done."

MONDAY, AUGUST 22. 2:22 A.M.
VANILLA GUMBALLS
COLLECTED: 5

Me

John took us to the distressingly impractical computer setup in his living room. After a few failed attempts to get his gesture/voice command system to work, he eventually just had us gather around his laptop on the sofa. Joy actually made us wait so she could go up and change into her pajamas, as if she were settling in to watch a movie.

When everyone was ready, I said, "Can you give me some hint as to what I'm about to watch here? When it was controlling us, did it make us put on a musical? Or perform . . . acts on each other?"

Amy said, "I don't think so. The subscriber counts would have gone through the roof."

John said, "No, it's actually weirder than that. So this recording is from about, let's see, sixteen hours ago, when you guys first got here this morning. Before I play this, think about what's the last thing you remember from before we blacked out and found that we'd fed the Magpie the bagful of teeth."

I said, "I can barely remember what happened on the trip from the driveway to this room."

"I had suggested feeding it a single tooth," said Amy, "just to see how it reacted. Then the egg howled, and I felt like an invisible dentist was drilling my eardrums. Then I think I asked you where you keep the teeth; you said you had them locked up. David said to destroy the egg, then I started to say something, and my next memory is that everything was suddenly quiet and I was standing across the room."

John nodded. "Yeah, that's how it was for me, too. More or less. We all agree that's about where the haunted toy took us over?"

This seemed like a really important point to him.

I said, "Sure?"

"Okay, I'm going to pick up the video right before that point. Here it goes."

He clicked, and appearing on his screen was a fairly poor-quality video of the three of us in John's garage. All three of us were holding our ears like there was a terrible noise, but nothing like that could be heard in the feed. I thought for a moment that maybe there was no audio at all, but then, on the screen, Amy yelled to John, "Where are the teeth?!?"

Shouting, to be heard over a noise that wasn't actually there.

"Locked in my gun safe, in my bedroom!" answered John in the video, also shouting for no reason. "I didn't know if something was going to come to life and crawl out of there, looking for a snack. Want me to go get them?"

"No!" I heard myself reply loudly. "Let's fucking destroy it!"

Amy said, "Wait! I think we should feed it one! To see if that calms it down!"

That sentence was new to me, so we were now in the period that none of us could remember. On the screen, John raced out of the room, presumably to get the teeth. Amy backed as far from the glass box as she could, as if the horrific howling wouldn't be quite so bad over there. So far, none of us seemed to be under the influence of mind control or anything else. We just seemed like ourselves, plugging our ears like we were impatiently waiting for someone to shut off a shrieking smoke alarm. I noticed that in the video, my hair looked like I'd spent the night in the belly of an anxious whale, and I involuntarily ran my hands through mine as I watched.

On the screen, John returned to the garage, and I saw myself take the bag of teeth from him. He dug a key from his pocket and opened the padlock on the glass case.

I watched myself yell, "Do you have a pair of tweezers or tongs or something? I don't want to touch the bloody teeth with my hands!"

On the screen, instead of getting tongs, John walked impatiently over to me like he was just going to reach in and grab a tooth from the bag, like I was being silly for not wanting a mutilated stranger's mouth juices on my fingers.

Then all three of us flinched and went to our knees.

John clutched his ears like he was trying to keep his skull from splitting open. Amy tried to crawl toward the door to exit the room, but the pain of the egg's psychic shriek was apparently so debilitating that she couldn't manage it. I dropped the bag of teeth. We were reacting like the noise had increased a hundredfold, though the room was, as before, completely silent.

I then watched myself struggle to my feet and snatch the tooth bag from the floor, fighting to take steps as if I were giving a piggyback ride to an invisible child through an equally invisible ball pit. I stumbled over to the glass box, opened the end panel, and flung all of the teeth inside, scattering them around the Magpie.

Just as we'd witnessed in the kennel, the plastic egg opened slightly along those zigzag seams. Then those tiny strands emerged, like knotted whips of hair, snatching up the teeth from around it a few at a time, drawing them inside the plastic shell. I watched the version of me in the video recoil at the sight of the eating process and quickly step away, the empty bag in his, or my, hand. At that point, the noise must have stopped, because Amy and John both got to their feet, breathing hard, like they were trying to equalize the pressure in their skulls. Then we all seemed like we'd just spaced out for a moment.

On the screen, I looked around and said, "What the fuck?"

John stopped the video. "After that point, it plays out as we remember it."

I said, "Incredible. It took us over but made it undetectable to observers. It played a version of ourselves that's like five percent less competent."

John nodded. "Exactly. But that five percent is important because it drops us below the crucial twenty percent competent threshold."

Amy said, "I don't think it mind-controlled us at all. I think we just lost our memories."

"Well, no," I said, "because I wouldn't have dumped all the teeth in there. I'd have given it one to see if that calmed it down, like you suggested. You give it the whole meal, you're starting the new feeding cycle, and we knew it was going to want something worse than teeth. So no."

"I think you can say that because you're sitting here, without the noise blasting in your head. Did you see how we were reacting in the video? That's debilitating pain there. Pain is a form of mind control. It's like how you can sit here all day and swear you'd never give up secrets under torture, but you don't know that until you're feeling it. I think if we had to do it again, if it happened right now, we'd probably do the same thing. Any of us."

Without agreeing or disagreeing, I asked John, "What do you have for the six hours we were out this evening? Is it more of us acting like slapdicks?"

"I can show the clips to you," said John, "but it's the same story. If you didn't know any better, you'd say it's just us being us, only worse. In our conversations, instead of working through ideas, we just make a bunch of dumb jokes and then get distracted. We apparently contacted the Simurai and then just kind of waited? We hung out. We ate tuna salad sandwiches. We took care of some business stuff, looks like Amy replied to a guy in the general inbox about selling one of the haunted dolls . . ."

"Exactly," said Amy. "That supports my theory. It's even kind of coming back to me. I remember the sandwiches being really good."

John said, "I always butter the hell out of the bread. But then there's the final clip, recorded just before we left. Let me find it."

For this one, the back door camera had activated when John passed under to enter the garage through the kitchen. He then returned holding his obsidian knife, and the following exchange occurred:

JOHN: *You could circumcise the Thing with this blade.*

ME (off-camera): *What thing?*

JOHN: *No, the Thing, capital T, from Fantastic Four. Made of rocks?*

ME: *Well, he wasn't made of rocks as a baby, so that's not saying much.*

JOHN: *You could circumcise him as an adult. Though you'd need a really sharp blade either way, so I feel like my point stands regardless. Who wants it? It's the only weapon I have small enough to be concealed. The next smallest is my revolver, and its barrel is fourteen inches long.*

AMY (also off-camera): *Is that going to work? I mean, will it be vulnerable to knives?*

ME: *He didn't say. He just said that Swallow will hatch. That can't be stopped. So I'm thinking we have to tell them whatever we have to so that after they complete the feeding, we can deal with what comes out, before it can go on a rampage.*

JOHN: *Well, I'm not giving them my tongue.*

ME: *He said they already have them.*

JOHN: *I'm going to park the van as close as possible. I'll crank the stereo and shut it down. I have a remote starter on my key chain. All I have to do is hit the button from wherever we are and the music will flood the space. Loud enough that whatever emerges from that egg should wind up flat on its back.*

ME: *Then we can circumcise it.*

On-screen, John walked out of the room, and the camera went back to sleep. I reached over and played the clip again, scrolling forward to the last words I'd spoken, beginning with, "He didn't say."

I paused it. "Who am I talking about there?"

John said, "Exactly. You talked to someone or met with someone. Any memory of that?"

"No."

Amy said, "Could have been a call. Check your phone."

I did. No calls during that time period. No text messages. No relevant email. John and Amy did the same, in case I'd borrowed one of their phones to do it. Nothing.

Amy said, "But you can agree that we weren't being mind-controlled in that clip, right? That's just us being us."

"Don't rub it in. So, at some point in the evening, I spoke to someone in person, but the cameras show no visitors at either door and don't show me ever leaving. And this person gave us advice that we all believed, and that advice was to, I guess, let them lock us in the goddamned kennel? Who would we trust with advice like that? Marconi?"

Amy said, "How, if there's no call? You think he flew here, then climbed in through a window to tell you that? And only you?"

I got up and paced around the room, partly to think and partly to keep myself from falling asleep.

"Man, there's too much going on at once. I mean, if these blackouts weren't the monster manipulating us—and it seems like it didn't gain anything other than making us slightly more confused than usual—then what caused them? And what's to keep them from happening in the future? Only this time, maybe we go forward days, or weeks."

"Or months," continued John helpfully. "Or years."

I said, "Wait, are we about to live out the plot of yet another Adam Sandler movie? I'm going home before we're forced to go back to elementary school to earn an inheritance."

"I think you should sleep here," said John. "And somebody should stay up to keep watch."

"Keep watch for what?"

"The cult of nerd wizards whose plan we just ruined? Maybe they're all scared straight, maybe they're not. Maybe the head wizard shows up with vengeance on his mind. I can take first watch."

"Oh, Jesus Christ. All right, I'm sleeping on the sofa. If you have to thrash some dipshits, do it quietly."

MONDAY, AUGUST 22, 4:34 A.M.
VANILLA GUMBALLS
COLLECTED: 6

Amy

Amy had told Gracie that she sometimes dreamed about running from monsters, only to find her missing hand was impeding her escape. That was extremely rare, though. Oddly enough, monsters hardly ever turned up in her nightmares at all.

Amy's most common dream was one where she finds out her family is still alive, like she runs into them at the grocery store and learns that it had all been a mix-up at the hospital somehow. She had lots of dreams where her hand had inexplicably grown back. As for nightmares, the most common was where she finds herself somehow back in high school and has to take a test in a math class she'd never attended and/or has forgotten her locker combination. Occasionally, she'll have the one where she has to pee but is in some situation where she can't find a bathroom, walking around and around some huge facility only to find that every women's room is out of order, or locked, or something.

The really traumatizing nightmares, the ones that leave her drenched in night sweats, aren't about any kind of danger to herself. Instead, she'll dream that John has overdosed on drugs or that David is trying to drive after having had too much to drink and she can't talk him out of it. Sometimes she'll dream she has a helpless pet that she never even owned in real life (a hamster or a bunny rabbit) that she accidentally allowed to starve or drown. But tonight, for the first time, Amy dreamed about her children.

These were children she didn't have, children she'd never planned to have, but there they were, just the same. A little boy with Amy's freckles and copper hair, who was skinny but with a round face, like he had been chubby but had suddenly lost all the weight, and a beautiful little girl with chestnut hair who, when cleaned up, would look like she could be a model someday.

Both of them were filthy, starving, and racked with terror.

It was dark. There was no sky above them. It was damp and cold. Moans echoed off unseen geography, a tortured noise like the whole world had a metal roof that was straining under too much weight. They were running, but the kids were struggling to keep up. Their little legs couldn't go as fast as Amy needed them to go, and they were begging her to stop, to rest. Amy was shouting for someone, but her shouts were weird; they came out as whispers, because in the dream, she was trying to yell but without being heard by whoever or whatever was chasing them. She didn't have her glasses. She wasn't wearing shoes, and the ground was slick and gritty and sticky beneath her bare feet. Her clothes were so dirty that they were stiff. Her son wasn't wearing a shirt. He had a layer of black grit on his face and his tears were washing clean streaks down to his chin. Her daughter was—

Gone.

Amy stumbled to a stop. She shouted/whispered the girl's name, a name that weirdly didn't register in the dream, like it was being censored by her own mind, coming out as garbled static. She shouted it again, now as loud as her lungs could manage, no longer caring who or what heard.

There was no response.

Amy froze. Going back for her would risk her son's life, even if she left him here while she doubled back alone. There was no good choice, so, in that manner that people do in dreams, she just stood there, stupidly, while the things that were chasing them through the darkness drew closer and closer. Then she saw that what was chasing them *was* the darkness, people made of shadow with glowing eyes. And the whole time, the thought that pounded through Amy's head was that this was her fault, all her fault.

Something grabbed Amy's shoulder, and she startled herself awake. She had no idea where she was. It was Joy, gently shaking her. They were both in Joy's bedroom.

"You were moaning in your sleep again," whispered Joy. "Grinding your teeth."

Amy rolled over. "Mmm. Nightmare."

"Was it the one about the math class?"

"Don't remember."

Me

When I dream, I often dream about myself, only I'm outside myself, talking or arguing with my doppelgänger. A court-appointed counselor once implied that it's because I'm a narcissist. I had replied that that can't be true, because in my dreams, this alternate version of me is often calling me a loser. The therapist had said that being a narcissist doesn't necessarily mean you think you're great; you can just as easily obsess over your flaws, that it's narcissists who lie in bed and beat themselves up over something embarrassing they said back in middle school. Ultimately, he said, some people just struggle to understand that the whole universe does not revolve around their problems. I told him that another sign of a true narcissist is you feel qualified to lecture other people about how to live their lives and then demand payment for it. They switched me to another therapist after that.

The point is, when I opened my eyes and found a man standing near John's sofa in the dark, I had no problem recognizing it as a Dream David.

I muttered, "Hey."

This one was fit, easily forty pounds lighter than me. Well-dressed. Not in a suit but in casual clothes that were just *better*. Clean, effortlessly matched, quality brands. He had a silver watch. Neatly trimmed beard. So not just Dream David, but Fancy David. But it was me. I'd know me anywhere.

His eyes darted around the room. "What is this? This place you're living?"

"Hmm? I don't live here. It's John's house."

"He's alive?"

"Last time I checked."

"That explains it. What do you do for money?"

"We charge people to fix their weird problems. And charge other people to watch."

"Where are the kids?"

"What kids?"

"You don't have kids?"

"No. How would that even work?"

I closed my eyes, which was a weird thing to be able to do in a dream, but whatever.

"Hey," he said. "What day is this? And how many days until the egg hatches?"

"Hmm? I dunno. Hopefully never. We squished the little eyeball monster."

"Have you talked to Marconi yet?"

"No? Why would I?"

"What a waste. You don't remember our last conversation at all, do you?"

"Leave me alone. I'm trying to sleep."

He actually did for a moment. But then he said, "How much do you weigh?"

"What are you, my doctor?"

"Do you exercise?"

"All the time. I'm doing it right now. You can't see it, but I, uh, clinch my muscles in my sleep."

"Don't you care?" he asked in a tone like he was too sad to be as pissed off as he wanted to be. "About anything?"

"I feel like getting enough sleep is really important."

"There's something different about you. You're not me. I can't put my finger on it, but something's off. Something happened with you, and I can't see it."

"I'm doing my best."

"Who's that woman upstairs? One of John's girlfriends?"

"Camouflaged hive of interdimensional insects. Name is Joy."

"You're not making sense. You know what? Forget it. You're a lost cause."

"Mmm. Probably."

"There's no point to me saying it because I know you'll fail even without looking, but I'm gonna say it anyway: *You have to kill Sebastian Galveston*. If that means you have to kill the rest of the family, do it. It's the only way. Don't get distracted by anything else. Don't go trying to puzzle out the deep, dark conspiracy behind all this. It's just Bas; he's the only one who matters. You kill Bas, you save everybody. If you have to keep it from Amy, do it. Easier to apologize later. But you at least have to try." He scoffed, and I could hear him shaking his head. "What a waste."

It took a moment for my sleeping brain to register what he'd said, but when it did, my eyes snapped open. The other me wasn't there, but of course he wasn't, because this time I had opened my eyes for real. I closed them again, tried to process what Fancy David had said, but instead immediately fell back asleep.

John

John was walking around in his childhood home, apoplectic because tomorrow was picture day at his elementary school, even though he was an adult and he had no pants to wear and all his teeth had fallen out. He was hurrying around the house looking for his guitar so he could use it to glue his teeth back in. Then he found his guitar and put it into the toaster, because his guitar was waffles. The toaster was a human butt. How was he going to play a waffle guitar when he performed at the Super Bowl halftime show tomorrow at elementary school picture day?

John walked out of his childhood kitchen and into the kitchen of the apartment he'd lived in for a few years after high school. There, he saw a ghostly figure emerge from the wall. A muscular man in a dark suit.

"I have granted your friend's request," said the man. He stepped out of the wall and into the center of the room, becoming solid as he did so.

"You have returned," said John. "What is your name, spirit?"

"They call me the Time Captain. I cannot stay long."

"Why do they call you that?"

"Is it not clear? Time obeys my command."

"I do not understand. Is this a vision, Time Captain, or is it a dream?"

"What do you think it is?"

"What request is it you have granted? You said you were giving us a second chance. What mistake are we trying to rectify?"

"What do you think it was?"

"Why can you not speak plainly, spirit?"

"Can you not grasp what I have spelled out for you? John, *you have done all of this before.* It went terribly wrong, and at the moment of calamity, I was asked to rewind, to give you this second chance."

"How is such a thing possible?"

The Time Captain made a motion with his right hand, sweeping past his groin. His suit disappeared, drifting off his body like smoke. He was suddenly nude, his tan organ erect.

"It is possible because I am the Time Captain, and the time is twelve o'*cock.* Follow me to the pool."

Suddenly they were at the public swimming pool in town next to the park, the very place where John had seen his first naked boob. They were not alone. Nearest to John was a short-haired young woman, whom John recognized as Joyce Hyser as she had appeared in the 1985 film *Just One of the Guys.* Next to her was another woman who John immediately knew was *Red Alert 2*–era Kari Wuhrer, accompanied by early-'90s Shannon Tweed. John heard a noise behind him and turned. Out of the shadows of the pool's brick restroom hut stepped Jessica Rabbit.

"To control time," said the Time Captain, "I must harness sexual energy. Together, we must fuck a hole in the space-time continuum."

John nodded and said, "I suspected as much."

The Time Captain stepped forward, smiled, and said, "Mount up."

BOOK II

AN EXCERPT FROM
PROJECTIONS INTO THE VOID,
BY DR. ALBERT MARCONI

Somewhere, at this very moment, a teenager is holding in her hands an envelope she has just received from a university. Her eyes are closed, praying passionately to her God that the envelope contains an acceptance letter. This teenager, without realizing it, is making a request of the Almighty that not even the most zealous believer would attempt: for Him to reach back and alter the past.

By the time the envelope in question landed in our supplicant's hands, it of course already contained what it contained. The acceptance decision had been made days or weeks prior, the document printed and added to the mail soon after. If the prospective student's request was answered by the Lord and the document transmogrified from a rejection into an acceptance, the faculty would simply dismiss it as a forgery or an error—their decision would remain unchanged. Therefore, what is really being requested in this prayer is that the entire chain of events leading up to the creation of the document also be altered, including the very thoughts and inclinations of those who made the decision, along with the many factors that influenced them. It is effectively no different from kneeling by one's bedside and praying that the Holocaust be erased from history in its entirety. A noble request, to be sure, and one a merciful God would seemingly be eager to accommodate. But it is not one that any believer I've ever met would be inclined to make or reasonably expect to be granted.

Yet, based on what we know about the universe, *every* appeal to a higher power for intervention is, in fact, asking for said intervention to occur in a timeline that has already been firmly cemented in reality. We only know of a crisis when a certain domino is poised to fall: after symptoms of the tumor have manifested, after the aircraft's engine has failed, after the employer's business has gone under. Avoiding it requires infinite shattered teacups to be reversed, reassembled, and their contents unspilled. To pray for a son to make it home safely from a war, under the assumption that he'd have been killed or maimed in the absence of such a prayer, is to pray that the circumstances leading to his averted death all be altered retroactively, that his orders take him a little farther away from where the lethal bomb was destined to land or that the enemy bombardier chooses to execute his duties of the day differently or not at all. And why not make such a prayer? An omnipotent God would surely not be shackled by something as trivial as our linear perception of time, not when we have observed particles in our own universe that seem to disregard it.

But now let us say that the prayers of the believers do in fact affect the outcome of events and that it is routine for the Lord to rewrite history to accommodate this. How much of your own past has thus been rewritten at the request of total strangers, ones whose interests differ wildly from your own? Our teenager's acceptance to her college of choice means someone else's rejection, the bomb that missed the soldier may have annihilated another platoon instead, or changed the outcome of the war entirely. If you reply that surely an all-knowing God can still see to it that all is well for everyone involved, I would tend to agree. But I would then ask you to imagine what a devil would do with the same power.

Me

Amy was shaking me awake. I knew it had to be some kind of terrible emergency to awaken me in the middle of the night like this and to also perform some kind of sorcery to make it appear to be midmorning outside.

I said, "What time is it? Why didn't anybody wake me up to take watch?"

"John fell asleep. But we just got good news! We sold Oksana."

"Who?" In my half-awake state, I couldn't think of how "We sold Oksana" could be describing any transaction that wasn't a felony.

"It's one of the cursed dolls. We've had it in storage forever. Name is Oksana. She's supposedly possessed by a little murdered girl? Apparently, she got up and walked a few steps in the storage unit, and I posted the clip to the site with a five-hundred-dollar price tag for the doll. We actually got three offers and accepted the one who said they could pay cash and get it to us today. They're picking it up in person! They're on their way!"

I blinked, trying to clear the cobwebs. "Really? This is the first I'm hearing of any of that."

"Me, too! I didn't remember it. The clip was posted while we were out of it yesterday afternoon."

"Wait. Stop. So before you went to the theater and broke your glasses, and while you were in a period of lost time, you arranged a deal that, by coincidence, would pay for the glasses you were about to break?"

"Maybe we just got lucky. It happens. Don't make that face—if it's some kind of a trap, we just have to risk it. I'm no good to us if I can't see."

"And did the doll actually walk, or is that, you know, a thing we did to drum up the price? Some fishing line or digital trickery?"

"They agreed to meet out at the storage locker," said Amy, ignoring the question. "If they show, we can go right to the glasses place. Let's go. I want to go home and get a shower first and a change of clothes. The only thing Joy has that fits me is this tiny leather skirt, and if I wear that, you're going to start demanding I dress like that all the time."

I fought a brutal, five-second battle against gravity and managed to sit myself up on the sofa. "We, uh, we have to find Sebastian. I think?" I squinted, trying to remember why that was so urgent.

"We will. The faster we get this thing done, the sooner we can—"

She was interrupted by the sound of thumping on the stairs, John's slippered feet descending at full speed. He sprang into view in the living room, wearing a black kimono.

"Stop!" he shouted. "Stop everything!"

"We weren't doing anything."

"I've got it. I know what's going on. Guys, *we've done all of this before.*"

Amy said, "We've done it a bunch of times, at this point."

"No, I mean this exact situation, these days, these hours. We've lived them before. Last night, I had a vision. In my sleep."

I said, "A dream, you mean?"

"No, listen. It makes sense. I was visited by the guy who we saw get chopped up in my wall the other day and then totally forgot about. He said he was a time traveler. The second chance we asked for? That was us asking him to rewind time and let us try again. All of this that we're doing, we did it before, and it went horribly wrong. This is our chance to do it right."

I just stared at him for a long, hard moment. "Just to be clear," I said, "you have no memory of that previous attempt."

"No, I guess our memories don't come back with us. It's like he just rewound everything, so everything we experienced and learned would be rewound, too. But remember when I said I had déjà vu yesterday? I've been getting it over and over. Everything feels like a repeat. That's because *it is*."

Amy said, "You mean like he reloaded a save after we all died trying to beat the final boss."

"No," I said. "No. Stop. Both of you just . . . stop." I rubbed my eyes and decided that this was, without a doubt, the worst conversation any human had ever been forced to have immediately after waking.

I took a breath. "I have been awake for less than two minutes. The only reason I haven't gone to take a piss is because my legs don't work yet. I am sitting here, still struggling to process Amy's haunted doll news, and then, in the course of like three sentences, you"—I pointed to John—"fly into the room to announce that time travel is real, and you"—I swung my finger to Amy—"just casually imply that you actually bought the *Matrix* nerds' claim that *we're living in a fucking computer simulation*."

"Oh, no," she said, "I was just using that as a metaphor."

"Thank god."

"But still," she continued, triggering a groan from me, "think about it. All these oddities, you guys remembering alternate versions of events, you running into that other version of John in the parking lot at the apartment, us skipping forward in time—they're like glitches. Isn't this what the cult says Xarcrax is going to do? Mess up the system until it crashes? Corrupts the OS or whatever?"

"Okay," I said, "I realize we made it a rule that no theory can ever be dismissed as 'too weird,' so I'm not saying that. But, just for simplicity's sake, let's table the simulation talk for now and focus on John's time travel news. John, when the guy from your wall visited you last night like the fucking Ghost of Christmas Future, what did he say we need to do? If he granted us a second try to get it right, how did we do it wrong before?"

"He didn't say."

I threw up my hands. "Oh my god. Amy, let's go."

"No, listen," said John, "I'm not even saying the guy actually came to see me last night. Maybe it was just information leaking through, in the form of a dream, something I already knew but my brain couldn't process. And the reason we don't know what we did wrong last time is that the Time Captain didn't get a chance to tell us before the wall squished him."

"Did you say 'Time Captain'?"

Amy asked, "But what good does this information do us, then? Even if all this is true, the time reset, the . . . other stuff, if we don't know how we messed it up last time, how does it affect what we do next?"

John thought for a moment. He got out a cigarette, started to light it, then Joy threw a sofa pillow at him that knocked it from his hands. I hadn't even known she was in the room.

"Oh. Right. Sorry. Okay. I say we just think about what we'd have likely done wrong last time and then do the opposite."

I said, "So we're going to do the opposite of our first impulse from here on out? Like that *Seinfeld* episode?"

"Yeah, yeah, like that *Seinfeld* episode. Where they're like, what we've been doing hasn't been working, so we're not gonna jerk off anymore."

Amy said, "So we just look at each situation as it comes up and try to see where potential mistakes could have happened last time around."

I said, "In other words, we have to become the kind of people who carefully consider actions and their consequences in advance? People who *aren't* just constantly screwing up all the time? If we were capable of doing that, it feels like we would have done it before now."

Amy headed toward the door and said to John, "Well, we're meeting a guy for a haunted doll pickup. Is there any reason to think *this* is the wrong thing to do?"

"I don't know. Did either of you have dreams last night?"

We both thought for a moment and said, almost simultaneously, "Not that I can remember."

I passed a row of roll-up doors to find there were four dead birds in front of our storage locker, which was around the normal amount. The owner of the place had complained in the spring, saying it was illegal for us to store dangerous chemicals in there, but we let him examine the contents to confirm it contained no such materials. A good number of the items were clearly cursed, of course, but that's not technically in violation of the lease. Still, he had raised the rent by ten bucks.

The dolls were heaped on a set of metal shelves along the back wall so that they were all in view of the live camera perched in the corner next to the door. To the left and right were piles of other junk we'd collected, mostly items people had mailed to us for evaluation and/or disposal. There was an aquarium full of water containing a severed hand that was forever making that sarcastic "jerk off" motion. There was a jar of peach jam that could not be opened by any human means. There was a pair of sneakers that supposedly could make anyone extremely bad at basketball. There was the discarded shell of a locust that was thirty-six inches long. We never saw the live creature; this was shipped to us from someone who included a note that said, "Keep it. Where I'm from, there are plenty more."

Oksana the Doll was lying in the middle of the floor, I guess where it had ended its supposed walk. If the camera wasn't lying, this would definitely make it the most sellable doll we'd ever owned. Plenty of them were probably cursed in some way, but always in a manner similar to what you'd find in a million listings on eBay—the dolls emanated a sense of dread, or caused nearby plants to die overnight, or "talked" in a voice that only one person could "hear." All stuff that, in an online ad, would come off as just another of the fakes.

I picked up Oksana. Just a porcelain doll, probably an antique, no creepier than any other. No fishing line was attached. Its floppy legs seemed to have no internal mechanism for walking. No immediate signs of possession or other weirdness. I shook it. Nothing. I tried standing it up to see if it would walk; it just slumped over.

"You David?"

I turned to find a chubby guy in a Hawaiian shirt and baggy shorts.

"That's me."

He shouted, "Ricardo Porkfart!"

I stared. "What?"

"That's my username! On your message board? Is that Oksana? I've been on the road since midnight!"

I felt a cold wind flow through my soul.

One of our message board weirdos may now know where we live.

"Yes, sir. Can't you feel the dark energy emanating from her?"

"Some comments are saying the video was faked."

"I don't know what to tell you." I hadn't even watched it.

"Can you make her walk for me?"

"She's not a puppet. She'll walk if she decides to."

"Can I have a refund if she never does anything?"

"No, but I'll give you the original video clip of her walking."

"What does that do for me?"

"Well, if you decide she's not worth it, you can use the clip as evidence to sell her to somebody else. In the listing, just say that she was too haunted for you. You'll find somebody willing to pay at least six hundred, I guarantee it."

This doll is cursed . . . by capitalism.

Ricardo took the doll from me, handling it gingerly. He examined it as if also looking for visible signs of possession.

"I'll give you three hundred."

"This is not a used car dealership. Five hundred was the price. Nothing has changed between the time you agreed and the time you drove down here."

He looked it over again. "I guess I just assumed it would feel spooky or something. What I'm looking at right now is just a doll."

"Five hundred and I'll throw in a second doll. Or all of them. As many as you can fit in your car. Pick out the most haunted ones. Here . . ."

I stood up and grabbed one at random. It had a tag on it that said, "STINKS." I handed it to Ricardo.

"Smell it."

He sniffed it. "Oh, god. It smells like . . ." His eyes glazed over. "Like an old person's house. Only worse. Like that and chemicals. Like a hospital. No, that's not right—a hospice."

I said, "It smells like your worst childhood memory. Take it home. Let your friends try it. It's the perfect trick to utterly ruin any party."

"What do you smell?"

"And old gym teacher's cologne."

After another twenty minutes of haggling, I got $450 from the guy, and he went home with Oksana, the smelly doll, the block of resin that contained the parasite thing from the Fourth of July, and a margarita machine that functions normally aside from making the sound of a crying baby when you're using it. He paid in cash and, I would find out later, didn't make it home that night.

John

John pulled his hair into a ponytail and set about making some extra-buttery coffee. He checked his phone to see if he'd heard anything from Regina Galvatron. As instructed, he'd texted her the night before to warn her about the situation:

> John: hey youll want to close the door and windows to gracies room tonight let us know if anything tries to get in
>
> Regina: ?
>
> John: also if bas is home see if he has that magick book we confiscated and if so take it from him but also wrap something around it to keep it closed like some duct tape or if you have some of those big clamps carpenters use to hold wood together when they are gluing it but if not then some kind of bungie cord might work
>
> Regina: ??
>
> John: bungee
>
> John: is it bungie or bungee

There had been no follow-up, but John figured that just meant Dalton Galvatron had demanded his wife cease all contact. That meant that they, at the moment, were operating even more in the dark than usual.

Joy appeared—John wasn't sure that she didn't literally materialize into rooms from time to time—and said, "Are we recording today? We got about forty questions."

Their relationship advice podcast relied on listener-submitted questions, and Joy had the task of sorting through them to find the genuine questions among all of the stealth boasts ("Hey, guys, my model girlfriend always gets jealous when other attractive women openly hit on me in public. What do I do?").

"No," replied John. "I have stuff to do. I don't know if you were listening earlier, but we have to get to the bottom of this monster toy situation, and it's gotten complicated. It sounds like we biffed it so hard last time that we had to reboot the whole universe."

"What time do you think that'll be over? I need to get some sleep before work."

"I don't know, Joy. I need to get ready because we're about to get a surprise visit from the cops."

"We are? How do you know?"

John froze. "I . . . don't know. But Detective Coiffure is going to be here in about ten minutes."

John could picture it clearly, the sedan pulling up, the man striding toward the gate and trying to decide whether or not to ignore the bizarre warning signs. It was déjà vu in advance.

"Or at least, I think he is. No, I'm sure he is."

"Are you in trouble?" asked Joy in a tone like she would find it very amusing if he was.

"Oh, we definitely are. But what else is new?"

Me

I have little triggers for my depression, and it usually doesn't take much—a financial setback, a sad story on the news, Tuesday—but the oddest one is probably missing letters and/or burned-out bulbs in store signs. I swear that 70 percent of the business signs in Undisclosed have partially broken signs due to the owners deciding it's just not worth the cost to fix them. It's a small thing, but it feels dystopian, like a civilization slowly going dark out of negligence. So it was even worse than expected when we drove past the Cashdollar Salon, realizing that the owners were probably sick with worry over what had happened to their weird son, only to be reminded that their sign was missing the R and the second A. Hell, it was even sadder that the place was open at all, as they presumably could not afford to lose an entire day's revenue just because of a life-shattering family tragedy. I briefly wondered if it would be more psychologically scarring to know exactly what had happened to Jonas or for him to remain missing and for them to forever not know, half wondering if he'd just walk back in the door someday. See? Depression trigger.

I dropped Amy off at One Hour Vision knowing that I'd have to kill at least two hours before they were done with her new glasses. It actually said FREE EXAM underneath, but that sign was also dark (the X missing in this one), and I assumed that meant they didn't offer that deal anymore. I walked a block over, already breaking out in a sweat on a day that was hotter than a deep-fried tractor tire. I ducked into Sammy's Smoke Shop, a tiny space with a few shelves of tobacco supplies in addition to liquor, energy drinks, ice cream, adult magazines, knives, a few guns, profane T-shirts, and about 85 percent of the legal ingredients and equipment you need to cook methamphetamine in your home (I noted that *their* sign was perfectly intact).

I stopped at the front counter, near a little glass warming bin full of the best soft pretzels in America and probably the world. I don't know how they were made, but they tasted like they were deep-fried; they actually had kind of a crust on them, dusted with cinnamon and sugar. There's nothing spooky or dramatic about them, so I suppose I could just skip this part, but you know what? Fuck it, I'm going to eat a giant pretzel, and you're going to read about it.

I grabbed the biggest one and went to the register. There was nobody there, and after waiting for what seemed like enough time, I held the pretzel and a five-dollar bill up to the security camera in the corner and then laid the fiver on the counter and weighed it down with an ashtray. I wandered around the store, wanting to eat my pretzel in the air-conditioning rather than in my sticky car. I browsed a magazine rack, my eyes skipping across the newest issues of *Guns & Ammo*, *Gun Digest*, *Shooting Times*, *American Handgunner*, *Firearms News*, *Bullet Parade*, and *The Gun Street Journal*. At the end of the one row of non-gun magazines, something caught my eye.

It was a magazine called *JAWBREAKER*, and the cover was a screaming woman's face, her mouth held open by a metal bracket, while a pair of hands was shattering her teeth with a hammer and chisel. I picked it up. The first article was headed with a huge picture of an old man's teeth being destroyed by a metal file held by a pair of hands in bloody leather gloves. The accompanying text was gibberish:

> Old Wittaker bared ivory on the walk like he was king chimp and thought he had the biggest balls on nut mountain but the rasp had him yelling for mommy in five ticks flat but the JB kept going until the old man was guzzling gravel and pulp and

after three days strapped to BIG CHONKEY Old Wittaker forgot his own name and cried and cried but it was too late you knew the risk when you tried to lord the pearlies over the peasants like we don't have balls and now it's time to CHORTLE THE ROCK SALT

It went on like that for six pages. I put it back and noticed that next to the magazines was a vertical rack of baseball caps that said GOD SINGS YOUR BLOOD??? in Comic Sans. Next to them, a whole shelf of jars of what appeared to be human feces, bearing commercial labels like:

HERMAN GARRISON
MEATLOAF AND MASHED POTATOES
(COLLECTED UNWILLINGLY)

In the cooler case on the other side was what I think were shrink-wrapped human fetuses with labels like "RUSSIAN–FEMALE–27 WEEKS" and blocks of "Vaginal Cheese."

I froze for a moment, blinking, then took a step back. I slowly looked down at the pretzel I was eating.

Okay, it was still just a pretzel. I took another bite.

"We meet at last," said a gravelly voice from behind me.

An old man had appeared. He was dressed in a fine suit of unfamiliar fabric and eccentric design, leaning on an elaborate walking stick.

I said, "Well, no conversation that began like that has ever gone anywhere good. Who are you?"

"You and I have known each other for a long, long time," he said through words filtered by a lifetime of cigarettes.

"I'm pretty sure I've never seen you before." Though his face did seem familiar . . . "Are you the head of the Xarcrax cult thing?"

He didn't respond, but his smile implied I'd guessed it in one.

I said, "Well, that worked out. You're just the man we need to talk to."

"Let's go for a ride."

"No, thank you. That would violate at least three personal rules of mine. How about we—"

And just like that, I was in the back seat of a car next to the old man, rolling down streets that were unfamiliar to me. I was still chewing on the same bite of pretzel.

"Let me ask you," said the man as we watched the storefronts roll by outside, "when's the last time you shit your pants? While sober, I mean."

I took a moment to make sure I'd heard the question right, then said, "Don't remember. Never?"

"Then you're a coward. You're not putting yourself in situations that test your limits. You're never away from the comforts of a restroom, never pushing your physical body or capacity for terror past the breaking point. You know who shits their pants? Marathon runners. Soldiers in battle."

We were passing storefronts as we drove. One was called Christian-Owned Baked Goods. Another was a clothing store called Mothers of Modesty. The sidewalk was bustling with pedestrians, and about a third of them wore a tinted plastic mask that covered his or her entire face. Faint graphics flashed across the masks as if the wearers were watching and interacting with a full-screen display from the inside.

Where the hell am I?

I said, "Uh-huh. So you're the one who recruited Sebastian Galvatron into this thing, right? And gave him that book? All this bullshit with the toys, this ritual, or whatever it is, this is your project?"

"Word for word," said the old man, "the same question as last time. Word for word."

"Because we've done this before."

He sighed as if bored.

I said, "So John is right, isn't he? This is all a replay. And you're aware of it, somehow."

"This time, rather than waiting for you and your people to jump through the hoops required to contact me, I decided to skip ahead and come see you, get it over with. I confess, I was secretly hoping for a different conversation this time, but I suppose when your adversary is the intellectual equivalent of a hot dog stand, you cannot show up expecting foie gras. Your next question will be something to the effect of, 'Why Sebastian Galveston? What's so special about him?'"

That was, in fact, my next question. "We've seen him do tricks nobody his age should be able to do," I said. "Is he some kind of an occult prodigy? Did you scout him out or something?"

His only answer was a playful smirk, like you'd give to a toddler who's asked you where the last Christmas presents are hidden.

"Your project," I continued, "this thing you're trying to summon into the world, you need Sebastian's help, don't you? Otherwise, why get him involved?"

The old man turned away from me as if he'd mentally moved on to his next appointment.

"Rabbits have evolved to smell the remnants of their relatives in the feces of predators," he said, gazing out of his window. "There is no human equivalent of that emotion, but there will be. How will you feel when you see knots of red hair in the heaps of scat?"

"If you think that just because you're a frail old wizard that I won't beat your ass, you're wrong. If anything, that just makes it funnier."

"What I am doing has already been done. The book is written; I can flip to the ending right now, if I so desire. So can you, if you are honest with yourself. You will not stop this. I am not boasting; I am reporting to you the future that already exists."

"Then why bother with this dog and pony show? It kind of feels like you're trying to talk me into backing off. Like maybe you're disturbed by the fact that we exploded your little monster last night, that all your wizard plans can be undone by a small group consisting mostly of drowsy idiots."

He gave me that knowing smirk again and said, "Just like last time. Word for word."

We were no longer in the car. The old man and I were now in a dim basement that smelled like a sweaty zombie. Water dripped from rusty pipes overhead. A huge man in a leather apron and a metal mask was standing over a table, upon which was an assortment of sinister tools. Rusty metal tongs, curved shears, hooks, and dozens of blades of every shape and size. He picked up a tool like an enlarged version of a thread ripper and left the room, passing through a heavy metal doorway. A moment later, there was a primal scream from behind that door that descended into wet sputters.

I tried to take a step toward that doorway, but found I couldn't move. I got the sense that we weren't actually here, if any of this was even really happening at all. I turned my back to it and took another bite of my pretzel.

I said, "It's weird that you think I'm so simple and predictable and yet also thought this bullshit would scare me. What is this, an alternate dimension where society has fallen apart and people get tortured to death? I've had the internet since I was a kid. I used to have torture videos as my signature on message boards. I fall asleep to shit like this."

"Who says I'm trying to scare you?"

"Listen to me," I said, trying to assume a serious tone. "I don't care who you are or what powers you have. If some entity from out there, some being from the void, has convinced you to summon it into the universe, then you need our help more than anybody. I don't know what this thing promised you, but you're not gonna get it. And I don't even mean you'll get some ironic version of it, like a wish from a genie. It'll just swallow you up like everything else."

"The assumption you made just now sums up the entire difference between someone like you and someone like me. You assume I'm in this for personal gain, because that's the only motive you can imagine for making the kind of sacrifices I've made. I have other goals in mind."

"Uh-huh. I know you're dying for me to ask, so what exactly are those—"

Before I could finish, the old man was gone and I was back in the Smoke Shop. I immediately turned to the vertical rack of baseball caps, each of which now said TITTY INSPECTOR above the bill. Everything was back to normal.

John

A peek at the security monitor revealed nothing at all, because it had apparently fallen off its mount into the grass. But a look out the window revealed Detective Coiffure was at the gate, studying the "shot by robots" warning sign and, from his expression, considering trying his luck. Just as John had pictured it.

"Let me guess," John said as he approached the gate, "you're here to give us an award for taking care of your problem last night. Do we get the key to the city? Actually, is that a real thing, or is that just something they do on TV?"

"Let's go inside. It's hotter than a camel's asshole out here."

John wasn't crazy about letting law enforcement into his home for a number of reasons, but honestly, if this guy wanted to arrest him, he could pretty much do it any time he felt like it. John's crew was mainly protected by the fact that nobody wanted that hassle. He let the detective into the kitchen, and as soon as he entered, Coiffure's eyes went right to the DO NOT OPEN cabinet next to the refrigerator. True to his nature, he immediately reached out to open it.

John said, "DON'T. I'm serious. Not unless you want a mess you'll be cleaning up for a long, long time."

Coiffure gave John a hard look, but decided not to press the issue and withdrew his hand. John led him into the living room, where he declined John's offer to sit down. He glanced around the room, then spotted the camera in the corner near the ceiling.

"Take that down."

John did, then Coiffure examined it to make sure it was off. John expected him to ask if they were alone, but he apparently had just assumed that they were. Joy was nowhere in sight and was making no noises. John wondered if she hadn't just evaporated completely. That was a thing she could do, if she wanted to avoid a conversation badly enough.

Satisfied that he was not being recorded, the detective said, "I'll make this short. I got a visit from Dalton Galveston just now. He seems pretty sure you guys might know something about the missing kid and the multiple mutilated victims we have on our hands after last night. And he seems even more sure that the department is in on it somehow or turning a blind eye at the very least."

"Yeah, I talked to him. You remember Amy asking you last night about a missing toy? And a spooky book? We still need those. But the big thing is we need access to his son, and that's a problem if Dad is determined to get in our way. What do you think we can do?"

"Oh, did you think I came here to *help you*? Fuck no. See, the problem is, Mr. Galveston has money, notoriety, and some prominent friends back where they're from. He says whoever or whatever is doing this is posing a danger to his family, and he's threatening to turn this into a Thing if it doesn't get solved posthaste."

"Right, that's what I'm—"

"Let me finish. Early this morning, Mr. Galveston apparently decided that I needed a little extra motivation. So he picked up the phone and got a private investigator friend to dig up dirt on me online. He turned up some unfortunate incidents from my youth that would maybe not reflect well on me professionally. Which, in turn, could unearth some of the shit I've had to do to try to keep some semblance of peace in this hellhole, much of which was very much *not* by the book. He threatened to use all of this against me if I didn't solve this to his satisfaction and disregard whatever arrangement I have with you people."

John said, "So? All the more motivation to solve it."

"Ah, but see, it's not going to get solved, is it? These never get solved. The thing about crime is that it only exists if there's enough evidence for a prosecutor to take it to court. That's why forty percent of murders don't result in an arrest. It doesn't matter if everybody knows who did it; if there isn't evidence to present at trial, or at least to convince a defense attorney to plead out, then it didn't happen. That means that if, for example, somebody disappears and leaves no evidence or credible witnesses, we technically don't even know if there has been foul play. Maybe they took off to go start a new life, buying their way to South America with a series of trucker blow jobs."

"You're losing me."

"It means somebody needs to solve Dalton Galveston instead."

"That doesn't help."

"I mean," said Coiffure, taking a step toward John, "if he were to disappear, all of my problems go away. But he would need to truly disappear. See, if he dies and his body turns up, it gets investigated like any other crime. If he just vanishes from the face of the earth, it won't."

"Are you . . . asking us to kill Bas's father for you?"

"If he continues walking around, I'll have no choice but to pursue the case, and it only leads in one direction: right here." He pointed to John's feet. "And, knowing how reluctant the state's attorney is to prosecute you numbnuts, that may require me to satisfy the doctor's request by other means."

"So we make Dr. Galveston disappear, or you make us disappear."

"I cannot control what you infer from my statements."

"What makes you think we can even do that?"

The detective just stared.

John said, "Oh, come on. You're not still buying into that bullshit about Dave, are you? Even if that were true, if he could, I don't know, transform into something inhuman, he'd turn into some kind of big, friendly animal. Like that bear in *The Shining*."

He turned to head for the door. "I've had to get my hands dirty plenty of times, in the course of doing my job here. This time, I'm delegating."

"Wait," said John as the detective reached for the door. "In your several minutes spent actually trying to solve this case, did you ever look up the other Galvatron kid? The dead one?"

"Yeah. She jumped off a mountain or building or something while on vacation in Mexico. There was a whole anti-bullying crusade at her school the next year. Inspiring shit."

"There was nothing weird about it, before or after? Nothing that points back to Bas, or monsters, or occult summoning rituals?"

"Nope, and I don't care if there was. Daddy Dalton is a public figure and has a team of people in charge of maintaining his reputation. The second any reporter doubted his story, they immediately got buried under an avalanche of accusations that they were harassing a grieving father. Fortunately, all of that is your problem now. Have a nice day."

Me

I was heading back to the vision place when my phone rang, displaying an unfamiliar number. I normally don't take strange calls—you never know when it's a stalker or, well, anyone else—but this seemed like a day for making an exception.

I answered with, "Who's this?"

"Uh, is this David?"

"Pretty much, yeah."

"This is Griff White."

"Who?"

"The bus driver who lost an eye to a demon last night?"

"Oh. Oh yeah. Uh, glad you're doing okay."

"I am not. I'm calling you from the hospital. A detective gave me your number."

"Oh, okay. Yeah, the monster, we blew it up. There was nothing left of it. I guess we should have let you guys know so you'd rest easier."

"You did not."

"Yeah, like I said, we should have."

"No, I'm saying you did not blow up the creature."

I came to a stop on the sidewalk. "What do you mean? Did it come after someone else?"

"I believe so."

"The detective told you that?"

"No, sir, nobody knows about it, as far as I can tell."

"How do *you* know?"

"Because I can still see out of the eye it took. I'd have told you that, too, if you'd asked."

"What? You can? How can you still see out of it?"

"You ask 'how' about that but not about the existence of the creature itself? The answer is the same: It's some kind of devilry. It doesn't want body parts, it wants to torment us. The other man who lost an eye, the old gentleman with his johnson out, he died. Had a heart attack before he even got to the hospital. Ranting about seeing through two bodies at once."

"Tell me what you saw. Through the other eye, I mean. As much as you can remember."

"It was inside your banjo box, dark, noises from all around. Then there was a pair of hands reaching for me, or it, and suddenly, it was in somebody's car, with a bunch of arguing white kids all dressed up in black. One of 'em pulls out a book, and then somehow I was in a prison. My eye, or you know, the thing with my eyeball in its belly, went after a prisoner, a skinny bald guy. At that point, I got so worked up and scared the nurses came in and sedated me. Don't know what happened after that. I'd have preferred to have stayed awake and tried to gather more information for you, but I suppose it's my fault for losing my composure."

"Where is it right now? The eye?"

"Don't know. It's all dark. Hear occasional noises, nothing I can make out."

"But you're sure it's still alive and intact?"

"Feels like it. Just think it's someplace dark."

The inside of the egg, maybe? God, I hope not.

"Well, that's not good."

"I could've told you all this last night if somebody'd thought to ask me."

"Yeah, you said that. We'll try to find this thing again, and, uh, if we can recover your eyeball, maybe the doctors can put it back in?"

"Not sure I want it back, to be quite honest. Getting old already feels like several of your body parts are haunted. Don't need a be-deviled eyeball rolling around on its own at all hours."

"I have to say, you're taking this very well."

"Oh, I've always known what's up in this town. It's a demonic place. Always has been. There are legends about this land going back since before we had the words. You live here, you know something will eventually come for you. Maybe some kind of beast, or a beast that looks like a man, or a walking shadow with eyes like a couple of lit cigars. Sooner or later. My home has got protection, crosses all over. But the devil thought he could get me on the bus. It was meant to happen. It's why I never moved away. I was meant to be here, to have this encounter. When this unclean thing took my left eye, I prayed to the Lord, 'Bind this demon,' and he did. Long enough for you to do your work. Or try to anyway. The Lord only offers so much help."

"Well, let him know that any additional help would be appreci-ated, because it's kind of too late for at least two people and by now, probably more."

"God does not give us a tunnel; he gives us a shovel. Got to dig it ourselves. Goodbye."

I hung up, and Amy emerged from the One Hour Vision door, saying, "All done. I made it through that thing where they blow the air into your eyeball without blinking, so I deserve a big knotted churro." Then she saw the look on my face and said, "What?"

"I'm, uh, kind of not sure where to start."

MONDAY, AUGUST 22, 2:02 P.M.
VANILLA GUMBALLS
COLLECTED: 8

ME

We were all in John's kitchen. The three of us had exchanged text messages explaining what had happened while we were apart, but the stories were nonsense when distilled down like that, so we'd had to just do it all again verbally.

I said, "I'm starting to think Coiffure isn't a very good cop."

Amy said, "I don't even want to talk about that. We're obviously not going to murder an innocent man who is a famous pillar of the community and also a grieving father. The detective can do what he wants to us, that request goes straight into the trash."

John and I shared a glance and pretended we'd both been thinking the same thing.

John said, "How do we find that old man? The one who talked to you in the store, not the bus driver."

I said, "Considering that he seemed to have the ability to hop between worlds without much effort, I'm thinking it won't be easy."

Amy shook her head. "He's not the most pressing issue either way. The app shows Swallow has all eight gumballs but that the Magpie hasn't been fed yet. And the stomach meter thing says it's going to start shrieking for its meal soon."

"Man, we're idiots for not checking the app after we blew up the box."

"We were just so tired at that point," said John. "I nodded off while I was wiring up the explosives. More than once. I was sure we were gonna die."

Amy said, "That's no excuse. We have to be better."

"That's what I've been saying!" said Joy, who'd apparently popped into the room at some point. "This is why I didn't go with you to the fireworks last month. Remember I said I had to work? I actually just didn't want to be seen in public with you."

"So," I said, "we have to find either the egg or Mr. Swallow, or both, before the feeding. The problem is we have no idea where to . . ."

I stopped myself.

I have a tendency to forget my dreams the moment they end, but the one I'd had last night suddenly leaped back into mind, wholly intact, including some very specific instructions from Fancy David. Then a whole bunch of things fell into place at once, and I was suddenly dizzy.

Amy, looking alarmed, said, "What?"

"We don't have to find the egg, or Swallow, or that stupid book. We just have to find Bas."

Amy heard something in my voice she very much didn't like. "Why?"

"When we reviewed the video from when we were out of it, we found I'd talked to someone, someone who gave me guidance. I think I know who it was. I think it was me. Some more functional version of me, who's trying to fix all this. He appeared last night, right in there, by the sofa. And he told me this is all about Bas, in the end."

"Last night?" said John. "You mean, *in a dream?*"

"I don't know. That's the problem with seeing actual, tangible craziness in your everyday life; you don't know what's worth paying attention to and what's just your brain misfiring. If Fancy David is real, I don't know where he's from or how he got here. Maybe it's reality glitching out, like Amy said earlier. Either way, he was berating me over how we were handling this, and it seemed like he knew what he was talking about. I don't know how to explain it; he felt like . . . like the most professional possible version of myself, I guess? The version of me that would exist if I tried harder. But then I woke up, and it turns out he was right: We'd fucked this up. And the advice he gave me last night, man, it makes sense."

I stopped myself again. This next part was what I couldn't say out loud, which is *why* it made sense. If John's thing about this all being a repeat was correct, then killing Bas is what we wouldn't have been able to do last time. Amy wouldn't have allowed it, would have insisted we find some alternative, holding off until it was too late, like with the guy who almost ruined our Fourth of July. In Bas's case, it just comes back to that fundamental truth, the first thing they'd teach you in school if anyone offered classes in whatever you call this work: that for the most part, houses and dolls aren't haunted; *people* are haunted. There are millions of these toys that are apparently harmless, not because of any properties of the toys but of their owners. If we destroyed the Magpie, Bas could have another one tomorrow, and he has the power to start it all over again. In fact, it's likely that he *alone* has that power. That's why he was chosen.

The toy didn't have to be stopped. *Bas* had to be stopped.

Stopped *to death.*

"If Bas's abilities make him special, then all of this other stuff is irrelevant," I said, choosing my words carefully. "You have to go to the source. There's no point in cleaning up the sewage until you've fixed the broken pipe. That's what Fancy David told me. Whether he's some me from another plane or just the smartest part of my brain manifesting as a vision, I think he's right."

John said, "So do we just go to Bas's house? Mount an assault while he carries out some occult version of *Home Alone* to fend us off?"

I imagined us pulling up and just riddling the house with bullets, then imagined little Gracie getting hit in the process. Then I imagined waiting until Bas left the house, tailing him, and blowing his brains out while he waited at an intersection on his motorcycle. Then I imagined little Gracie afterward, howling with grief. Then I forced myself to stop imagining things entirely.

"Actually," said Amy, "he's at school. He just posted a pic from there." She held up her phone so that I would know how she had seen said picture. "It's their first day back. We could intercept him on the way home."

I nodded. "Then that's what we do."

Amy said, "But then what?"

"We have to stop him from doing magick attacks on us, for one thing," said John. "I don't know what all tricks he can do, but just the one I saw is enough. He has what occultists call *the invisible touch*. He can just reach in and tear you apart."

I said, "How do we stop him from doing that?" while thinking that just shooting him in the head would probably be one way.

"He had to do his hexes verbally. I heard him. I think you have to disrupt his speech and then bind his hands somehow."

Amy said, "Already this is getting more violent than seems necessary for someone who, again, is probably standing at his locker right now and ranting to his football team buddies about which girls gained weight over the summer."

I said, "If your complaint is that he's just a kid, note that we started trying to kill Mr. Swallow from the second it was born."

John said, "We can stop him from doing verbal spells with the speech jammer."

That was a gadget John had bought off the internet (about 30 percent of John's income went to bootleg devices he found online, many of which were either illegal or more dangerous versions of legal things). It was absolutely diabolical: You pointed it at someone, and when they tried to talk, it would echo their own voice back to them in real time, only much louder and with a tiny delay. This, if you've never experienced it, absolutely breaks the brain's mechanism for generating speech. You need to be able to hear what you're saying in real time; that delay throws off the process so much that you'll actually get light-headed if you keep talking. We'd tested it out at a party and one guest got so frustrated by it that he tried to rip it out of John's hand and smash it on the floor. But to be fair, I'd had a couple of drinks at that point.

I said, "If it works, then it'd just be a matter of tying Bas up, sitting him down, and getting him to give up all his cursed objects and tell us how to destroy them. And to swear off the occult lifestyle forever."

Amy asked, "How do we convince him to do all that?"

John said, "Could we offer him weed? Maybe he just needs to chill out."

I said, "We have to make him understand. One way or the other, we have to make him see what's out there, waiting to get in. And that if he persists, well, we can't be held responsible for what happens next."

Joy said, "Uh, while you guys are doing that, I'm going to go across town and shop somewhere crowded. You know, so I have an alibi."

An hour later, I sat behind the wheel of my sticky Impala a block down from the Undisclosed High School. The bell would ring at any minute. The day was hotter than Ghost Rider's curling iron.

John's van was parked a block down the street, since if we were going to stop Bas anywhere short of his parents' driveway, we'd have to box him in en route, which meant two vehicles. We had a designated location in mind, a somewhat secluded spot near a row of abandoned houses that he'd definitely pass if he took the shortest and most convenient route home. If he detoured to get gas or something, we'd have to play it by ear. I mean, sure, this town still bore the scars of our previous attempts to play things by ear, but you can't get better without practice.

The high school was, to be fair, a nice building. Or rather, it had been, back when it had been built nearly a hundred years ago, all ornate concrete pillars and archways framing a body of red brick. That original building, however, was flanked on each side by two startlingly mismatched wings of glass and painted cinder block that had been bolted on in the 1980s, back when the city was actually growing and they'd quickly needed more classroom space. The sign on the front lawn welcomed students to the first day of the fall semester (the words *High School* were missing the *I* and *S*). Christ, I could still smell the floor polish in the hallways, the rooms that for some reason always stank like Elmer's glue. I'm not saying I have bad memories of high school, but I will say that I actively avoid driving past it whenever possible, as if the faculty might rush out and drag me back in, insisting I'm still four credits short.

The final bell rang, meaning kids would soon begin oozing out of the main entrance.

Amy said, "Oh. Oh!"

"What?"

"I had a dream."

"Just now? Were you asleep?"

"No, last night. But it just came back to me, like my brain had suppressed it until this moment."

"Did it contain useful information? If so, you need to spill it fast."

"I don't know. In the dream, I had kids, two of them. Boy and a girl. I was searching for someone. Maybe you. I don't know. But we were being chased by shadows. Then I lost the girl, and just as they were about to catch up with us, I woke up."

"It would obviously be very hypocritical of me to say, 'It was just a dream,' so I'm going to instead ask you what you think it means. Was it the future? Or something?"

"I don't know. Everyone was dirty and starving. I had this sick feeling in the dream, and I think it was just hunger, extreme hunger. But then I remember that starving version of John you saw in the parking lot . . ."

"Maybe he's who you were looking for. Maybe that's why you couldn't find him in the dream. Maybe he was here, eating out of the dumpster."

Amy thought for a moment, then said, "I don't know what to make of that."

"Here he comes."

Bas emerged with a group of guys who seemed more like his football friends than his wizard buddies. I bet they never attended the same parties. I started the Impala, then watched Bas head to the parking lot and straddle his motorcycle. He pulled out of the exit right in front of us, swerving around the line of cars waiting to leave. I saw John pull out down the street, a couple of vehicles in front of Bas. I let one car out and then lurched forward, cutting the next one off before it could get between us.

Amy said, "When you said you were visited by some other version of yourself last night? There's some part of it you're not sharing. I can tell."

I shook my head. "Amy, I don't know anything for sure. But I have a strong feeling that before this is over, we may have to do something that we don't—"

A disembodied tongue licked my ear.

"AAAHHWHATTHEFUCK—"

I lost control of every one of my limbs. I hit the steering wheel with a knee, and the Impala swerved left, across the oncoming lane, landing in a grassy ditch and jolting us to a halt. Amy was yelling frantic instructions I couldn't hear. I thrashed around with my hands and slapped something moist and toothy, but then I felt it jump away and lost track of it.

"IT'S IN HERE!" I shrieked. "GET OUT! GET OUT!"

Amy flung open her door and jumped out onto the street. I heard tires screeching, and a car swerved to miss her.

"WHERE?" she yelled, scanning her own body for a wad of several eyeballs, oblivious to the fact that she'd almost gotten run down just now. "Where did it go?"

I tried to throw open my door, but we were tilted into the ditch, and it was blocked by the grass. I crawled across the passenger seat and joined Amy in the road, both of us breathing heavily, looking frantically in every direction, seeing nothing.

Amy turned toward some students who were approaching the scene of the after-school excitement. "Stay back! There's . . . gas! It could catch fire!"

One of the kids said, "Is it that eyeball-stealing monster?"

I said, "Yes! Back off!"

"But Bas said it has all it needs," said another kid.

"Jesus Christ, just get back. It could be going for some bonus eyes! You don't know! We're the experts!"

A girl said, "You're clearly not," and I suddenly wondered if the Swallow's true evil intention was to just put me back in high school again.

I was about to tell the girl that her hair looked stupid when a vehicle pulled up behind us, presumably some helpful person making sure we were all right, or perhaps another student eager to taunt us for our inability to stay on the road. We both ran toward it to ward off the driver, then realized it was the silver BMW SUV owned and driven by Regina Galvatron.

Amy waved her arms wildly. "GO! KEEP DRIVING! THERE'S A TINY MONSTER HERE!"

Instead of doing that, Regina pulled over, rolled down the window, and said, "What?"

Trying to catch my breath, I said, "There's a little creature that made us run off the road. It's made of tongues and teeth. Or, to you, it's made of human eyeballs. Don't take our word for it. Ask anybody."

"I need to talk to you. Dalton came home this morning and—AAAAAHHHHHHOHMYGOD!"

Regina howled in a way that suggested she'd just seen a clump of eight twitching human eyeballs crawl in her window and amble across her lap. She flung open the door of the SUV and jumped out, landing on her knees in the middle of the street. She scrambled to her feet and slammed the door closed, then peered inside the vehicle. The window was still rolled down, so the little creature not only wasn't sealed up in there, but Regina had her face right where it could leap onto it if it wanted to.

Amy yelled, "Get away!"

Regina did not take much convincing. She backed away until she was standing on the opposite shoulder, across from where the Impala had landed. Cars were creeping between us, parents and teenagers peering out of the windows as they passed, either hoping for a glimpse of a monster or thinking they'd run across some grown-ups having some juicy domestic drama in public. I ran up to the other side of the SUV and peered into the windows—

"SHIT! SHE BROUGHT THE EGG!"

Amy rushed over. The Magpie egg was sitting in the back of the SUV, and as we watched, the wad of hovering eyeballs, each one twitching and spinning as if their owners were remotely operating them, calmly walked up to it. The egg opened just enough for Mr. Swallow to squeeze through and then the plastic polka-dotted shell snapped closed again.

"YUMMY! THANK YOU, MOMMY, I WUV YOUUUU!!!"

I closed my eyes and put my hands on my knees. I stayed like that until I heard Regina, who must have decided from our manner that the immediate danger was over.

"I-I found the toy in Gracie's room. I don't know how it got there. I grabbed it and ran out of the house. I saw the news about the bus. I was headed here to confront Bas about it. I didn't know if he would come home. People . . . people are dead! *What is happening?*"

I said, "Get out of town. Take your kids and go. Don't even stop to pack."

"I would if I could! Dalton won't hear of it!"

"Then go without him. You've got access to your money, right? Do what the rest of us wish we could do. Get away and spend every night thanking God you and your children dodged this bullet."

"I can't. Even if I wanted to. Dalton, he . . . You don't understand."

"Oh, I understand just fine. This town finds ways to keep you ensnared. Why do you think we're still here?"

"What *is* this place? Are all of the stories true? *How is this real?*"

"What context could I possibly give you that would make any of this better? We're going to take the toy and I don't even know. Try to destroy it? Try to get help? Try to do something. I don't know."

"But what can I *do?*"

I didn't answer. I'd already told her what to do. I opened the back door of the SUV and grabbed the egg. It didn't weigh anything, or rather, it weighed what you'd expect a cheap piece of plastic with a stuffed animal inside it to weigh. If we pried it open, I suspected we'd find nothing unusual. I also suspected we'd never actually get it open, even with a whole construction site's worth of equipment.

Amy said, "Tell Dalton that if he insists on staying here, we can't guarantee the safety of anyone. Not you, not him, not Bas. And especially not little Gracie. That thing that just crawled over you? Bas made that by feeding it parts, and some of those parts came from your little girl."

Regina clenched her jaw and in a trembling voice said, "Dalton would kill Bas if he knew that."

I didn't hear what Amy said in response. I walked away and inspected the front end of the Impala. The bumper had dug itself into the dirt a bit and the front license plate had come off, but otherwise it seemed fine. Whatever Amy said to Regina had convinced her to drive off, so I got behind the wheel and, after just twenty minutes of slapstick failure, managed to get the car out of the ditch. I was faintly aware that like fifty high school kids were now watching me from across the street, several of them recording me with their phones.

I got out of the car, walked over, and set the egg in the middle of the school parking lot, then ran over it with the Impala while the crowd of confused students watched. I backed up, ran over it again, then repeated this six more times. When I got out and examined the toy, I wasn't surprised to find it actually looked better than before—not even black smudges from the tire rubber marred the surface. I picked it up and showed it to my audience.

"Look at how haunted this toy is, you assholes! *Look at it!*"

I stomped back and stuck the toy in the trunk of the Impala, but didn't close the lid. I just stood there at the back bumper, looking at it, waiting for some solution to all of this to magically occur to me. Instead, I heard that other, better David taking over my internal monologue:

What if—and hear me out, Loser David—this just can't be solved? You got a second chance, but the only factor that matters is you, and you're still here. Even if you had a third or fourth or fifth try, you're still a fuckup.

Amy joined me at the rear of the car, her phone already in hand. "The app didn't even wait for us to feed it the gumballs. It just reset itself when the eyeballs came home."

"I guess somebody should text John to let him know not to keep pursuing Bas."

"He knows. He's pulling up right now. See? We should move. We're blocking the way for the people who are still trying to leave."

"I'm almost afraid to ask, but what's Magpie want for the next meal, again?"

"Uh . . . three gingerbread men. What would that be?"

"I don't know. Like, just, three whole people?"

She studied her screen. "Maybe. The picture of the cookies, they're kind of flat, and their eyes and mouths are just black. Is it possible it's not the whole person, but just their . . . oh, god."

John pulled into the parking lot and hopped out of the van. A teenage girl yelled that he had left his coffee on his roof.

"What happened?" he asked. "Bas turned down a side street. I think he saw you. Is that the—"

I said, "Yes. And Mr. Swallow just crawled into it." I slammed the trunk lid. "Do we think Bas is going home? If so, I say we just go confront him there, right now. If the dad gets in the way, we'll just do whatever we have to do."

"We don't need to do anything. We've got the egg, right?"

"That doesn't matter. I know that now. Let's go. If he's not there, we'll find out where he is. We'll stay on it until we do. I'm all the way sick of this shit."

Amy, with sudden urgency, said, "Oh! I missed a message while all of that was happening. Guess who it is. You're not going to believe it. Seriously, you won't."

John got a serious look and said, "*Molly?*"

I said, "Whatever it is, it can wait."

"No," said Amy. "He specifically said we shouldn't do anything else until we talk to him."

"Who? Because considering the situation, there's exactly one person on earth who'd make me just drop everything."

MONDAY, AUGUST 22, 5:35 P.M.
GINGERBREAD MEN
HUNGER AT 11%

Me

Dr. Albert Marconi is either a larger-than-life hero or a sad wannabe celebrity grifter, depending on whether or not you are really into cable shows about ghost hunting and cryptozoology. He has authored a dozen books on various such subjects, has played himself in at least one low-budget movie, and was portrayed in satirical fashion in a *Saturday Night Live* sketch. He also was the subject of some backlash when it was pointed out that many of the supposedly cursed ancient artifacts in his possession were obtained through a process that, in any other circumstance, would simply be called grave robbing. Also, the doctor has been known to sell the film rights to stories that are "his" only in the sense that he spent a single weekend investigating the home of a family who'd been dealing with a haunting for the entire previous decade.

These days, young people largely know him through his social media channels, on which he offers helpful if somewhat pithy debunkings of paranormal photos and videos (trying to trick the doctor has become something of a pastime for skeptics who consider him a charlatan). Thus, a blurry photo of a "ghost" captured by a security camera in a convenience store parking lot yielded a reply of, "This is a moth flying four inches from a dirty camera lens. Enjoy your afternoon." A more elaborately staged video of a flying winged creature was met with droll advice on the production ("In the future, try to avoid using a patch of sky with utility lines in the foreground, as they can make the compositing process difficult and create telltale artifacts, as you can see at the thirty-one-second mark. Enjoy your weekend.").

Dr. Marconi has been to Undisclosed enough times that he has a favorite restaurant in town (Chubby's Catfish Saloon), though he hasn't been back here since the last incident involving a missing girl and a supposed cryptid that prowled the night sky on leathery wings, locals describing it as a combination of a giant mantis and a bat. There was a mess in the aftermath in which some accused me, John, and Amy of inconsistencies in our accounts of the incident and even went as far as to publish supposed evidence that I and the creature had never been seen at the same place at the same time. The doctor had remained conspicuously silent on the subject, and these days, we mostly communicate via terse email replies in between messages from his assistant informing us that if we would like to enlist the doctor's services, she could set us up with a consultation and discuss rates. If I didn't know any better, I'd say he was worried that any perceived relationship with us would sully his reputation. This is why I was fairly shocked to hear Amy say the doctor had called us. Shocked and oddly proud.

We went back to John's place, and Amy initiated a FaceTime call. If you're reading this in the future and you don't know what that is, I'll just say that technology in this era was deviously designed to alternately coddle and torture introverts. For example, a FaceTime call would suddenly make a stranger's big, scary face appear on your phone out of nowhere, and answering it would automatically turn on your own camera, so it had the psychological impact of someone barging into your bathroom to demand a meeting while you are struggling with a stubborn poop. I mention this only because it's the reason we could see that Dr. Marconi was in bad shape. Thinner, pale. He had clear plastic tubes running from his nostrils.

Wait, is he in the hospital?

The idea that this man could age and even die like a normal human being briefly flattened me. He was our sage old mentor, our Dumbledore, our Obi-Wan Kenobi, our Qui-Gon Jinn, our Mufasa, our Wade Garrett from *Road House,* our Mickey from *Rocky III.* People like that can't die.

As a greeting, Marconi said, "I understand you have an urgent situation? By all means, distract me from the tedium of this room. The boredom is wearing holes in my brain."

I said, "Wait, didn't you contact us?"

Amy said, "Ah, some wires may have gotten crossed. But yes, it's urgent."

He said, "The note here says you have multiple deaths and you believe a haunted toy is to blame?"

"Sort of. Are you all right?"

"If you're referring to the state of my health, I appreciate your concern, but I prefer to keep such affairs private. I do not wish to die in this room, but wishes count for little in rooms such as this. I've long known that my habits were too reckless—and frankly, too enjoyable—to be healthy, and I have already outlived my parents, so good genes will not be my ally. Do you have the toy in question?"

"It's not a haunted toy," I said, scooting aside so he could see the Magpie egg behind us on John's living room floor. We didn't have it in any kind of protective case because 1) our glass containment box had been destroyed in the explosion, and 2) that hadn't prevented the toy from escaping last time, so what was the point? "It's called a—"

"I can see it. It's a sacrificial altar."

"Well, it's a plastic egg, when you feed it—"

"I know what it appears to be. I'm telling you what it actually is. I've been tracking this project for some time. It is a mass summoning ritual. There are at least twelve of them active at the moment, but they are summoning a singular entity."

I said, "We gathered that much. Do you already know about Swallow? The little creature it manifested that collected eyeballs for it?"

"I know enough. Yours is the only instance that has been reported so far; the others have likely completed their collections undetected. Some of these are located in parts of the world in which victims can be more easily made to disappear."

"The nerds we got this one from think we're living in a simulation, that they're trying to summon something that will cause it to crash or shut down. And, apparently, so does Amy. Are we living in a simulation, Doctor?"

"You already know my beliefs on that subject. I am a Christian man, in my own way, so of course I believe we are living in a simulation, yes."

John said, "Wait, you do?"

"The very first words of the scriptures state that our universe is a creation and a temporary one at that. Considering that, on at least one occasion, God and Satan placed a wager on the outcome of human affairs, calling this a simulation, or even a game, seems entirely appropriate. But this is all semantics. The real issue is whether or not this entity is capable of corrupting it, and one thing we know for certain about our universe, simulated or not, is that it is eminently corruptible."

I said, "You know how I try to maintain a positive attitude about these things, Doctor, but I've got to say, is this really all it takes to invite some game-breaking entity into our world? Somebody feeding a few body parts to a toy? It seems like anybody can do that at any time, and it's kind of exhausting to think about how hard it is to stop it when it does. We've been running ourselves ragged for a couple of days now and have accomplished absolutely nothing."

"This is actually the first time in human history—and the first time in the history of the known universe—that such a project would have been possible on this scale. These altars are scattered around the globe, their feedings orchestrated to occur simultaneously down to the second, via mobile technology and the game software. Then, in addition to the altars being fed human tissue, there are more than five million users playing the game on their phones, all of whom are participating in the ceremony to some degree, whether they know it or not. Think of it as a sort of mass prayer or incantation."

"Hold on," said Amy. "You're saying everyone playing that little kids' game is a part of it? All of the little girls and boys with plastic eggs and stuffed birds?"

"That little kids' game," said Marconi, "was developed by neuroscientists who are experts on the addictive nature of dopamine release intervals. They believed they were simply boosting 'engagement' by making the software as addictive as possible to young minds. But gods and devils gain their strength by subsuming the will of followers, by the molding of human behavior to their own ends. This software manipulates will on an astonishing scale, locking in the user to performing mindless, repetitive tasks instead of living out their own purpose as human beings. Watch anyone on their smartphone and tell me their state of mind can be called anything other than a 'trance.'"

I said, "Are you sure you're not just old and scared of technology?"

"Never forget, David, that devils have soft hands. The most effective manipulation always comes with the illusion of choice; it feels less like a whip and more like quenching a thirst. What is the next step in the ritual?"

John jumped in. "The app says it wants three gingerbread men, which in reality is—"

"Three whole human skins," said Amy.

"Oh yeah, that makes way more sense than what I was going to say."

I said, "And if they get those, that's it, right? The egg hatches and the Magpie, whatever it actually is, is birthed into the world? Then what?"

Amy said, "Magpie the Pie Pilferer is the name of the toy. You're supposed to keep feeding it pies until it becomes an adult and flies free to fulfill its destiny."

The doctor nodded. "Let us hope the world never experiences whatever that represents. As for the current stage, skinning a person is a very difficult task. It requires time, privacy, and equipment. It involves evading the police and witnesses both—this is the kind of crime that would gain international media attention if detected, especially if it were occurring in multiple locations around the globe simultaneously. I would say that in this circumstance, it is your adversaries who have an unenviable task in front of them, not you."

I said, "Ah, well, they've found a way around that. They have a portal to some other location, or some other time or universe, for all I know. It's embedded in a book. I think they're getting their body parts from there, or that was their plan anyway. We saw them orchestrate a trade for human tongues."

"But they didn't use that to collect the eyes."

"Right, ah, that might be our fault? Thinking about it now, that probably was their intention, to send Swallow through the book to get the parts. But then we showed up and disrupted it. I think it just went rogue after that."

The doctor said nothing, but his expression said it was very late in this conversation to be bringing up such an important point. He had the look of a dad at a neighborhood barbecue watching a rival dad overcook the steaks.

I said, "We really are doing our best over here."

"Are you?" asked the doctor, trying to sit upright, though the angle of the bed wasn't really allowing it. "When I was your age, I was traveling the world, discovering that multiple tribes across times and places who'd never contacted each other all worshipped the same cruel demigod. There was no one I could turn to; the authorities considered me a con artist, academics considered me a crank, the church considered me a heretic. Yet I pursued this dark thing across years and borders, because there was no one else. I have been fired five times in my life, arrested four, declared bankruptcy twice. Then again, I was raised to believe anything is possible, if one refuses to quit. You were raised to believe, well, something else, apparently."

I said, "Look, you're clearly not feeling well. You're probably frustrated that you can't come down here and film a special about this because you're laid up. But I don't think we have the energy to listen to you bark at us. It's been a rough week."

"David. You are not a child, and you need to abandon the childish concept of being 'in trouble' because the grown-ups are criticizing you. I am trying to address you as I would address a colleague, with appropriate frankness and urgency. And what I am trying to convey, what should have been obvious without me saying a word, is that *I am old.* I feel the weight of my miles and years every time I roll out of bed. This society now mutates so quickly that I feel myself straining to keep up, becoming a fool in real time. I worry that there is no one to hand this work off to, no one who will take it seriously as a discipline, the way a true master must learn all of the quirks and intricacies of a craft, all the mistakes and pitfalls that must be anticipated and avoided. You and your friends were my hope for that. What you are hearing in my voice is not anger but fear. Fear that I have failed to pass on what I know, that I have wasted my life. These are the thoughts one has when he is detained in a small, pungent room, deprived of entertainment and drink."

I said, "Well, maybe the fact that we're so bad at this should motivate you to just find someone else."

"The entity that is going to emerge from this ritual is not going to arrive in Russia, or Australia, or South Africa. It's going to emerge there, where you are. The altars are a tool to summon, but the door through which any entity would be summoned is within walking distance of where you're sitting. It is always there, where the veil of reality has grown thin. Why do I have to keep explaining it? Who will you go to for answers when I'm gone?"

John said, "We kind of assumed we would die long before you."

Amy said, "I know you didn't want to talk about your health situation, but seriously, is there anything we can do for you?"

"Yes. You can allow me to put my mind at ease and recuperate in peace. I am in no condition to travel. I ask only that you do your best. Your true best, not the watered-down version of it our decadent society has set as the standard. Be what you can be, what I know you can be. Now, if you don't mind, a nurse is giving me an angry look and holding a terrifying medical implement. Is there anything else?"

I wanted to ask him if he'd ever been forced to kill a teenager in his line of work, or at least ask how he handled cases where the apparent solution was morally questionable. Just as I was figuring out how to phrase the question, Joy appeared in the room and leaned down in front of Amy's phone, so that her face presumably now occupied the entirety of Dr. Marconi's screen.

"DR. MACARONIIIII!!!!!!" shouted Joy. "How's it hangin'?"

I pushed her out of frame. The doctor seemed briefly confused, then intrigued.

"Is it still with you?" he asked. "Or rather, is she—"

"You already said 'it'!" shouted Joy. "You referred to me as an 'it'! Everybody heard."

I said, "It's a long story. But, we're, uh, handling it."

Marconi said, "I see."

"Ha!" yelped Joy. "They're not handling shit!"

"Thanks for your time," I said and ended the call.

I faced Amy and said, "Well, that didn't help."

"What do you mean? He told us the solution. He's right; catching and skinning a person is hard, to the point that I don't think any of the kids we saw in the theater could actually do it even once, let alone three times."

John nodded. "Yeah, these amateurs couldn't skin a baby."

"That's why they need the Xarcrax book," said Amy. "That's how they intend to get the skins, from that terrible place on the other side. That means we don't have to go after Bas at all. We just need to get that book."

She seemed incredibly relieved by that.

I said, "Even if I agreed, we have no idea where—"

John's phone rang.

He glanced at the screen and said, "It's Momma Galvatron."

He answered and listened for a moment, then stood at attention.

"You think they're together?"

Pause.

"Well, did you call his weird friends? Okay. Yes, I heard you. We'll see what we can do."

He hung up and said, "She's freaking out. Bas and Gracie are both missing."

I said, "But we just saw Bas leave school."

"Yes, he went missing after that. She said he's missing in the present, not in the past."

"I'm saying somebody isn't missing after a couple of hours. He and Gracie could have gone to see a movie or something."

"Do you think that's what happened?"

"Fuck no."

I was waiting for Amy to chime in, but she appeared to be on the verge of collapse. She had her hand over her mouth.

"Are you okay?"

"*David*. The egg is demanding human skins. Bas went home and got his sister and took her somewhere. I can't breathe. I-I'm going to be sick."

"Oh . . . no," I said. "No, that's surely not—"

"We have to find them. Now."

"We can swing by the Dollar Cinema, see if they—"

John said, "His mom was calling from there. It's empty, they've abandoned it. Which means they've set up somewhere else. What are the places we know Bas goes? Other than home or school?"

I threw up my hands. "We don't know anything!"

"What about the pool?"

"*What pool?*"

"The first time we went to the Galvatron house," said John,

thinking, "Bas was coming back from the pool. His mom said so. That's where they are. In fact, I'm sure of it."

"How can you possibly be sure of that?"

"I think . . . I think I heard it in my dream."

"How would a cult gather and do cult shit at a public pool? The only building is the little toilet hut."

"That's not true," said Amy, her eyes wide. "The old community center is right next to it. And it's empty. It's just storage. City couldn't afford to staff it. Tons of room, lots of privacy. You know what? That's it, I'm sold. Let's go."

I shook my head. "Man, that is some thin reasoning considering that going there means leaving the egg here unprotected. Hell, I'd almost think they planted the pool thing in John's dream so they can come here and steal the Magpie while we're away. Or to trick us into bringing it along."

"Someone has to stay here and guard it."

"All right, who's doing what?"

John said to me, "I'll let you pick. One of us stays here, watching the egg and listening to Joy get irrationally angry watching *The Bachelor,* and the other one will engage in a terrifying wizard battle in an abandoned building."

"Somehow those sound equally bad to me. Let's flip for it."

He dug out a coin. "Call it. Winner goes to the pool."

"Heads."

It was tails.

John said, "I'll take the van. Let's gear up."

He headed toward the garage. Amy grabbed her purse and followed him.

I said, "Where are you going?"

"He can't go alone. And you'll have Joy here."

"What can Joy do?"

Joy, who had gone into the kitchen and was currently rooting around in the refrigerator, said, "What can *you* do? Juggle?"

"I'm leaving the shotgun here," said John, "since you have terrible aim and it will generally hit anything in the same room. There's more to pick from in the gun safe in the bedroom. The combination is you just pull on the door really hard until it opens. I'm taking the speech jammer in case we run into wizards trying to shout spells at us, plus we'll have the stuff in the van, including the sound system. We should be fine."

"*You* should be fine," I said. "What if Bas comes and teleports his hand inside my guts and squeezes my liver in half before I can even point the gun?"

John thought for a moment. "I'll be right back."

He went to the garage and returned a few minutes later, holding a vest made out of connected loops of leather, like chain mail woven out of cured skin.

"This hasn't been tested yet," said John, "but I believe in it. You remember in the Old Testament, King Saul tells David to collect for him a hundred foreskins from Philistine men as a test of loyalty? Then David collects two hundred, just to show off? Well, legend has it that those two hundred foreskins were crafted into a vest, which would grant the wearer immunity from any evil influence. Dave, *this is that vest.*"

"Instead of asking where you got that, I'm going to ask the more relevant question: What did you pay for it?"

"Less than you'd think. Put it on."

"Just leave it on the counter."

Amy said, "And if Bas shows up here, don't just shotgun him in the face. Try to talk him down. Let's go."

MONDAY. AUGUST 22. 5:55 P.M.
GINGERBREAD MEN
HUNGER AT 32%

Amy

Amy nervously watched the van's dashboard slurp up the road. They were heading right into the sun, the windshield feeling like a heat lamp that was turning them into jerky.

Just a couple of minutes out from their destination, John said, "I know you don't like to fixate on worst-case scenarios, but let's say we get there and find that Bas has, you know, already done the thing. With the human skins. And let's say he's done it to his little sister. What do we do? With him, I mean?"

"We call the police and have him arrested. That is a crime. I'm sure I've heard that somewhere."

"But what if we think the police can't hold him, due to his, you know, special abilities?"

"Then we offer whatever help we can to the police in holding him."

Amy felt like her tone made it clear she was done discussing it, and John apparently picked up on that, allowing Amy to stew in silence. They drove past the city's park with its dilapidated basketball courts and arrived at the mostly full parking lot by the fenced-off public pool. Up on a hill behind it was the dormant community center.

"Look at that, motherfucker!" screamed John.

Amy followed his pointing finger and saw that in the parking lot was an Undisclosed PD patrol car and, next to it, Detective Coiffure's sedan.

Amy said, "Oh, god. If the detective is already here . . ."

"It means my dream was dead-on. Dave can suck it." John took a photo of the cars and texted it to David, presumably with an attached message telling him to suck it.

"Did anything else happen in the dream that might come true? Anything that might help us right now?"

John hesitated, as if thinking. "It, uh, seems unlikely."

Amy immediately noted the dense, damp crowd around the pool. This wasn't a town where a lot of people had good pools of their own, so this one stayed busy. It was open until seven, so there was another hour of having lots of mostly naked bystanders in harm's way.

Amy said, "We have to pass through the pool people to get to the community center. I assume that means you can't go striding through them with a giant flaming sword or whatever you've got back there."

"Yeah, all those little kids would be bugging me to let them hold it. Let's see what we've got."

They circled around to the sliding side door of the van. John pulled it open, and then both of them recoiled at what they found inside.

Little Gracie Galveston was sitting there, a pink backpack on her lap, fiddling with one of the "white magick" dolls John kept on hand.

Amy said, "Oh, it's you! You're alive! Oh, good. Wait, how did you get in here? Were you back here the whole drive over?"

"He said you would give me a ride over here if I got in the back and kept quiet. You should always check in the back before you drive away. What if instead of a girl I'd been a murderer or a bear?"

"Bas told you that?"

"Your husband did."

"He did? When?"

"Last night, in my room. He said either he or his friend would be here, depending on who won the coin toss this time. He said if I give you the book, that you can get Bas out of trouble. Is that right?"

John said, "Do you have it?"

"Can you get Bas out of trouble?"

Amy said, "We can do our best. Is he here?"

"Somewhere around here. I'm supposed to meet him."

Gracie reached into the backpack—it was decorated with cartoon ponies—and brought out the Xarcrax portal book. She held it out to Amy.

Gracie said, "I'm starting to get scared."

Amy took the book and asked, "When all this began, did Bas tell you what the toy would do? Did he say what would come out of it?"

"He said everything would be better. He said I'd get to see Silva again. He said he could make everything right. With her, I mean."

"But you don't believe that now."

"I don't know. It all got weird. What is that book about? I tried to read it, but the words are all spelled wrong."

"It's not about the words," said Amy. "Remember when I said your brother could do magic? Well, this is a magic book. It opens to some other place. It's like a little window. But it's very dangerous."

"Bas does tricks for me. He can go into his room and make his hand come out of a drawer in mine. The first time he did it, I got really scared, and he had to come apologize. One time, I spied on him in the backyard, it was night, and he was standing there talking and I thought he was on his phone but he'd left his phone inside. He was just talking, having a conversation with the air. I watched him for a long time. I'm scared. I know I said before that I was just starting to get scared, but I was scared before, so I guess that was a lie. My stomach hurts all the time."

"Let me call your mom. She can come pick you up."

"I don't want to go home! I have to go to Bas. He's looking for me."

"You can't go to Bas. He's trying to . . ." Amy had no idea how to explain this without traumatizing the girl. "You could get hurt. What he wants to do, it might hurt you. You parents are probably worried sick."

"Then let me stay with you!"

Amy leaned toward her and, in her most reassuring voice, said, "Gracie, you can't. We're about to do something very dangerous." Amy pulled out her phone, and in the moment it took her to figure out she didn't actually have Regina Galveston's number in her contacts, Gracie had taken off.

"Hey! Gracie! No!"

Amy only needed about five steps of pursuit before she realized Gracie was much, much faster than she was. The little girl flew out of the parking lot and down the sidewalk, pink backpack bouncing all the way. Amy pursued as best she could, then Gracie turned and ran into the park, across the basketball courts, into a playground where a few families were hanging out. Amy slowed to a stop, imagining having to explain to them why she was chasing down this child who clearly wasn't hers, especially if said child screamed bloody murder the moment Amy got close.

Defeated and sweaty, Amy returned to the van to find John rooting around inside for gear.

He glanced back at her and said, "Whole family's fast."

"At least she's some distance away from Sebastian and whatever is about to happen here."

John emerged from the van with the speech jammer (which just looked like a blocky black speaker attached to an elongated microphone and a pistol grip) and a "music gun" he had rigged up. It was a megaphone attached to an MP3 player that, at a moment's notice, could trigger "In the Air Tonight" by Phil Collins, set right before that drum part. John went to give the latter to Amy, but she had the Xarcrax book in her only hand.

"I don't want to leave this here," she said, imagining some teenager stealing it out of the van and getting sucked into the Phantom Zone. "Do we have something we can put it in?"

John dug around in the van again until he found one of those ribbed metal suitcases like you see in spy movies. He opened it, dumped onto the floor bundles of some kind of foreign currency, and then locked the book inside the case and handed it to Amy. They ventured through the fence into the pool area, Amy carrying the suitcase, John dual-wielding his two ridiculous sound gadgets.

They weaved through the pool crowd. Amy had confronted David in the past about the way he always described the town as an unending carnival of despair. No, not every structure was falling down, not every business was dying, and not every citizen was shambling under the weight of crushed expectations and meth withdrawal. The people at the pool, for instance, were having fun. Little kids were chasing one another around, parents were laughing, the pool was functioning just fine as a pool, aside from a couple of Band-Aids Amy could see floating around in there.

Past the pool there was a sidewalk and a set of wide concrete stairs that led up the hill to the dormant community center, a two-story building audaciously built from not one but two shades of tan brick, with a row of tinted windows around the top like a headband (only one of the windows was broken, as far as Amy could see). The words *Undisclosed Community Center* were printed on a sign positioned among the overgrown landscaping so that it appeared to be hiding in the bushes, like it was waiting to jump out and surprise them. If David were there, he'd note that the Y was missing.

They didn't have to walk far before they found Detective Coiffure talking to a uniformed officer who looked young enough to be a trainee.

The beat cop said, "Stop right there," but the detective waved him off and said, "I know these assholes." Amy took some pride in the fact that he didn't exclude her from the group description.

John said, "Is Sebastian Galvatron here?"

"You think he might be?"

"Isn't that why you're here?"

The beat cop said, "There's a missing security guard."

Amy sucked in a breath.

Coiffure caught it, groaned, and said, "Tell me what you know."

"Regina Galveston said her kids are both missing," said Amy. "We found Gracie in the parking lot, but she ran off."

"And in response to this report of missing children, you decided to come yourselves instead of calling it in?"

John said, "We knew you'd already be here. You're always a step ahead."

"Shut the fuck up. A security guard said he heard screams inside the building. He went to check it out, immediately disappeared into thin air. That was a couple of hours ago. Pascal here got the call from a witness and then he got spooked by what the witness told him, so he called me and now we're waiting for the janitor to come unlock the building. What's in that suitcase?"

Amy said, "Magic book." She glanced at the uniformed police officer, Pascal, not sure what details of their weird case could be shared with the rank and file. "There's a real good chance that your missing person may be tied to all the other stuff that's going on. With the, uh, group. The one that's collecting stuff from people."

"The little floating bundle of eyeballs?" asked Pascal the Beat Cop.

"No," said John, "this is being done by something even more terrifying: motivated nerds."

"There's the janitor," said Coiffure. To Pascal, he said, "If we see anything weird, stay vague on the radio. If the others down at the station think it's monsters, they'll all show up. Everybody wants to be the goddamned X-Files until they have to do the paperwork."

The elderly janitor took an infuriatingly long time to get the door open, then Coiffure pulled a gun out of a shoulder holster and gestured for Pascal to do the same.

To John and Amy, he said, "You two stay out of our way."

Me

I was on the sofa with the shotgun in my lap. The Magpie egg was on the floor where I could keep an eye on it. John's laptop was on the cushion next to me so I could monitor the exterior camera feeds, but the one watching the front lawn had gone out. Joy said the bird had turned up earlier and pecked the camera free of its mount, knocking it into the grass. She insisted we couldn't fix it until the eggs in the nest had hatched and the baby birds had moved out; otherwise, we'd be disturbing them. Joy had not been interested in arguing this point further. At this moment, she was finishing watching a recorded episode of *The Bachelor,* which had made her extremely angry.

She turned off the TV, stood, and said, "Don't make a lot of noise. I have the midnight-to-eight shift, so I'm going to go get some sleep."

"Noise may be coming our way, whether we like it or not. Also, do you actually need to sleep?"

"Do *you* need to sleep? Is it hard with your big floppy shoes and your nose making that honking sound all night?"

"I'm asking a serious question. I may need your help if things go wrong. And by 'go wrong,' I mean if they go the way they do in ninety-five percent of situations like this."

"What kind of help? I'm not going to help you kill anybody."

"That's the same as saying you're not going to help at all!"

She shrugged and answered a text she'd gotten.

Who texts Joy?

Without looking up from her phone, she said, "Oh, do you want some of that German chocolate cake I brought home? Or do you just eat clown food?"

"Can we be serious for a moment?"

"Oh-oh. Are you going to say you're in love with me?"

"I just want you to answer a question. Really answer. Will you do that?"

She met my eyes. "Depends on the question."

I sat up straighter on the sofa and said, "Why are you here?"

"Why are *you* here?"

"So we just can't have this conversation? You're just going to keep dodging and repeating my questions back to me?"

"I have this conversation all the time, with other people. John got drunk one night, and we talked for hours. He even cried. When we were in Japan, Amy asked me if I age or if I have dreams when I sleep. I told her. But no, I don't like having this conversation with you because you should already know. If those people out there, the normies, figure out what I am, they'll show up with torches and burn me alive."

"And me along with you!"

"That's right. So it's like a hyena accusing a sheep of being a wolf."

"Nobody is accusing anybody. We're in a situation here where I may have to depend on you to not let me die. And to this day, I don't know how you operate. Or why. I don't know what you are when nobody is in the room with you. I don't know if you have thoughts of your own or if you just reflect back what you think we want to hear, as part of the camouflage, or whatever you call it."

She crossed her arms. "Why are you wearing pants right now?"

"What?"

"I'm making a point. Why are you wearing pants? Think and then give me your best answer."

"Uh, because everyone gets mad if you walk around with your dick out?"

"Right. And why do those people get mad?"

"Because . . . it's not the thing you're supposed to do."

"In other words, they get mad because unspecified other people expect them to get mad. So you wear pants because other people expect you to, and those people expect you to because other people expect them to expect you to. Our personalities are just like water in mud puddles, filling in the holes of other people's expectations."

"No. That's where you're wrong. I exist as an individual outside of what I'm doing to please others. I mean, that's why I don't have any other friends."

"You've never squashed a thought inside your head because it's too weird or gross? You've never thought, 'What would Amy say if she knew I was thinking this?' When you're making a decision, you never stop to ask yourself how it's going to look to others? What you think of as your amazing, unique, individual personality would be totally different if you'd been raised on a desert island."

"At this point, I don't even remember what my question was, but I definitely regret asking it."

"Do you want some of the cake or not?"

"Wait, I remember now: Why are you here?"

"Why are *you* here? Answer that, and then you'll know."

"Where else would I go?"

"Nowhere, and it's for the same reason as me: because you like it here."

"That's ridiculous."

"Do you want the cake or not?"

"Obviously I do."

"It's on the counter. Go get it yourself. I'm putting on my pajamas."

She went upstairs, and I headed for the kitchen, taking the shotgun with me and occasionally glancing back at the Magpie on the floor of the living room.

From above me, Joy shouted, "Hey, I, uh, think you need to come take a look at this."

John

The community center was as hot as a dwarven forge and smelled slightly worse. Detective Coiffure and Pascal the Beat Cop had gone inside and told John and Amy to stay put, orders that they had broken about two minutes later. They ventured in to find a lobby still decorated with a faded banner welcoming everyone to the Kids' Safety Safari, featuring a cartoon monkey with his arms around a happy little boy and girl. There were stairs to their right, but John advanced through a set of twin doors directly in front of him, into a gymnasium that was the only other room on the first floor.

There were no windows in the gym. The space was all heat and shadow, the kind of stifling lightlessness you'd expect from Hell itself. John immediately found himself at the entrance of a darkened tunnel surrounded by tall fake plants. The tunnel was constructed out of PVC pipes and trash bags and decorated with plastic vines, set up as some kind of kid safety presentation. At the entrance was a life-size plywood gorilla with a speech bubble saying, "WELCOME, KIDS! Do YOU have what it takes to make it out of the other side of the MONKEY TUNNEL alive?!?"

John chewed a breath off the airless room and tightened his grip around both of his weapons. He heard the floor creaking and squeaking inside the tunnel—the shoes of the detective and the beat cop, or someone else? John turned to face Amy, the apprehension on her face lit by the meager shafts of light spilling from the doors behind them. Did they, in fact, have what it took to make it out of the other side of this tunnel alive? John didn't know, and he sensed that she didn't know, either. If you think about it, isn't life itself one big Monkey Tunnel?

He nodded, and together they stepped past the plywood sentry and into the black, crinkly bowels of the Kids' Safety Safari. They had brought with them no flashlights, and John was already wondering if this was a fatal mistake. Illuminating the way with the meager light on Amy's cell phone, they soon passed another wooden primate, this one in a tiny cartoon car with a speech bubble above it that said, "If a stranger offers to pick you up, tell a grown-up right away!"

John took a step toward a blind corner. In the shadows beyond, he thought he could hear shallow breaths, could sense tense muscles coiled for an ambush.

He raised one of his weapons; he couldn't remember which one was in which hand. He pivoted around the corner—

And found himself face-to-face with a tall figure sculpted out of hate.

Its hair was perfect.

"I told you to wait outside," said Detective Coiffure. "There's nobody in here."

Amy said, "I didn't think there would be. The guys we're looking for probably need some more enclosed, private space to do their work."

As she was speaking, John saw a shadow looming behind the detective.

John drew his other weapon, pointing it over Coiffure's shoulder. "GET DOWN!"

He didn't.

The shape drew closer. John saw light reflecting off a pair of unfeeling eyes.

"Yeah, nobody here," said Pascal the Beat Cop. "This place got a basement?"

"No, the second floor is it," said Coiffure. "Let's go. You two, go outside and wait. Or go home. I don't give a shit."

The detective pushed past them and headed out toward the lobby and the stairs, his partner in tow. Instead of walking back through the Monkey Tunnel, Amy jiggled at the frame, and it all instantly collapsed around them. Something rustled under the plastic sheeting, and a very fat, annoyed raccoon waddled out.

John caught up to Pascal just before he reached the door. "Hey," whispered John, "the detective said the witness's story scared you enough to call him in. What spooked you?"

"It was called in by a girl who works the concession stand. She knew the guard. Says Louis—that's the guard—heard the screams but said the screams he heard were his own voice. Sounded like he was being tortured. He thought maybe it was some kind of prank, but where would somebody get a recording of his voice to do that? And why? Then the guard disappeared, and the concession girl called it in." He nodded toward the detective in the next room. "We got a standing procedure: When this kind of thing comes up, it gets dumped on him."

John nodded. "If this turns weird, stay back and follow our lead. Got it?"

"What do you mean by—"

Pascal was interrupted by the sound of a man's scream, from upstairs.

He drew his gun and ran through the twin doors to the lobby. John and Amy followed, trailing the cops through the lobby and then up the stairs. They reached the top, turned, and emerged into a long hallway lined with doors. Shafts of sunlight stabbed into the hall from a window behind them, stretching their shadows along the tiled floor. The two cops were on high alert now, trying to prepare themselves for something no cop had ever trained for, unless they'd learned under some rogue instructor who began every class by dropping a buttload of acid.

Keeping his voice low, John said, "This is hard to explain, but if one of these rooms contains a bunch of gingerbread men cookies, let me know, because that means there's been a terrible misunderstanding."

Pascal threw open the first door, and both men swept the room through their gunsights from outside, then stepped in to check the corners. Stripes of sunlight from venetian blinds illuminated stacks of folding chairs and wall posters listing the twelve steps of an addiction recovery program.

"What the hell is that?" whispered Pascal.

He was referring to a trio of square plastic vats on the floor. They were positioned where the meager light from the blinds would hit them, the walls coated with droplets of condensation, the bottom few inches filled with dirt. John approached, and the two cops let him, apparently figuring if it was a booby trap or toxic substance, why not let him take the brunt of it? Inside each tub were some kind of mushrooms, dozens of them, vibrant purple with red at the tips.

"Either somebody is growing 'shrooms in here," said John, "or else they did a terrible job of cleaning their storage tubs."

They moved on to the next room, across the hall. Same procedure: scan from outside, check the corners. Inside were stacks of what appeared to be gymnastics mats and a big wooden box with a curtained window for puppet shows. John thought that would have been a pretty good place for a killer to hide, but found that kicking over the box while screaming revealed that no one was crouched back there. When he turned to head back out of the room, however, he froze at the sight of a tangle of gnarled faces piled in one corner.

"HEY! FACES! SHIT! WE GOT SEVERED FACES! FACES!!!"

Amy popped into the room, her green eyes wide. But as soon as she did, John realized it was just a pile of puppets. Still, he went over and gave the pile a thorough kicking, then closed the door securely behind them when he left. John had never been attacked by a puppet, but it was for the same reason he'd never been bitten by a snake: He knew when to exercise caution.

From somewhere came another scream, sounding like the same man from before—their missing security guard, apparently. It was impossible to tell where the sound was coming from; it almost seemed to be emanating from the hallway itself, like the missing man was already a wraith haunting his crime scene. If so, he wasn't visible in the hall.

The two cops threw open the door of the next room. The floor was all but covered in three-foot-wide spheres that John immediately assumed must be some kind of giant monster eggs, but closer examination revealed them to be yoga balls.

Two rooms left.

In the next was stacked boxes of plastic cups, paper plates, and printed T-shirts for the Undisclosed July 4 Forest Fire Recovery Fund Fun Run.

Amy said, "Look. By the door."

She was looking at the floor, where there was a cluster of black, circular stains, like dried blood from a robot that had cut her finger. John knew why she'd called attention to it, but he knew this wasn't the black substance they called Arby's Sauce—that stuff didn't stay put. A further search of the room revealed a couple of boxes of used black candles, which was absolutely part of any Occult Summoning Starter Kit. The room, however, contained nothing more of note.

Just as they stepped back into the hall, there was another scream, emanating from every direction at once. John suddenly had a memory of their first feeding of the Magpie, a cry beamed directly into their heads. They moved on to the final door.

Locked.

No—stuck. None of these doors had locks on the handles. Something was blocking it from inside.

Coiffure motioned to Pascal, both men moving silently now. The beat cop reared back and kicked the door. It didn't budge. Another attempt, same result. Coiffure gave it a try, but it was like it had been nailed shut.

Almost as if in response, there was the sound of a hollow knock, a single bang of a fist on a surface. But the sound wasn't coming from the other side of the closed door.

It was coming from Amy's suitcase.

There was another knock, then a jolt that shook the suitcase in Amy's hand.

The lid burst open.

Me

I found Joy in her bedroom, standing in front of her closed closet door. She was wearing a tank top and very short Lycra shorts. My gaze lingered one second too long, and the next time I blinked, she had instantly changed into baggy pajama pants and a T-shirt.

I took a bite of the cake I was holding on a saucer and said, "I'm going to start a 'I think you need to see this' jar where we have to put a dollar in every time we say it."

She said, "Open the closet."

"I know it opens into John's room now. I helped knock the wall out."

"*Open it.*"

I really wanted to ask Joy what I was going to find in there, but knew she wouldn't tell me. In theory, I should just get a view into John's bedroom, obstructed only by hangers full of Joy's blouses and skirts. I handed her my cake saucer, sighed, and pulled the closet door open.

I was looking at water. A vertical slab of it that stood a few inches into the closet.

I expected it to splash into the room and flood the house, but it just stayed there, defying gravity. The surface was perfectly smooth, no ripples or waves. Beyond it, I could see daytime sky—like we were looking up from just below the surface.

I said, "Huh."

I stuck my finger into it. Just water. Nothing special about it, aside from the way it was behaving.

Joy, through a mouthful of my cake, said, "You see the water, right?"

"Yeah."

"If you go in John's room and look from the other side, it's normal. Just the hole in the wall and either my room or the back of the door, depending on whether or not it's open."

I again said, "Huh."

"So what do we do?"

"I . . . don't know. I mean, is this a portal to the ocean or something? What happens if you go into John's room and try to walk through from the other side?"

"No idea. Go try it."

"I'm definitely not doing that. Best case is I get wet, worst is I get teleported to god knows where. Maybe we should try throwing something through it instead."

She took another bite of cake and said, "Why?"

"I don't know. See if we can figure out how it works?"

Joy pointed at it with her icing-smeared fork and said, "I know I'm not the professional here, but maybe we should instead be preparing for if something dangerous comes swimming out of it?"

John

Detective Coiffure and Beat Cop Pascal turned their guns toward Amy just in time to see an entire human skin fly out of the suitcase she was holding. It flopped to the floor of the hall with a slimy *thwap*. John saw ragged cuts and veiny fat, he saw tangles of matted, bloody, salt-and-pepper hair at one end. He saw features that said this skin had belonged to a large, middle-aged man, and then he forced himself not to look at it anymore.

Amy dropped the open suitcase and screamed.

Pascal said, "That's him! That's the security guard! They fucking skinned him!"

Coiffure pointed his gun at John, even though Amy had been holding the suitcase that had just unleashed the hide. John felt like that was somewhat unfair; clearly this act had been performed by some kind of supernatural means. Wouldn't a small woman be just as capable of that?

John dropped his sound gadgets and put his hands in the air as a show of surrender. "Everybody be calm," he said, despite knowing that the human nervous system does not respond to voice commands. "It's not what you think, but it's going to be hard to explain."

With his hands held above him, John moved toward the suitcase and, in slow motion, grabbed the Xarcrax book and held it up.

"I know this doesn't make sense," he said, "but the skin came from this book. The people doing the skinning, they're at another location. We don't know where. But they're using this book to pass things through."

"You stupid asshole," noted Coiffure. "If somebody asks why you have human body parts in your suitcase, you say, 'That's not my suitcase.' Get on the ground and put your hands behind your head."

John got to his knees, but no further. Amy did the same.

To Pascal, Amy said, "If you've never handcuffed someone like me, you just cuff my right and put the other cuff around a belt loop in back."

"Shut up," barked Coiffure. "I'm not dumb enough to arrest you; the paperwork is a goddamned nightmare. I need you to tell me exactly what is about to happen here and who else is in danger."

John said, "It's actually not complicated. The weirdos collecting body parts need two more skins after this one. We don't know whose, and we don't know how they intend to get them. Sebastian Galvatron is one of the weirdos, maybe the main weirdo, and we only came here because we knew he hangs out here and had no other ideas. That's it. That's all we've got."

Amy said, "And sometimes objects fly out of this magic book. But I know that's a sensitive subject, so we don't need to dwell on it. We need to find Bas. And if I had to bet, I'd say he and his cult have been using that locked room to do cult stuff. As for who's in danger, in the short term, any of us. In the long term, all of us."

Coiffure turned to say something to Pascal, who was staring at the bloody pile of skin on the floor and looking like his brain was spitting out nothing but blinking red error messages.

"Hey. Look at me. We need to—"

Coiffure stopped at the sound of footsteps behind him, on the stairwell.

John said, "Oh, there he is now."

Bas did not look surprised to see them.

Coiffure aimed his gun and said, "YOU! ON THE FLOOR! RIGHT NOW!"

Instead of obeying, Bas reached out and, just as John had seen him do back in his yard, made his hand vanish. John just had time to think, *I should have worn the foreskin vest,* before Bas's disembodied hand appeared right above the Xarcrax book in the open suitcase. It grabbed the book and then both hand and book vanished. When John turned back toward Bas, he was holding the book, already heading back down the stairs.

"AFTER HIM!" screamed John as he scrambled to his feet, picking up his sound gadgets. "IF HE GETS AWAY WITH THAT BOOK, THE UNIMAGINABLE HAPPENS!"

Everyone ran after Bas, John leaping down the last four steps, stumbling and almost falling on his face. Bas blew through the front doors and ran outside, toward the crowded pool area. John slammed into the doors just as they were closing, knocking them open again with his face and forearms. He aimed his Phil Collins gun at the boy's back, having no idea if it would have any effect but also knowing that two decades of smoking cigarettes would not allow him to catch up to the teenager on foot. John squeezed the trigger, and the "In the Air Tonight" drums blasted out at ear-piercing volume.

Bas, who apparently mistook this for gunfire, instinctively dropped to the ground. John ran up and kicked the book from Bas's hands as the two cops arrived, their guns trained on the teenager's back. The crowd of pool revelers nearby went silent, some drifting over to see if this particular situation promised hilarity or unimaginable horror.

John leaned over Bas. "Are there any more victims? I know you need two more. Do you have them somewhere? If they're still alive, it's not too late. Are they up in that room? If they're just partially skinned, the doctors can probably fix it, easy as re-peeling a banana."

From the ground, Bas said, "You wouldn't understand the answer even if I told you."

"What would your parents think of this?"

Bas laughed. Amy showed up, picking the Xarcrax book out of the grass and holding it against her chest with both arms.

Coiffure nodded toward Pascal and said, "Cuff him. We'll get an answer."

John turned to the gathered crowd of damp rubberneckers and said, "Back off, everybody. This is none of your business. He's just a kid and—"

The Xarcrax book Amy was holding belched out another full human skin, like a snake from a can of prank peanuts. The children in the crowd shrieked in terror.

Amy dropped the book, then got down and put her knees on the cover, like she could somehow save the next victim by keeping the cursed book closed. It was very rare that John saw Amy at a total loss as to what to do, and it wasn't doing wonders for his confidence.

"Oh my god," she said, through hitching breaths, looking at the twisted suit of skin in the grass. "We're too late. John. Oh my god . . ."

The detective brought his gun closer to Bas and said, "WHO IS THAT? WHERE IS THE BODY? WHERE ARE YOU KEEPING THEM? TALK OR I WILL PUT A HOLLOW-POINT IN YOUR KNEECAP!"

John leaned over the wad of skin, noting that it was covered in dark body hair, along with smears of blood in the shape of strong, grabby fingers and—

"Look at the arms," said John as he kicked a tanned strip of deflated human skin. "This one has a full sleeve of tattoos. Should be identifiable."

Pascal the Beat Cop, looking like his sanity was clinging by sweaty fingertips, rushed over.

He took one look at the skin and said, "Bullshit. B-bullshit. That's . . . that's BULLSHIT!"

Amy said, "What?"

"That's bullshit!" He pointed his gun at Bas. "How are you doing this? What the fuck is going on?!?"

Coiffure said, "Hey. Get ahold of yourself. I take it you recognize him?"

Without a word, Pascal simply rolled up his sleeve.

John said, "Uh . . ."

Amy said, "Now, be calm. It's just an illusion. He's trying to mess with you."

"Or maybe the victim just had the same tattoo."

Pascal said, "That's ME. Look at the hair. Look at the other shoulder—same tattoo over there. How is this possible? TELL ME!"

From the ground, Bas said, "You'll find out."

Pascal gritted his teeth and kicked the boy in the ribs like he was trying to punt him out of the city.

John sensed Amy struggling at his feet. She was wrestling with the book, trying to keep the cover closed with all her meager weight. Someone from inside punched the cover so hard that the book bounced out from under her, landing facedown in the grass a foot away. She reached for it at the exact moment another sticky suit of human skin puked itself out from inside. More children screamed. Several adults joined them. John wondered exactly how they would describe these events in the police report.

A brief check of this third skin told John what he'd already guessed. The hair on it wasn't as perfectly sculpted as it was on the detective standing in front of him, but it was clear that it once had been.

Coiffure said, "Oh, fuck off," and snatched the book off the ground.

He examined it as if it would contain some kind of explanation that would cause all of this to suddenly make perfect sense.

Amy, her voice shaking, said, "Be careful with that." John thought she was on the verge of fainting.

Coiffure opened the cover and actually held his gun up to the book, like he was ready to shoot whatever tiny human-flaying gnomes lived inside. He was visibly disappointed in what he found, which to his eyes was likely just a nearly unreadable book by and for nerds.

He said, "How is it—"

A brick flew out from the book and smashed him in the nose.

"Ow! What the—!"

Coiffure dropped the book, blood squirting through the fingers he'd pressed to his face. Bas seized the opportunity. He sprang to his feet in a way that should not have been shocking for a high school athlete and yet still managed to surprise everyone involved. He snatched the book and sprinted through the crowd of damp swimmers, rounding the pool and heading toward the restrooms—a small white cinder block building with two openings for the men's and women's.

John pursued, shouting at the clammy bystanders to clear the way. He had no idea where Bas thought he was going, if he had any plan at all. The restrooms were a dead end, and if he intended to circle around them, he'd find a fence that he'd struggle to climb before John caught up. That meant either Bas was operating out of blind panic—and nothing about his manner said he was—or he had some kind of unthinkable curveball in mind.

Bas headed right for the men's room and slipped inside the door. John skidded to a stop and took a moment to remind himself which hand held the speech jammer. He pulled open the men's room door and raised his gadget.

What he should have seen, if his memory was correct, was a few feet of floor and then a white brick separator to block the view of the people pissing inside. Turning and walking a few feet should have given him a view of a stall to his right and two urinals to his left. He saw none of that. Instead, he was looking at a vast, dim interior, a space fifty times larger than the building housing it. There were puddles on the floor. It smelled like ten thousand infected wounds. It wasn't the exact room they had glimpsed through the window of the Xarcrax book, but it could easily be another wing of the same facility or another spot in a world where everything looked like that.

Detective Coiffure arrived and shoved John aside. Leading with his gun, he stepped into the impossible space, seemingly oblivious to the fact that he was no longer in the small restroom that should have been there.

He yelled, "BAS! Give yourself up before you make this worse! You're a minor; they'll go easy on you! Make this hard and they'll never get the chance! You hear me?"

Pascal showed up next and stopped cold, first staring inside the impossibly vast room and then looking around at the small white hut it existed inside, as if to confirm he hadn't taken a wrong turn somewhere. His gaze landed on John, wordlessly pleading for guidance.

John said, "Wait," and then shouted to Coiffure, "Get the hell out of there, man! Look around you!"

Coiffure, so inflamed with rage that the logic part of his brain had gotten swallowed in the blaze, kept going and motioned for Pascal to follow. He dutifully obeyed, gun aimed at the floor, presumably thinking about all the people in his life who had told him not to take this job. John stood at the entrance and watched as the two men moved farther away, now so far from him that by all rights, they'd not only be outside of the restroom but on the verge of crossing the parking lot outside the fence. Coiffure's posture was that of a man who knew the situation was insanity and was so pissed off by it that he was determined to find the cause and shoot it until the world returned to normal, even if it meant taking a break halfway through to go buy more bullets.

Something grabbed the back of John's shirt. He jumped and readied himself to Phil Collins the assailant to death, then saw it was Amy, pulling him back. "Get away. John, get away from it." She yelled to the cops, "Hey! It's a trap! Get out here and help get the kids away!"

John turned back to see that the "kids" she referenced were several teenagers from the pool crowd that had wandered over, thinking they were going to see some kind of high-stakes toilet standoff between the cops and one of their classmates, if not the resurrected zombie of Ed Gein. At least three already had their phones out, recording. It was just a reflex for them at this point. John turned back to the portal and recoiled so hard he almost fell down.

A huge, sweaty, hairy man had materialized in the restroom doorway, facing inside. The reason he seemed to "materialize" is that, as far as John could tell, the portal was freestanding in that other world, and this guy had walked through it from John's direction, so there was actually a split second where John thought he could see the pink interior of the man, complete with beating heart. But now he was looking at the dude's sweaty back, which was crisscrossed with leather straps. He appeared to be wearing an apron, a heavy one, like you'd see in the part of the slaughterhouse where they have to chop entire cows in half. He was striding steadily away from John and toward the cops.

Then a second figure stepped into view in exactly the same way, a glimpse of innards and then a broad back and a bald head. He wore modern but weathered armor and tattered black fatigue pants, all of it looking like it had been pulled off a corpse on a battlefield. In one hand, he held what appeared to be an axe whose handle was made of a human thighbone, the head a ragged piece of scrap metal with a serrated edge. On his other hand was a set of wrist-mounted hooks that extended forward like foot-long talons.

Talon Man himself seemed briefly confused, looking left and then right before turning to face John and Amy. That's when John saw that the man wore a mask made of chiseled black stone, with two narrow slits for eyes and a yellow cross painted on the bottom half. He started walking in John's direction. John felt Amy tugging on the back of his T-shirt again, urging him away, but for some reason, John had it in his head that the Talon Man couldn't leave the place/time/dimension he existed in, even though the two police officers had just made the trip in the opposite direction with no problem. Mainly, John couldn't visualize this giant Mad Max motherfucker just wandering around the Undisclosed public pool, striding through the wet moms and crying toddlers wearing their pool floaties. And yet, the man stepped right over the threshold of the two worlds, emerging from the restroom into the sunlight. He turned his masked face up to the sky, as if briefly fascinated by the color.

John backed up far enough to be out of axe-swinging range several times over but not, as he noted to himself, out of axe-*throwing* range. The Talon Man advanced once again, and John retreated in turn.

"HEY! TURN AROUND!" yelled John to the cops inside. They were far enough into that other world that he wasn't sure they'd be able to hear him. They did. Coiffure and Pascal pivoted to see the hairy man in the leather apron right behind them, now with some kind of curved blade in his right hand. Coiffure raised his gun and yelled cop commands. The Hairy Apron Man ignored them. There was a gunshot and then a man's scream, but John didn't see what had happened because he'd turned his attention to the Talon Man, who was continuing to move steadily toward him. John heard parents behind him urging their kids away, the bystanders finally realizing that the only thing between them and the unfathomable horror was John, and there was always that tiny chance he might let something slip past.

John pointed the speech jammer at the Talon Man, hoping he would mistake it for a real gun that could actually damage him.

"STOP! DROP YOUR WEAPONS!"

He stopped, but nothing about his posture registered any kind of alarm. He did not drop his weapons.

Inside the restroom dimension, John saw that more weirdly armed butchers had shown up. The two cops started firing. One filthy dude went down, then another. Amy yelled for them to get out of there. Pascal looked toward her, but there were now several men between him and the doorway, and Detective Coiffure was focused on the fact that there were still some people in that world he hadn't shot yet.

John said, "Wait here!" to Amy and headed in their direction, with no plan for how he would extract the two men whose skins were lying in the grass behind him. After just two steps, the entire world containing the Hairy Apron Man and the two cops just . . . shrank?

The entrance became smaller and smaller until it was a foot-tall square on the floor, and then it fell over, and a leather cover slapped closed. Where the threshold between worlds had been now was only the Xarcrax book, lying on concrete that was damp with pool-water footprints. Beyond it was now just the restroom's familiar interior of white-painted brick covered in ink pen graffiti. And, standing right inside the door, was Bas. The teenager snatched the book off the floor and ran out of the restroom, toward the pool.

John said, "HEY! Let them out of there! Those are cops, Bas! Hey!"

Bas ran up to the Talon Man, who was still standing where John had told him to stop. It was then that John realized the man had merely been waiting for Bas to show up with instructions. As he ran past, Bas barked something at the man that didn't sound like English, then inexplicably continued running right toward the swimming pool.

Bas stopped at the edge, chucked the Xarcrax book into the water, then turned to face John. He opened his mouth to say something.

Panicking at the thought of having some kind of spell cast on him or, even worse, Amy, John raised the speech jammer and squeezed the trigger. Bas started to say words that were immediately echoed back much louder, creating a sort of sonic double vision that immediately gave John a headache. Bas tried talking through it, as everyone does when faced with the speech jammer, then confusion washed over his face and his mouth fell closed.

Bas scanned the people around him as if trying to spot someone, then dove into the water. A moment later, Talon Man followed his lead, jumping in feetfirst.

John ran up to the pool with Amy in tow. When he arrived, he found the pool was empty, aside from the Xarcrax book, which floated there silently. Amy jumped in, opened the book, then said something that John almost thought was an expletive. She tossed the book up onto the tiles at poolside.

John said, "What is it?" then opened the book, keeping his face out of the path of any projectiles.

There was no need. The book was, now, just a book.

He asked, "Did you hear what Bas was trying to say before I jammed him? Was it a hex?"

Amy climbed out of the pool and said, "I only heard the first two words: 'Where's Gracie?'"

Me

I shut the closet door, noticing for the first time that on the other side, Joy had hung a presumably fake newspaper clipping. It was a photo of her holding a clearly photoshopped fish, under the headline:

LOCAL WOMAN SNAGS RECORD-BREAKING TROUT

I said, "How about we barricade it? If something is going to come through the magic water, we can at least make it harder for them. Or buy ourselves time to do something."

"Barricade it with what?" asked Joy. "And don't tell me to scoot the bed over here. That's a new mattress. I don't want some squid creature sliming it up."

"Let's see what John has in his gara—"

Something crashed against the door, flinging it open. Bas Galvatron flew horizontally out of the water, landing on the floor, soaking wet. He tried to stand up and immediately tumbled over, as if gravity was running in a different direction from what he'd been expecting.

I reached for the shotgun and realized I hadn't brought it up with me, because I'd been carrying the cake.

I said, "Stay on the floor! Where's—"

Before I could finish my question, a second, much larger man came sailing into the room like he was doing a flying dropkick, accompanied by a spray of water.

His boots slammed my back, and I fell on top of Bas. The teenager shoved me off him—he was stupidly strong—and jumped to his feet. I rolled over in time to see Bas bark an instruction at his henchman, then run out of the room.

Whatever language or jargon Bas and the henchman were using, I now knew the phrase for, "Kill that fucking guy." The masked man raised a truly ridiculous weapon, some kind of bone axe, and brought it down. I rolled out of the way, and the axe crashed into the floor behind me so hard that it shook the house.

I said, "Joy! Run!"

I rolled back over just in time to see Joy break the cake saucer over the masked man's head, which he barely noticed. He swung at her with a wrist-mounted claw thing and missed. Joy had dropped to the floor, where she grabbed the sharpest shard of broken plate and stabbed it into the back of the man's leg, behind the knee.

He definitely noticed that. The man stumbled backward, reaching down to extract the embedded shard. Joy pulled me to my feet and dragged me into the hallway. We closed the flimsy wooden bedroom door behind us and bounded down the stairs. We spilled out into the living room and found that the Magpie egg was gone and so was Bas. The front door was still standing open.

The shotgun was still on the sofa where I'd left it. I ran over, grabbed it, and went back to the bottom of the stairs just in time to hear the door to Joy's bedroom explode and the huge man stride to the top of the staircase.

I aimed the laser dots right at his chest. He was wearing some kind of black tactical gear that looked plausibly bulletproof, but I wasn't a skilled enough shot to do anything but aim vaguely at the center of him and hope for the best.

"I hope you like your ribs BARBECUED, bitch!" is what I'd think to say later but didn't at the time.

I pulled every trigger I could get my fingers around. I think three barrels successfully fired their shots. The masked man dropped like a sack of pig heads.

I tried to catch my breath, then found Joy next to me and said, "We have to go after—"

I heard a groan from above. The masked man was, in fact, still moving. I had no more shells for the shotgun, and the ammo was stored up in John's gun safe, behind the spot where the huge man was in the process of rallying himself to his feet.

I said to Joy, "Do you have any, uh, special abilities? In your other form, I mean?"

"Do *you*?"

"What do you mean? I can't do anything like that."

"David, *what do you think we've been talking about all this time?*"

The huge masked man was now in a sitting position. He had a ragged tear in his chest armor but I didn't see blood. The man stood, adjusted his mask, and looked around for his axe.

Joy grabbed my elbow and said, "Come with me!"

Joy pulled me into the kitchen, heading toward the door to the garage. I heard pounding footsteps behind us and took a detour around the kitchen table, past the refrigerator, scanning the crowded counter for anything that would possibly kill or at least slow the masked freak:

John's block of knives. A food processor. The coffeemaker. I knew from memory that the three drawers below them contained silverware, baggies of weed, and fast-food condiment packets, respectively.

In the one second it took me to scan all that, the masked man had entered the kitchen, now right behind me. I reached for the first thing my hands could find:

The door of the black cabinet next to the refrigerator.

The one with the DO NOT OPEN sticker on it.

I braced myself, then I yanked it open just as I heard Joy say, "No!"

For a tense, silent moment, nothing happened. And then, the avalanche came.

Out from the cabinet sprang hundreds of compressed, crumpled wads of plastic grocery store bags, years' and years' worth. John kept insisting he was going to recycle them someday, claiming you weren't supposed to put them in the trash.

The masked man was startled by the spray of bags falling and unspooling at his feet. He'd apparently never seen them before and was thus unsure of what the second stage of the assault would entail. It only took him a couple of seconds to realize there wasn't one. He swung his axe, which whooshed through the open door of the bag cabinet and turned it into a cloud of splinters. The axe embedded itself into the floor.

Joy said, "Duck!"

I did. She'd picked up the glass decanter from the coffee machine. It was full, the coffee had been sitting on the burner all day, and even when fresh, John's coffee could strip the grease off an engine block. Joy bashed the pot into the huge man's mask so hard that it exploded. Hot brown acid poured in through the eyeholes. He growled and stumbled backward, then tripped. He smacked his skull on the edge of the counter behind him with a noise like a baseball bat connecting with a watermelon. He went down, but I was sure he wasn't dead. I wasn't even confident he was knocked out.

I grabbed the next appliance off the counter. The food processor. I yanked off the plastic bowl to expose the blade, punched the highest speed, and then lunged the spinning blade toward the prone man's groin.

The machine died in my hands. I had pulled its stupidly short power cord from the socket.

"DAMN IT! Joy, find me an extension cord!"

Instead of doing that, Joy said, "MOVE!" and grabbed me again, pulling me toward the garage. As soon as we were inside, she slammed the door behind us, even though we both knew it wouldn't delay him any more than a chalk line on the floor that declared the garage was outside of the Combat Area.

I assumed Joy would grab some hidden arsenal John had stashed

out here, but instead, she ran over to the camera that was still focused on the spot of floor where the containment box used to be.
She checked it to make sure it was off.

She said, "It'll be easier to clean up the mess out here."

"What? What are you going to do?"

"We're going to do it together."

"Do *what?*"

The door exploded off its hinges. The masked man stepped into
the room and twirled his bone axe like it weighed no more than a
plastic toy. He showed no sign that the damage we'd inflicted so far
had even mildly inconvenienced him. If anything, he just seemed
invigorated by it, like he needed to take a couple of blows to really
get into an ass-kicking rhythm.

Joy said, "You already know how to do it. Just feel what you're
clinging to inside and . . . let it go."

Amy

John was driving too fast. They'd hurried to the van for two reasons: They wanted to get away from the pool before more police came and tied them up with impossible questions, and because they had both tried to call David and gotten no response.

John said, "The bad guys are already at the house. I know they are. They have the skins; they just need to feed them to the egg."

John was one of those people who comforted himself by repeating the main plot points out loud. As for the three human skins, right after Bas and his partner dove into the pool, John and Amy had doubled back for them, only to find greasy pink smears on the ground where they had been. Either Bas's Xarcrax nerd friends had followed behind and gathered them up in the chaos or they'd been zapped away by some otherworldly means—it was the same result either way. If a bunch of pool kids had just grabbed the skins and started playing with them, they'd have noticed.

Amy had the damp Xarcrax book in her lap, holding it closed with her hand but not getting the sense it was necessary. To her and John both, the pages were now just regular, wet paper, full of corny text written by some cult leader talking about how reality isn't real, et cetera. She studied the weirdly complex pattern on the cover. As a logo, it was hopelessly overdesigned, hundreds of interlocking lines that branched off into grids, like the whole thing had been scrawled without lifting the pen from the paper. As a religious symbol, it wasn't exactly the kind of thing you could wear on a chain around your neck. How were these idiots going to be the ones to ruin the world?

Wait, what was she saying? Of course it would be someone like this.

John said, "We're here," in case he was worried Amy thought they were pulling up to a different black-and-yellow house.

The front door was standing open.

Her heart dropped.

John stopped the van in the street and ran in through the gate and the open front door. Both of them immediately looked to the spot in the living room where the egg had been, saw that it was gone, and didn't say a word about it.

Something caught John's attention, and he headed through to the kitchen. Amy followed and sucked in a breath when she saw the door to the garage had been obliterated.

She pushed past John, and the first thing she saw was a lot of blood on the floor. There was a man lying in the middle of it with a ragged hole in his chest. The hole went all the way through, like his heart had been dug out of him. His severed head was lying across the room near splatters that implied it had bounced off a wall.

David was sitting against the big white garage door, looking dazed. Joy was standing on the other side of the room, her eyes wide, breathing hard. Whatever had occurred, they had just missed it.

Amy said, "Oh my god! What happened? Are you okay?"

"Yeah," said David as if he was surprised to find himself there. "I think so? I . . . blacked out. Or skipped forward. Did anybody else?"

Amy said, "No. I don't think so. Joy, are you all right?"

Joy blinked. "What? Sure. Yes. Everything is fine. A teenager flew out of your closet and stole your haunted toy. He got away. This guy came, too. And now he's dead. That's his head over there, I think."

"What happened to him?"

"Uh, I don't remember," said Joy. "I also skipped ahead to just now. Both of us. We both have just . . . no memory of what happened here over the last few minutes or so. Everything is fine. Fine. Fine."

David said, "I'm not feeling well."

John said, "They got their skins. All three of them. One of them belonged to Detective Coiffure. He's gone. I think? It was confusing, I think they collected his skin before they killed him. Like they had the result before the process, because of time magick. Or something. The cops might be after us. I have a headache."

Amy said, "I'm not worried about the police coming here. They have dozens of witnesses and a bunch of videos showing two officers entering a restroom and never coming out. I don't see how they arrest us for that. I mean, we do have a dead body on the floor, I guess."

David said, "I think I'm going to be sick."

He stumbled to his feet and went into the house, through to the tiny bathroom on the first floor. Joy followed him, for some reason, and Amy followed her. David closed the bathroom door behind him, and Joy pressed up against the door and said something to him that Amy didn't quite catch.

But it sounded like, "Close your eyes. Don't look at what comes up."

MONDAY. AUGUST 22. 7:37 P.M.
GINGERBREAD MEN
HUNGER AT 55%

Me

John and I started wrapping up the corpse of the huge masked man in garbage bags, having decided we'd just drive him to the nearest bridge to chuck him into the river. We discussed chopping him up and incinerating the parts in the garage, but that would have taken hours, and really, what would have been the point? Nobody's going to report this guy missing. John kept the dude's chiseled black mask, though, saying he wasn't sure if he wanted to sell it or just stick it up on the mantel. I didn't have to ask about his bone axe—there was no question we were keeping that shit. During this process, Amy and John had both endeavored to find new ways to ask me what exactly had happened to the guy, but at some point, they accepted my pleas of ignorance as genuine. I actually didn't even know why it mattered. If it's clear self-defense, who cares if that defense is delivered with a little flair? Why would killing be the one activity where we *deduct* for style points?

When we got to the bridge, we found the guardrail had been torn and scraped in what looked like a fairly fresh car accident. This registered to me only as an easier place to dump the body, since we could just roll it through the gap instead of lifting it over the rail.

We did exactly that, only on impact, we heard a thump instead of a splash.

John looked over the side and, at the top of his voice, shouted, "RICARDO PORKFART?!?"

Protruding from the surface of the water below was the ass of an enormous pickup truck with dual rear tires. Sitting on the back bumper was the man in the Hawaiian shirt and shorts who'd bought our haunted merch earlier in the day. He was now studying the plastic-wrapped corpse that had landed on the bumper next to him.

He looked up, his face lighting up with joyous surprise. "John! Dave! Did you hear?"

John said, "What are you doing in the water, dude?"

"Oksana attacked me! I was driving, and she jumped out of the passenger seat and grabbed the wheel! It was amazing! Hasn't done anything since, though." He held up the doll, as if to demonstrate. "I thought that's why you came, figured you heard about it. Is this a dead body?"

I said, "Evil henchman from another world. Just roll him off into the water. You need us to call somebody?"

"Cops are already on their way," he said, while shoving the corpse into the water with both feet. "Hey, I want to apologize for doubting you about the doll earlier. This thing is haunted as fuck!"

John said, "Hold on."

He went to the van and rummaged around until he found one of the "white energy" dolls he kept in there for emergencies. He returned to the broken guardrail, holding it up. This one was a Barbie-size doll in a wedding dress.

"Her name is Marienne. She makes infections heal faster and can restore rifts in relationships. For your trouble." He dropped it down to Ricardo. "Tell your friends we got the real shit."

By the time we got back, Amy and Joy had cleaned most of the blood out of the garage, but there had been another thirty minutes of work stuffing the plastic bags back into the cabinet and taping up cardboard to replace the shattered doors.

The four of us eventually landed in chairs around the kitchen table. I wasn't hungry, but everyone else was eating junk they'd scavenged from around John's kitchen. Amy had a jar of olives she'd found in the refrigerator, John was eating loose slices of American cheese with potato chips, Joy had somehow found a container of Planters Cheez Balls, even though I didn't think those were being manufactured anymore. Our drinks included a Fight Piss, a brown bottle of some obscure IPA, a can of Dr. Thunder cola, a bottle of water, a cup of greasy coffee, and a two-liter bottle of Surge, which again I thought had been discontinued.

John had turned on his police band scanner and, from what we could gather from the cryptic cop-speak, Bas and Gracie never made it back home. The cops were on the hunt for the rest of the members of the Xarcrax club, but they, like us, had no idea where any of them were. All their old haunts were presumably off the table; the community center was a crime scene as was the old Dollar Cinema, and the cops were already searching each of the members' homes. Then again, if there were new developments, we might not hear about them, since the police here knew when handling true Undisclosed weirdness to get off the radio and switch to cell phones. That monster stuff tended to attract crowds. Not just locals, either—once internet rumors about the pool incident got out, gawkers and their cameras would come from all over. Hell, some were probably already here, prowling around and waiting for signs of chaos.

I'd have said we were completely at a loss, but we did have one lead: a giant, now-readable (if very wet) book that was a wealth of information about the cult's belief system. Amy was flipping through it, seemingly unconcerned about the olive juice she was getting on the pages in the process. Though, from what she had said, "readable" might be giving it a little too much credit. It was in English, but it was like the author's typewriter was missing letters or their hands were missing fingers. The opening lines were:

Th wrld as u kno it is a chain wraped around ur mind. Th systm kils any1 who dares reveal that it hz all bin a pack of lies. Mankind will nevr b free until enuf of us stand up n prclaim the truth 2gethr. They canot kil all of us. It jst takes 1 2 break the dam n start th flood. Xarcrax is the 1. Xarcrax is th flood.

That went on for more than six hundred pages. It must be hard to write a good bible, because it seems like most of them badly need another editing pass.

To John, I said, "How long?"

"About four and a half hours, I'd say."

He was watching the egg toy's app. Amy had wondered if they could feed the egg early since they already had the skins, but it apparently didn't work that way. The ritual functioned on a schedule, and feedings happened when the Magpie cried for them.

"That would put it around midnight," continued John, "which seems appropriate from an occult standpoint. If so, I'm thinking they're planning a special ritual for the birth. I don't know if I mentioned this, but that's a big thing with these toys. All the kids go live on social media to watch their birds hatch and see if they got one of the fancy ones."

Amy said, "And maybe they'll do a special first feeding, the way they tried to have eyeballs ready for Mr. Swallow. But yeah, they'll want to gather somewhere and make a thing of it. So I guess our first task is figuring out where."

Joy said, "We have to do it soon, too, because I have to be at work at midnight."

I said, "I've been putting off asking this, but what are the 'pies' that Magpie the Pie Plucker is going to want, in real-world terms?"

John held up his phone. "They just look like round pies, like apple or cherry or something. But if you look real close, here—see the little holes in the top of the crust, how they kind of form two eyes and a mouth?"

"So they're what? Heads?"

"Ah, they're flat, and the holes are kind of vacant so maybe just faces?"

"Well, that's not so bad, compared to whole skins. How many does it need?"

John seemed confused for a moment. He showed the screen to Amy, and then she was confused, too.

Amy said, "I think . . . ten? It's glitched out. There's a one and a zero but the zero is kind of smeared so that it runs off the edge of the screen. See? It's the same on my phone."

She showed me. The zeroes overran the menu along the side, the digits overlapping each other.

I said, "Unless they want . . . There's like twelve overlapping zeroes, so unless it's going to emerge asking for a trillion faces, then yeah, I guess it's broken."

John said, "I mean, that's more people than even live on earth, so let's call it ten."

"The good news," said Amy, "is this book might actually be useful. But there's just *so much* of it."

I flipped through one corner of the pages with my thumb. Dense text in a book five inches thick.

"What, do they have like two million commandments?"

"It's a history," she replied. "The timeline of the Xarcrax cult, in excruciating detail. Decades of it."

"They've been around for decades?"

"Well, that's the thing. It's all phrased like it was written about fifty or sixty years from now. It's referencing the future, but as history, not prophecy. I just skimmed through a whole chapter about the time their leader spent in an Arizona prison, from September of

2043 until July of 2051. But if it's just fiction that the nerds wrote, it's awfully dry. They've got exhaustive details about this guy's court appearances and appeals and how he had to fire his attorney. There's all sorts of stuff about grievances with the local government where they set up their compound and all of these zoning issues. And it's all written in this weird compressed spelling, like they were trying to save on ink."

John said, "It sounds like you're trying to say this is a book from the future, without actually saying that."

She shrugged. "Sure, why not?"

I said, "Wouldn't that be good news, if so? We'd have advance warning on everything that's about to happen."

"Maybe, but that's the other thing: It's not in chronological order. It says their leader, the prophet, doesn't experience time that way, so it's all jumbled up. The second chapter is just a list of grievances against his ex-wives. I found a basic description of their belief system inserted halfway through the book. 'Xarcrax' isn't the monster they're summoning. I mean, it is, but the prophet is also Xarcrax, and the ritual is Xarcrax, the collective will of the followers is Xarcrax. That's just a name for the overall system, the time-spanning mechanism that will break the simulation."

"I hate that they're forcing us to say that name over and over."

"From what I gather," she continued, "their followers in the future all use what they call a 'looking glass,' which I thought was a metaphor, but the more I read, the more I think it's some kind of augmented reality thing, like they have a display in front of their faces telling them how they're doing in the faith in real time. It watches everything they do and shows a literal score. They get points for promoting Xarcrax to others, a whole bunch for actually converting someone—or rather, for 'discovering' a stranger is human. Then they lose points for sinning; telling a lie costs them ten points, but only if they tell it to another member of the faith. It's fine to lie to the Empties. And the points come with real-world rewards; they hand out jobs and raises based on score. All romantic partnerships are arranged, so you can win a better partner with a higher point value. You have to earn sex acts with good deeds. All of them, even if it's, uh, with yourself."

John said, "And the guy at the top gets to set the scores, right? So if you ever want to know what that dude's vices are, look at the rule book and see which sins come cheap."

I said, "It's kind of genius. Imagine living your life where all the messy complicated stuff was stripped away and you just had this system telling you what to do. You always knew exactly where you stood. No ambiguity, no doubts. If you wake up in the morning and see you're ten points behind the pace, you know you have to go help an old lady across the street to get back in the game. You can watch yourself level up to righteousness in real time."

Amy frowned at me. "It's a terrible idea. The moment you put black-and-white scores on something, people lose all common sense and just start optimizing for the easiest stats. It's like those terrible teachers that just teach around passing the standardized tests; you can see them squeezing the life out of the kids. You're making a human think like a robot. Then again, it sounds like the future agrees with you. This religion is hugely popular, according to the book anyway. It says it exists in six countries."

I shrugged. "Having lived my whole life wishing society would just explain what I'm doing wrong, I'd love it if somebody just gave me clear instructions. Does it say what I need to do to join?"

Instead of answering, Amy bolted to her feet, saying, "Ooh! Ooh! Oh my god!"

"Jesus Christ, what is it?"

"Look. There are pictures in the back. Look! Here. Oh, this makes so much sense."

She was stabbing a page of the book with her finger like a bomb would go off in her skull if we didn't notice it fast enough.

John and I leaned closer. On the final page of the book was a grainy photo of an older man in eccentric dress. The quality was bad on purpose, like somebody had manipulated it in Photoshop to appear old, like that would lend it an air of legitimacy.

She said, "That's the prophet, who wrote a big chunk of this here book. Recognize him?"

I did. "That's the fancy old wizard who came to me while I was in the Smoke Shop and you were getting your glasses. You knew the picture just from my description of him?"

"No! No! Look. *That is Sebastian Galveston.* Only older. Look at the eyes! Look!"

John said, "Holy cow, you're right."

I didn't see it, but I decided to take their word for it. Then what she was saying finally hit me.

I leaned back in my chair. "So, Bas is like this whole religion's Joseph Smith? Their L. Ron Hubbard?"

"Well, he's going to be," said Amy, "if this book is true and it's not just some weird fanfic Bas wrote about himself. He's going to grow up and, apparently, start one of the world's major religions."

Joy said, "See, this is why I like watching you guys work. It's like you're simultaneously very good and very bad at this. It makes me feel like I could do it."

Joy took a picture of the old man and started furiously typing on her phone. Was she live-tweeting this meeting?

I said, "Hold on. I'm lost again. Bas had a copy of a holy book that he himself contributed to as an old man? So the guy behind all of this, the guy who presumably brainwashed Bas into the cult, is the old version of Bas himself? He grew up and reached back to indoctrinate himself so that he could grow up to start a cult so he could reach back and indoctrinate himself? How does that work? It's just a closed loop. God, I hate time travel shit."

"Get ready to be even more confused," said Amy, rapidly reading the several pages of what I guess was the prophet's biography. "All the way on page five-fifty-five, it says this religion began when young

Bas miraculously survived an attempt on his life by the simulation itself. It then says he will die of old age, but prophesizes that he'll be resurrected once the church reaches a billion followers worldwide. It even gives a date—the year 2112. At that point, Bas will be magically reborn from a crystal in the earth. The billion followers will then join in a ritual that will usher in the end of the simulation, and all true humans will be freed, and so on."

I said, "They'll do that by summoning Xarcrax?"

"It's all Xarcrax," said Joy. "The whole process is Xarcrax. Try to keep up. I knew that, and I'm only half paying attention."

John said, "But that means the apocalypse isn't coming for another hundred years or so. Surely we'll be able to figure out something by then."

"Well," said Amy, "it says once they break the simulation, it will be retroactive. It will be broken in the past, too. Since time itself is an element of the simulation, you see."

I said, "I swear to God, science has not yet invented the kind of ass-beating these nerds deserve."

John said, "So the assassination attempt he survived in his youth, is that us? Like, later tonight? Or whenever we run into him again?"

Amy read for a moment. "It actually says the simulation cast down a star from the sky to smite him, but I assume that's symbolism or something. And it doesn't specify the date."

I said, "But it makes sense, based on what we know, right? Everything will go to hell if he avoids an assassination attempt and rides that legend to the top. So if someone were to, say, *successfully* assassinate him, none of this happens. That's what the fancy version of me was saying, that we have to see it through, make sure the job gets done. It's like if we had a chance to go back and kill baby Hitler. All philosophers agree that, in that situation, you'd yank that infant from his mother's breast and three-sixty dunk that shit straight into a wood chipper."

"Or," said Amy, "we prevent this situation altogether so that the assassination attempt doesn't even have to be made."

"Fancy Me seemed pretty confident that wasn't possible."

"And we're sure Fancy You is all-knowing? What are we basing that on? Oh, and here's something else," said Amy, quickly hurrying to the next subject before I could answer. "Look at the cover."

She closed the book and showed it to us.

"What about it?"

"Look hard at the design. Does that mess with your head a little?"

John said, "Kind of. It's almost like one of those Magic Eye posters people used to have."

I knew what they meant. I studied the design on the cover and once again felt like my brain was struggling to comprehend the complexity. It was almost like it got more complicated in between viewings.

I said, "You took a picture of this, right? When we first saw it in Bas's bedroom?"

"Yeah, hold on."

She found the photo on her phone, held it up next to the cover, and said, "Oh, I think you're right."

"Would you let me say what I think before replying to it? You're messing up the whole rhythm of the conversation." To John, I said, "Look, the cover is different now. See how the pic in the phone is unfinished? Like someone has drawn more of it in since then."

John's reaction implied that he did in fact see this but that he also didn't understand what it meant.

I said, "Now look close at the cover. Both of you." I pointed to an area down at the lower left corner, near the spine. "See it?"

Amy said, "No? Wait . . ."

John said, "It's moving."

I said, "It's filling itself in. Very slowly. The cover is drawing itself."

Amy said, "I think I see it. What does that mean?"

I rubbed my thumb across the design. Some of the ink came off. I held up my thumb.

"Still wet, too."

With some alarm, Amy said, "The stain on your thumb is moving."

John stood up in his chair. "Dave, that's not ink."

I groaned and said, "I am *not* in the mood for this."

And then the world went away.

?. ?. ?
?????
? ? ?%

Me

The Sauce, a.k.a. Shadow Jizz or Armus Sauce or whatever we were calling it now, is a drug in the same way that a land mine is a pedicurist. It creates a sensation of detachment from time and space by actually detaching you from time and space. If life is a video game, the Sauce is a hack that glitches you through all the levels and then causes a meteor to fall on your house.

My first sensation after watching the blackness crawl across the whirls of my thumb was of a bunch of information fleeing my head, like when you walk into a room and suddenly forget why. Next, there was an odor. It was the sickeningly sweet scent of coconut, or rather, the chemical they put in suntan lotion to trigger that association in the brain. For me, it wasn't the smell of the beach but of the video store where I'd worked after graduation. There was a tanning salon next door run by the same owners, and the sweet tropical stink of the baking customers was so strong that it had lingered in my khaki work pants long after I'd quit the job. To this day, the scent triggers memories of mean drunks arguing about late fees.

And then my sight came back, and I was in the sky, flapping leathery wings and looking down from bird height at that video store and its tiny parking lot with the Dairy Queen across the street. I was rising fast, the streets and neighborhoods shrinking until the whole town was in view. A black line, thin as a strand of raven hair, drew itself out from the center of my vision. Then it spawned bristles and branches and grids, laying out a complex design that was beginning to look familiar, even though I no longer remembered where I'd seen it. It was something about a magic book and, I think, a missing charging cable?

I blinked—or maybe the world blinked around me—and suddenly I was back at my apartment above the porno store, standing in the living room area. But it was a little off; there were unfamiliar curtains on the windows, and outside those windows, there were customer cars in the parking lot, like the store below was still open. Then I blinked again, and the cars disappeared and the apartment was more like the one I knew, only the kitchen table was different and the counters were buried under drifts of trash. I saw maggots on a plate of half-eaten macaroni. Then I blinked again, and I was in a small house, the bungalow I had lived in several years ago, the one that, like so many structures in the city, had burned down in an event the news would call a mass panic. But I was in a version of that house that had never existed, one with a current-model television and a fresh coat of paint on the walls. It was as if that house had managed to survive those events, and as a result, I apparently was still living there. I glimpsed a framed photo on the wall of Amy and me at . . . Disney World? Really?

Blink.

I was now in a dilapidated version of that house that seemed to have five strangers living in it, one person sleeping on the sofa, two on the floor. A man was yelling from the kitchen that someone had eaten his leftovers.

Blink.

I was in a tiny apartment that was unfamiliar to me. The walls were plastered with thousands of clippings from magazines and printouts of internet articles. The only piece of furniture was a computer desk with four monitors. I thought I saw myself hunched over in front of it, but—

Blink.

I was now in a trailer and could hear at least two screaming babies. A football game on TV had been cranked up to drown out the sound. Someone was on the sofa, and they looked like—

Blink.

I was in a neat, middle-class house. Not a mansion but a respectable place where a husband and wife would live if, say, one was a schoolteacher and the other an insurance salesman. I heard gentle laughter from the next room, and I turned (or shifted my view, somehow—again I had no sense that I was physically there) to see a dining table and at least six people sipping wine over a finished meal. A dinner party, the kind that you always see on TV but that I assumed never happened in real life. I heard multiple small children playing nearby. Had I fallen into one of those prescription drug commercials where they show you what your life can look like once you get your Crohn's disease under control?

Then I saw that eating at the table was Fancy David, that cleaned-up, bearded version of myself who had visited me in the night, though the details of that visit were now fuzzy in my memory. I thought I could also see Amy. From where I stood, I could only catch a freckled shoulder, but in a fancy dress she did not own and wouldn't wear if she did. I didn't recognize any of the other voices. I didn't see or hear John. I tried to take a step that direction, but of course I couldn't move, I wasn't actually here, and "here" didn't actually exist. And yet . . .

I made eye contact with Fancy David, and just for a moment, he reacted like he was seeing something impossible, yet oddly familiar. He stood up from the table, politely excusing himself in a way that I never would, then stepped into the room where I was/wasn't. Then the house vanished from around him, but he remained. I was now in John's house, in the upstairs bathroom, face-to-face with this other version of me. Somehow, we were in mid-conversation.

He was saying, "I don't know if you'll even remember this. I was there, at the first feeding, with the teeth. I watched it happen and saw your face go blank. I think that was me, I think me being there messed it up, made you glitch ahead in the timeline."

I heard a question come out of my mouth. "Wait, back up. How are you here?"

Then I was momentarily confused, because why was *I* here? But that was a stupid question—I was in John's bathroom; it was Sunday evening. The Magpie was asking for strawberry Popsicles, its hunger meter had tipped over 70 percent and we still had no plan. We knew Bas and his weird friends would be at the Dollar Cinema, but had no idea what to expect or how to approach the problem. Then I'd gone up to take a piss and found this fancy version of myself watching me.

He said, "There's no time to explain."

"Nope, sorry," I heard myself say. "Put a dollar in the 'no time to explain' jar. It's *always* worth it to explain."

He seemed frustrated by this but somehow knew I was right.

He took a moment to gather himself, then said, "When I first came in contact with the Sauce, I saw, mapped out before me, a whole lot of paths that all converged in the same place. That place is very bad, and I am trying to avoid going there. So I am hopping from path to path, trying to understand the bigger picture. The paths are alternate realities. You're in one of them. There are others. Many of them are living nightmares. I think if we can fix this, then all of the timelines consolidate to just one. The good one."

"It seems like that was actually really easy to explain. So that thing where we skipped ahead in time, you're saying that was you?"

"I'm watching your timeline like a movie, and I can fast-forward it whenever I want. When you skipped ahead earlier, when doing the feeding with the teeth, I had the thought in my head that I wanted to skip forward, and then it did, only you skipped with it."

"Are you saying you fast-forwarded our entire reality because you got *bored*?"

"I didn't do it on purpose. I don't have buttons I can push. But right now, I know the next thing that happens, because it's always the same, and I'm eager to get to it. If that causes me to jump ahead, I'm afraid you'll jump with it. I think the longer I stay here, the more likely that becomes. Thus, 'There's no time to explain.'"

I asked, "So what should we do tonight?" though on some level I knew it was a nonsense question, because it had already happened. Right?

"It's going to get its tongues. The Simurai already have them. Swallow will hatch. All of that happens, in every timeline. You can't stop it any more than you can stop the world from turning."

"So you're saying we have to kill Swallow after it comes out."

"The fact that you think you can do that, despite what I've been saying, doesn't surprise me."

"Of course. You're me. I'm you."

"No. I'm pretty sure you're not."

"So how are we supposed to—"

And then he was gone. I turned to leave the bathroom, to tell John and Amy what I had learned, but of course, that was pointless. This was twenty-four hours ago, we'd already gone to the theater, already had the whole thing play out just as Fancy Me had said, including the part where we skipped forward without our memories.

Then the bathroom changed around me. The picture on the wall over the toilet (a cartoon turd with a word bubble saying, "SHIT'S ABOUT TO GO DOWN!") turned into a painting of flowers. Then the house was erased from around me, as if a shock wave had puffed it away like a dandelion. I was left in a vacant lot under a strobe flash of day-night cycles, surrounded by rubble. Then, after some unknown amount of time, a large concrete foundation covered the entirety of the lot and those surrounding it, overtaking John's old neighborhood completely. Girders and walls and glass appeared, and then I was rising, as if floors were being built beneath me and carrying me upward. Soon, I was surrounded by offices full of workers in booths communicating with clients via banks of video screens. Then they were gone, along with their cubicles, and the building appeared to be abandoned. I watched windows grow grimy with dirt that apparently no one was responsible for cleaning, saw tiles overhead turn brown with water damage. Graffiti appeared on the walls, none of it comprehensible to me. I saw repeated use of a symbol, a letter X painted in red, with a pair of black curves on the top and bottom to turn it into an infinity symbol.

I waited for the world to zip away again, but this one lingered, as if we were now on play instead of fast-forward. I scanned the vacant office space, finally noticing that the floor was covered with decaying corpses. No, not corpses—living people, if you could call them that. Their chests were rising and falling ever so slowly, like they were all in hibernation. Their spindly limbs seemed incapable of supporting their weight should they try to stand, their skin pale and papery. There were dozens of them scattered around the floor on old cushions and folded blankets. Their faces were covered by those clear plastic masks I'd seen on the shoppers during my hallucination earlier in the day. Only these had grown cloudy with filth and scratches, still with data scrolling and blinking faintly across them. The living corpses all had IVs in their arms, the clear plastic tubes snaking over to nearby attachments on the floor.

I heard a grunt and saw the living corpse closest to me—almost touching where my feet would be had I actually been standing there—was moving. Its limbs flailed slowly, like gravity was too much for it, the way a baby struggles to get off its back. He was reaching up for the mask, and I noticed that the skin around it was oozing and encrusted, as if the mask hadn't been removed for months or years. He pawed at the mask like he was trying to get it off, like it was suffocating him. A strap that was holding it on had turned brittle and crumbled at the slightest pull, and he was able to get the mask off himself.

His face came off with it.

I saw pink, twitching muscle stretched across bone and heard the man screaming and then—

Blink.

I was in a classroom full of bored teenagers. Outside the window, approaching across the lawn, was a single figure, entirely black but with burning orange eyes. It strode slowly but purposefully toward the school, invisible to everyone there until it reached the window and passed through without a pause.

In its wake, the world changed.

The windows were bricked over, the doors replaced with bars, the students replaced with a moaning, tangled crowd of starving, naked prisoners.

Blink.

I stopped hallucinating and found things had gone back to normal. I was back at work, at my desk, the surface vaguely greasy and gritty under my hands. I sensed that there was a stink in the air that I couldn't smell, like it was there but I was breathing it through a nose that had gotten used to it long ago. There was a bundle of stapled sheets of paper on the desk that had been snow white when they'd been delivered but were now mottled with my own smudgy fingerprints. The din from outside my office was deafening. I couldn't think. Something had gotten the pigs riled up. The noise of this place was worse than the stench. The stink you could adjust to; the shrieks and the howls and the groans never faded into the background because they were constantly changing.

My guts were stewing in anticipation of an argument I was about to have, one with probably an 80 percent chance of turning into a brawl. I'd welcome it. It'd break up the boredom. The fight was going to be with that fat fuck Mauser. It was day shift's job to clean out the drains, and he, as the day manager, swore up and down to the bosses that he cleaned them like he was told, but every night, they'd back up with shit and hair and everything else that got rinsed out of the pens and we'd have to go snake them out. So after last shift, I left a bottle in front of the valve, right where you'd have to move it if you were going in to clean, and what do you know, I get in at midnight and there's the bottle, undisturbed. And here's the log saying the drain was cleaned. My shift ends at noon, that's when Mauser gets in, and when he does, I'm gonna fill that bottle with sludge from the drain and pour it on his big fat head. Then we'll see what happens after that.

The pigs were more stirred up than ever, kicking on the metal doors and howling their incoherent noises. That meant they had too much energy, which meant they were overfed and we could skip lunch. That was my call. Maybe I'd feed them anyway, let them stay stirred up for day shift. Or maybe mix in the rancid rations from the broken freezer and let Mauser deal with a diarrhea outbreak all day. Maybe he didn't like cleaning because he didn't get enough practice. Maybe I should give it to him.

"What are you smiling at?" Zig had shown up in the office at some point.

"I'm happy. I love my job. What's got the swine so riled up?"

"Screws cut the tongues out of a couple."

"Just for fun or on orders?"

"Orders. Guess the screws dragged 'em out of their pens and did it out on the floor, where the rest could see. Now they're all goin' nuts."

"Yeah, that'll do it. Thinkin' about skipping lunch. It'll make 'em mad for a while, but then they'll get sleepy."

"Don't have to ask me twice. It's fish meal day. If I don't have to put my hands in that slime, then that's a win. Did you fix the lock on B-66 yet?"

"First I'm hearing of it. If the lock is broken, why aren't the pigs running all over the place?" There were twelve of them stuffed into that particular cage.

"It's busted the other way; it won't unlock."

There was a moment where I had a strange, out-of-body feeling, like for a moment I forgot who I was or why I was there. Did I know how to fix a stuck lock in this place? Where was this place?

I squeezed my eyes shut and blinked, even though there wasn't a damned thing wrong with my vision. Of course I knew where I was. This was Purity Camp Bravo. I came on as a janitor and worked my way up to night warden through pure attrition, after the last one got cholera and crapped himself to death.

I pulled a dented metal case off a shelf behind me and opened it up. I cursed out loud. All sorts of tools missing. The good flat screwdriver, the good wire strippers, the good needle-nose pliers. Somebody on day shift had probably borrowed them to fix the monitor in the employee cafeteria and left them on the floor, because why take the extra one minute of effort to put them back? I gathered up the next-best tools, wondering if maybe I shouldn't stuff something sharp in my pocket for Mauser. I decided against it.

I went down the hall, and there again was that floaty feeling like I didn't know where I was going, like I had never been here before, but again it passed. My feet were already turning right, toward the B-block, and when I came to a heavy steel door, I knew which of my keys opened it and the door behind it, and the one behind it. I stepped out onto the floor, the rows of grated doors on each side of me, another row above, a third above that. The pigs were chanting slogans and taunts at me. I had no idea what they were saying and definitely didn't care. I found the supposedly broken cell and—

There was a scuffle of boots behind me, and suddenly my arms were being wrenched back. Two of the B block guards had grabbed me, and I thought they were doing a prank, but then I heard Mauser's voice back there somewhere.

"So which is it, Wally?" That was his nickname for me, I had no idea what it meant. "You a sympathizer or just incompetent? Not that the result is any different."

"What the fuck are you talking about? Get your fucking hands off me."

The guards shoved me down the hall until we passed through yet another door, the one leading into the solitary box and the bank of coffin-size vert cells. I saw the third one on the right, saw that it was empty, and my stomach dropped.

Mauser said, "Mind telling us where she went?"

And here I had that floating sensation again that I both knew and didn't know, that all of this was both strange to me and intimately familiar. I heard myself say, "Who?" but on some level, I knew it was a lie of a question, a stalling tactic.

"The ginger pig that got put in here after her third escape attempt, who was supposed to stay in here until there wasn't enough left to want to escape or do anything else. The one you kept feeding after a starvation order. You sneak her home in your lunch box?"

"You're full of shit," I heard myself say, but of course I had in fact rigged the lock. The bolt was misaligned by a millimeter, but I'd set it so that it wouldn't throw up an error in the guard booth when it failed to slide into place. I made sure that it would appear to fail in the exact way these janky locks failed all the time on their own. And here I got really confused because there was no logic behind this decision in any circumstance, considering the best possible outcome from an escape would be she got caught in the hallway and stuck back in the cell only with both legs and both arms broken.

I said, "These locks break faster than they can be fixed, you moron. And if a pig got out, it's probably running around the C-tunnel or crouched in a pipe access. Check the tracker and get off my dick."

"Tracker comes back 'no signal.' Either it made it out of the building or dug out its tracker, and nobody can find either one. You've lost a pig, Wally. Even worse, you let one out. You know what that means, right?"

And in that moment, I tried to process two thoughts at once, the first being the full realization of what that did mean if the tribunal agreed with Mauser, that it meant having my hands and feet cut off and the rest of me stuffed into one of these cells, that betraying the cause meant I was worse than a pig. The second thought was that somehow, someway, she had made it out, had slipped through three locked doors and past two guard booths and the gun towers in the yard. And I thought that maybe if that miracle had occurred, that whatever else happened was okay, that maybe she would live and have kids and tell them about me, even though she never knew my name.

I had just enough time to feel the impact of a billy club across the back of my skull before I blacked out and—

MONDAY, AUGUST 22, 8:08 P.M.
GINGERBREAD MEN
HUNGER AT 55%

Me

I was sitting at John's kitchen table again with John, Joy, and Amy all staring at me. Each of them had paused in the act of putting a piece of food in their mouths, holding a slice of cheese, a pretzel, and an olive, respectively.

I said, "How long was I out?"

Amy said, "Were you out? You said you got the Sauce on your finger like five seconds ago."

"It . . . seemed longer than that."

Amy grabbed her phone and set it to record audio. "Tell me what you saw. Before you forget. Anything that might be important."

I shook my head. "Man, I didn't learn shit. I saw, I guess, a bunch of alternate lives I could have lived? Some where I was rich, some where I was poor. One where I was . . . working in a POW camp or something? The details are already fading. I don't know. It was weird."

John said, "I tried rubbing my fingers on the book, but it didn't work for me." He looked around the room. "Or *did it?*"

I stood up. "I need air."

I actually wasn't sure what I needed, but I'd always heard people on TV say they needed to go outside for air, so I figured I would try it. I think I really just needed to know I was free of that place I had been. I could still smell it, like I'd brought back particles in my nostrils.

I stepped out onto John's porch and instantly broke into a sweat. The sun had gone down, but the nights in August were just the smoldering coals left over from the day. I breathed in the steamy air and tried to ground myself in this world, remind myself that I wasn't surrounded by brick and wailing humanity, that above me were stars and across the street was a bunch of giggling kids doing stunts on kick scooters and recording them with their phones.

The door opened behind me and in a low voice, Joy said, "You're acting strange, and it's scaring Amy."

"You said I was only 'gone' for five seconds. Then I came out here. What's scary about that?"

"You changed. In those few seconds, like the look on your face got all weird, like you were a different person for a moment, then you came back and you kind of still look like that other person."

Before I could reply, the door opened again.

"You need a drink?" asked John.

"Nah, just give me a second. Just need to gather myself."

He lit a cigarette. "Want to take up smoking? This could be the perfect time."

"No, thank you."

The door opened once more, and Amy appeared, holding the Xarcrax book, one finger poked into the pages to mark where she'd left off.

Before she could ask, I said, "I'm fine, I really am. It's just disorienting, it always is. On one hand, I only perceived several minutes of time while I was away, but also it felt like I'd lived several other lifetimes, or briefly lived as someone with all of their years and baggage and stuff in their heads, if that makes sense. You know how sometimes you'll have dreams where you get really mad at me, then when you wake up you're still kind of mad? It's like that."

I turned to face them.

"And I have to say, I actually don't remember what we were doing before I started tripping. I mean, I remember the general scenario, but not what we were talking about."

"We have to rudely interrupt a summoning ritual," said John, "and we either have to not attempt to kill Bas at all or we have to absolutely kill his ass all the way but nothing in between. The one thing that cannot happen is we try to kill him and fail, because that's fulfilling a prophecy, I guess. And we still don't know where he is or where the summoning will take place. You didn't happen to have a vision about where this thing will happen tonight, did you?"

"I had a vision about this." I pointed at the cover of the Xarcrax book behind Amy's forearm. "I saw the town from overhead, overlaid with this design. Whatever my brain was trying to tell me, it should have been less symbolic and more literal because I have no idea. The book doesn't give us any clue?"

Amy, happy to be back on task, sat on the steps of the porch and opened the book in her lap.

She glanced back at Joy and said, "Light."

Joy activated the light on her phone and shined it on the book.

"Everybody stay quiet and let me just find this. It has to be in here somewhere."

Instead of staying quiet, John said, "You said there are pictures in the back, right? Start there."

"Why?"

"Because a picture is worth a thousand words, so that's just more efficient, time-wise."

"Seriously, hush, we don't know how much time we—oh, you're right, here it is. It's the last picture before the one of Sebastian. It's a drawing, not a very good one. It's called *Defeating Death,* and I think it shows . . . Is this Bas, stepping out of a UFO?"

We gathered around under Joy's cell phone light. The illustration was in the style of an old-time etching and depicted a group of soldiers attacking a man standing proud in front of a large black disk. Corpses littered the ground at his feet.

John leaned over the drawing. "That's not a UFO. That's the turd polisher."

I said, "The *what?*"

"The, uh, wastewater treatment plant. Down the road from the water tower? See those little buildings behind him? I've been out there, when Tyler used to work security. That big black circle is one of the clarifiers, the big pools where the water sits so the solid poop can settle to the bottom. You can see another one in the background."

I squinted at the drawing. "Are you sure? How in the hell would you hold cult rituals at the wastewater treatment plant? I feel like the staff would notice."

"They actually wouldn't," said Amy. "Half of it is closed. It got damaged in the flood, and they decommissioned a whole section, because the town's population has dropped so much they don't need it anymore."

John nodded. "Yeah, three of the pools are just sitting there. Tyler said they got in trouble with the state because mosquitoes were breeding in the stagnant water."

I thought for a moment and said, "Wait. Let me see the cover of the book again."

Instead of showing it to me, Amy checked it herself and said, "I think you're right."

"You don't even know what I was going to say!"

She pointed to a spot in the lower left of the complicated design and said, "That's the treatment plant down there, right? And all these little lines are sewer lines running under every street. It's a map of the city's drainage."

"Yeah. But why? Is drainage a major part of their religion? Are they going to put poison in the water?"

"I haven't seen anything like that in the book but, you know, I've just been skimming."

John stood up straight and tied his hair back. "Doesn't matter. We've got our time, and we've got our location. Let's go up to the gun safe, see what exactly I have for this strangely specific scenario. We'll flip for who gets to wear the foreskin vest."

Joy said, "I knew you guys could do it! You're the filthiest! Let's go eat their hearts out."

Everyone made their way to the door. I stayed put.

I said, "Just . . . give me a minute. Just . . . let me think. The 'prophecy' is that the world will end in 2112, right? But the part with Bas surviving an assassination attempt and starting this nerd religion—that's not prophecy. That's already happened. We know that, because this book exists and Bas has been in active contact with an older version of himself who will only exist if that exact thing happens tonight."

"Right," said John. "That's what I was saying."

"It doesn't make sense."

"Why not? Maybe if we do it right, this book vanishes. Or maybe it'll turn out to just not be true." He flicked his cigarette into the yard and headed into the house, saying, "I'm thinking those riot control beanbag rounds for the shotgun. That'd take the fight out of him, right? Would getting pelted in the gut with a beanbag count as an assassination attempt in their songs and legends?"

They all headed inside, toward the stairs. I reluctantly followed everyone up to John's bedroom. He went to his gun safe in the corner—it was the size of a wardrobe—and I leaned against the wall.

Then I turned, glanced at the patch of wall next to John's bed, sighed, and said, "Oh, *kiss my shit.*"

Amy said, "What?"

The patch of wall I was staring at was the part that would be on the opposite side of Joy's closet in the next room, which I knew because I had a vivid memory of having knocked out a whole section of that wall because a corpse had gotten embedded in it. The wall I was looking at, however, was untouched. There was no sign of fresh paint or repair.

I said, "Did . . . did we fix this?"

John studied my face. "Fix what?"

"The hole in the wall. Where the guy came through."

Amy and John exchanged glances.

Joy said, "Ew, this is too creepy. I hate this. Somebody make him stop."

Amy led me over to the bed and gently sat me down. "You're mixed up. Probably because of the Sauce. You normally take more time to recover than this."

I stared at the wall, rubbing my chin. Trying to make sense of it.

John said, "Try to remember. I called you, right? I said I had a vision of that happening, the ghost in the wall. Then you got here and everything was fine. Same as with your laundry getting folded weird and a bunch of other things, our memories are glitching out. That's all."

Without answering, I stood and headed back down the stairs, then out to John's backyard. I headed for the spot in the corner near the fence where we had buried the wall guy's ashes and bones, the stuff the incinerator couldn't quite get rid of. Even in the darkness, it was clear that the spot was nothing but a patch of undisturbed weeds.

I heard Amy's footsteps behind me. "What are you looking for?"

Without turning to face her, I asked, "Is this real? Am I here?"

"I don't know how to answer a question like that. I kind of wish I hadn't brought up the whole simulation thing. It's messing with everybody."

"It's not you; it's all of this. Everything getting garbled up and mixed around. It's making me feel like . . . like nothing I do matters."

"But you know that's not true. If not for things you did up to now, I wouldn't be here, John wouldn't be here. Joy wouldn't be here."

I said, "I still don't know why Joy is here."

"I do. We all made choices and here we are, all still alive, all able to make more choices. That's the best you're going to get, the chance to keep trying. If it turns out it's all an illusion or a dream or whatever, so what? Your choices are your choices, they're the only thing that's real because they're the only part you can control."

"Are you sure? That we can control them, I mean?"

"I'm sure that if I'm wrong, then nothing matters anyway."

John joined us in the yard. "Sounds like somebody needs to put a dollar in the 'free will argument' jar."

Amy said, "He just needs to get his bearings."

I said, "Sure." I reached out to take her hand, mostly to confirm to myself that she, too, was real. Her fingernails were painted green. Had they been like that before? Would I have noticed?

John said, "Let's load up. We need to make a list of what we think we'll need, and we have to make it all fit into one van. As for what we actually have to do tonight, we'll figure it out when we get there. We always do. I mean, eventually."

Based on what John had packed into the van, we were ready for just about every possible scenario and at least a dozen impossible ones. That's why it was a little discouraging when, even before we'd left the rural highway that would lead us to the wastewater treatment plant, Amy asked, "What did you bring to get through the fence?" and got only awkward silence as an answer.

I could see it as soon as we turned off onto the inlet road that encircled the plant: a tall, serious fence topped with razor wire. It made perfect sense—you don't want a terrorist or disgruntled employee dumping toxins in the water—but it stopped our plan in its tracks. Right now, that plan consisted entirely of wandering around the dormant part of the facility until we stumbled across a bunch of nerds setting up for a summoning ritual. If we got arrested for trying to break in, no story we could tell the cops would get us back out here before it was too late.

I asked John, "Does Tyler still do security here? If so, is he working the booth at the gate?"

"No, he got fired," replied John as he made his way down the access road. "Security camera caught him pissing in one of the clar-ifier pools."

Amy said, "It's interesting that you see the cause of his firing be-ing the camera catching him, rather than him doing it." She pointed at the windshield. "Who's that?"

John skidded to a stop. Standing in the middle of the road was a man in a suit, looking like he'd been calmly waiting for us. With-out a word, John pulled over and hopped out, acting like he knew the guy. The man had a muscular build and long, blond hair.

I'd seen him before: in slices, on the floor of John's bedroom.

As the rest of us approached, John said, "Dave, this is the Time Captain."

Joy said, "Whoa, déjà vu."

"That is not my name nor my job title," said the Time Captain. "I am here to keep you on track. But I can't stay long."

I said, "Great, how about you start by telling us exactly who you are and who you work for and what's going on in general. And then I have several other questions once you're done with those."

"My name is Tim. Tim Kaplan. I am just a man. I moved here a few years ago, from Peoria. As for who I work for, I like to think I work for the universe. Like you."

"Oh, no," I said, "I am in no mood for cryptic answers that are clearly designed to elicit a follow-up question. I'm asking who em-ploys you, who signs your paychecks. I've never gotten one signed by 'the Universe,' and I'm very sure that we do not work for the same employer."

"You were paid just yesterday. The universe arranged a sale from your collection, right when you needed it."

"You mean our sale of our doll that barely covered the cost of Amy's glasses? So you're saying we do the work, and the universe swoops in later and takes credit? You know what, that does sound like an employer."

Amy said, "We think we've done all this before and that you re-set the timeline. Is that right?"

"It is."

"So you are, effectively, a god."

"No. I can reset from this specific point, because of what happens on this specific night. I would say it's purely due to happenstance, but as I said, I believe the universe placed me here to fix all of this, if it can be fixed. I believe I acquired my abilities the same way you acquired yours. But they are limited; for example, it is a tremendous strain for me to remain here, right now."

I said, "If we screw it up again, you can just let us retry it?"

"Yes, but doing so comes at great cost, more than you can comprehend. And there is no guarantee you will even make it back to this point."

John asked, "Fine, so can you give us a strategy guide on how to successfully beat this next part?"

"The gap in the fence you require doesn't exist yet, but it will. The Simurai will arrive in about twenty minutes and cut a hole right down there. See where the light is out on the utility pole? It is also a blind spot for the security cameras. Wait patiently, and you can follow them in through the same spot, undetected."

I said, "Okay, and then what?"

"You will either successfully kill Sebastian or you won't. From this point forward, that is all I know. The entity orchestrating this will attempt to thwart you, but I cannot predict its strategy."

"Next question. I, and only I, have a distinct memory of your death, of your corpse in pieces on John's bedroom floor."

I paused, and Joy said, "That wasn't a question."

"Oh, right. Uh, so what's the deal with that?"

"You are experiencing interference between realities and possible realities but are struggling to keep them separate in your memory," said TC. "As you can see, I am standing here, intact. You can touch me to see if I am solid, if you have doubts. I am not immortal any more than you are, and I do not reset with the universe—if I die, I die."

Amy asked, "Why are you so sure killing Bas is the only way to stop him?"

"Ask yourself: If you successfully discovered a way to turn him away while leaving him alive, what would prevent him from simply trying again? I know that you do not prefer this path, and I understand that. But that is how this universe works; we purchase safety and comfort with suffering. The Black Death bought us the Renaissance. Death now, life later."

I said, "And just to be clear, you have no other abilities that can help us? You can't go back and blink Bas out of existence? Prevent his conception, whatever?"

"I can only pull this one lever that is available to me. All of us—me, you, Sebastian—are playing within the rules of the game, all of us are but pawns moved by powerful, incomprehensible forces."

John said, "And the universe's ability to assist us at this stage extends only to having you reset and then tell us where the nerds are going to cut a hole in the fence?"

"I assure you, extreme measures will be taken, should you fail." He pointed to the sky. "It will be as if God himself has cast down a star to smite them."

I said, "Consider this me asking the obligatory follow-up question that your cryptic statement requires."

"There is a space-based weapons platform, in geosynchronous orbit thirty-six thousand kilometers overhead. But it is a blunt weapon, designed to pulverize concrete missile silos, not kill individual human beings. If all else fails, keep Sebastian here until it impacts. But I assume you agree that we would all prefer a solution that is more, let's say, surgical in nature."

Joy said, "And when you thought 'surgical,' you immediately thought of these guys."

"I'm sorry," said Amy, "I just want to make sure I'm clear on this. You're now threatening to blow all of this up with your space laser if we don't successfully kill Bas ourselves?"

"It is not a laser. And it belongs to the United States government, run by the innocuously named Defense Support Program. The order to fire will come from a military official whose name none of us will ever know. Again, I have only seen these events play out before; for me to know that the satellite will strike is not the same as me making it so. The Simurai will be here soon. Bas and Gracie will arrive shortly after. You should get out of sight until they are inside the fence. If word leaks that there is a hostage situation involving a child, the police will come, and that will only complicate matters. Which, again, I know only from experience. I do wish you luck. But I must be going."

Amy said, "Just one more question. Why do we keep suddenly skipping ahead in time?"

The Time Captain seemed confused by this, but I realized in that moment that I actually knew the answer.

I said, "Oh, that's not him or the Magpie. That's caused by the other version of—"

Before I could finish the sentence, Amy and the rest of the world disappeared from in front of me.

TUESDAY, AUGUST 23, 12:21 A.M.
GINGERBREAD MEN
HUNGER AT 98%

Me

"The fire order has been given! We're getting the fuck out of here! You've got just a few minutes until impact! Probably! I don't even know! Good luck!"

I was about to ask who was talking and what they were talking about, but then heard gunshots and ducked. I smelled gunpowder and sulfur. I was standing in front of a giant concrete pool, round and maybe a hundred feet wide. Lit black candles had been placed around the rim, though I noticed several had gone out. There was a maintenance catwalk across the pool that led to a railed platform in the center. On the platform stood Bas and, sitting at his feet with her legs dangling over the side, Gracie. Next to her was the Magpie egg. Bas seemed rather calm, considering the rapid gunfire splitting the air and the several corpses of his friends lying just outside the pool. It appeared the Xarcrax cult had chosen this spot to make their last stand, and we'd missed it.

I turned to the voice that had spoken to me and said, "What?!?"

The man was in full SWAT gear, his whole body covered in black aside from his eyes. He wore a helmet with night vision goggles attached to the brim, flipped up out of the way. He was already shouting commands at several other guys dressed the same. Immediately, they all began a rapid but disciplined retreat, shouting dispersal commands at several bystanders I could see farther back, many of them recording the scene with their phones.

Only one member of the cult remained standing that I could see, a chubby kid with an AK-47 that looked comically wrong in his hands. He was awkwardly trying to return fire. One of the SWAT guys paused in his retreat, turned, and put a bullet in his head. The kid stumbled—forward, oddly enough—and did a face-plant into the grass, landing inches from my feet.

I found John to the right of me, crouched in the grass, his shotgun in his hand. Amy was to my left, kneeling, quickly trying to orient herself. She had some blades of wet grass stuck to her face and glasses, like she'd recently hit the deck to avoid bullets. I didn't see Joy anywhere.

Amy said, "We skipped forward again!"

I said, "Goddamn you, Fancy Me!"

I was so disoriented that it took me a bit to figure out where we were, even though we'd just been discussing it from probably less than a quarter mile away. I saw that a short distance behind us was another of those concrete pools—the clarifier pools, John had said—next to a trio of small brick buildings with fat metal pipes sprouting from their sides. I heard the hum of machinery—pumps or whatever—but the sound was coming from a distance. We were, of course, in the dormant section of the wastewater treatment plant. The shouted commands of the SWAT team faded as they fled, all of them heading toward the front gate of the facility. I saw swaying lights back there that never retreated all the way, surely the cameras and cell phones of bystanders who'd shown up to watch.

John muttered to me, "What did the SWAT guy say to you before he left?"

"He said we had just minutes until impact and that we should get the hell out of here!"

"Impact? From the space weapon thing?"

"Probably? I honestly wouldn't be surprised if something unrelated was about to land on us. How did we not have a plan for if we got fast-forwarded? Fuck!"

Amy said, "Hey! David, you have to be calm because we don't have time for you to be anything else. Bas's right there. We just have to talk him down."

"Do we even have enough time to get to safe distance? Like if we left right now?"

Amy ignored this rather important question, put her hand up like she was trying to get the teacher's attention, and got up on her knees.

"Bas? Can we talk?"

I couldn't see a weapon on his person and guessed it wouldn't make sense for him to have one. Once you can kill somebody with wormholes, a gun probably feels like going backward. Gracie looked shell-shocked, like she didn't understand anything that she'd just seen. But she didn't act as if she was being held against her will. She wasn't afraid of Bas; she was afraid for him. She reached up, and he took her hand, muttering reassurances.

To us, Bas said, "I already know what you're going to say. And I already know that you're gonna say it anyway. So get on with it, I guess."

Amy stood up, slowly. John did the same. I faintly heard the last of the SWAT cops in the distance and the sound of vehicle doors slamming shut.

Amy hissed, "Put that down!" to John, who didn't realize until that moment he had his shotgun in his hand. I wondered if he'd loaded the beanbag rounds or real ones. I wondered if there was a way to find out without just shooting the kid and seeing what happened. Maybe it wouldn't come to that. John set the gun in the grass but seemed to be making a mental note to remember its location.

Next to the third corpse from the right.

Amy approached the lip of the concrete pool, which came up to her chin. This was as close to Bas and Gracie she could get without actually climbing over and wading into water so filthy that she could probably just walk across. John, meanwhile, casually made his way to the left, where there was a short set of metal stairs to access the catwalk leading to Bas and Gracie's perch. Gracie was crying now. Bas was trying his best to comfort her. The sulfur stink of the pool hung in the humidity around us, like we were trapped in a Balrog's sauna.

Before mounting the stairs, John said, "Mind if I come up? I don't have a gun."

"It wouldn't matter if you did," said Bas.

John mounted the catwalk but didn't get too close to the two of them. I didn't know what he was planning, if anything in John's head could be called a plan, but I assumed he wanted to be in a position to force the issue somehow if Amy was unable to talk Bas down. I approached the pool, stepping carefully around the corpse of a kid I thought I recognized from the Dollar Cinema that night. I reached Amy, taking a spot at the lip next to her.

I said, "Just real quick, I need to get clear on something. The SWAT guy, before he ran away, said we only had a few minutes until impact. Are you aware of that whole, uh, situation?"

Bas said, "The egg will open, and right after, the simulation will try to kill me and it and everything around us. It won't work."

"Right, what I'm trying to figure out is the blast radius. And how much time we actually have to get to safety, if it's not already too late."

Bas shrugged. "Don't matter."

Amy said, "At least let us take Gracie away from here. Let John take her. He'll drive as fast as he can to get away from whatever's about to happen. In the meantime, you and I can talk."

"Gracie can do what she wants. Gracie, do you want to go with that weird guy in his windowless skin-tone van?"

She shook her head.

"Bas," Amy said. "Look around. All of your friends are dead. All of their families are going to find out soon. Think of all the funerals. Think of all the grief, all the pain. This can't go on. You know it can't."

"I'm doing this," Bas said, "*because* it can't go on."

I said, "You have to see by now how this stuff really works. The pain is all these things want; it's their food. They're always happy to trade for it, but I'm telling you, man, they always come out ahead in the end. Look at how this has all worked so far. Can't you see that this Magpie thing, whatever it really is, never wanted the body parts? It just wanted the suffering that comes from collecting them, the pain of the victims and the corrosion of the collectors' souls. It's using you!"

"And you're not? We're putting an end to this, and I mean *all* of it. To people using each other. People getting tortured and raped. This whole universe is like a big machine that cranks out animals that it can shit on. I'm pulling the plug. Somebody has to."

Out of the corner of my eye, I sensed John was taking another step closer on the catwalk. Bas didn't seem to notice. Or maybe he was intentionally letting him get close?

Amy said, "Bas, you don't get to make that choice for other people."

"They didn't choose to be born!" screamed Bas. "None of us agreed to this! If nobody had chosen for them already, they wouldn't be hurting. I'm just giving back what was taken from them—the peace of not existing. If you stopped this, and you can't, but if you did, then every starving child, every burn victim, every cancer patient—all their suffering is on you. Every war, every plague, every earthquake, all of it."

"There's happiness out there! Right now. Even in this town. Look! You can see the lights out there, all the houses and apartments. There's birthdays and babies and people falling in love.

Right now. If you asked them all if they want to go on, they'd say yes. I can prove that, because they make that decision every day, to keep going. Because even with all the other stuff, survival is better."

"No, they do it because they're told things will turn around someday. But for every single one of those birthday parties, skip to the end and you see all those people dying alone. The one who survives longest gets to attend all their friends' funerals, then they go out, too, confused and crapping their pants. This right here is mercy."

John took a step closer on the catwalk.

Time was running out.

I said, "Even if we granted you all that, this isn't going to go how you seem to think it will. There are no clean endings. It doesn't work that way."

"Every single thing the old man told me has come true," said Bas, "exactly like he said."

Amy asked, "Do you know who he is? Who he really is?"

Before he could answer, the egg cracked open. A thin, black appendage snaked out from inside.

Gracie saw it and screamed.

Amy said, "Gracie. We can take you away from here. We can take you back home. Go with John. He won't hurt you."

John drew closer still.

The egg opened a little more. Gracie screamed again and, this time, stood up. She tried to pull away from Bas to meet John on the catwalk, who was now just a few feet away. Bas grabbed the little girl's arm, and John pulled something from his back pocket.

John lunged forward, past the little girl, and pressed the object against Bas's thigh while screaming something I couldn't quite hear. John had jabbed his obsidian knife into the only nonfatal spot that would still have a chance at incapacitating his target. Bas fell hard against the rails, then collapsed to his knees. The ivory handle of the knife was jutting from this thigh, and I think he was more shocked than anything.

John grabbed Gracie, and the two of them ran for the stairs leading off the catwalk. Amy and I ran over to meet them.

Bas gathered himself, reached up with his hand, concentrated, and did . . . something. John collapsed as if he'd been flicked by a giant finger, banging his face off the metal grating. I heard bones crunch on impact.

As I write this part down, I'm tempted to draw it out. I want to describe the dawning horror of the situation as it unfolded, as I realized exactly what Bas had done and what it meant. I want to play it in slow motion for you, squeezing every drop of drama out of the moment, to really chisel it into your imagination as the pivotal event that it was.

I've written it, then deleted it, over and over. Because it's all bullshit.

The truth is, I didn't even realize it had happened, when it happened. The kid did something and John fell, and I thought he'd just tripped or gotten knocked over by whatever attack Bas had flung his way. There was maybe a split second of vague recognition that the way John fell wasn't the way a living person falls, instinctively stopping themselves with their hands, keeping their face off the ground at all costs. Actors even do it when they "die" in movies, always trying to make their fall look somewhat dignified. You never see their heads just bounce off the floor.

Real dead people don't fall with dignity. Just as they don't, outside of rare exceptions, go out in some emotional crescendo surrounded by loved ones wailing their name. They also don't get any kind of profound last words; those fortunate enough to live long lives usually spend their final breaths asking for another blanket or to turn up the TV so they can hear *Wheel of Fortune*.

As such, it actually took a while for me to register what John had said when he'd stabbed Sebastian a few seconds prior to this, the phrase that would go down as his last words.

I'm pretty sure it was, *"Knife to meet you!"*

Gracie screamed again. So did Amy.

The girl recovered and sprinted down the catwalk, jumping off the stairs and zooming past Amy and me, dashing away into the darkness, vanishing between a pair of the brick pump houses.

I was frozen in place. Amy ran up the stairs to the catwalk, breathing John's name over and over again. Bas was struggling to his feet, pulling at the knife stuck in his thigh meat.

Amy made it to where John lay. From where I stood, I could see his eyes were half-open and blank. His nose was bleeding and malformed. Amy fell to her knees and cradled his head in her hand.

I told my body to go up there and join them, but I found myself running the other direction, scanning the grass as I ran.

Third corpse from the right.

I heard a splash and saw that Bas had rolled himself off the platform into the filthy water, disturbing a layer of algae on the surface. He swam toward the edge.

I heard Amy saying, "John. Hey. Can you hear me? Wake up." She turned in Bas's direction. "WHAT DID YOU DO? IS HE DEAD? FIX THIS! HEY! UNDO IT! HEY!"

Bas climbed up onto the concrete lip of the pool, coated in so much gunk that he looked like Swamp Thing.

I found John's shotgun and snatched it out of the grass.

Bas jumped down just in time for me to pivot and point the gun right at his face. I stepped closer, wanting to pull the trigger a foot away from his eyes, figuring even if these were nonlethal rounds maybe it could still do the job if it was point-blank. Bas made a motion with both of his hands, and I fired every barrel.

He fell through the grass like he'd dropped through a trapdoor. I stopped and looked down to find nothing at all. He was nowhere in sight—the kid had teleported away.

It was just the three of us now.

You mean the two of us.

I heard a noise like a jet engine or a rocket launch, masses of air being violently compressed and then ripped asunder. Above me, a pinprick of light smeared up into the sky. It really did look just like a star was falling on us, just as the holy text had said.

Amy said, "Look!" but she somehow wasn't talking about that. She was standing up on the catwalk and pointing at the spot where a giant pipe joined the pool, the inlet valve for all the town's flushes. I climbed up on the lip of the pool to get a better view.

In through the valve was flowing swirls and tangles of blackness, like streams of living oil, the dark tendrils reaching out and grasping like tentacles.

Amy said, "It was in the drains! The Sauce, the Armus. And it's all gathering here!"

As if it mattered now. Who gave a shit about all that? John wasn't breathing. He wasn't John at all; he was a husk, a spent firework, all his chaotic, vibrant life gone.

And in that moment, a series of scenes flashed through my mind, almost simultaneously. I saw John dead in the mangled remains of a car, dead on the floor of a party with a stoned kid trying to give him CPR, dead while flatlining in a hospital bed, dead of a gunshot wound to the skull, dead of a gunshot wound to the chest, his charred bones in the remains of a house fire, his body torn apart in a Las Vegas casino. Dozens of deaths, hundreds, flashing across my mind as if they were all familiar to me, even though they weren't.

It can only ever end this way. Deep down, you know that.

I blinked and tried to shake it off. The water was entirely black now. It had filled faster than should have been possible, but possibilities never meant anything here. The blackness was bubbling up from the surface, turning into vertical appendages and splitting into smaller ones, until the entire surface of the pool had become a mass of tiny, grasping black hands, like every soul in Hell reaching up at the rumor of a drop of water. The roaring was growing louder overhead, and I found myself rooting for it. The plastic egg was opened fully now—I hadn't even noticed the final hatching—and I saw writhing appendages emerge, something crawling out.

I ran over to the stairs. I had to move John's body from this spot. I couldn't let this newborn thing have him, even if what was left of him was just that limp, discarded meat. I joined Amy on the catwalk and told her to get John's feet. I checked the platform to track the progress of the horror being born from the egg, but it was no longer visible. A column of those black hands had reached up from below, twisting themselves into a single shape that swallowed up the platform where Bas and Gracie had been standing just minutes ago. They were forming a perfect black sphere.

Amy started to help me with John's corpse, but then stopped because she seemed to realize it wouldn't matter. That bright streak overhead was now lighting the whole area like a sunrise. The thunder it made filled the world. The end would come within seconds. Maybe it was already here.

And then, all was quiet.

?. ?. ?
PIES
COLLECTED: ? OF 1.000.000.000.000

Me

The bright thing in the sky remained but had frozen in place. The sound of crushed air had been abruptly muted. The dark orb now occupying the platform in the center of the pool sat still and silent. I turned to say something to Amy and saw that she was a statue, individual strands of copper hair hanging still in midair.

Time had stopped.

A voice said, "And so, we arrive here again."

The Time Captain strode casually into the scene, strolling between the corpses in the grass like it was something he'd done a thousand times before.

I said, "Okay, what the fuck?"

"I'm sure you have many questions."

"Really just the one."

"Your one question is 'what the fuck'?"

"You want me to elaborate? If you have the power to pause the entire goddamned universe, can you bring back John? If he is dead—is he dead?"

"He is. As are you and everyone in the vicinity. And yes, there is a way to bring you back. All of you. But as I tried to warn you ear-lier, it is not simple. And it is not assured."

I said, "Great, let's do it."

"I'm sure you're eager to know what transpired here and what it means."

"Not really. Bring John back and you can tell me your whole life story. If you don't bring him back, you can go strap on a bib and eat a giant, sloppy bag of fat dicks. Because I don't give a shit about any of the rest of this."

"This is your last chance. Once I do it, you will not be able to ask me questions."

"All right. So the object frozen in the sky that appears to be about one second away from killing us the moment somebody unfreezes time, your space weapon, how widespread is its damage? Like how far away do we need to get from it next time?"

The man glanced up at the burning projectile hanging above us. It looked like an angel was cutting open the sky with a blowtorch.

"The town will be a crater, along with the surrounding landscape. That object, by the way, is a gift from Project Thor. Your tax dollars helped pay for it. Well, other people's tax dollars. That projectile—a massive tungsten rod—was fired from a black project satellite that was launched by the U.S. military five years ago. That piece of metal will hit at a speed in excess of Mach ten; the velocity carries enough energy to impact like a tactical nuclear warhead. It was ostensibly designed to penetrate the buried bunkers of rogue nations—it will dig itself two hundred feet into the earth—but certain people at very high levels know that it can be used in . . . other circumstances, if the situation warrants it. The government will have a cover story ready to go in the aftermath."

"Yeah, I was about to say it looked like tungsten. But it's not go-ing to take out Sebastian, right? Otherwise, you'd have just let it fall. Boom, problem solved."

He nodded. "Bas transported himself and his sister to a safe dis-tance. His biography will one day claim that stunned witnesses watched him walk directly out of the rubble, unharmed. Which is true—there will be video—but it will only be because he transports himself back to Ground Zero immediately after the danger is over. He will become an icon, his movement will spread around the globe, and, generations from now, the Xarcrax process will complete itself on schedule."

"So how do we fix all of this?"

"You already know. I can take you back to any point of your choosing, but you must stop Sebastian. Your enemy, meanwhile, will be working every step of the way to arrive at this same point, regardless of what path you take to get here."

"The same as how a turd will wind up in this facility no matter what toilet it gets dropped into. So you could rewind several hours, long enough for us to try to come up with a different strategy—wait, no. If Amy wasn't frozen, she'd say that's not good enough. Several people had died by that point. So I think we have to go back to before we even got the call from the Galvatrons. So we can save the cops, all the rest. But then again, that's what we did last—okay, back up."

I had to stop and think for a minute.

Finally, I said, "To be clear, you would be giving us our third chance, right? Because we already figured out this was our second time around. So you and I have had this conversation before."

The man's only response was a kind of tragic smile.

I stared at him, then sat down on the catwalk. I let out a long breath and turned my face up to the sky, toward the bright death poised above us.

I said, "We've had this conversation a bunch of times, haven't we?"

"We have."

"How many?"

"That's not relevant. If you are successful, all timelines will be overwritten by the one. None of this will have happened. The dead you see around you, the soon-to-be dead, all will live and be none the wiser."

"You said I could go back to any point in the past. Can I go back to childhood? Relive my whole life from the start? Avoid all my mistakes? Become some kind of successful, productive human being? Make it so that by the time I get here, I have all sorts of skills and habits that actually make me an asset to society?"

"You can, but keep in mind, you will have no memories of the years hence, outside of a vague sense of familiarity and dreams that twist the remembered reality into shapes you won't recognize."

"Have I tried that before, rewinding my whole life? In the previous attempts, I mean?"

"You have. Sometimes to positive results, up to a point. Sometimes branching possibilities along the way turn the world into something very different from what you know. But as we have repeated the process, I believe we have dialed in on an optimal moment for rewind and a singular key to success. I know you don't remember the many other tries, but I do. This is the part where you express doubt or even accuse me of being in on it, because that's who you are. And I always have to convince you that you have no real choice but to trust me. Either we go back, or everyone here is vaporized in a microsecond."

I sighed in resignation, studying the Amy statue as if I could detect some kind of subtle movement that could be taken as advice.

"Okay," I said. "So take me back to this optimal moment."

"Early Saturday morning."

I nodded. "Just before the mother asks us to intervene, right? But we have to get a message back this time, we have to have something to work with; otherwise, we're just taking shots in the dark."

He nodded impatiently. How many times had we had this exact exchange?

"As always," he said, "there is a window of about half a minute in which I can become physically present in that time period before fading out again. It's enough time to impart a few sentences of instructions, no more. They must be simple, as I won't have time to repeat them. Having done this repeatedly, I can tell you that the instructions that bring you closest to success on a consistent basis boil down to little more than, 'You have been given a chance to undo your previous failure, and you must kill Sebastian, at all costs.' And those instructions are delivered to John, not you."

"Why him?"

"Because we have found that, with zero exceptions, if I appear in your presence out of thin air, you will physically attack me until I fade out again, hearing nothing of what I say. This is true even if I appear to you in childhood."

"Yeah, that sounds about right. But in that case, give him different instructions this time. Tell him to stay away. Tonight, I mean, so he doesn't end up getting wizard-murdered again. We'll handle it without him."

"I can tell you with absolute certainty that such a message will not be heeded on his part."

I considered this for a moment before it fully hit me.

"If I've asked to give that message before," I said, "it means he's died here before. Right?"

He said nothing, just gave me a knowing look.

I said, "It always winds up like this, doesn't it? With John, I mean."

"Usually long before now. But if not, then yes, right around this point. Every time. If this task will be accomplished, it has to be you."

"No. There has to be a way. And I mean a way that gets everyone through alive, including John. There has to be."

"*Why* does there have to be?"

"Because fuck you, that's why. Do your thing. Turn back the clock. Tell John that we're getting another chance, and this time, none of the other bullshit with the toy matters, that we can't stop the collection of the parts. We have to focus on Bas from the start and never let up. If there isn't time to say all that, then, I don't know, talk fast."

He said, "After you," and gestured toward the black sphere hovering at the center of the pool.

"What, we're going to walk into that?"

"That," said the Time Captain, "is the reason I can do this at all. The summoning is about gaining power to rewrite the timeline. But in creating this weapon, Xarcrax has also created the means by which it can be undone. I was shown this moment in a vision, what feels like many lifetimes ago, and shown how to manipulate this mechanism to our own ends."

"Who showed it to you? Somebody who's on our side?"

"I have been reliving this cycle for a very long time, and I am no closer to knowing the answer to that question than when I started. I have come to believe that the universe itself is guiding us, perhaps operating out of a sense of self-preservation."

"So you're stuck in this loop? Watching me fuck this up over and over again? Jesus, you must want to just slap the shit out of me."

"You have no idea. And yes, I am stuck in this loop, and I presumably will be, until we either resolve it or run out of chances. I assure you, I would give anything to be free of this. But my needs are nothing in the grand scheme of things." He once again gestured toward the sphere and said, "After you."

I stepped forward. Somewhere in the back of my mind was a tickle of doubt, a suspicion that I had been backed into this particular corner by design. The feeling was familiar to me, probably because I'd been feeling it my whole life.

I had to scoot around the Amy statue and step over John's frozen corpse to get to the big black magic sphere. As I approached, I again had that sensation of timelines and possibilities flashing through my mind, seeing myself approaching this orb again and again, in varying clothes and physical conditions and amounts of body fat, sometimes wounded, sometimes with Amy, sometimes alone.

The Time Captain appeared next to me. He did some Time Captain shit with his hands, and the black sphere expanded to engulf us and the entire pool, maybe the whole world. I again had that sensation of information leaving my mind, of experiences dissolving like smoke rings, a vague sense of mourning the loss of a person I had become but was no longer.

Familiar walls formed around us, and I turned to see John lying there on the catwalk, only now a bed was fading into existence under him, the Time Captain standing next to it. Walls grew around us, covered in framed posters for John's various bands. I had the strangest feeling like I was fading as the room and bed were becoming solid. I was in the wrong spot, I needed to be rewound back to my kitchen floor less than seventy hours ago, eating old pizza and vacantly scrolling on my phone. I felt a tug like an ocean current, urging me backward through time. I sensed plants getting sucked into the earth, larvae getting pulled back into their eggs, millions of turds shooting back through these drain pipes and flying up into assholes.

But for just the briefest moment, while I was still in John's bedroom watching a duvet cover fade into existence over the man himself, I saw a speck of white. It was floating past me, like a single petal from a dogwood tree carried on the wind. It was moving steadily toward the Time Captain, and just before the world was taken from my view, I made out what it was:

A white mouse, scurrying along John's floor, toward the Time Captain's polished black shoes.

The mouse reached his right foot and climbed up onto the cuff of his pants. The man reacted with mild confusion, but not alarm. It was, after all, just a mouse, nothing you wouldn't find in any random home that surely had plenty of crumbs on the floor. He shook the mouse off his pant leg, knocking it back a couple of feet. Then the mouse righted itself, charging back toward the same shoe.

The Time Captain took a single step back away from the weirdly persistent rodent, then kicked at it in annoyance. The mouse stopped, but did not retreat. It was just staring.

Waiting.

The walls were becoming solid now, which meant I was losing sight of them as I was becoming less solid at the same rate. But in that brief window of time, I noted that because of that single step backward, the Time Captain was now standing too close to the wall, was standing inside of it. He was speaking words I could not hear. Then it all went away, and my last thought before being yanked out of that time stream was that once that wall became fully solid, the front third of the Time Captain would slide wetly to the floor like a sliced roast beef.

I had time to think, *He's finally free,* before it all went away.

Me

I found myself back in my kitchen.

Wait, no. Wrong kitchen.

I was at John's place, at the table with John, Joy, and Amy all staring at me with almost comical anticipation, as if waiting for me to spontaneously combust. Each of them had paused in the act of putting a piece of food in their mouths, holding a potato chip, a Cheez Ball, and an olive, respectively.

I had the Xarcrax book in my hands. I dropped it and bolted upright, knocking my chair over in the process.

Amy said, "What?"

I looked around. "What time is it? And, uh, what day?"

John said, "Why, it's Christmas Day!"

"It's a little after eight, Monday night," said Amy. "You just had skin contact with the Sauce, and we're all here waiting to see if you vanish into another layer of space-time or something."

"When was that?"

"Just seconds ago. What was it from your point of view? Did anything happen?"

John said, "Were you greeted with visions of how your miserly ways have affected others?"

Amy pulled out her phone, like she was going to record me recounting my experience, just as she had last time around. I waved her off and stood, running to the stairs. I made it to John's bedroom and—

There was the ragged hole in the wall, opening to Joy's closet. Just where it should be.

Amy came up the stairs behind me, probably thinking I'd run up here to vomit in the bathroom again.

From downstairs, I heard John say, "He's going to come back with the biggest goose you've ever seen."

Amy asked, "What happened?"

"I need to think. Give me a minute."

I went back down and grabbed a Natty Light from John's fridge. Joy seemed mildly alarmed. John was just waiting patiently. He'd been through this, knew it took a bit to get your footing after coming down.

Amy followed me into the kitchen and started to ask a question, but I interrupted. "Just give me a second to gather myself. Please."

I took a drink. I glanced around the room, trying to orient myself in space and time, maybe hoping to stop short before the depression set in.

"Okay. So I just flashed back to last time. The last time we did this, I mean, I lived the entire thing while I was on the Sauce, the whole previous attempt before the reset, through to the end. Everybody wound up dead, and I know exactly what happened and exactly how we messed it up. Listen, and don't interrupt."

We'd gone out to the front porch so John could smoke. I was sitting on the swing with Joy. Amy was pacing around, thinking.

John said, "It's just like my dream. The ritual is to summon all the darkness into one place so that it can fuck a hole in the space-time continuum."

Amy said, "That guy's trick with resetting everything—he can't do that this time, right?"

I said, "I guess not. The Time Captain is dead in this timeline."

"Because he was afraid of a mouse?"

"I think it was just annoying him, but he lost track of where he was standing when he phased in."

"We think that's just a coincidence, that a mouse happened to be there?"

"Who knows, maybe the mouse was working for Xarcrax. Either way, yeah, I think this is our last chance."

"And there's a secret space weapon positioned above the town that's going to destroy us just after midnight, no matter what we do. It's kind of crazy to think *that* isn't the headline here."

"To be honest, I'm mainly impressed that the government built it and that it actually works. Looked like it was going to land right on our heads. We should find the guy who designed it and tell him he did a good job."

John said, "The doomsday satellite thing has been a conspiracy theory forever. The story is that the government approved the project after 9/11 as a secret black budget thing. Then there's another even conspiracier theory that there's an even more secret, blacker budget reason for the satellite, which is to take out unnatural apocalyptic threats if they should turn up. Supposedly, the brass in charge at the deepest levels have this town pinned on a map."

Amy said, "That means even if we succeed this time, we have no idea how to stop it from firing. Who orders the strike? What's the protocol? At what point in the process is it too late?"

I said, "You're saying we should just clear out, let the thing blow up the town, then take care of Bas after."

"What? No."

"Of course. I just wanted to, uh, make sure."

Joy asked, "What was I doing in the last attempt?"

"I didn't see you. I don't think you came along to the part at the end. Didn't you say you have to work tonight?"

"I wouldn't skip this for work!"

"Then I don't know. It doesn't—"

"You think I was shot by the SWAT team? We should be talking about that!"

John asked, "Would that even kill you?"

"You mean the way those cigarettes are going to kill your clown ass?"

"Maybe you hung back to drive the getaway vehicle."

"Well, I'm not doing that this time! I'm coming with you."

"Nobody said you couldn't!"

"Now," I said, "there's something else." I stood up, off the swing. "You guys might want to sit down for this."

John took the swing next to Joy. Amy sat on the rail of the porch. She said, "What?"

"Ah, I don't know how to approach this. It's about John."

Joy said, "John is secretly Bas, from the future?"

"No."

"John is Xarcrax."

"No, just let me—"

"John is secretly you, from the future."

"Stop. The Time Captain said that in all of the previous attempts, that there are some constants that play out the same way. I think, well, I guess it's like in a game of pool, you can break the balls in infinite ways, but the pockets are always in the same spot, right? And one of the constants, one of the things that happens every time, no matter what . . ."

I trailed off. I honestly didn't know how to deliver the news.

John said, "Dude, you refusing to say it is way worse than anything you could possibly say right now."

"You never make it. Whether you die at the end or at some other point, you never make it to the finish line tonight. And he seemed pretty sure that that part is written in stone, for whatever stupid, cosmic reason."

John nodded. "Yeah, that makes sense. By all rights, I should have died thirty or forty times by now."

"You're just going to hear that news and roll with it."

"I mean, obviously I'm not going to die this time. Or maybe I will." He shrugged. "I would get my affairs in order, but that shit is already ordered. I try to live in such a way that my every encounter with a person would also serve as a pretty sweet ending if it's the last."

Joy said, "What did he say about me? Do I make it?"

I said, "It didn't come up. I honestly don't even think you're supposed to be here." Before Joy could reply, I said, "But I think that's part of it. We're asking what we can do different from all the other attempts, but he said we're refining the process, getting closer each time. And I think part of it is just us, this particular version of us. Fancy Me didn't know Joy, and in his life, not even fond memories of John remained. And *I'm* different. That version of me, most versions aren't, you know. The way I am. This version of us, being alive at the very end, that's rare. And we have to take advantage of it. Last time, we tried to talk Bas out of it, convince him the world was worth saving. But that's what Amy would always do. And my way doesn't work, either. I think the Time Captain is wrong. We're never going to kill Sebastian if the military's trillion-dollar space cannon can't do it."

I turned to John and Joy on the swing.

"So, you two. Give me a plan that *only you could have come up with.*"

Joy said, "How about we all forget about it and just go get ice cream? Surely we've never done that."

John nodded as if taking that suggestion under advisement, then said, "It still has to start with finding Bas, right? Last time, we tried to meet him at the Turditorium, but that's too late in the process. He'd already have all his Xarcrax buddies around him; no way he could back out with his whole squad watching. Once they've all been shot by the SWAT cops, then there's definitely no way. Quitting means they'd have died for nothing. That means you have to catch him before all that, somewhere that it's just him and Gracie. So where are they?"

Amy said, "It's not in the book."

"No, it wouldn't be. This isn't part of the ritual. This is a big brother and his baby sister. They have to be someplace out of sight, but also where he could keep Gracie calm. I bet that cancels out all of the many creepy abandoned buildings around here."

John dropped his cigarette on the porch and crushed it under his shoe. Thinking.

"But it's more than that, right?" he continued. "On some level, he knows this could be their last night on earth, that maybe none of this works and they'll just get shot down by the police. What would you do if you were him, in that situation? You'd want to make her as happy as possible."

Amy said, "I'm coming up empty, because I wouldn't do any of it."

I said, "Maybe he'd try to knock Gracie out with cold medicine or something, get her to sleep through it."

"No, no," said John impatiently. "We were all wrong about the skinning thing. Gracie is the last person he'd have picked for that. He loves her. She may be the *only* person he loves. He'd want tonight to be special. Like they have to eat at some point. What would he get her for her possible last meal on earth? Probably her favorite, right?"

Amy glanced at Joy, looked like she was getting an idea, then went to work on her phone.

She said, "Ice cream. Gracie had a birthday last November. They took her to Chilly Whip for a banana split. She looks happy in the pics on Facebook. And hey, look at that, they took her there again in April, after she went to the dentist. Bas was there both times, so he knows."

John said, "That's the call, then. Either they've been there already or they're about to be there. I'm sure of it. He wouldn't let his little sister die without ice cream. Let's pack up the van."

Joy said, "In other words, we're all going to get ice cream cones, which is exactly what I suggested one minute ago. I think I should be in charge."

I said, "We're not getting ice cream. We're staking out Chilly Whip for a wizard ambush."

"Oh, I'm getting a waffle cone one way or another. I don't care what you guys do."

We sat in the van across the street from the orange Chilly Whip building, all of us licking ice cream cones. John had asked the girl at the drive-through if she'd seen Bas, and she said she hadn't (she hadn't needed a photo; she knew him from school). So we were waiting, knowing that we at most would have another thirty minutes or so because that's when the place closed. The main problem was we didn't know what vehicle Bas would be in, if he showed at all. The motorcycle would be too recognizable, and you couldn't really transport ice cream on one.

"There," said Amy. "She's signaling. Look."

The girl at the drive-through window was waving to us and pointing. A blue Honda Civic was pulling out, Bas at the wheel. He'd disguised himself as best he could, covering his head with a jacket hood and sunglasses, Unabomber-style.

I asked, "You going to pull up and block him in the parking lot?"

John shook his head. "No, we don't want a wizard battle at Chilly Whip. We'll follow him back to his lair."

I hated this idea, since our last attempt to follow Bas had ended in disaster. There was virtually no traffic at this hour, so the issue wasn't losing him but the opposite—we'd be extremely obvious if we followed him for more than a couple of turns. John hung way back, more than a block, and immediately two cars got between us. I felt like we'd already blown our last chance.

But then, after multiple instances of us almost losing sight of the blue Civic, I saw where we were heading and said, "You've got to be shitting me."

Bas was pulling into the Coral Rock motel, which was approximately thirty feet from my own apartment. I assume Bas didn't know that and only picked it because it was one of the joints in town that didn't ask questions. We noted the room he entered, then we just parked the van at my place.

Amy said, "Well, does anyone need anything from the apartment?"

I said to John, "You guys are in charge. What's the plan?"

"We wait."

"For what?"

"For Gracie to finish her ice cream. Give it like fifteen minutes, then we go."

"And do what, when we go?"

"Whatever pops into our heads."

When the time came, we walked over, Joy still finishing her ice cream—she was one of those people who ate at an infuriating pace—and went right up to the door of Bas's room.

John knocked and said, "Room service."

Bas opened the door an inch to peek out, and John shouldered his way in. Gracie was sitting on the bed. She was startled by our arrival but not shocked. Like she'd been expecting someone but just hadn't been sure who.

Bas put his hands in front of him, ready for a fight. His expression said this was the first true curveball he'd been thrown since this whole thing began.

"Don't make me hurt you in front of her," growled Bas.

John said, "We haven't called the cops. We aren't here to fight you. But I have something to say that you're going to want to hear. It's three words. Will you listen to three words?"

Bas didn't respond.

John reached out, put a hand on Bas's shoulder, and, in a tender voice, whispered, "I have weed."

Bas, John, and I retired to my apartment while Gracie, Amy, and Joy stayed in the motel room. We hadn't intended to split it up by gender like that, but Gracie couldn't be around the weed smoke, and somebody needed to watch her. When I asked Joy if she wanted to join us, she said she didn't want to get grease paint on her new shirt. I'd thought Gracie would protest, but she seemed oddly relieved, even while being separated from her big brother protector. As for why Bas agreed to go with us, I hadn't a clue. He just seemed curious, I guess, in that way teenagers are. Enticed by adventure but nervous about breaking the rules.

John and Bas took the sofa; I claimed the Big Shitty Chair near the window. We asked Bas if it was his first time, and he responded that he preferred to smoke because edibles and vapes made him paranoid. So we took that as a no. We turned on a marathon of *The Fairly OddParents,* grabbed some cans of Fight Piss, and John booked us three seats on Reefer Airlines.

We sat there watching the TV for some amount of time that didn't matter. Nobody said anything. I actually couldn't think of anything to say. I had kind of lost interest in the whole affair, to be honest.

Finally, Bas said, "You ever notice that if you barely watch a show, like you only stumble across it now and then, it's always the same episode? Or even like the same part of the same episode?"

I didn't answer. Then I laughed, because that was hilarious, if you think about it. Somebody just watching a TV show. Like the three of us, just sittin' here watching a cartoon in the cartoon-watching room. I thought about how it's weird that we have different rooms for doing different things and how the fancier your house is, the more rooms and walls it has. I wondered who invented walls and what he was ashamed of. Probably began with a guy hanging curtains up around his corner of the tent, like, "I don't want you to see what I'm doing over here." Soon, everything was walls and shame, in our houses, in our minds. The guy was probably just jerking off. What, like he's the only one? Now everybody else is ashamed to do it, because walls and shame isolate us, make us think we're unique in our vices. Thanks, wall guy.

We heard the first splatters of rain outside. We all sat and listened to the drops flicking the windows.

After a while, a few minutes or a few hours, or maybe just a few minutes, or maybe a few hours, Bas said, "Maybe that rain will cool it off."

John coughed and said, "Usually just makes it sticky."

"I swear, you get the worst of all weather here. It's humid like the South; winters may not be as cold as up north but what you get here is worse, the ice storms and the snow that turns to slush but then somehow sticks around for like a month after. Did you see that tornado that came through back in April or May or whenever it was? It got close enough to our house that we could see the clouds turning in the sky. Like something out of a movie."

John said, "You watch the Channel Five weather guy when they go live with that storm warning stuff? I swear he gets horny."

"How can you guys stand to live here?"

I said, "Weed. And other things. Got to build soft layers between yourself and reality or else the sharp edges will just shred you."

"I don't know how you don't just blow your brains out."

"You don't think the thought's occurred to me? But the more I thought about it, the more it was just another empty promise. 'End it all'? It doesn't end anything. Everyone who loves you is sad, and the ones who hate you are happy. Just makes the situation worse. That's the first thing you find out when you get old: all the easy exits are just fake doors painted on brick, like in those old Road Runner cartoons. Do kids still watch those?"

"When we first got here and we drove through that real bad

neighborhood by the population sign, Gracie started crying so hard she threw up."

"Yeah, that happens a lot. John used to live in that neighborhood, by the way. The big blue building? Next to the power station?"

John said, "Actually had a lot of good times there. Don't let Dave steer you wrong; he had a lot of good times there, too. For some reason, only the bad sticks in his memory."

Bas inhaled and then, through a cloud, said, "My dad is an asshole."

John asked, "For moving you here, or just in general?"

Bas thought about it. He had a look like he'd been presented a sandwich so big and complicated that he wasn't sure where the first bite should come from.

"Silva, that was my sister, she always got a ton of attention. She was girlie, you know. She wanted to wear makeup and earrings from the time she was like eight years old. She always looked older, I guess. Dressed older, you know. I used to give her shit about it, how she was still my gross, smelly sister who never flushes the toilet but she's acting like she's a fashion model. She would get catcalled by guys when she was eleven. Guess they thought she was older, all the makeup and all that. Or maybe they were just creeps, you never know. Dad, he got real weird about it, though. He was always yelling at her about it, dragging her into the bathroom to wipe the makeup off, telling her she was dressing like a slut. She went to a party a while back, just a little kid party for all these eighth graders, there were grown-ups there, but Dad saw pics she was posting of it online, and I guess he didn't like her outfit. It was nothing the other kids weren't wearing, shorts and like a tank top or something. But he drives there and drags her out of the party by her hair. A little while later, in the middle of the night, she gets kidnapped."

Bas stopped talking, and it took several seconds for those last words to soak into my brain.

I said, "Did you say *kidnapped*? By who?"

"They came in a black van in the middle of the night, woke Sil up, told her to get dressed, and when she tried to fight them, they put her in cuffs. Those plastic ones. She thought she was gonna die, or gonna get raped, or who knows what. But it turned out the kidnappers worked for this troubled teen rehab camp thing. Dad had hired them, said Silva was out of control, said she was a degenerate. He uses that word all the time. Everything is degeneracy, all the girls are turning into whores. I got in Dad's face about it, about having Sil taken away. He yells that if they don't save her now that she's as good as dead, that he's not going to have everyone thinking he raised a disease-ridden slut. Said he'd rather she *was* dead. Sil comes back from the camp two months later, and she's different. She won't talk about it. And Dad, he just keeps getting madder and madder over time. I guess she got into some trouble at the camp. She sneaked off with a boy, and Dad just wouldn't let it go. He took the door off Sil's bedroom, told her she couldn't close the bathroom door when she went in, like he thought she was playing with herself or something. I don't know what he thought. I mean, every dude I know is going wild on his meat like it's an Olympic event, but if a girl does it, it's the end of the world?"

Bas just shook his head. I came up with a bunch of comforting things to say, but none of them left my mouth.

John said, "What a fucking lunatic."

"She lost weight. She stopped bathing. One time, we were all eating at the dinner table, and Dad has one of his work friends over. Dad starts accusing Silva of having trimmed her pubes. Right there at the table. He asks her what corner she plans on working when she moves out, which n-word is going to pimp her out. Only he didn't say *n-word,* obviously. One day, not too long after that, Dad says he's going to start checking her from time to time, to make sure she's still a virgin; he'll do exams. So, a little more than a year ago, that summer, we go on vacation, to Mexico City. Dad is doing an appearance there or something, and they've got places you can go zip-lining, that kind of thing. I thought it'd be too hot, but it was nice. I guess the altitude keeps it cool. We visit one of those pyramids they've got, Dad and Silva say they want to climb it, there's like five hundred stairs going up, but Gracie didn't want to, so me and Mom went and got Popsicles instead. Paletas, that's what they call them. And we're in line for them when there's a bunch of yells and screams from somewhere. We find out Sil has fallen. There's this big part of the pyramid that slopes straight down, then there's a landing at the bottom, and she just hit that headfirst. And Dad, he says she did it on purpose, jumped the rails around the steps and ran over to that ledge, threw herself off it."

I wanted to ask Bas why he didn't just tell us this from the start, but I tried to think back to when he'd have even had a chance to.

John said, "Fuck, man. I can't even imagine. Jesus."

Bas inhaled, coughed, then said, "I can't prove this, but Dad did it. I know he did. I could see it in his face. He pushed her, or threw her off, or something. I swear, he had tried to get her to do it herself, before that. Tried to put the idea in her head, kept talking about how he'd rather she be dead than . . . whatever she was doing wrong that day. He started using this antique razor, not like a straight razor, but like an old double-edged razor where you insert the full blades into it. And he left the package of blades right there on the vanity, in the bathroom where she took baths, like he was dropping a hint. But like I said, I can't prove it. So anyway, after she dies, Dad finds in Sil's Instagram a couple of comments from girls at school making fun of her—and these are from months earlier—and Dad goes out in public and says the suicide was due to cyberbullying, like these couple of comments would have been enough. He does all these interviews in the paper and all that, using Silva as this prop to talk about how he cares about kids' mental health and the damage social media is doing and how he doesn't want any more girls to suffer like her. Pushing his books and seminars the whole time, like, I don't know, man. It was like he sacrificed her for a career boost."

Bas inhaled, exhaled.

"I told all this to Mom. She slapped me in the face. I told the cops.

Filed a report and everything. Hell, even if I can't prove anything about her death, why is it legal to pay somebody to kidnap your kid? Why doesn't any of that stuff Dad was doing count as child abuse? Somebody tells my parents, and the next thing I know, I'm talking to a therapist about my paranoia. I tell her everything, tell her about Dad's razors, I even looked up other complaints about that behavior camp or whatever they call it. It costs over a hundred grand! I printed out articles and gave them to her, said we've got to do something, because Dad's going to start in on my other sister next."

John said, "Is your dad sick, like in the head? He sounds like he needs a straitjacket at the minimum."

Bas waved him off. "His parents were weirdos, were hippies, or something, I dunno, maybe they messed him up. But you still don't get it. Nobody gets it. The problem isn't just him; the problem is everything and everybody. Look at who all had a chance to step in: all the government people; all the friends and coworkers and neighbors who saw what was going on. This went on for *years*. Everybody saw what he was like, and nobody gave a fuck. He's this famous guru or whatever; he's got fans. And he's this big bully of a dude. Everybody's scared of him. The teachers at school are scared of him. The cops are scared of him. So if you want to get justice for Silva, where does it stop? Do you go all the way back to Grandma and Grandpa for messing up Dad when he was a kid? To whoever it was that messed them up, to all the people who didn't stop whatever happened to them? There is no answer. The whole thing is rotten. All the way down."

We didn't reply.

"One day," he said, "I come home from swim practice, and Dad says we're moving immediately, before the school year starts. I can't even go back and say goodbye to anybody, my friends, my girlfriend, our other family—we all just left it behind and came here. He says the degeneracy has taken over California, we have to head east, to save Gracie, to save her from what happened to Silva, as if *he* wasn't what happened to her. We moved to the worst place in the world—I swear he picked this town on purpose. We move here, then early this year, just like I said, Dad starts getting on Gracie. We go out to that pool in the park, and she's wearing this little girl's one-piece bathing suit with Princess Bubblegum or something all over it, and he's like, when you're out of the water, you got to wrap yourself in a towel. He tells her all of the men at the pool are staring at her ass, that they're all going to jerk off to her later, that she's a piece of meat among wolves. And Mom is just sitting there, in her hat and sun-glasses, looking at Pinterest on her phone, and she'd maybe mutter something about not ruining the mood, but that's it. And I think, what can I even do? Take Gracie and just leave in the night? Then what? I got no money. So I'm just gonna sit here and watch this hap-pen, watch him break her, just like he broke Sil?"

I said, "I wasn't even there, and this is making me physically sick just hearing about it."

"Dude, if you'd met Sil, you'd feel a thousand times worse. She was the coolest fucking person I ever met. She was the middle kid, but she was the oldest, if you know what I mean. She'd give me ad-vice about how to dress, how to talk to girls. She'd get on my ass if I was being an idiot. She used to call me Crab. When I was being dumb, I mean. Everybody loved her. Everybody wanted to be her friend. There was like this light she had, you know? Like she lit up whatever space she was in. Then the world just came and . . . snuffed it out."

He wiped his eyes.

"Man, the last time I saw her," he said, "I yelled at her. At the hotel in Mexico City. She'd spilled cranberry juice on my new white shoes. I called her a bitch. That's the last thing she ever heard from me. Forever."

John and I stayed silent. There was nothing to say. Rain danced on the windows.

"Soon," said Bas, "I get a visit from somebody in the night, like maybe it was a dream and maybe it wasn't. An old man. He says, 'I brought you here, to this town. I arranged this.' He says this world is all a prison and he can get me out. Me and Gracie and the other people worth saving. And from that point on, every single thing that old man said came true. Every word. Every prediction. Until . . ."

I said, "Until?"

"Until you dickheads came along."

More silence.

Finally, I said, "Are you old enough to have seen that Johnny Depp movie about the guy who has scissors for hands?"

"I know what you're talking about, yeah."

"Well, I feel like that all the time, like whatever I try to fix, I'm just going to stab it a lot. I want to help you, I want to make the pain better. But everything we do just breaks it worse. I'm sorry about that. I really am. We got played. I thought I knew what was going on, but I didn't. You've opened my eyes. I get why you're doing what you're doing."

I got up and went to the kitchen, looking for something to eat. I found some Nutter Butter cookies. They were a little bit stale, but they were fine.

I said, "When I was your age, I used to lull myself to sleep at night imagining myself shooting up my high school. I had a list of who I'd kill first. Not just students, either. My adoptive parents didn't have guns in the house, so I researched how to make pipe bombs instead. And you want to know the best part? The reason I didn't go through with it isn't because I had some epiphany; nobody intervened and told me I mattered, that I was loved, that I had too much to live for. I was just a coward. Too afraid. That's it. That's the only reason I'm here today. So I've gotta say, part of what I'm feeling right now is envy. Nutter Butter?"

He reached for one, and I just gave him the package.

I said, "What sucks the most is that it shouldn't be you and me and John talking here; it should be Silva. It should be her story. But on top of everything else, death robs you of a voice. You know one of the most common requests we get, but never, ever take, is people wanting to talk to their dead kids or wives or friends? We can't do that, and as far as I know, nobody can. The dead, if their spirits are powerful enough or their will is strong enough, they can try to get messages through, but it's hard to hear. And even harder for me to hear, because I'm a dumbass. So I didn't hear what I was being told, over and over, these last few days."

I sat down on the floor next to the sofa. I reached over and took one of the cookies from the package on Bas's lap.

Bas said, "These are the best cookies I've ever had."

"Can I ask you a question?" asked John. "Why'd you agree to come over here and smoke weed with us?"

Bas said, "The mouse," then didn't say anything else for a little bit, like he intended to leave it at that. I didn't prompt him. Finally, he continued, "When I got back with the ice cream, Gracie swore her missing mouse, Penelope, had turned up in the hotel. Swore it was the same mouse, said it came right up to her on the bed. I didn't tell her it was silly, even though I thought it was. How in the hell is a mouse gonna get across town like that? And show up in that exact room? It's not like they're smart. But while we were sitting on the bed, after we'd finished our ice cream, it ran out from under the bed. It ran right to the door, slipped under it. Then there came a knock, and it was you guys. I don't know. It was like a sign, or something." He shrugged. "I don't know why I did it."

I said, "When your mom hired us, the thing that pushed her over the edge was she said the whole family was having bad dreams, where they were running from this darkness that was swallowing up everyone they knew. Amy had that dream, too. You said that the man you spoke to told you that he arranged for you to move here. But then those dreams, they made it so that John and me and Amy would get involved, so that we would wind up right here, in this room, throwing a wrench in the plan. Because those dreams, they were of the future you're about to create, and the one putting those dreams into our heads wanted us to try to stop it. You make Silva sound like an amazing person, but what I've seen her do, what she was able to pull off from the other side? Goddamn. She must have shined brighter than a star."

Bas bolted to his feet. The cookies went flying.

"You don't fucking know that's what's going on. You don't know anything."

John said, "Hey, man, we don't necessarily disagree with that second part. I mean, look around." He gestured to the general state of the apartment. "But the reason it had to be us is that the three of us understand something that most people don't. The devil is real, but he doesn't turn up in a red suit with hooves. You have to imagine him as like a disease that you get—you pass it on and you don't even know it. Educated people don't call it the devil; they call it *trauma*. It rewires your brain and tries to spread itself down to the next generation and the one after that, the pain rolling down through time. The old man talking to you in your dreams, I think you know that he's just you, the man you can wind up being if you go down this path. All that about the end of the world? The best and worst news you're gonna hear all day is this: There's no such thing. It's another one of Dave's fake painted-on exits. You try to end it, and instead of release, it's just waves of trauma. The devil wins. You hate your dad and you should; he poured all his sickness into you. But if you want to fight him, the way you do it is by making sure you don't pass on the trauma. That's how you kill the devil. The only way."

Bas had his hand over his eyes. I didn't know if he was crying or just trying to block out the world. The rain came harder now, rattling across the landing outside.

I said, "You know, on some level, that we're right. That Silva wouldn't have wanted this. She wouldn't want you to become that old man."

Bas punched me in the face. From the floor, I heard the door slam and footsteps bang down the stairs.

Amy

Joy was painting Gracie's nails, an act that Gracie was receiving with the mesmerized wonder of a child who's just been told she's a secret princess who has been accepted to wizarding school.

Joy said, "Now, if you learn to do this yourself, you'll save hundreds and hundreds of dollars over having to get them done at a nail place. Then you'll probably just go to the nail place anyway. Contrary to what grown-ups will tell you, sometimes you appreciate things *more* when others do it for you."

Amy was at the window, watching the rain pummel the cars in the parking lot.

She muttered, "I sure hope this rain keeps up."

Without looking away from her nails, Gracie asked, "Why?"

"So it won't come down!"

"Would you stop! God."

Joy said, "Hold still."

Bas burst in the door, so wet that he looked like he'd once again teleported in from the town pool. His face was flush with rage.

He moved toward Gracie and said, "We have to go."

Joy said, calmly, "One more finger, then we're done."

"We're done now." He took Gracie gently by the arm.

She stood. "I want to go to Japan!"

"What?"

"I want to go to Japan. Amy showed me pictures. Can we go?"

"No. I don't know. Not right now. Come on."

"I know we can't go *right now*. But later. Maybe at Christmas? Amy says they all eat fried chicken on Christmas over there."

Bas led her to the door. Amy went to intercept but didn't put her body in the way. She wouldn't win a physical confrontation with Bas even if he couldn't bend reality.

"Wait. Where are you going?"

He opened the door and faced her. Before he could speak, sirens emerged from the distance, wailing under the sizzle of the rainfall.

Bas said, "They're coming here. I'd get away if I was you. But I'm not you, so I don't give a shit."

He led Gracie out into the rain. They hustled over to their little car and pulled away. Amy had no way to give chase, so she instead ran across the parking lot to her apartment, to find David and John descending the stairs.

"What happened?"

"Not sure," said David. "I thought we'd made a breakthrough, maybe we did, but I really couldn't read his reaction."

"How did he react?"

"Punched me in the jaw."

John watched Bas's car head down the street, then turn out of view. "You think he's heading toward the sewer plant?"

David said, "Don't know. But that's where we're going."

Me

Joy was driving the van because John and I were both too high. She had awarded Amy the passenger seat, and John and I had to sit in the back among the weapons, guitars, and dolls. The rain had ended but had left behind so much humidity that Joy was forced to run the wipers anyway.

Before either of us had a chance to tell Amy what we'd gotten out of Bas, she said, "The kids can't go back to that man. Dalton. Their father."

John said, "I know."

I said, "I don't disagree, but how do you propose we stop that? The authorities wouldn't even listen to Bas. Why would they listen to our crazy asses?"

Amy, in a tone I'd never heard before, said, "I don't know. We'll figure it out."

A police car whooshed past us in the opposite direction, sirens howling. John's scanner suggested police had gone into manhunt mode over the missing child that, according to rumor, was about to be the subject of a ritual sacrifice. But they were, at the moment, heading back toward the motel we'd just left.

I was briefly encouraged by the little bit of a head start we had on them, then a few minutes later, Amy said, "What did you bring to get through the fence?" and got only awkward silence as an answer.

I could see it in the distance: a tall, serious fence topped with

razor wire. It made perfect sense—you don't want a terrorist or disgruntled employee dumping toxins in the water, plus I remembered
it from last time—but this still stopped our plan in its tracks.

Joy turned down the access road and said, "Seriously, nobody has
ideas?"

I said, "If I ask you if you have some special ability to slip through
fencing unnoticed, are you going to actually answer, or are you going to get offended and start calling us clowns?"

"I don't know. Ask me."

"Forget it."

"You could try driving through it in a tiny car with twenty of your
friends!"

Amy pointed at the windshield. "Who's that?"

Joy skidded to a stop.

Standing in the middle of the road outside the fence of the wastewater treatment plant was Sebastian Galvatron. Gracie was over by
the fence and peering in, like she was fascinated by this look behind the scenes of her bathroom stuff. Their blue Civic was parked
on the shoulder farther down, in the shadows of a dead streetlamp
that I vaguely remembered marked an important spot in the perimeter.

We all got out, and at the sight of me, Gracie said, "Joy told me
you can make balloon animals! Can you make me a bird?"

I said, "Don't have any balloons." To Bas, I said, "What's the plan,
Chief?"

"I'm fucked. That's all. It's like one of those janky old PC games
where you can accidentally save in a no-win situation. You're in the
arena with some big dragon or whatever, but you're out of health
and bullets and you can't leave. All you can do is die. Over and over."

John said, "Life isn't a game. In some ways it's worse, and some
ways it's better. Sometimes you get into a situation where you have
to eat shit no matter what, but if you look close you'll see some shit
isn't quite as bad, or maybe there's not quite as much of it. Then

one day you wake up and realize that a lot of those no-win situations only seemed like that in the moment."

Amy said, "In situations like this, it helps to work through your bad options, figure out which one you want to muddle through. Okay? Now, we can make this really complicated, but I think you have one primary concern here, and she's standing over by that fence."

Bas shot a glance over at Gracie. "Yeah. That's right."

I noticed Joy had joined the girl over by the fence, and I could faintly hear the two of them trading toilet anecdotes.

"So here's the choices," said Amy, "and tell me if I'm wrong. Choice one: You load Gracie into your car and go try to start a new life somewhere. Now, I say that's the kind of thing you could do fifty years ago, before cameras and credit cards and social media, but today, all that happens is you get caught the first time you try to buy gas or go to an ATM."

"Yeah. Like I said, we're fucked."

"Choice two: You go in there and tell your crew that the ritual is off. Say you heard from the prophet or whoever that the conditions aren't right or that you changed your mind, whatever you have to tell them. You give us the Magpie egg, and we'll do the rest. It'll be our problem."

"And then what? I just go back to my life? Go back home to Mom and Dad?"

I said, "We'll make you a deal. You call off this madness, and we'll make sure your dad never hurts you or Gracie. How about that?"

"How?"

"I know we don't look scary to you, but we can be scary when we want to be."

"My dad isn't scared of anybody."

"Bas, *I am guaranteeing you* that he'll never touch her. One way or the other."

"You'd have to kill him."

I shrugged. "If we fail, you can always get back at us later. You know where we all live, and you can cast hexes. Make us all tiny and chase us around with your motorcycle."

"Is there an option three?"

Amy said, "Option three is you complete the ritual. Dark seeds are planted that will sprout and, over time, blot out all light from the sky. You'll live a long life, and maybe Gracie will, too, during which you'll watch the world grow steadily colder and darker and you won't even notice, because by then you'll be so corrupted that you'll be seeing it through inhuman eyes."

Bas sighed. "I don't know if I can stop this thing even if I wanted to. The rest of the guys are coming; they've got the skins. This group, this ritual, it's all they have. If I drop out, they'll just do it without me. They'll feed the Magpie, or the Magpie will make sure it gets fed, one way or the other."

John said, "Again, leave that to us. Whatever the Magpie is, if it comes, it comes. We'll deal with it. This is what we do. Being a teenager means feeling like you're alone; getting older means realizing you never were."

"Even if the help you get isn't remotely what you asked for," I added. "Sometimes you're really hungry and the only thing open is a gas station. But, personally, I think if you stay out of it, the egg will open and nothing will be there. Just a stuffed bird, whatever. I have it on good authority that without you, none of this is anything. All this insanity, this system or spell or whatever that they're collectively calling 'Xarcrax,' it's always been about clearing a path for you. These ten nerds aren't anything; this ritual takes a billion nerds to complete. This is about a movement that will grow to that size a century down the line, and that movement starts with you. Without you, I really think it all just fizzles out."

"Why, though?" asked Bas, suddenly sounding very young. "Why me?"

Amy said, "I don't know if anybody is born a monster, but some people are born with a potential monster inside them. It's not fair, nothing is fair, but you play the cards you're dealt. I have chronic back pain; you have the soul of a tyrant."

John said, "The good news is, you tame that monster and you can put it to work for you. Achieve great things."

Bas scoffed. "What, like become a self-help guru?"

"Yeah. If you want. All we know is that there are certain people who stand out, for whatever reason. The crowd adopts their vibe; people naturally want to imitate it. It's like a superpower. You're probably not gonna save the world, but you can save individual people's worlds, and that's still pretty sweet."

Bas wiped sweat from his face using a shirt that was still soaked from the rain. "They'll be here soon. They're gonna cut the fence right here."

I said, "We know."

"And they have guns. Serious guns. They've been told from the start this is gonna come down to some big *Scarface* standoff."

"We know that, too."

"I'm saying that if I try to back out, if I try to ruin this for them, I don't know what they're gonna do. They may just start shooting. Think about it, man. There are deaths we can be tied to. Cops are everywhere. These guys, their lives are over. It's jail or worse. They've got nothin' to lose. I don't even know what I'd say to them."

"Aren't you their boss? The founder, or whatever? Won't they do what you say?"

"No, they've been around a while. They just decided I was their Chosen One after I joined. But you know what crazy people are like; they flip on you like a switch."

"Again, leave that to us," said John, who once got a casserole recipe so wrong that his kitchen exploded. "And trust me, the legal consequences really are the least of everyone's problems. How do you think we're still walking around free?"

"Well, you're not gonna fix this by giving them all weed, I can tell you that. They're already tripping."

I said, "Do you mean metaphorically, or . . ."

"It's part of the ritual. They have this mushroom tea they make. They all took it around nine thirty, figuring they'd peak right when it all goes down after midnight. I skipped it tonight, but they don't know that."

John said, "Hell, why didn't you say so? They're going to trip in the middle of a stinking facility full of humming machines and huge pipes, with the promise of some kind of monster coming their way? No wonder they're willing to let this thing eat their faces off."

"It's worse than that. They think they have to cut off their faces and give them to the Magpie when it comes out. Like a first feeding. They're ready to do it, man. Or they think they are."

John seemed visibly relieved, for reasons I could not begin to comprehend.

"Are you saying there's a way to offset the effects of the drug?" asked Amy. "An antidote or something?"

"Not a literal antidote," said John, "but if you're asking me how to manipulate the vibe of a small crowd of tripping weirdos, well, that's my specialty."

I said, "Oh, god."

"Now, the big problem with my plan," said John, clearly about to ignore all the actual big problems, "is I assume the Xarcrax club will freak out if they see any of us, right? They know we've been working against you, and they'll think we've turned you to our side. The only one of us whose face they haven't seen is—"

Before John could finish, Joy said, "Yes!" She had appeared six inches away from me at some point, thrusting her fists into the air. "It all comes down to Joy. Suck it, bozos!"

We all hung back from a safe distance and watched as the Simurai arrived. They crouch-walked up to the fence, plainly visible in the moonlight, then struggled badly to hack through the chain link with a pair of small wire cutters that apparently weren't up to the task.

At least one guy seemed to injure himself badly in the attempt. Eventually, they all made it inside, hauling gear that included several rifle cases and three black trash bags that sagged as if containing wads of wet laundry. John watched the last of them fumble through the fence and shook his head.

"Tyler would have never let this happen."

They all headed off into the darkness, in the direction of the three clarifier pools in the dead half of the treatment plant.

Amy said, "Those trash bags. Are they—"

"The skins, yeah," said Bas. "They've started gathering some flies, too."

"Oh, god."

"The last guy through had a black wooden box. That's the egg."

I said, "All right. We're going to go set up. You guys got this?"

Joy said, "You can't think *we're* the weak link in the operation." She turned to Bas. "Let's go save the day, cowboy!"

MONDAY, AUGUST 22, 11:11 P.M.
GINGERBREAD MEN
HUNGER AT 86%

Joy

Joy knew that David squirmed every time he thought about what she "really" was, which was 777 beings functioning in a hive. Humans are like that, or at least the ones she'd run into. The idea of a hive mind terrifies them because, deep down, they love individuality and hate cooperation. The idea that this many beings can unite so perfectly and willfully that it becomes its own beautiful thing is so alien to them that she'd never even try to explain it. David imagines it as an erasure of everything that makes life special, rather than as a kind of love that he can barely comprehend. That each individual human brain essentially operates as a hive, with competing impulses and agendas constantly warring for supremacy, well, that's a conversation they're just not ready to have.

When Joy looked at humans, she saw animals so detached from the food chain that their own boredom was eating them alive. None of their instincts made sense to them; they were primates adorning themselves in skins and shiny things, all swagger and posturing with no idea what it's for. They were grotesque and ridiculous, and she loved them so, so much. They were all doing their best, and their best was just an appalling disaster. That was why she loved the nursing home; the residents were humans stripped of all their pumped-up self-regard, scared and forced to put their whole trust in someone else for the first time since childhood. How could you hate humanity after seeing them in that state, helpless and afraid, watching their strength trickle away? Even the worst of them, when reduced to that, become something that just needs to be fed and bathed and comforted. They begin that way, and they end that way, and you can't really get too mad about the stuff they do in the middle.

Joy and Sebastian approached the ten boys who were busy setting up their ritual next to the big concrete pool of stinkwater. And they *were* just boys, even though one of them was pushing thirty. They all startled at the sight of her, not because there was anything special about her appearance but because they'd been expecting Bas to come alone. And they certainly hadn't expected him to show up with a girl.

They were each wearing belts that, on the right hip, held an ornate ceremonial dagger in a scabbard, all of them having been purchased online. The boys had been working in five pairs, each one with a black marker drawing on the face of his partner, making an outline like a mask around the forehead, cheeks, and chin. As they all turned to face her, Joy forced herself to restrain laughter.

Bas said, "Hey, guys, huddle up. Can you see the woman next to me?"

They all muttered in the affirmative.

"Good. This is the Oracle. She visited me with further instructions and now has made herself visible to all of you. If you have doubts, that's okay; she's not offended. She's happy to show you."

Bas turned to her and nodded, like, "Do your thing."

Joy spread her arms, relaxed, and allowed herself to disperse. She felt wind flowing through her body, swirled herself around the group of boys, and came together behind them, re-forming in an instant, all parts effortlessly embracing in formation without a single bump or shove or tangle of wings. Just for fun, she changed her outfit in their eyes, into a flowing white gown that she figured would stand out in this damp campus of smelly concrete and steel. She threw a little cleavage in there, but not too much. These guys would find the hint of it ten times more intriguing than if she gave away the whole game. She was now looking at the backs of their heads, not all of them having processed the fact that she'd just vanished from their view approximately two seconds ago.

"Do not be afraid," she said from behind them, knowing that human language contains few phrases more unsettling.

One by one they turned and, for the second time, startled at the sight of her.

One skinny kid raised an assault rifle. The barrel shook, like he could hardly bear the weight of it.

Joy smiled. "You can shoot, if you wish. It will not harm me, and I will not hold it against you. It is okay to be fearful. When we do not allow ourselves to show fear, the emotion simply comes back in a much uglier disguise. If that piece of steel and plastic helps you deal with your fear, by all means, use it however you see fit. I would suggest that you instead acknowledge that you are afraid, examine your fear and the reasons for it, and then, once you know it well, simply set it aside. When you have done that, you will find you no longer need your weapon."

Bas said, "Everybody be cool. She's here to help us get to the finish line. She says the vibe isn't quite right yet. You're all too tense and worked up. It's the wrong energy for the first feeding. Leave the egg on the platform and follow us. The Oracle is going to get your mind right."

This, Joy knew, was the pivotal moment. Bas turned and headed back toward the gap in the fence. None of the ten boys took a step in that direction, all of them exchanging looks, suddenly anxious about deviating from what for them was already a terrifying, dark path.

One boy asked, "Where are we going?" He wasn't being aggressive, but clearly had doubts. "We haven't even got the candles set out yet."

Bas said, "Just up the hill, out of the Magpie's sight. That's what I was told. Don't worry about the egg. If anybody tries to touch it, they'll get their heads bitten off."

Another kid said, "But why? Nobody said anything about this."

Bas spun on him, rage flushing his cheeks. Joy didn't think he was acting.

"*Because*," snarled Bas, "I told the prophet we were ready, but the Magpie is detecting doubt. Faithlessness. Some of you, and I'm not gonna say who, are wavering. We can't have that."

Joy knew what Bas sensed, which is that every single one of them had doubts, waves of them, blasting through their blood and bones like electricity.

"Now," said Bas, "I asked if instead of rooting out the faithless, if we could all step away from the ritual site, go off and get ourselves right, as a team, as a family. But we have to do it away from the egg because right now, the Magpie is so disgusted with the doubters that it can't stand the sight of us. You understand now? Will you all come with me? Or do I have to start naming names?"

They let that hang in the air for a moment. Then Bas stomped off, not even looking back to see if he was being followed. Joy smiled, gracefully extended a hand in the direction of the fence, and said, "After you." Then she made brief eye contact with each and every one of the ten boys. One by one, they dropped their eyes, then followed Sebastian.

He led them out through their hole in the fence, then instructed them to get into their vehicles and follow him a couple of miles away, along a rural road that passed through some cornfields and then snaked up a hill to a spot next to the town's water tower. When Joy joined them at their destination, she did her costume change trick once again, now in a short red skirt and top under a black trench coat. The boys were, once again, amazed.

They had chosen this spot because it was the highest point. All of Undisclosed stretched out below them. A campfire was burning. The plan had called for a "bonfire," but John, Dave, and Amy had apparently not had time to build something on that scale, or maybe they'd just struggled lighting whatever damp wood they'd found (it appeared they had wound up smashing and burning several items from John's van, including a broken boat paddle, a pair of wooden Dutch clogs, a framed painting of a woman having sex with a squid, an entire rocking chair, and at least a dozen copies of John's self-published book of erotic poetry, *Welcome to the Hog Storm*). The plan had also been to surround the fire with blankets for everyone to sit on, but apparently, the van had contained only one blanket, one beach towel, one sheet of some kind of reflective foil, and a black trash bag. They'd been placed around the fire in a semicircle so that viewable beyond it would be the lights of the town.

Bas said, "All right, guys, gather over here."

One kid, an overweight boy with bad posture and cheeks scarred by acne, said, "I'm not doubting, Bas, I'm not a doubter, you know that, but, uh, do we have time for this?"

Bas struggled for an answer, but Joy stepped in. "Bernie," she said, because it always freaks them out when you know their names, "time is like happiness. The moment you start thinking about it, it fades away."

Joy hadn't known how that sentence was going to end when she'd started it, but she was fairly pleased with how it'd turned out. She examined the boy closely. What she saw in his eyes was starvation. Outside of doctor visits, horseplay, and attacks from bullies, he'd not physically touched another human in seven years. He lay in bed at night and fantasized, not about sex but cuddling. He was terrified of actual sexual contact with a woman—afraid of embarrassing himself, disgusted by his own body. As a result, all his masturbation scenarios were unfulfillable fantasies, perfect girls who were enslaved or brainwashed, if not literal cartoons. He was a ball of unfulfilled desire that had congealed into a black sludge of bitter narcissism and petty rage.

Joy stepped toward him. She reached out and lay a hand on his cheek. He flinched, but then let her. She sensed his heart skip a beat when he felt how soft her skin was. Even though she was creating the sensation herself, she knew how to mimic the feeling down to the molecule. That was the part he could never build into his fantasies, the feel of the skin. Her warm palm on his cheek was the greatest moment of his life, she saw it in his eyes. He never wanted the moment to end. It wasn't just the hand but the aura behind it, the sense that Joy did not find him disgusting. This part was not a performance. She felt pity, mourned for the loss of the good man he could have been.

She took away her hand, then hugged him. He initially froze—not even his own mother did this; his wasn't a hugging family. But then he gave himself to it, squeezed her back, and smelled her hair.

Joy put her lips to his ear and in a whisper as gentle as a kitten yawn, said, "All you ever wanted was for no one to ever have to feel the way you were made to feel."

Slowly, she backed away. For a moment, she thought the boy wouldn't keep his feet, but he did. She gestured to the blanket/towel/trash bag around the fire.

"Please, sit, sit. As many of you as can fit on each mat. Sit so that you are looking out over the city, at the streetlights, at all of the people tucked away in their homes. And I want each of you to hold hands with the person next to you. Good. You two—hold hands. Good. Scoot closer together. Don't be afraid. These are your brothers. They're ready to die for you. We must harness that energy right now. Breathe in, deep breaths, slowly. Taste the air. Don't talk, don't think, don't look at your watches or the clocks on your phones—we have all the time we need, time obeys *us* now. Let go. Let yourself drift free from time. Use all of your senses and feel what is happening around you. The world, the brotherhood."

They sat in silence around the crackle of the fire. It was apparent now that John had included some dried sage to add a slight ceremonial spice to the air. Then, from somewhere in the darkness behind them, came the soft strum of a guitar, then a gentle drum. Then, an echoey voice gently reassuring them that he'd never meant to cause them any sorrow or pain. It was Prince, via John's van stereo in some unseen spot in the distance, stating his aching desire to see the world bathe in his purple rain.

Joy said, "Can you hear the music?"

They all nodded.

"Can you *see* the music? Allow yourself to see it."

None answered either way, but their mesmerized expressions answered for her. John had said he didn't know exactly what fungus they'd used in their tea, if it was even something from this world, but he was putting his faith once again in the music, in allowing the power of song to flow through their elevated sense of consciousness. It appeared in this moment that he had been right. Whether they could see it or merely feel it, they were all bathing in the purple rain. They lay immersed in the music, soaking in it. By the time the iconic guitar licks kicked in halfway through, none of the ten boys seemed to remember what planet he was on. They were in a world of music, of life and light and fire and the faint spice of the smoke.

And then the guitar took on a different tone, became closer, realer. Into view stepped a man playing a guitar that was covered in thick black fur, wearing a mask of chiseled black stone, a vest of human foreskins, a winged speedo like the one Sting wore in *Dune*, thigh-high leather boots, and nothing else. He played out the guitar and vocalizations from "Purple Rain" for several minutes after the song ended, fading it out as he slowly backed away from the camp, the music easing gently into the distance like a mother's hands withdrawn from an infant that has finally surrendered to sleep.

Silence fell over all of them like a blanket.

Joy said, "Now lie back. All of you. Say nothing. Release the hand you have been holding. Look up at the stars, and listen to the music of the world. The crackle of the fire, the breathing of the person next to you, the breeze through your ears. Time means nothing. This moment is ours, for as long as we want it. But listen to what I am about to say, because it is the most important instruction you will ever receive, in this life or the next. The fate of your eternal being depends on it.

"If, while you listen to the melody of the silence, you feel like there is somewhere else you should be, if there is someone you never had the chance to say goodbye to, someone you'd like to see one more time, you have the permission to leave. You are released from your obligation to Xarcrax without recrimination or loss of privilege. This is not a trick or a test. You have served well, and your reward will be great. But you cannot leave business undone. You cannot proceed past this point with lingering ties to this world. Now, I will be silent. So will you. If any of your brothers rises to leave this place, you will not speak, you will not try to stop them. If they leave, it only means they were always destined to. In doing so, they are showing more bravery than any they have shown so far. If none of you choose to leave, it will be a profound disappointment, because it will mean some of you are not capable of following your truth."

Five minutes of silence passed, but none had left. Joy waited.

Fifteen minutes.

Thirty.

Joy, making no noise whatsoever as she passed over the grass—she could do that—went to the heavy boy she had embraced earlier, kneeled beside him, and put a hand on his shoulder.

She leaned over so that, once more, her mouth was all but touching his right ear. "You will meet her in three years," she whispered. "But only if you turn yourself into the man worthy of her. Go. Shed the skin they forced you to wear."

The boy considered, then stood, then walked away, back toward the lane. Then he ran, as fast as he could.

A moment later, another boy joined him.

Me

I sat with Amy and Gracie on the rear bumper of the van, parked on a narrow gravel lane in between dense green walls of cornstalks. John had finished the "Purple Rain" guitar solo a while ago, and at this point, all we could do was wait.

Gracie whispered, "I don't understand what's happening."

I said, "If you intend to keep living here, you'll just have to get used to that feeling."

Amy said, "Well, I actually don't understand why John had to be there in person."

"I think he just wanted to be close by in case Joy messed it up or Bas changed his mind."

"What would he have done, if so?"

"I don't know. All I can say is that John has this steadfast belief that he can just guitar his way out of any disaster scenario. He keeps one by his bed."

"But what if the music hadn't—"

"The cops are coming!" yelled Gracie. She'd jumped to her feet and was pointing. "A bunch of them. Is that bad? All the boys smell like drugs."

Sirens were wailing in the distance, and she was right: It was a lot of them. It was impossible to tell from which direction the sound was coming, but it didn't take a genius to figure out where they were heading. We scrambled to get into the van. Whatever was about to happen when it came time for the egg to open, if anything, we needed to be there when it did. We had to protect the cops from it, if nothing else.

By the time I'd driven back to the poop improvement plant, there was a SWAT van and probably all of the city's cop cars parked at the main gate. I suspected if we tried to enter that way that we wouldn't be allowed in, so we drove back toward the Simurai's hole in the fence.

As we slowed to a stop, I told Amy, "Take Gracie and keep her out of sight for the moment, over in those trees, wherever. Text John and tell him where you are. Everyone can come meet you there. I'll go in and try to explain to the cops what's going on. If they show up at the spot with their guns ready and see us standing there with Gracie, they may decide we're keeping her hostage and just headshot us all."

"Why don't you watch Gracie and let me go in?"

"You know why. If something does emerge from the egg, if it tries to force the issue even without Bas, there's a good chance that it will be visible to me but not you. Otherwise, yeah, I'd agree that you're more suited to talk down a pack of trigger-happy agents of the state."

Amy said to Gracie, "It's better out here anyway. It doesn't stink quite as bad."

Gracie asked, "Are we going to jail?"

I said, "No," but didn't clarify that I did think the chances of us all getting perforated by bullets were still extremely high. The last time I reached this point, the ground was a carpet of corpses.

I crawled in through the fence and made my way to the middle concrete pool. I found the array of ritual gear the Simurai had left here earlier, including three plastic bags swarming with flies, a bunch of unlit black candles, and a few gun cases from the kids who'd left theirs behind. The Magpie egg was still sitting on the maintenance platform at the center of the rusty catwalk that bisected the pool, unchanged. I heard approaching voices and tried to assume the least threatening posture I knew. Several members of a SWAT team showed up first, six or seven of them. I guess they acted as the tip of the spear since they had the most armor. Then I noticed that in the distance, pinpricks of headlights were heading down the same road the cops had just traveled.

Spectators. Word, it seemed, had gotten out.

The SWAT guy nearest me made what I presumed was eye contact through his tinted visor. Instead of waiting for him to ask, I just went ahead and lay down in the wet grass, my hands in the air as high as I could hold them.

I said, "Everybody be calm! We've found the little girl—she's safe. Her brother, too. Everything is fine! It was all a misunderstanding!"

SWAT guy kept his assault rifle trained on me. I don't know how many AR-15s I'd had pointed at me over the years, but it's a lot. This was one of the better ones; they'd gone with the vertical grip on the front, holographic sites.

"WHERE IS SHE?!?" he yelled.

"Close. She's going to go meet up with her brother. My girlfriend is with them. They'll be here in a moment. Everything is fine. We fixed it."

He flipped up his visor and pulled down the black cloth mask that had been covering the rest of his face. He had a bushy Lemmy Kilmister mustache-sideburns combo and the expression of a kid who's just reached the front of a six-hour line to get onto a ride at Disney World.

"We heard there was a huge monster coming," said Lemmy the SWAT Cop. "Sometime after midnight, right? Did we miss it?"

"Some kids were trying something like that, but we talked them out of it. Sort of. It's over, is the point."

"Are you sure? What about all these candles? Should we light them?"

"The good news," I said, "is that we've also solved the disappearance of your missing detective, police officer, and security guard. See those trash bags? They're full of the remains of the three victims. Specifically, their skins. A DNA test or whatever should confirm it's them. I guess I shouldn't have phrased that as *good* news, but you know what I mean."

I could hear other cops farther back yelling at the spectators who'd apparently shown up. It wouldn't work. If they couldn't get through the front gate, they'd just encircle the facility and find another way in, just like we had. The professional monster enthusiasts would happily deal with a trespassing charge if it meant livestreamed video of a demonic summoning and/or a child sacrifice. A spot on the speaking circuit, book deals, podcasts, a chance to host their own show—that silly little fence wasn't going to stand between them and a place on the paranormal expert gravy train. Meanwhile, by now, word would have made it back to town that exciting events were happening at the crap carnival, so we'd also be getting locals who'd always wanted to see something freaky up close. Everybody here wants their own anecdote. I mean, if you run into somebody from Loch Ness, what's the first question you ask them?

The rest of the SWAT guys were sweeping the area with their gun barrels, I guess to see if I was just acting as bait for an ambush. I heard one on his radio talking to a street cop over at the gate, learning that this spot was about to be overwhelmed with rubberneckers. Meanwhile, Lemmy moved slowly toward the nearest trash bag. He prodded it with the barrel of his AR-15—it had a fancy side-vented muzzle brake on the end—then pulled open a flap.

Still lying in the damp grass, I said, "Dude, isn't that evidence or something? Aren't you contaminating it for the CSI people?"

"There's nothin' in here." He checked the other two bags, kicking them open with his boot. He was about to ask me about them, then heard a noise and spun, raising his assault rifle to a spot on my left.

I heard John say, "Don't shoot! We've got Gracie! She's fine, everybody is fine!"

Bas was walking hand in hand with Gracie. John, Amy, and Joy were behind them, all three with their hands up. They were supposed to have waited for some kind of all clear from me before approaching, but apparently somebody had overruled me on that.

Joy said, "Any other crises you need solved? Line 'em up!"

I said, "Bas, the human remains of the detective and the rest that you guys, uh, found, where are they?"

"In those bags."

"Not anym—"

"YUMMY! THANK YOU, MOMMY, I WUV YOUUUU!!!"

Every gun barrel in the vicinity whipped toward the toy egg sitting unattended on the platform.

John stepped forward, put his hands over Gracie's ears, and said, "Oh, kiss my fucking shit."

Amy said, "What happened? Did it get the final meal? How?"

I said, "I don't know! Bas, get Gracie away from here!"

The egg clicked, cracking open just a bit.

Gracie screamed. I saw Bas start to hustle her away, but he didn't seem to know in which direction safety could be found, if it could be found at all. I was reminded of Amy's dilemma in her nightmare.

Lemmy said, "What is that thing? An egg?"

Nobody seemed to care about me anymore, so I went ahead and stood up. "Uh, everybody remain calm. It's not a real egg; it's just a plastic toy. But it's also kind of a real egg. But maybe not."

The egg was in that first stage of the opening process, with a quarter-inch gap so you could just see inside, if you were close enough. I imagined little kids all around the world trying to peer in to see if their Magpie had gold wings. Its spot at the center of the pool was fifty feet from all of us, and it was dark, so nobody had any kind of preview of what was to come.

There was another small click, and the shell jumped, some spring-loaded mechanism inside opening the egg a little more. In a movie, this is where everybody would cock their guns, but that's kind of not how automatic weapons work—these rifles were as cocked as they could get before they'd even arrived at the scene. Voices were muttering from behind us, and I saw an undulating constellation of camera and cell phone lights moving between the pump houses. The oncoming monster tourists had sensed something awesome was about to happen and were picking up the pace.

I said to the SWAT cops, "Don't bother shooting the egg. If it's nothing, you'll just be sending stray bullets into the countryside. If it's something they've summoned, bullets probably won't even leave a mark."

"WHAT IS THAT?!?" yelled one of the SWAT cops. "LISTEN! EVERYBODY, SHUT UP AND LISTEN!"

The egg was chirping. It was a recorded sound from the little speaker inside, singing "Happy Birthday" in birdsong. Some tourists had arrived with their cameras now. Lenses and gunsights focused on the hunk of white and green polka-dotted plastic. No one said a word.

The egg finished its song. The shell clicked one final time, springing open fully, like a flower in bloom. Whatever was inside was now fully exposed. Several people trained flashlight beams on the platform, spotlighting the egg like it was about to sing the national anthem before a basketball game.

A small stuffed bird sat silently in the center of the open shell.

Then, with perfect comic timing, it flopped over and rolled off onto the metal platform.

Trying not to make any abrupt movements, I made my way around the pool to the metal stairs and mounted the catwalk. I reached the platform at the center and picked up the stuffed bird. I tossed it across the pool to Lemmy, who took one hand off his rifle to catch it.

"See?" I said, "Just a toy." I looked toward Gracie and said, "It's got some reflective gold trim along its feathers. That's the rarest, right?"

Gracie barely raised both fists and, in a deadpan tone, said, "Woohoo."

Amy let out an exaggerated breath and ran her hand through her hair. "Does that mean we did it? Is it over?"

"For you, maybe," said Lemmy. He turned his gun to his left and said, "Bas Galveston. You are under—"

John shouted, "Look!"

He was at the lip of the pool, and I already knew what he had seen: blackness oozing purposefully into the fetid water like a sentient oil spill. Several of the SWAT cops ran to the edge so they could get a look, thrilled that something was finally happening. A few of them were aiming their guns like they were expecting to see sharks swarming in there.

"What is that?" asked one of the cops, watching the black streams zipping quickly into the water. "Are they snakes? It looks like hundreds of snakes—"

"It's the tarry, hot semen from the balls of Satan himself," said John. "We call it Arby's Sauce."

"Back away from it!" I shouted before Amy could correct him. "That stuff is toxic in ways you wouldn't believe. Don't breathe it, don't look at it, don't listen to it. And for the love of god, don't get within grabbing distance of it."

I sprinted along the catwalk toward the stairs, leading by example. "Grabbing distance?" asked Lemmy. "What are you—"

Another cop started yelling and fired six shots into the pool.

"Hands!" he was shouting. "There's black hands coming out of it!"

Someone else fired. I ducked at the noise and jumped down to the grass. "Get back!" I shouted, flailing my arms to demonstrate what direction "back" was. "Back! Back! Shooting it won't do shit! You, get back! You, too!"

Incredibly, some of the cops acted on my advice. Or maybe they just saw hundreds of grasping oil-black hands rising from the pool of unthinkable filth and decided they probably couldn't arrest them. Meanwhile, the spectators who were near enough to hear the commotion edged closer to get a better view.

"Look!" said John again. "The egg! Something's coming out!" His tone implied he was relieved we weren't disappointing the people who'd taken the trouble to be here tonight.

Several flashlights flicked up to the platform once more. The egg play set was now just a plastic nest with a pair of white shell pieces lying flat on either side. Something was crawling up from the base. Amy had been right, of course—inside the toy had been a portal to god knows where and, ritual or no ritual, something was coming through.

Amy yelled to the cop closest to her, "You have to get the people away!"

I agreed with her, but had no idea how this would be accomplished short of just shooting several of the bystanders to start a stampede. The SWAT team, meanwhile, was focused entirely on the creature being birthed on the platform, eager to have something tangible to train their sights on. I could only make out a shape, something smooth and hard and dark, followed by writhing appendages. When it emerged fully, it was maybe the size of an expensive crab.

But then, it grew. The SWAT members held their fire, like they were waiting for its final form before taking it down. The creature rose as if being inflated, reaching a height of six feet or so, growing a pair of appendages on each side like arms. Its bottom half separated into a pair of legs.

Sebastian, a look of dread and anticipation on his face, stepped forward toward the pool, putting his body in front of Gracie.

"Of course," said Bas softly, watching the horror he'd helped birth into our universe. "We summoned the most terrifying creature of all: *man*."

Several cops groaned in disappointment.

Lemmy said, "Oh, come on! That is bullshit!"

Joy yelled, "Boooo! Boooooooooooo!!!"

John said, "Hold on! It's probably going to turn into something else! Just be patient, goddamn it!"

The newly born figure on the platform caught just enough light for me to get a glimpse. It was a man; he just looked like any regular, droopy middle-aged guy. Then I saw his face.

I know that guy.

"That's him!" said Lemmy. "The missing security guard! Lou! Hey! Are you okay?"

Amy said, "Lou? Oh! Lou!"

I said, "Who the fuck is Lou?"

"The guy!" said John. "From the Fourth! Had the thing on his head!"

He was right. And there was Eve, perched at the top of him. Not sucking on his brain, as we now knew, but inflating the man below it using a skin it had stolen earlier this very day.

While we all gawked at him, Lou took a step back from the egg. A column of those black hands then reached up from below, twisting themselves into a single shape that swallowed up the platform. For some reason, this is what finally convinced the cops to start shooting. Gracie screamed at the roar of gunshots splitting the air. Some of the onlookers hit the deck.

I yelled, "STOP! STOP! I know for a fact that you're not going to kill that guy! Don't ask me how I know!"

Nobody could hear me. Amy had put Gracie on the ground and thrown herself on top, though I couldn't imagine Amy's body preventing a high-velocity 5.56 millimeter rifle round from punching through her body and Gracie's both. On the platform, the black shapes were writhing and twisting and merging, forming a black knot, all the Sauce in the pool collecting to one form and purpose.

John shouted, "Look! It's fucking a hole in the space-time continuum!"

Some of the SWAT guys stopped shooting, as if that was the reasonable response to what John had just said. The swirling knot of blackness was smoothing itself into a perfect sphere, at least eight feet in diameter, as if huge invisible hands were sculpting it like a snowball. Lou turned, made eye contact with me, waved, then walked into the sphere, which swallowed him whole. As he passed through the surface, there was a sort of disturbance or ripple across the sphere, and in that moment of interference, I could see into it, like a crystal ball. I saw a distorted view of Amy, answering the door of my apartment. Then I faintly heard Lou say, "Sorry to bother you, miss, but the cops just dropped me off and I don't know what in the hell is going on . . ."

The sphere vanished with a faint *thwap*, like a child's hand slapping a clown's bare thigh. This was followed by the dead silence of now dozens of people who also, in fact, did not know what in the hell was going on. Everyone had stopped shooting, some of the cops taking this opportunity to reload for whatever came next. But the open Magpie egg, now truly spent, just sat innocently on the platform. An inert hunk of plastic.

"Where did he go?" asked Lemmy.

I waved him off. "He's gone. He traveled back in time; it's a whole thing. Don't ask me to explain anything time travel–related; I'll just get mad."

Amy was helping brush grass off of Gracie. Bas asked her if she was all right, then sat down next to her, as if exhausted.

Bas said, "I don't think I understand."

John said, "I'm also confused."

Amy said, "According to the book, the prophet is going to be reborn from 'a jewel in the earth.' They're talking about your resin cube, the one we trapped Eve inside, the one that wound up in the river after Ricardo ran off the road. They're going to find it in 2112, crack it open, and then Eve is going to inflate a guy, and he'll claim to be the prophet reborn. Everything on the Fourth, selling the doll, all of that, everything we did, was orchestrated by Xarcrax to fulfill that prophecy."

I said, "Wait, did the prophecy come first, or did Xarcrax see how the Fourth of July thing played out and then write the prophecy around it, so that it would appear to be predestined?"

"And is everyone still doomed?" asked John, which probably was the more relevant question.

I thought I knew the answer, which was that it wasn't up to us to break this causal time loop situation. Only Sebastian could do it, and for whatever reason, we were still on track to get the bad ending.

"That black oil is gone," said Lemmy, ignoring us and peering into the scummy water. "Where did it go? Is that stuff in the water supply? What *is happening?!?*"

We had no good answer for him. I faced the tourists, each marked by a twinkle of light attached to a recording device.

"Show's over," I said, knowing that apparently wasn't true. "Nothing to see here. Just go—"

I was interrupted by an electronic buzz, like this was a quiz show and whatever I was about to say was declared the wrong answer in advance. It was emanating from all around us, from every cop's radio. It was some kind of alert, a much angrier and shriller version of that obnoxious Amber Alert noise I can never figure out how to get off my phone.

Lemmy pulled his radio off his belt, looking confused and alarmed by the noise. The SWAT members were exchanging glances. It was like they knew what the alarm technically meant but hadn't expected to ever actually hear it.

John asked, "What the hell is that?"

Lemmy held up a hand to silence him. The buzzing ended and a stern-sounding female voice took over, playing like a chorus from all directions at once:

"Attention all units. A Class Omega emergency has been declared. This means they are going to destroy the fucking town as soon as the satellite can be armed and fired. I repeat: Get the fuck out of there. This will be the last announcement. We're all leaving. Holy fucking shit. Over."

Another SWAT cop asked Lemmy, "Is that real? The Class Omega thing? I remember it from training but always thought they were just messing with us."

Instead of answering, Lemmy turned to the bystanders. "Listen up, everybody! You know how in some zombie movies, the government just blows up the whole town to stop the outbreak? And how they've tried to do that here at least once before? It's happening now! Again! The fire order has been given! We're getting the fuck out of here! You've got just a few minutes until impact! I don't even know! Good luck!"

Amy said, "Well, tell them to call it off! We stopped the summoning! It's over!"

"Look!"

I don't even know who said it, but it wasn't necessary anyway. The area was being lit from a bright speck in the sky. Apparently we hadn't gotten quite as much warning this time around. I heard terrified gasps from behind us.

Thor was coming.

I yelled, "What are we going to do?!?"

Amy hurried over to Bas. "Can you teleport everyone out of here?"

"No!" he said. "There's too many! I could do me and Gracie and maybe one more."

"Then get Gracie out of here! At least save her. The rest of us will just run for it."

I didn't think even the most athletic person here could run to a safe distance, not if the Time Captain had been right about the destructive power of this thing. I heard that familiar air-rending roar from above. I tried to remember how much time we'd had last time, once it'd reached this point. One minute? Less?

"No!" yelled Gracie, in the angriest little-girl voice she could manage. "We're not going! Bas, send it away. Make a hole down here and just . . . get rid of it."

"How?" he asked, staring up at the doomsday projectile. "And where do I send it? It'll just blow up something else."

I said, "Outer space?"

"I can't do outer space! Not without help."

The object was now too bright to look at directly. I swore I could already feel the heat.

I said, "Then send it to Siberia or something. Siberia a hundred years from now. Or a hundred years ago. Can you do that?"

His expression said he had no idea if he could or not. Still, Sebastian ran up to the pool. He did some wizard moves with his hands, working frantically, muttering alien words I couldn't make out. Gracie watched him with a look of apprehensive pride, like she was rooting for him to make title-winning free throws in a game in which he'd already scored forty. Like the rest of us were about to see him do what he did best.

I could feel the swirling energy in the air, making the hairs on my arms stand up on end. The effect of the spell was barely visible, just a weird little ripple hovering in space directly above the pool where the egg had been. Bas was trembling with the effort, like he was being asked to hold a burning car aloft while a dwarf whaled on his nuts. He fell to his knees, still verbalizing the spell, spittle flying out with each word as he strained to channel the immense power through his body. One leg of his pants turned dark as his bladder let go. Blood oozed from his nose.

The rift fluctuated and blinked, fading in and out of reality. I sensed that if the Thor projectile struck while Bas's spell was waning, that it'd smash right past it, impact the pool below, and vaporize all of us before we even felt the shock wave.

The projectile streaked down. Everything was heat and light and a noise like the entire planet had been dropped into God's coffee grinder. Then, instead of detonating with the force of a large nuke, the white-hot, telephone pole–size rod passed through the portal Bas had created and blinked out of view.

Instantly, the sound dissipated, the displaced air washing over us like a hot wind, strong enough that it pushed some bystanders to the ground.

But that was it.

Bas collapsed as if he'd taken a sniper round to the skull. I ran toward him.

The boy was not moving or breathing. When I arrived, I saw blood streaming across his cheeks.

From behind me, I heard Lemmy ask, "Was . . . was that it? Was that the satellite thing?"

Amy came and joined me in kneeling over Sebastian. The tourists were starting to draw in again. The ones in back had presumably never been clear on the danger at all; they just heard some people shouting and briefly saw a bright flash. I could hear them back there asking each other what happened, what had they missed.

John and Joy arrived, all of us gathered around Bas's body. We exchanged looks, no one sure what to say. We just stood over him, and I think we all had the same thought, that maybe this was, in fact, the only way the Xarcrax cycle could have ever been stopped, that this is how it had to be. This worldwide spell with all its millions of components was like a piece of supernatural software, and maybe the only thing that stops it from running is deleting a particular line of code. But in that moment, I couldn't escape noticing that the apparent linchpin of the apocalypse just looked like a dead seventeen-year-old boy.

I glanced at John, had a sudden flashback, and thought, *At least Sebastian got his big hero moment at the end. And what were his last words? Oh, right. "Not without help."*

John lit a cigarette and said, "He could have gotten himself to safety, easily. He had that power. Instead, he used it to save all of us. And nobody out in the world will ever know."

He was talking to Gracie, I think, but she wasn't listening. She stepped right past John and nudged Bas with her foot.

"Hey. Get up."

Amy said, "Honey, he's gone."

"Hey. Sebastian the Crab. Get up."

I said, "All that power. It felt like I was standing next to lightning that just kept striking and striking. It was too much for him. I think something just popped in his brain."

"What, because his nose is bleeding?" said Gracie, annoyed. "He gets nosebleeds all the time. He gets them when he thinks too hard about algebra. Get up, dork."

Bas lay there, lifeless, the crowd around us having again gone dead silent. How do you explain it to her?

"HEY!" Gracie screamed.

Everyone flinched.

Including Bas.

His eyes blinked open. He felt the wetness on his cheek and wiped at the blood. He noticed his piss-soaked jeans and let out a disgusted grunt.

In a raspy voice, he asked, "Did it work?"

"No," said Gracie, "we're all smushed. The whole town. It all blew up. Stop being dramatic and get up."

Gracie pulled him to his feet. Amy gasped with relief, chuckling a little to herself.

"Okay," she said, "*now* it's over."

I said, "What he just did would have killed any normal man. But he withstood it, thanks to the electrolytes and four hundred milligrams of caffeine in Fight Piss energy drink."

Lemmy found the collector's edition Magpie on the ground and kicked it. The toy bounced off the concrete wall of the clarifier pool, rolling to a rest in the damp grass next to a scatter of spent shell casings. The tourists behind us were muttering to each other, now browsing around the area for something interesting to film.

"No," said Lemmy. "That can't be it. That sucked! We didn't even get to do anything!"

Amy stood, brushing grass off of her knees. "What, because you didn't get to kill a monster? When this is done right, it never comes to that. I'm sorry to disappoint y—"

John

"SHUT THE FUCK UP!" said Gracie. "LOOK! THE BIRD!"

All eyes shifted to the discarded stuffed Magpie on the ground. John spun toward it, fists at the ready.

The bird was twitching.

No—its wings were flapping.

The Magpie was, in fact, alive.

"LOOK!" said the SWAT cop who had the facial hair of Civil War general Ambrose Burnside. "IT'S A GENUINE HAUNTED TOY! KILL IT!"

He pulled out a sidearm and pumped bullets into the ground, missing the tiny stuffed bird entirely. The toy righted itself, testing its wings. Its stuffed head turned from side to side as if surveying the strange world it had just been born into. Other cops gathered around and opened fire, pummeling the grass around the toy and sending hunks of moist dirt into the air.

"HOLD YOUR FIRE!" said Burnside the SWAT Cop. "I think we got it!"

It appeared the bird had stopped moving. John, however, wasn't convinced.

John said, "Joy, go get the—"

"SHIT!" said Burnside. "IT'S STILL ALIVE!"

The bird, now riddled with bullet holes and bleeding wads of white stuffing, once again righted itself and flapped its wings. A couple of bystanders saw it and drew closer, including a group of college kids with a camera and strong portable lights, probably pros doing a livestream. More tourists were flocking in behind them, hoping to salvage some usable video from this fiasco.

The Magpie, flapping its tiny, battered wings, rose a few feet into the air. Everyone gasped. It flew higher and higher, reaching an altitude of about twenty feet.

Amy said, "Everybody calm down. We don't even know if it's dangerous."

With a shriek, the stuffed bird tore itself apart in midair. Something was erupting from within. Vast dark wings unfurled from the sides of the plush animal, wicked talons sprouted from below, a serrated beak burst from the top. The surface of the newly born monster was squirming and rippling. In the wings, John saw rotting rats and tiny flopping fish skeletons, as if the creature was constructed from every pet that had ever been flushed down a toilet and every rodent that had ever drowned in sewer water. Before their eyes, the bird grew to the size of an eagle, then a pterodactyl, then a single-engine airplane.

The bystanders' and SWAT cops' reaction to this was total indifference. The shredded remains of the original Magpie toy fell to the grass, and the eyes of the gawkers followed it down.

"It's dead," said somebody, totally oblivious to the giant-and-still-growing monstrosity spreading its wings overhead, now blotting out half of the stars from John's view.

John found Dave in the crowd, and without a word from John, Dave said, "They can't see it!"

"See what?" asked Burnside.

Above him, the Magpie grew and grew. Its serrated beak was now long enough to bite a car in half.

"It doesn't matter!" shouted John to Burnside and everyone else. "Run! Now! There's, uh, another projectile coming! This is all gonna blow!"

If the bystanders heard John, they apparently didn't believe him. Amy made her way over, probably reacting to John's and Dave's panic rather than the presence of the bird. She was probably just about to ask what it was that she couldn't see up there, when everyone flinched and clutched their ears. The Magpie had opened its massive beak and emitted that same psychic cry that had debilitated John and his crew when it was still in the egg. The bystanders who couldn't see the creature, it seemed, could definitely receive that terrible screech in their skulls.

The Magpie, now the size of a Learjet, lowered its head to scan the crowd. It cried out again, then reached out with a set of black talons big enough to palm an elephant. It went right for Officer Burnside, aiming for his midsection. The man had no idea what was coming.

With two massive claws, the Magpie reached out and snatched with them, just to the side of the man's hip. John initially thought the creature had missed in its attempt to disembowel its victim, but then it pulled back, and John saw what it had pinched between those two talons.

"Watch out!" shouted John. "It's got a gun!"

The Magpie began firing wildly into the crowd. One tourist took a bullet to the chest. A SWAT cop was shot in the thigh. The other cops, still unable to see the Magpie itself, fired at whatever poltergeist was holding the stolen Glock. Handfuls of undead mice and fish flew off with each impact; otherwise, the Magpie didn't seem to mind.

The monster reached down with its other foot and grabbed the tourist who'd just been shot. With one quick snip of its massive beak, it bit off the girl's face. It then screeched with a volume that shook the ground, flapped its wings, and then faded from sight, becoming just as invisible to John as it had been to everyone else. All that he could see was the hovering handgun and—just as with Swallow—the severed face sliding down its gullet.

The disembodied face, somehow, was still screaming.

Gunfire roared, the entire SWAT team and at least two armed bystanders shooting at the space in front of them that, to their eyes, was now just a floating screaming face and, twenty feet below it, a hovering semiautomatic pistol. The Magpie apparently responded by picking up three more people in the crowd and snipping off each of their faces like they were the tips of new cigars (that's only "apparently" what happened because from John's viewpoint, three screaming people floated into the air before each of their faces peeled themselves off from their skulls—it's not 100 percent certain that something unrelated hadn't caused this to happen). Regardless, the end result was a quartet of howling, disembodied faces now swirling around the air, inside the Magpie's invisible belly.

That, at least, solved the problem of the crowd refusing to evacuate. Everyone was in a full stampede now, including the SWAT team. Everyone was sprinting in the same direction: toward the main gate, where all the vehicles were parked. The swirling bundle of screaming faces floated along with the crowd, the invisible Magpie having no problem whatsoever keeping up. Hell, the thing was being kept aloft by magick; for all John knew, the bastard could zip along at the speed of light if it wanted.

Another tourist, an old man, got snatched into the air. Two seconds later, his body landed on the grass, his face a bloody half-eaten lasagna.

Amy ran up and yelled, "We need to occupy it so everyone can get away!"

Dave responded by running back toward the bird. "Hey!" he shouted to the space where he assumed the creature was. "It's us! It's John and Dave! We're the face versions of collectors' items! Forget those people, take us! But not Amy—we fired her! She sucks!"

They had no way of knowing what the Magpie's reaction to this was, if any. John sensed movement, a shifting of the wind or maybe just the hateful psychic energy that radiated from the creature. Whatever it was, John felt it brush past him. And then there was a scream.

A child's scream.

It was Gracie.

Bas was right next to her, but could see only that Gracie was in distress, was being squeezed by something invisible to him, as if the sulfur stink in the air had somehow solidified and gone on a rampage. Amy ran over with the intent of grabbing the little girl and pulling her away. She found her path obstructed by invisible talons, trying in vain to pry the child loose. John and Dave both ran in that direction, John with his obsidian dagger at the ready. The Magpie snatched both of them with its other foot, an invisible curl of squirming dead things squeezing him and Dave together and lifting them into the air.

Dave said, "If it swallows our faces, let's just chew our way out!"

John could think of at least three flaws in that plan. The Magpie was pulling Gracie toward its maw first; it fed on pain and must have instinctively known that was the most dickish thing to do.

There were gunshots from below. Bullets whizzed past. Bas had collected one of the cult's discarded rifles from the grass and was firing it at the Magpie in a fit of blind rage. It had no effect. Even from his spot suspended in the air, John could read the boy's expression, his realization that he was too late. His change of heart, his attempt to redeem himself from the dark side—it wasn't going to matter. The horror he'd set into motion was too far gone. Now Gracie was going to pay for it and, after her, the whole world. Bas presumably had not known prior to today that a single human being could fuck up this hard, but John could have told him, if he'd asked.

At the exact moment when it all seemed the most hopeless, John spotted a flash of flesh tone out of the corner of his eye, plowing their direction. It was the Anal Massage van, roaring between the pump houses and rumbling against the current of fleeing tourists, their bodies lunging aside like toppled bowling pins.

The van ran full speed toward the Magpie, braked, and spun around in the grass. The rear doors flew open, and out from inside came a spray of tiny, flailing figures.

A flock of twenty haunted, positive-energy dolls flew across the night air and attached themselves to the Magpie like a swarm of angry bees. The Magpie shrieked and dropped all three of its prizes to the grass below. John thumped onto the ground and felt the crack of broken ribs.

Joy jumped out of the van and ran to where he and Dave had landed. "That won't hold it long!" she said, "Get in! We'll hit it with the music!"

They didn't need to be asked twice. Not eager to get snatched up by the monster's talons again, Gracie sprinted toward the side door of the van. Amy headed for the passenger seat. John headed for the driver's door, only to be shoved aside at the last moment by Joy.

She pushed her way in and said, "Get in the back! You never let me drive!"

"You drove us here! And do you even know how to work the stereo?"

"John," she said, placing a hand on each of his shoulders, "*I am more competent than you.*"

She got behind the wheel, and John headed for the side door, where he encountered Sebastian, climbing in ahead of him. Gracie was already inside, having pressed herself against the far wall and pulled her legs to her chest. Ready for the grown-ups to fix the problem.

Before pulling himself inside, John tried to check the status of the invisible monster overhead. It was now firing around with its stolen pistol, shooting haunted dolls off its body. Then it ran out of bullets and John saw a tiny pistol magazine float off the corpse of a slain SWAT cop and toward the suspended pistol. The two objects weren't quite merging in the air. The Magpie was trying to reload but seemed to be struggling to do it with its gigantic, invisible talons.

John climbed inside and slammed the door closed. "Everyone, plug your ears!" He leaned up between the front seats. "Joy, hit the power button, then scroll to the track labeled DEFCON 5."

"DEFCON 5? Screw that. Where's DEFCON 1?"

"DEFCON 5 is the last resort track; that's the most serious situation!"

"No, it's not! The scale goes the other way! DEFCON 5 means everything is fine!"

Amy said, "She's right!"

"Either way, the track is called—"

Everyone tumbled to the side, like they were on the bridge of the *Enterprise* and it just got hit with a torpedo. The whole van had been lifted into the air. Dents and holes were punctured in the roof by a serrated beak they could not see.

"It's got us in its mouth!" said Dave. "Hit the music!"

Joy was in the process of scrolling through the tracks for DEFCON 5 and struggling to find it (John had alphabetized the playlist by the surname of the band's lead guitarist) when the entire van tilted down, going entirely vertical, ass-up.

They were being swallowed.

Everyone tumbled down to the cockpit. John fell between the seats and landed on the windshield, his face pressed against the glass, granting him a view of the ground about fifty feet below. Joy was on top of him, Dave was on top of her. John tried to snake his hand over in the direction of the stereo console. A thigh and a butt were in his way. He heard a chorus of inhuman howling from outside the windshield. On the other side of the glass from John was the mass of swallowed faces, each contorted in a state of pain and despair. That meant the van was in the Magpie's belly now, the bird having apparently decided to just swallow the vehicle whole and collect the faces inside at its leisure.

Dave said, "John! Move your foot like six inches to the right!"

He did.

"No, your other ri—"

The windshield gave way. It didn't shatter; it just popped out whole. John tumbled out into the nothingness, landing on the squishy wall of the Magpie's invisible stomach, feeling squirming undead creatures writhing under him. Joy landed on top of him, then Dave, then Amy. John twisted around to see the van suspended above, twitching in the Magpie's throat or its pyloric valve or whatever. Bas was hanging out of the windshield and slipping, with seemingly no hope of getting back inside. That kind of dangling-off-a-ledge grip strength only exists in action movies.

From within the tangle of limbs, Dave said, "John, if we die here, I want my last words to be this: Our life together was *da filthy*."

Amy and Joy voiced their agreement. But John thought he could make out movement inside the shadowy interior of the van. Tiny limbs and blond hair. John assumed Gracie was climbing out to try to help Bas, but instead, she was trying to work the controls on the dash. Everyone was shouting instructions at her that she almost certainly couldn't hear.

But then, after a seemingly endless stretch of tense moments, DEFCON 5 erupted. It was "Free Bird," cued up to begin at the four-minute, fifty-five-second mark, right as Allen Collins's guitar solo is unleashed. Every watt of the van's sound system was cranked to the max, blasting sonic waves like the orgasmic cries of a climaxing Zeus.

The effect on the Magpie was that of a grenade detonating inside a chicken. Whatever unfathomable dark energy had stitched the creature into being was torn asunder. The monstrosity shrieked, and John had the sensation of being thrown free from the blast, only he and the others weren't flying away from the belly of the creature but from the universe, from time and reality itself.

There was tremendous noise, and then there was an even tremendouser silence.

Me

For a moment, I thought I was dead. It wasn't the first time, and I recovered quickly. I assume when I actually die for good, I won't think anything at all.

The events that had led up to this moment were all a hazy blur. John's account will have to suffice, which I know is unfortunate, but my memory of the climax exists in seemingly hundreds of different iterations, always ending in some kind of gruesome failure. Until this one, which seemed to have ended in a time-out, as if Xarcrax had rage-quit the game. All was silent, the total stillness that I recognized as a world in which time had been paused. I tried to get a sense of my surroundings.

I was at the wastewater treatment plant, or on the patch of land that had at one point been the wastewater treatment plant. The clarifier pools had been replaced with some kind of white-domed structures. Farther in the distance, I saw horizontal tubes, hundreds of feet long. They were filled with some kind of bright green organic substance under artificial light, like they'd been stuffed with guacamole. I saw no staff on-site, but it was a working facility—mechanized units were paused in the act of crawling over the tubes, and some kind of drones hovered silently overhead. Though, considering the world was frozen in place, for all I knew they were in the process of plummeting to earth. Where the town had been on the other side of the cornfield were now three high-rises, and farther in the distance, I saw vast, low buildings surrounded by layers of fencing interspersed with narrow towers. Several black objects shaped like diamonds hovered silently overhead.

I heard faint voices. I walked toward the sound, near where the fence used to be (there was now just a row of hovering white pillars that I assumed served as some kind of security apparatus). Strolling along there was Sebastian and the old-man version of himself who'd accosted me in the Smoke Shop the other day. Bas seemed confused to be there, like he'd been suddenly abducted into the encounter just as I had been, back when I was trying to eat my pretzel.

"When did you figure out my identity?" asked the old man.

It took Bas a moment to orient himself before answering. I got the impression he had been conscripted into spontaneous meetings like this before, whisked away to strange times and places he knew not to inquire about.

"I dunno," he said, briefly glancing at one of the hovering security pod things as they passed. "At first, I thought you were nobody at all. Thought all the stuff with Silva and the move had broken my brain. Then when you were showing me things, predicting events, I thought you were some kind of ghost from the future. When I figured out you were me, it wasn't like some huge jaw-drop moment. I felt like I kind of always knew. Kind of like when a memory comes back to you, I guess."

"Then there is no question as to whether I want the best for you," said the old man. "You are me. I am you."

"See, I don't think that's true, though," replied Bas.

I followed them out of fear of letting the conversation get out of earshot. I saw no indication that they knew I was there, or cared. Hell, maybe I wasn't actually there at all.

"There was a point, not too long ago," continued Bas, "when I thought, 'I don't really wanna do this,' but then I thought, 'Well, I've come this far, might as well.' Like I was only doing it because I was doing it, you know? And now, I think when you get old, it's just that, over and over. You're a thousand miles down some path you set way back when. So the thought of going back is crazy to you, even if the path you're on is the craziest possible bullshit in the universe. So I think you're just me, only if I didn't turn around when I saw things going in the toilet. You're a me that has gone too far down the path."

The old man sighed. "If we back out now, she will have died for nothing. Everyone we hate will be laughing at us. Dad will be laughing at us. He'll have gotten away with everything."

"Okay, but, see, this is what I figured out tonight. When I was sitting there stoned earlier, I was thinking, 'This is still all about Dad, you know?' Remember when—or maybe this was too long ago for you—when I was showing Gracie something on a Pokémon game and Dad saw us and told me I was too old to be playing it? And I wasn't playing it; I was just showing her something on her game, but I got so mad that I started playing it. I don't even like those games, they all suck, but I did it just to spite him. Think about how dumb that is. I was still putting him in charge of how I spent my time. If I turn myself into a negative image of Dad, that's still a picture of Dad. You say he's laughing at us. Why do I care who he's laughing at? Let him laugh. I just want to be free of him, all the way, forever."

"It's not about him," replied the old man, the exasperation evident in his voice. "It's about all the people like him! All the hypocrites and clergy, pushing shame and callousness. Do you remember how fast the other kids moved on from Sil? The day of her funeral, everything at school stopped, but then the day after, it was like nothing had ever happened. Kids laughing in the halls."

"You're asking if I remember? Dude, for me, that all literally just happened last year."

"Well, when you leave high school, you'll find the whole world is still just that. High school. All those kids with their cliques and fads, they're the ones who make people like Dad rich. Have you seen it yet? The results? The Magpie, I mean, in its final form. Look."

The old man looked to the sky. So did Sebastian. So did I.

The sky, however, was gone. Regina had described the sky in her dream as having been blotted out, but I sensed the blackness overhead as a living mass, a swarm. I detected fluid movements of Shadows twisting and swirling in the air and glimpsed hundreds of pairs of burning eyes, bright with malicious, alien cunning. Then I blinked and the blackness was gone, and what replaced it was a river of human faces, howling and weeping. Millions of them, enough to occupy our entire field of vision in every direction. Over the chorus of the shrieking faces was another, worse noise, a high-pitched laugh that chewed into my eardrums like a pair of ravenous worms. It was the laugh of an immense, broken mind, of a child whose only hobby is torturing neighborhood cats who's found he suddenly has the powers of a god.

Bas had stopped walking. It seemed to me like his terror was making it hard for him to stay on his feet, but he was trying to hide it. Like any teenager, he didn't want to show fear in front of the older guy he wanted to impress.

"This is because of me?" asked Bas. "Because of us?"

"No," replied the elder Bas. "This is because of *them*. This is the world getting what it deserves, which is to be burned to the ground. Before it blinks out of existence, let Silva's name be the last they hear. Let her name be the word that brings about the nothingness."

"No. I don't want this."

"We're doing it for her. If you take it back, it's the same as killing her all over again."

Bas seemed to have no answer for this, but then I noticed that he was merely distracted. This would seem impossible, considering the howling cloud of the damned rolling past overhead, but he was entranced by something moving on the ground. Something alive, in a world that was supposedly frozen in place.

A speck of white.

A mouse.

It was so white that it almost glowed, scurrying across the invisible boundary marked by the hovering security pillars, heading toward the nearest dome. Bas broke away from the old man and followed the mouse, intensely curious. The old man shuffled after him with his cane, demanding Bas stick to the mission, that he not throw it all away.

The mouse followed the curve of the dome until it vanished from view. Bas chased after it, jogging now, and I chased after him.

I made my way around the dome and had to skid to a halt. Bas had abruptly stopped in front of me, in a state of shock.

Sitting in the grass before him was a girl in her mid-teens, wearing a yellow sundress with sneakers and a baseball cap. She wasn't glowing, she wasn't translucent, she didn't have wings. She was just a girl, dressed for the heat, maybe looking the way she had on her last day on earth.

Sebastian fell to his knees. Then he started bawling, crying in a way that I wasn't sure his body could survive, like it was tearing itself apart with jerks and spasms of grief. In between ragged breaths and sobs, he was saying he was sorry, so sorry.

The girl smiled, then looked embarrassed. "Get ahold of yourself, Crab. You're making a scene!"

"I've fucked everything up, Sil. All of it. I've fucked it all up. I'm-I'm sorry. I'm so sorry."

"You can make it right," she said softly. "You know why? Because you're alive. Do you have any idea how much easier that makes everything? I'm jealous. Trying to affect stuff from this side is like trying to play chess by blowing on the pieces. I do *not* recommend it."

"I don't know what I'm supposed to do."

"Of course not, you're still a kid. Don't overcomplicate it; you'll just give yourself a nosebleed. For now, find something that's broken and fix it. If you're gonna ask me where to find broken things, well, just start walking and you'll run into one. That's all I can offer you from over here."

"I don't know if I can. I'm not who you think I am, Sil."

"You're not who you think you are. This can all work out. Not just you, either. All of this. I know for a fact it can. I've seen it."

The old man arrived at the scene, brushing past me as if I either wasn't there or simply wasn't worthy of notice.

"It did work out!" he sputtered. "This was all for you! And others like you! Don't you see that? You owe it to all the rest, everyone like you, to let us finish our work!"

Silva just sighed, rolled her eyes, and ignored him. The old man was still just her dumb big brother. He was being a baby, and she just needed to wait for the tantrum to pass.

Old Bas reached out and grabbed his younger self by the arm, pulling him away.

"That's not even her," he snarled. "It's a trick. If she were really here, she'd tell you—"

Bas yanked his arm out of the old man's grasp and said, "Dude, would you fuck off?"

It was the voice you'd use to dismiss an annoying drunk at a bar or what an embarrassed teenager would use to make his little brother stop demanding to play with the older kids. *I have tolerated you, but I have decided to do so no longer. And that decision is final.*

And with that, the prophet of Xarcrax vanished. There was no sound, no howl of rage, no fade or dissolve from reality. He just wasn't there, because he had never been. Of course he hadn't. How would he? It was ridiculous to even suggest it.

Sebastian and Silva resumed their conversation, but I found I was being led away by my elbow. Grabbing my arm was my own hand, only it had a manicure.

Fancy Me said, "Let them have their privacy. The two don't have long together, and what they say is none of our business."

I saw that there were, once again, stars overhead. "Is this it? Is it over? I feel like I've asked that a million times, and it never is."

"Looks like it to me," he said. "And now I know why I could never see past a certain point, when playing out these scenarios. It's because only yours makes it this far."

"I'm gonna be frank. I'm not at all clear what has happened here."

"That doesn't surprise me."

"The mouse, was that Silva? So did Xarcrax's prophet's dead sister kill the Time Captain? Did she do it on purpose?"

"First of all, I want you to think about how your life has gotten to a place where you can say that string of words out loud and have all of it make sense to you. But the answer is yes."

"Why? Why would she kill him, I mean?"

I saw on his face the very look I've probably given to a thousand slow drivers I've gotten stuck behind in a no-passing zone.

He said, "The idiot that you are for some reason calling the 'Time Captain' is Tim Kaplan, a local mattress salesman and amateur bodybuilder. He survived a dose of the Sauce and experienced a vision that told him that he alone could reset the world if we jacked up our chance to save it. It was Xarcrax that gave him the vision, to make sure he would be here, where the hole in time would appear, again and again, to loop us back through, over and over."

"But why would Xarcrax keep giving us chances to undo the ritual?"

"Jesus, you're like a walking public service announcement for brain fog. Those repeated attempts *were* the ritual. It required more spiritual suffering than was available on the planet. So, it created a cycle, to repeat this same loop of time, the same cult getting started in each one, like an Old West evangelist hopping from town to town, leaving behind a new church in each. Only instead of towns, it's parallel timelines. Looping the process over and over, planting the same seed that would grow into the same movement in each. Us and the Time Idiot were, unwittingly, part of the mechanism, reaching that crisis point and asking for another chance, again and again and again. The result was that the same minds and souls were getting enslaved across hundreds of possible variations of their lives, and they all counted toward the ritual. All of those shackled minds, all of those collected faces, all of those nightmare timelines running in parallel. That's what Xarcrax is, this cycle of pain looping until it reaches critical mass. Until Kaplan was killed in John's bedroom wall, finally stopping the loop, breaking the mechanism."

"And we—meaning my timeline's version of me and John and Amy and, I guess, Joy—we did the rest, right? It's all fixed, collapsed into the good timeline. The bad timelines won't happen. They'll be erased now, just like the old, corrupted version of Sebastian Galvatron."

He—or I—turned to face me.

"What are you talking about?" he spat. "Yours is all that will remain, yeah, but yours *is* one of the bad timelines."

"What are *you* talking about? Everybody is making it out alive. I mean, not *everybody*, but—"

"I won't. My Amy won't. And . . . others that you don't even know about. Don't you get it? When I leave this conversation, I won't be anymore. I'll have never been. It'll just be you."

"But that was going to happen to all of us but one, regardless. So it sounds like you're mad that it wasn't me who got erased. And my version is the only one who did this correctly, soooo . . ."

"You did this right and absolutely everything else wrong. In my world, Amy has health insurance. We travel. We have friends. We have . . . we have a lot. More than I can even make you understand right now."

"But you don't have John."

"Look around at your life. Where he is, it always looks like this, all the mess, the chaos. He always ends badly, and, yeah, that's tragic or whatever, but the world is full of tragic fuckups, and you need to find better friends. You owe it to yourself, you owe it to the world."

"If I hadn't met John, I wouldn't be here at all."

"Well, my John died in a drunk driving accident seven years ago, and I'm here."

"No," I said, studying his face. "No, you're not me. That's what you said, that night you came to me when I was sleeping on John's sofa. You said I'm not you, and on that, we agree. There's something missing from you, something he brings out of us. Something I wouldn't give up from myself, not for anything."

Fancy Me was now showing the same annoyance that Old Bas

had shown with his younger self. "Don't romanticize people's flaws. That's what's wrong with our culture."

"No. What's ruining the culture is worshipping people who pretend they don't have flaws. We're all broken. And you couldn't pull this off because you didn't have John."

"Keep telling yourself that. And when you go back to your little life, try to remember what was lost to give it to you. What had to be sacrificed. Every moronic decision you make wipes out a universe of better possibilities."

"I'm doing my best, dude."

"You can tell that to anybody else on earth, and maybe they'll believe you. But I know for a fact it isn't true."

He sighed and rubbed his face in a way that I'd done a hundred thousand times in my life.

He shook his head, smiled a little, then stuck out his hand. "I never did enjoy my own company. Look, you saved mankind or whatever, so that's pretty good."

I shook his hand. He had a strong grip.

I said, "I'll be better."

He turned his face up at the stars, taking them in for the last time.

"You'd better be." He sighed and closed his eyes. "All these moments will be lost in time, like piss in a sewage plant. Give your Amy a hug for me."

Before I could reply, I was gone.

MONDAY, JULY 4, 2:12 P.M.

Me

"Who the fuck could that be?"

I say that every time someone knocks on my door, even though there are lots of people it could reasonably be on any given day. Though that was less true on this day; John was already there, and I wasn't expecting any deliveries, since it was a national holiday. We hadn't ordered food, and I don't have a landlord who drops by . . .

Amy went to the door. John had been in the middle of explaining his Fourth of July outfit to us, even though neither Amy nor I had asked when he'd shown up in the novelty patriotic Stetson and insufficient denim shorts. When Amy passed me, the chemical coconut scent of her sunscreen hit my nose, and a rush of bizarre memories flew through my head, too quickly to register.

Wait, what day is this?

Amy opened the door, and immediately, I sensed something was wrong. Whoever it was shouldn't be here. As for who *should* be at the door, or why, I couldn't quite bring it to mind.

Amy said, "Hey, I thought you had to work!"

Joy pushed into the apartment, looking enraged.

She threw out her hands and said, *"Okay, why is it the Fourth of July again?"*

John asked, "What do you—"

He couldn't even finish the question. We all exchanged confused glances.

I sat down. "Are . . . are we dead?"

"I'm not!" shouted Joy. "I just lost like seven weeks of my life! And my big hero moment! I saved everybody, and it got wiped out because you people reverted to the last save point."

"Why would it throw us back here?" asked Amy. I was kind of surprised she could remember the bit that had been rewound.

John said, "This is where Eve went. Maybe that forged a path, or something? They fucked a rupture in space-time and then we were flung through the glory hole."

"But if so, where's Lou and Eve?" I asked. "Shouldn't they have arrived ahead of us?"

"Well, Eve doesn't exist, right?" replied Amy. "Bas doesn't grow up to be the prophet, and so none of that stuff happened, because the prophet isn't there to reach back and make it happen."

"So how do we get back to where we were?"

Amy shrugged. "I guess just live it out?"

"This is so stupid. What the hell do we do now? Like right now, I mean."

Nobody seemed to have any suggestions.

After some awkward silence, John said, "Uh, we go to the fireworks, I guess?"

I said, "I am in no mood for that."

"I think we have to go," said Amy. "Just to make sure the stuff that happened last time doesn't happen this time."

"And I kind of am in the mood for fireworks," said John. "Or rather, fireworks viewed through the haze of a dozen beers. Joy, you want to come this time?"

"No, I have work."

I said, "You already admitted to us that was a lie, in the other timeline."

"I just got called in. There's an emergency. The, uh, old people are stampeding."

"Come on."

"Wait, do you *want* me to come?"

"Amy wants you to come. And we should probably all be together, just in case."

"I'll come to the fireworks if you say you want me to come."

I stared her down.

"Come on," she said. *"Admit it."*

The four of us found a nice spot in the shade this time, which was good since the day was as hot as Godzilla's meth pipe. While we were settling in, Amy spotted someone, or something, in the crowd.

"I'll be right back."

She headed out to where a familiar family was getting situated: the Rossmans, the people whose cooler we'd borrowed last time around. I followed her over there, more out of curiosity than anything, but hung back when she struck up a conversation with Mr. Rossman. I hadn't had enough alcohol to talk to strangers yet.

"Excuse me," Amy said, "this is going to sound weird, but I love this cooler. Do you know what brand it is?"

Mr. Rossman didn't know, but seemed extremely pleased that someone was complimenting his discerning taste in coolers. He said the brand and model was noted on the interior. Amy opened the lid, took a picture of the inside, and thanked him. The man settled back into his lawn chair, satisfied at already having won some Dad Points for the day.

I headed back toward our spot under the trees, in what I was already thinking of as the first-class section of lake fireworks viewing. Then I noticed that just three blankets down from us was the Galvatron family. Mom and Dad were looking at their phones. Gracie had a pad of paper and seemed to be drawing the couple sitting in front of them.

Bas, however, was staring right at me.

It was a look of recognition, which made no sense, because on July Fourth, he had never met any of us.

Unless . . .

He stood up and headed back toward the woods, motioning for me to follow. Against my better judgment, I did.

As soon as we were out of earshot of the crowd, Bas turned to me and said, "You remember?"

"Depends on what you're referring to."

"The rest of this month and most of August. The next . . . fifty days, I guess."

I nodded. "Yeah, we all do. The four of us."

"Mom and Dad don't. Gracie says she doesn't, but I know she does; she just doesn't want to talk about it. When I asked what she wanted for her birthday this time, she asked for something else, instead of the egg like last time. Asked her why. She said she didn't want to play the game, said she wanted to spend less time on her phone. What little kid says that?"

"I say let her forget."

"I haven't forgotten what you promised. Do you remember? About Dad?"

"Yep. Nothing has changed on that end?"

"Why would it? I'm holding you to it."

I just nodded, then turned to walk away.

"Hey," he said to my back. "I, uh, just wanted to say thanks. For your help with all that stuff. The world doesn't know, but I do."

"You can thank us by not wasting your second chance."

"All those people, they're back alive. Jonas was just on Instagram. They're all back, I think, the whole gang. They're texting me about coming to the next meeting. I'm just gonna ghost them, though."

"Try to get them turned onto a different hobby. Something that will force them to interact with normal people. Maybe start a band, learn to play something pretty."

I headed back toward our spot and found Amy, John, and Joy huddled over Amy's phone.

"What is it?"

Joy said, "She's showing us all your dick pics."

Amy turned her phone toward me. It was a photo of the interior of the Rossmans' cooler, but I couldn't see anything special about it.

She said, "There's a logo inside, etched into the plastic. So when we made the mold with the resin, it pressed that logo into the side. I'd show you the pictures of the mold, but, of course, they're not on my phone anymore since they now never existed. The point is, this logo you're seeing on the inside of their cooler would have been on the side of the resin block when somebody dug it up a century from now. You know, the 'crystal' that will 'hatch' the reborn prophet?"

She zoomed in on the spot. The logo said "X-Treme Arctic Tundra Icebox" but something sticky had been splattered on the side of the cooler and filled in several of the letters. All that remained to become part of the resin mold was:

X   Arc   ra   x

I said, "I don't understand. What does it mean?"

Amy put on her hat and pink sunglasses and reclined in her lawn chair. "Who said it meant anything?"

Joy said, "What time does Chilly Whip close? I want to ditch the fireworks and get ice cream."

I said, "We just had ice cream like five hours ago."

"We literally did not! That was all erased!"

"Fine. I don't care."

"Good," she said, putting her own sunglasses on. "I want to get something different this time."

"Ooh!" said Amy. "We get to go to Japan again!"

"Since you already had that experience," I said, "wouldn't it make more sense to just save the money?"

"No," she said, "because this time you're coming with me."

"No, thanks."

"I'm requiring it. That's one thing I've decided I did wrong last time. You, my friend, need to remind yourself that this"—she waved her hand around at the general area—"is not the whole world."

"How can we afford it?"

"I'm working on that."

MONDAY, JULY 11, 8:48 A.M.

Me

Amy chronicled our experience in an extremely long email to Dr. Marconi. A week later, a cryptically worded response from his assistant informed us that he was flying in and wanted to meet us at what is now the best coffee place in town: McDonald's. My first impulse had been to inquire back to see if his health had improved, but Amy reminded me that his health crisis had presumably not yet occurred in our timeline, if it was going to occur at all. I'd thought that maybe this meant we could warn him somehow, but after his assistant informed us that 8:00 a.m. was the latest he could meet due to his production schedule, I decided he deserved whatever he got. I became even more certain of this when, after we arrived on time, the doctor kept us waiting until a quarter to nine.

"First of all," he said as he settled into the plastic booth and stirred his coffee, "I should say well done. Even before I'd read the details of what occurred, I could sense the magnitude."

John said, "You could?"

He was on Marconi's side of the booth, Amy and me facing them. The restaurant was packed; in the booth next to us was a loud old woman regaling a group of other old women with an anecdote about her and her husband's disastrous attempt to take a swing dancing class. They were laughing so hard they were crying.

"My team was aware that the pieces were being meticulously moved into place for a worldwide summoning," said Marconi. "And then, quite abruptly, the project was snuffed out. All signs of it instantly gone, as if the event had been surgically removed from reality."

I said, "Does this mean the whole world is going to repeat these next forty-some days? It doesn't seem right."

He shrugged. "For all we know, these kinds of shifts and loops occur all the time. Though, this does shed light on something I'd been curious about. For the last several weeks, I'd been ignoring clear cardiac symptoms out of pure pigheadedness and a secret fear of doctors. Then, one night, I had a vivid dream of suffering a heart attack while walking back from the studio on a brutally hot day. In the dream, I collapsed on a sidewalk in Midtown Manhattan, my life saved only due to the actions of a few quick-thinking strangers and an especially heroic cab driver. I suspected that the details were far too specific and logical for a dream, including the prophetic nature of the setting—I am scheduled to shoot a studio segment in New York next month, you see. I didn't know what to make of it, taking it as my body trying to send me a message. I booked an appointment with my cardiologist; he found a blockage and congratulated me on catching it in time. But I suppose I should be thanking you, instead."

"So it's all better?" asked Amy. "We were worried."

"The cardiologist tells me that all I require is a regimen of medications that each carry obnoxious side effects and also to give up every single vice that makes my life worth living." He pulled out a flask and poured a generous amount into his coffee. "But I am certain I can rise to the challenge."

"Also," Amy said, "I'm not sure if we've totally fixed this other thing. This whole process was supposed to play out over decades, until 2112 or so. And part of the prep for the end was creating this huge, well, I guess it's not a cult once they have a billion followers, is it? A new religion. A major one."

"I am aware of that aspect," said the doctor. "The Simurai existed prior to this, and regardless of whether or not they will reattempt a summoning, I would prefer such a faith not take a foothold in the mainstream. It is rather eliminationist in its beliefs, among other things. For safety's sake, it might be wise to see to it that its mythology is destroyed as well."

I said, "The book, you mean? It doesn't exist, as far as we know."

"The fledgling faith's writings can be found online. The ceremonies and bylaws, if not the laborious biography of the prophet."

John asked, "How do you destroy a mythology, considering that killing the people in charge tends to just make the faith run hotter?"

Amy said, "Someone needs to rewrite it. Like in a way that makes the whole thing doomed to fail. Right?"

Marconi nodded. "For example, if the group adopted strict new rules that would send it in a radically different direction. A new version of their sacred texts that could be distributed online, one that could be made to seem authoritative, may do the trick."

I asked, "Are you suggesting we write it? Why would they take anything we write to be authoritative?"

"You've lived a preview of the next six weeks, have you not? If you were to turn up with some extremely specific predictions of events you remember, that would earn you a great deal of credibility for whatever you were to say after."

John nodded. "Yeah, we can do that."

I said, "Can we? The prediction part, I mean. I'm not sure I remember anything from the news. It's not like we were playing lotto or tracking the stock market."

"I can. I won a bunch of money betting preseason football games last time around; I remember the scores."

Amy said, "We're not betting those again, in case you were considering that." To Marconi, she said, "Did you come all the way down here just to go over this with us? I don't see how you'll get a TV show out of it."

"Not this specifically, no. We received word that the youth here are experimenting with a new kind of hallucinogenic mushroom, in an effort 'to see beyond the illusion of reality.' I have a sample in my possession; they are quite sinister to look at. We hope to interview some users, some concerned parents. It will make a nice segment, particularly considering the persistent theories that this entire town is under the thrall of some kind of mind-controlling fungus. Enthusiasts are always hungry for another explanation for why this place is the way it is."

There was a lull in the conversation, and I exchanged glances with John and Amy. We hadn't really decided who was going to say this next part, and I'd assumed it'd be Amy. But apparently not?

I said, "Let me ask you, if you found a way to forever safeguard the toxic leak in reality that is this town, if you could come up with a permanent solution, what would you be willing to sacrifice? To beat this thing you've been battling your whole life?"

"Anything," said Marconi as he attempted a sip of his coffee. "I've dedicated everything to this cause, at the expense of my health, my relationships, and every opportunity for a normal life. As you are well aware."

"Sure. So our proposal is that the next time something terrifying sticks its head out and we're forced to stop it, that *we* document the whole process on camera, *you* get the footage to use on your TV show, and—this is the most important part—you pay us for it."

"You can speak to my producer about fees for video. It typically depends on what phenomena you capture and how clearly it can be seen."

"No," said Amy. "We're not talking about a fee, we're talking about a full-time salary. All three of us. It's not charity. You get content; you get full rights to write books about it or whatever makes you the most profit."

"Even so, I doubt that what you produce would pay for itself."

"Who said it would?" said Amy, leaning forward on her elbows. She appeared calm, but I'm telling you, those green eyes were on fire. I found myself physically scooting away from her.

"You know," she continued, "for someone with such keenly honed perceptions, you seem to miss a lot of the obvious stuff. Did you see the sign when you pulled it, where it's advertising two-for-one Quarter Pounders but the *O* and *U* are missing? Those letters have been gone for a month, and I'm telling you right now that nobody will ever fix it. It's like that all over. Look around."

"I'm afraid I don't understand."

"This town, Doctor, *is dying*. There are no jobs here. Not real jobs, with benefits. We, the three of us, I mean, are about to slam headlong into our thirties. We need something stable, and that probably means moving away. Unless . . ."

She gestured to him to signal that he was the "unless."

"You would seriously leave the town unguarded, in the name of pursuing economic opportunity?"

"Would you?" Amy shot back. "Because we're giving you the chance to guard it, by paying us to do the job."

"I am just disappointed to be having such a conversation over something as trivial as money."

"Not money," said Amy. "Something much bigger and more important than that: health insurance."

"We can discuss it. To be frank, I do not believe you quite know what you're asking, in terms of finances."

"You drive a two-hundred-and-fifty-thousand-dollar car. You could have bought John's house three times over for that alone. You keep apartments in New York and London. You charge seventy-five thousand dollars for a speaking event. You can throw us on your production company's payroll as consultants, and nobody will blink."

John said, "Hey, and if it makes your financial books look worse, that's a small sacrifice to keep humanity safe. As you said a second ago, you're willing to do anything. It seems like this falls under the umbrella of 'anything' since, and I'd have to check a dictionary to be sure, that's literally what the word means."

Amy said, "You want us to take this work seriously? This is America. There's only one reliable way to make sure we do that."

"In that case," said Marconi, "I suppose we need to discuss salary."

"Send us an offer at your earliest convenience," said Amy. "I'm sure you'll be fair."

"You do know that this means there will be expectations, in terms of the quantity and quality of work," replied Marconi. "You would earn your pay. And I assume you can all pass a standard employment background check?"

In near-perfect unison, John and I said, "Oh, *fuck* no."

WEDNESDAY, JULY 13, 10:10 P.M.

Me

The problem with staking out the back seat of somebody's car is that you don't really know when, or if, they're going to show up.

Dalton Galvatron's Audi was parked along a lane outside of a wooded area south of town. Bas had tipped us off as to where to find it, saying his dad liked to come out here to hunt. Coyote was the only thing in season right now, but he seemed like the kind of guy who would shoot whatever the law would allow at any given moment. Still, it was only legal to hunt until sundown, so that meant he should be returning to his vehicle at any time.

I'd been there for almost two hours, rehearsing what I would say when he sat down in the driver's seat in front of me, trying to anticipate how he would react to getting ambushed. At some point, however, I'd apparently dozed off. I was awoken by the man knocking on the glass next to me.

"Hey! Get the fuck out of my car!"

Through his window, I said, "I know where Bas and Gracie are. Get in."

Sebastian had run away from home just after the Fourth, taking Gracie with him and leaving behind a note recounting his allegations about his dead sister. My guess is that Dalton had destroyed the note immediately. At the moment, Bas was at an older friend's

412

apartment, and Gracie was at John's house, getting her nails painted by Joy.

"I'm calling the cops! Get out!"

"I'm not holding your kids hostage; I just know where they are. They're scared to go back home. They're scared of you. We're just some friends who are trying to help them. Get in the car."

He did, then said, "Tell me where they are, right now. I'm going to get them, and then we're getting the hell out of this town. Then I hope this whole place falls into a sinkhole. My wife has been having crazy dreams, something about an alien egg. She gets confused about what day it is. I think she's been drinking. Now my son is having these paranoid fantasies."

"This is going to sound like an idle question, but it's not. *Why did you move here?* I know you'd heard of this place. You had to have been expecting weirdness. You don't go to Woodstock assuming you'll never see a hippie's dick."

"It's none of your business."

"Humor me. I'm asking for a reason."

"It was a mistake," he grumbled. "We wanted to get away from the coast. The warm sun has turned everybody soft out there, decadent. I looked up what part of the heartland had been hit the hardest in the last few years, with the opioids and the unemployment. I immediately got the name of this city. The Realtor said that in some parts of town, land is so cheap that you can get it for free if you take on the responsibility for tearing down whatever structure is rotting there. He told me not to come, said there was fungus growing everywhere, psilocybin, said all the unemployed addicts and burnouts here are constantly seeing ghosts and monsters. But I'm writing a book about all of this, about the degeneracy, about what's happening to the world. I figured this was Ground Zero. Should have just rented a room here and left my family somewhere safe. If there is such a place."

"Is that what you did with Silva? Tried to keep her safe from all of us degenerates?"

Dalton went cold. His eyes flicked to the rearview mirror, meeting my gaze.

"I did everything I could to save Silva. Everything. To save her from the rot and, yes, from people like you. Wouldn't you love it if you could pin that on me, to prove to yourself that I'm a monster, a hypocrite? Because then maybe you wouldn't feel so bad about your own life, wouldn't have to wear sarcasm like armor to hide your failure. Just looking at you turns my stomach. Are you ever up before noon? What do you build, what do you produce? What do you *do* all day?"

"You don't know this, because there's no way you could know it, but Sebastian got into some weird occult stuff for a while. Rituals, summonings, spells, hexes. All of it."

"*What?* When?"

"Listen. What Bas was trying to do with all of that, was to summon something horrific into the world, to get justice for Silva. To bring it all down. Did you ever have that urge, growing up? To just burn it all?"

"No. It's the losers who always want to take their ball and go home. I'm from a culture that still believes in going out and competing, planting a flag. Staking a claim. Everybody else can go home if they want, but if so, I'm keeping the ball. Whatever Sebastian is doing, I'll put a stop to it."

"It's already over. I think, in the end, he figured out that he only *thought* he was mad at the world when he was actually just mad at you. I suspect that's the case for a lot of angry young men."

"Of course he's mad at me. I'm spoiling the party. I'm sure he'd have loved to see his sisters sucking cock for crack by the time they're old enough to drive. What does he care if Regina and I wind up raising some bastard babies born addicted to god knows what, while Gracie is in jail or rehab, Silva shacking up with some homeboy who's keeping her enslaved with drugs? Better that than to be told to obey the rules, to learn a work ethic, to have some respect for himself."

"Did you kill your daughter?"

"I did everything I could for that girl. I gave more to her than you've ever given to anybody. I sacrificed for her, over and over. I gave her as long as I could, and what happened in Mexico, tragic as it was, was the best thing that could have happened because now she gets to be frozen in everyone's memory as this young, cute, bright little thing. Nobody has to watch her get chewed up and rotted out from the inside. What she was, that was as good as she was ever going to get. A father knows."

"That sounds like a confession to me."

"A confession implies wrongdoing, and I am guilty of none whatsoever. What, was Bas trying to call up some demon from Hell to punish me? Guess what, pal, Hell is all around us. There are vacant houses out there with no power or water and a dozen people sleeping on the floor, dog and cat feces everywhere, and everybody so wasted on painkillers that they can't even smell it. We're sitting in the underworld right now, my kids are getting burned up in the flames, and I'm trying to get the survivors out while there's still something to salvage. Maybe I'm too late. Maybe it's too late for everybody. The filth in this place runs so deep that the kids here even have a slang term for it—"

"Bas and I have had our . . . differences," I interrupted, "but he paints a very different picture of Sil. And Gracie, she seems like a pretty normal kid to me. So are you sure it's not just you?"

"You're just proving my point. I'm sure Gracie does look normal to *you*. Look at the standard you're using to judge. She's being conditioned to be the exact thing you want in the world. Girls with no standards, no self-control, no self-respect, no belief in anything but the next pleasure passing through the next orifice. You admire Gracie like a vulture admires a limping animal in the desert: as an upcoming meal." Dalton shook his head and set his jaw. "I won't let her become that. Won't let the press throw it in my face at every appearance, like I'm not qualified to give advice because my own daughter succumbed to the rot."

"Yes, that would be very bad for your brand. So here's what I've decided. You're going to disappear. I don't know how your kids will do without you, but it seems like their best bet is to find out. Maybe Regina will meet somebody new. I don't know."

"You're wasting your time and mine. I'm not going anywhere."

"You misunderstand. I'm not requesting that you leave. I'm informing you of what's going to happen. I don't know why I'm informing you; it's not like it matters. I guess I just wanted you to know. You see, Bas's vengeance summoning ritual worked. His avenging monster has arrived. It's not what he was expecting, but"—I shrugged—"here it is, just the same."

"Are you threatening me?"

"Do you think your family would be more upset if your body was discovered as a bloody mess in your car or if you just disappeared entirely? I think the latter would be better. But I can do either."

"What, am I supposed to be scared? I'm a public figure. What do you think you can do to me and get away with?"

"You'd be surprised."

"I can bench two-fifty and I've been training in Muay Thai for six years. The last guy that tried to mug me wound up facedown in an alley in a pool of his own teeth. I have a loaded rifle in the seat next to me. You can see it. One of us is about to get a major reality check."

It seems fitting to me that those should be Dalton Galvatron's last words.

THE NEW COMMANDMENTS OF THE SIMURAI: A TRINITY OF TRINITIES

The following are the commandments received within the simulation by the Oracle. There are three commandments that each contain three sub-commandments, collectively known as the Trinity of Trinities. The legitimacy of the Oracle has been verified by members of the Simurai around the globe via a series of successful predictions observed in real time, intentionally restricted to inconsequential events whose foreknowledge could not be used to turn world affairs. These included the results of more than thirty NFL preseason games down to the exact score, except for one game where the Oracle was off by seven points because the simulation did not account for the losing team scoring another touchdown in garbage time. Now that all doubt has been cast aside, here are the new commandments as handed down by the Oracle:

1. **Everybody Calm the Fuck Down**
   A. Humans act like assholes when they're scared. Anybody who's trying to keep you scared all the time just wants to breed more assholes into the world. Don't let them do it.
   B. Exactly 100 percent of religious apocalypse predictions have turned out to be hilariously wrong. The odds that the next one will be true seem pretty low.

C. If you truly think you've somehow stumbled across a superior way to live, there is only one way to spread the word: Live that superior life and let others see how cool, happy, and successful you are. They'll spend the rest of their lives trying to imitate it. If they choose not to, just **calm the fuck down** and let them.

2.   **You Don't Have All the Answers (and That's Okay)**

A. Every human believes in some kind of simplified Grand Theory of Everything that explains existence. The problem is that there are multiple competing theories. In fact, there are about seven billion of them, one for every human on earth. Admit that the odds are pretty slim that you alone have it exactly right.

B. Uncertainty is scary. It is also impossible to eliminate uncertainty from the universe, so you need to learn to just cope with it instead of trying to pretend you know everything.

C. If you embrace a Grand Theory of Everything that gives you permission to treat other people like shit, it's likely that you started with the urge to treat people like shit and just worked backward to form your theory. Open your eyes, dude: They're not heretics, they're your neighbors.

3.   **Never Forget That You Are Meat**

A. The one thing we know for sure about our possibly simulated world is that we are experiencing it via meat. All your thoughts are running through meat, and therefore, a lot of what you're perceiving about the universe is just meat stuff. Feel like the world is doomed? There's a good chance that's only because your meat isn't getting enough sleep. Mad at everyone? It might just be that your meat is hungry. In a state of panic? Take deep breaths—you might just not have enough oxygen in your blood. If the world feels off to you, always check your meat first.

B. Your meat needs physical and emotional contact with other meat. Humans are social animals, and you need a pack to call your own, whether that's friends, family, or whatever. Do you find your mind going to dark, freaky places if you spend too much time in a quiet room? That's just loneliness corrupting your meat. If your current group makes you miserable, find a different one. **Do not try to go it alone.**

C. Unless you're a toddler, you shouldn't need a list of rules about what exactly you should or shouldn't do every day. Your meat has impulses, and some of them cannot be satisfied without harming yourself or others. Deep down, you know which ones those are. This is a battle you'll be fighting every day from now until you die, and you have to take each situation as it comes. The good news is that you're not alone: Billions of other people are going through the exact same thing and, believe it or not, most of them are trying their best. We're all in the same boat, united by meat and our desire to be something more.

Now turn off whatever machine you're reading this on and go the fuck outside.

These commandments are brought to you by Fight Piss brand energy drink; click here *and enter offer code XARCRAX to receive a coupon for a free can. Offer expires January 1, 2015.*

AFTERWORD

Before we go, there are three bits of housekeeping I want to take care of, if you don't mind:

1. Every book in this series has, in at least one of its editions, carried some form of the following disclaimer:

   None of the supernatural elements or events described in this book is based on reality. The "Shadow People" are not real, as far as I know, and I don't personally believe that any kind of ghosts or demons interfere with our daily lives.

   I try to take time to say this now and then because I have absolutely received fan mail over the years from readers who believe otherwise. This is because "Shadow People" do routinely turn up in visual hallucinations. I understand the phenomenon to be caused by a misfire in the part of the brain that senses the location of other people nearby, signaling that a person is in the room with you but substituting a blank figure in the absence of any visual feedback (note that I am not a scientist and am probably explaining that incorrectly). Others have seen similar shadowy figures during episodes of a well-known phenomenon called sleep paralysis, in which a person wakes up enough to be conscious and aware, but not quite enough to stop dreaming. It's always good to keep in mind that just because lots of people have seen a thing, doesn't mean that thing necessarily exists. We're all experiencing the world through similarly flawed brains and sense organs.

If you are experiencing any kind of unnatural phenomena that is causing you distress or interfering with your life, please talk to your doctor. It is objectively far more likely a misfire in your senses than a real malicious entity determined to torment you. If you truly believe your home is haunted, well, to my knowledge, history has not recorded a single death, injury, or illness at the hands of a ghost, so it may be one of those problems you just have to learn to manage.

2. Note that this is the fourth novel starring these characters (this can be a source of confusion, as reissues and new editions can complicate things if you search purely by publication date). They can all be read independently, and if this is your first, I assure you that having read them all in sequence would do nothing to alleviate whatever confusion you're feeling now. In order, they are:

   John Dies at the End

   This Book Is Full of Spiders: Seriously, Dude, Don't Touch It

   What the Hell Did I Just Read: A Novel of Cosmic Horror

   The first was turned into a feature film with the same title and is surely available on at least one video streaming service you have access to. If you are a loyal fan and have been following this series from the start, first of all, thank you, and second of all, please note that all plot and continuity errors, as well as timeline inconsistencies, are intentional. Or at least, my choice to not worry about them is intentional.

3. Longtime readers have no doubt noticed that this is my first new book released under my own name. I'd previously published under the pseudonym David Wong (taking the name of the protagonist of this series, as if he were writing the books autobiographically). All five of my previous novels (the previous three books in this series, plus the two in the science fiction

Zoey Ashe series) have now been rereleased in paperback with *Jason Pargin* on the cover; those are now available wherever books like this are sold. If you are a fan, one way you can help is to gently let someone know the situation if they ask why "David Wong" stopped writing. Same author, different name—nothing else has changed aside from me continuing to get older and sleepier.

I assume there will be another book in this series at some point. On one hand, four John and Dave novels feel like a lot, but on the other, there are literally like nine hundred episodes of *Doctor Who,* and they're still going. And fans of that show will tell you that every single season, without exception, has been better than the last. If you want to keep up with me in between novels, you have many options:

linktr.ee/jasonkpargin

Thanks!
—Jason

TURN THE PAGE FOR A SNEAK PEEK OF
JASON PARGIN'S NEW NOVEL

I'M STARTING TO WORRY ABOUT THIS BLACK BOX OF DOOM

Available Fall 2024

Abbott

Abbott Coburn had spent much of his twenty-six years dreading the wrong things, in the wrong amounts, for the wrong reasons. So it was appropriate that in his final hours before achieving international infamy, he was dreading a routine trip he'd accepted as a driver for the rideshare service Lyft. The passenger had ordered a ride from Victorville, California, to Los Angeles International Airport, a facility Abbott believed had been designed to make every traveler feel like they were doing it wrong.

He rolled up to the pickup spot—the parking lot of a Circle K convenience store—to find a woman sitting on a black box, one large enough that she probably could've mailed herself to her destination with the addition of some breathing holes and a piss drain. It had wheels and she was rolling herself back and forth a few inches in each direction with her feet, working out nervous energy. The millions of strangers who'd become obsessed with that box in the coming days would usually describe it incorrectly, calling it everything from a "footlocker" to an "armored munitions crate." What the woman was actually sitting on was a road case, the type musicians use to transport concert gear. This one was covered in band stickers, a detail that would have been inconsequential in a rational society but turned out to be extremely consequential in ours.

Abbott rolled down the window and braced himself, doing his usual scan for reassuring signs that the passenger is Normal (he'd developed a sixth sense for the weirdos who, for example, wanted to sit in the front). The woman on the box wore green cargo pants and a dazzling orange hoodie that looked to Abbott like high-visibility work gear. Though, if she was on the job, the bosses weren't strict about the dress code: She wore a faded trucker cap that said, WELCOME TO THE SHITSHOW. Below that was a pair of oversize sunglasses with lime-green plastic frames and, below that, smeared lipstick that looked like it had been hurriedly applied in the dark. Her hair was short enough that it looked like it had been shaved without a mirror while driving down a bumpy road. It did not occur to Abbott that all of this would be an excellent way to thwart security cameras and facial recognition software.

Abbott, his nervous system already hovering a finger over its big red Fight-or-Flight button, asked, "You got the Lyft to LAX?"

He was hopeful she'd say no, but there was no one else in the vicinity aside from a rail-thin man by the tire air machine having a tense argument via either Bluetooth or psychosis.

"Oh my god," said the woman on the box, "I have a huge favor to ask you. HUGE. I am in so much trouble with my employer."

She removed her green sunglasses, as if the situation had become much too serious for such eyewear. Her eyes were bloodshot and Abbott thought she'd either been recently smoking weed or recently crying, though he knew from personal experience that it was possible to do both simultaneously. He was now absolutely certain that the favor she was about to ask was going to be illegal, impossible, or just a string of nonsense words. He wasn't sure how to respond without accidentally agreeing, so he just stared.

"Okay," she said, after realizing it was still her turn to talk. "Yes, I ordered a trip to LAX, but in the time I've been waiting, I found out that's not going to work. This is a big problem. BIG problem."

Her voice was shaky and Abbott decided that she had, in fact, been crying. He instantly sensed two opposing instincts in his brain quietly begin to go to war with each other.

"This box I'm sitting on?" she continued. "The guy who hired me has to have it by Monday, the Fourth of July. I can't ship it, because I can't let it out of my sight—I have to stay with it, wherever it goes. And I can't fly, for reasons that would take all day to explain. Now, I'm going to ask you a question. It's going to sound like a hypothetical or a joke, but it's an actual question. Okay? Okay. So, how much would you charge to drive me to Washington, DC?"

Abbott took a moment to make sure he'd heard her right before replying, "Oh, that's not something you can do in a Lyft, the maximum trip is only—"

"No, no. You'd clock out of your app or however you do it. I'm asking you, personally, as a citizen with a beautiful working car— what is this, an Escalade?"

"A, uh, Lincoln Navigator. It actually belongs to—"

"I'm asking what you would charge to take me all the way across the country. And your reflex is going to be to say no amount of money because I'm talking about totally putting your life on hold for more than a week, without notice. Restaurants, hotels, lost business, canceled Fourth of July plans, additional stress—it's a lot to ask. But I'm willing to pay a lot. Or rather, my employer is willing to pay a lot. Look."

She twisted around and dug into a tattered duffel bag that Abbott hadn't previously noticed. When she came back around, she was holding two thick folds of cash, each bound with rubber bands. He physically recoiled at the sight of it, mainly because not a single reasonable person has ever carried money that way.

"This is one hundred thousand dollars," she said, waving the cash around like a mind control amulet. "The guy who hired me has this kind of money to throw around and no, he's not a criminal, he's a legitimate rich guy, if such a thing exists. No, I can't tell you who he is. All I can tell you is that he needs this box by the Fourth at the latest and it has to be kept quiet. Today is Thursday.

We can make it easily, we don't even have to travel overnight. Four days of leisurely driving and we'll get there Sunday evening, no problem. One hundred K is my starting offer for you to make this drive. Make me a counteroffer."

At this stage, Abbott was considering this request in the exact same way he'd have considered a request to be transported to Venus in exchange for a baggie of rat turds: he just wanted out of the crazy conversation as quickly and safely as possible.

He said, "I'm sure there are plenty of people within a few miles of here, probably a million of them, who'd love to take you up on this. But I really can't. I'm sorry."

She shook her head. "No. No, you're perfect for this, I can tell already. And I can't keep asking people, I have to get on the road and I have to do it now. The more drivers I have to ask, the more people know about this, and that's bad. Secrecy is part of what I'm paying for. And I'm not crazy, I know how I look. Though I will have to tell you about the worms at some point. But no, I'm dressed like this for a reason. How about one fifty?"

A third fold of cash was added and Abbott had to force himself to look away from it. He prided himself on not being enslaved to mindless greed, but way back at the rear of his noisy brain was a tiny voice pointing out that this amount of money would let him move out on his own and tell his father to fuck off (though it would definitely have to be done in that order). It would be *freedom*, for literally the first time in his life. Abbott imagined a factory farm pig escaping into a sunny green pasture and seeing the clear blue sky for the first time. Though he was having trouble imagining the pig looking up. Could pigs do that? He'd have to google it later. Wait, what did she say about worms?

The woman grinned and sat up straighter, the posture of an angler who's just seen the bobber plop under the surface. It kind of made Abbott want to refuse just to spite her.

"But there are rules," she said, a finger in the air. "You can't look in the box. You can't ask me what's in the box. And you can't tell anyone where we're going until it's over. After that, you can tell anyone anything you like. But no one can come looking for us."

"Well, there's certainly nothing weird or suspicious about that. So, why don't you just rent a car and drive yourself?"

"No driver's license. I used to have one, but the government took it away. They said, 'You're too good of a driver, it's making the other drivers look bad, you're hurting their self-esteem.'"

"I just . . . I really can't, sorry. You say I'm perfect for this, but I assure you I'm the absolute perfect person to not do it. That's, what, like, fifty hours of driving? I don't even like to drive for *one* hour."

"You drive for a living!"

"Oh, I just started doing this a couple months ago to—"

"I'm just teasing you, I know you probably didn't grow up dressing as a Lyft driver for Halloween. But no, you're my guy. You're not married, right? I don't see a ring. No kids, I can see it on your face. If you have another job, it's one you can walk away from, it's not a 401K and health insurance situation. You probably live with a parent, so even if you have pets, there's somebody to feed them while you're away. You're old enough that nobody's going to assume you were abducted. You're, what, twenty-four? Around there?"

"Twenty-six. Did you just deduce all that on the fly?"

She smiled again and made a show of leaning forward, narrowing her eyes as if to examine him. "Ah, see, there's something you need to know about me: I can *read minds*. I can tell you're skeptical, so let me give it a shot. Ready?"

She narrowed her eyes further, comically exaggerating her concentration. At this point, Abbott was 99 percent of the way to driving off and marking the ride as canceled.

"You have trouble getting to sleep at night," she began, "because you can't turn off your brain. Usually it's replaying something stressful that happened in the past or rehearsing something stressful that could possibly happen in the future. You then have to down constant caffeine just to function through the day—I bet you've got one of those big energy drinks in the center console right now. You sometimes get really good ideas in the shower. You can't navigate even your own city without software that gives you turn-by-turn directions. You get an actual, physical sense of panic if you can't find your phone, even if you know it's still somewhere in your home."

She was rocking in her seat, rolling the trunk's tiny wheels back and forth, back and forth.

"You don't have a girlfriend or a boyfriend," she continued, before Abbott could interrupt. "You've never had a long-term relationship and, at least once in your life, you thought you were dating someone while the whole time *they* thought you were just friends. You actually don't have any close friends. Maybe you did when you were in school, but you don't keep in touch. You've replaced them with a whole bunch of internet acquaintances—maybe you're all members of the same fandom or a guild in a video game—but you'd be traumatized if any of them suddenly showed up at your front door unannounced. Sometimes, out of the blue, you'll physically cringe at something you said or did when you were a teenager. When you use porn, you may have to sort through two hundred pics or videos before you find one that will get you off. You're sure that humanity is doomed and feel like you were cursed to be born when you were. Am I close?"

Abbott had to take a moment to gather himself. Forcing a dismissive tone with all his might, he said, "Congratulations, you've just described everyone I know."

"Exactly. It describes everyone *you know*."

"I really do have to get back to work, I don't—"

"Don't get offended, please, none of that was intended as an insult. I'm only saying that I know you're an outsider, just like me! I think the universe brought us together. But I'm not done, because this is the big one: The reason you're hesitating to make this trip, even for a life-changing amount of money, isn't because you're worried that I'm a scammer or that my employer is a drug lord and this box is full of heroin. No, what you fear above all is *humiliation at the hands of the unfamiliar.* What if you get a flat tire on a highway in Tennessee, do you even know how to change it? What if we wind up the wrong lane at a toll road and the lady in the booth yells at you? What if you get a speeding ticket in Ohio, how do you even pay it? What if you get into a fender bender and the other driver is a big, scary guy who doesn't speak English? Then there's the absolutely *terrifying* prospect of spending dozens of hours in an enclosed space with some weird woman. What if you embarrass yourself? Or, worse, what if I say something that makes you embarrassed on my behalf? You'll have no mute or block button, just unfettered raw-dog, face-to-face contact, with no escape for days on end. What if I'm so unhinged that we literally have nothing to talk about, no shared jokes, no way to break the tension? What if, what if, what if—all of these scenarios that humanity deals with a billion times a day but that you find so terrifying that you wouldn't even risk them for a hundred and fifty thousand dollars in cash. So the question is: Would you do it for two hundred?"

She fished out a fourth hunk of bills. The escalating amounts actually didn't make an impression on Abbott; at this point, the dollar figures all registered as equally impossible sums of money. But the hand that held the cash was trembling and he sensed the thrum of desperation inside the woman, the vibe of one who has exhausted every reasonable option and is now trying the stupid ones.

"A hundred now," she said, "and a hundred after we arrive in DC. If you think it's a trick, that we'll get there and I'll steal back the money at knifepoint, we can swing by somewhere and you can drop off the first payment. You can even take it to your bank, let the teller do the counterfeit test on the bills. If we hurry."

"How do you know I wouldn't do that and then just refuse to drive you?"

"Because *I can see into your soul.* You would never do that. Not just because it's wrong, but because you'd be torn apart by the awkwardness of that conversation, of having to see the look on my face when I found out you'd double-crossed me. Also, you'd soon realize that you wouldn't just be screwing me, but my employer. And even if he's not a criminal, you can guess that's probably a pretty bad idea. He could send guys in suits to your house to demand the money back and just think how awkward *that* would be."

Abbott heard himself say "Can I have time to think about it?" and knew that his automated avoidance mechanism had kicked in. He'd been developing this apparatus since his first day in kindergarten when the Smelly Girl had asked him to play with her and, in a panic, he'd had to come up with a plausible excuse not to (he told her his family's religion forbade touching plastic dinosaurs). These days, it was pure reflex: if an acquaintance invited him to trivia night at the bar, a ready-made, ironclad excuse would fly from his lips before he'd even given it a thought.

Sure, sometimes he'd find himself wondering if maybe he should be filtering these invitations before they were routed directly into the trash. Here, for example: on some level he knew this offer deserved more consideration. But his request for time wasn't about that, it was just one of the stock phrases he deployed to get to a safe distance where plans could be easily canceled via text or, even better, by simply avoiding that person for the rest of his life. Sure, this woman was in some kind of distress, but that would be no burden to him once she was out of sight—

"No, you can't have time to think about it," said the woman on the box. "I meant it when I said we have to leave right now. *Maybe* we can swing by your place to pack up some clothes and whatever medications you're on—you're on a few, right?—and to tell the parent or grandparent you live with that you'll be back late next week. But it has to be real quick, in and out."

"I can't even tell my dad where I'm going?"

"You'll tell him that a friend needs you to help with a job that pays a bundle, that it's being done on behalf of a celebrity and has to be kept quiet so the press doesn't sniff it out. And that it's nothing illegal. That's, like, ninety percent true. Or eighty percent. It's mostly true."

"Is your employer a celebrity?"

"He's not a movie star or anything, if you're trying to guess who he is. But your dad shouldn't question it." She waved a hand in the vague direction of Los Angeles. "Out there, you've probably got a hundred professional fixer types doing jobs like this as we speak."

"Then go find one of them. If you think I'm such a loser, what makes you think I can even get us there?"

"All right, enough of that." She stood and put on her lime-green sunglasses. "You don't even have your heart in it anymore. Come on, help me load the box, it's really heavy. We've been sitting out here too long and people are starting to stare."

In the coming days, many words would be spent speculating as to why Abbott had agreed to the trip. Was it the money? Or did he genuinely want to help this woman he'd never met? The truth was, not even Abbott himself knew. Maybe it was just that by the time she was lugging the box toward the rear of the Navigator, it'd have simply been too awkward to stop her.

Malört

Considering he was two hundred and seventy-five pounds, bald, covered in tattoos, and wearing mirrored sunglasses, Malort could have wound up with many nicknames. But, a drunken bet in a Milwaukee dive bar decades earlier had resulted in a bicep tattoo of a Jeppson's Malört bottle, the Chicago-area liquor so infamously bitter that the label featured a lengthy paragraph apologizing for the taste. His friends had all agreed the tattoo and nickname fit him, but never dared to explain their rationale in his presence. He did have to drop the little dots above the O in recent years as nobody knew how to add those in text messages.

The man they called Malort rolled up to find that the Apple Valley fire department had apparently arrived just in time to turn the shack in the desert from a smoldering ruin into a wet smoldering ruin. Only two and a half walls of the flimsy structure were still upright, exposing the charred interior like a diorama. It told a fairly simple story of a loner hiding from and/or rooting for the Apocalypse. From where he sat, there was no sign of the black box and he had a sinking feeling it was long gone.

He stepped out of his metallic red Buick Grand National and approached a young man whose build and face made him look like a kid who'd dressed up in his dad's helmet and turnout coat. He was hosing down the aftermath to cool the embers and looked like he would have a stroke if two thoughts appeared in his brain simultaneously. He noticed Malort and a beam of curiosity pierced his haze.

"This your property?" asked the kid.

It was a dumb question, thought Malort. The type of guy who sets up in a wilderness survival shack probably doesn't get around in a sparkly Buick that surely lists at least one pimp in its Carfax report. He took the dumbness of the question as a good sign. Instead of answering, Malort pulled out his phone and pointed the camera at the scene, acting like he had an important job to do. Generally, if you can project enough confidence and purpose, all the uncertain nerds of the world will just part like the Red Sea.

He stepped toward the smoldering structure with his phone and, without looking at the kid, grumbled, "Is there propane?"

"There was, it already popped, that's what blew out the sides here. The ruptured tank is on the floor, there's some kind of apparatus attached. Maybe a booby trap, or maybe they were trying to deep-fry a turkey? You ever seen one of those go wrong? Nightmare. So, uh, are you a friend? One of the neighbors?"

Malort peered into the half-standing structure from afar, trying to stay out of the hose splatter. The other firefighters hadn't seemed to register his presence, most of them distracted by the task of spraying down the landscape to keep stray sparks from triggering a brushfire.

"The strangest thing just happened," rumbled Malort. "You know the big house over the hill there, behind the fence with all the barbed wire? The crazy bastard who lived there owns all this, it's all his property. So, I was chasing an intruder through that house, then they went 'round a corner and vanished into thin air. I looked all around, saw neither hide nor hair of 'em. A few minutes later, I looked out the window and noticed the smoke over here."

"Oh, really?" said the kid, who didn't seem to understand what that had to do with this.

"Nobody dead in there, I take it?"

"No, sir. Looks to me like they either left the propane to blow on purpose or left it unattended on accident."

"So there's no corpse in *there,* but if you go over the hill and look in that house behind the barbed wire, you'll see the owner is dead on the floor of a workshop where he was making Lord-knows-what. Though I wouldn't advise poking your head in unless you've got a strong stomach. They'll have to identify him by his teeth and prints, considering the condition his face is in."

Malort studied the smoking remains of a bed, now just a blackened frame and springs. The morning sunlight and the spray of the hose was decorating the scene with a festive little rainbow.

"Is that true?" asked the kid, trying to piece together the implications. "Did you call it in?"

"I'm not much for callin' things in. Though you should tell your people to wear protective gear when they go over there. I don't know what the guy had in his shop, but there were homemade radiation warning signs on the door. You can decide for yourself whether a homemade radiation sign is scarier than an official one." Malort studied the shack's exposed ashy guts and asked, "Have you seen any sign of a road case? One of them black boxes with aluminum trim, about the size of a footlocker?"

"No, sir. I mean, we haven't dug around inside there, but I haven't seen anything like that. Hey, uh, Bomb and Arson are on their way, you should tell them about the dead body."

"Nobody has come to take anything from the scene?"

"Not since I been here. I didn't catch your name?"

"And nobody saw the occupant leave? Or what vehicle they were driving? Might have been a blue pickup."

"No, sir." The kid was glancing around now, presumably for someone senior to come to his rescue.

Malort zoomed in with his camera, focusing on the bit of intact wall at the foot of the bed. There was a schizoid scatter of pictures and drawings pinned to the wall, blackened and curled. The residue of a mind gone to batshit. He snapped a photo. He then studied the floor around the bed. . . .

"Point your hose away," growled Malort. "I'm gonna check somethin'."

He stomped toward the shack, kicked over the burned-out bed fame, and yanked away a waterlogged rug underneath. There it was: a hatch that opened with a metal ring.

"Huh," said the kid as Malort yanked the hatch open. "They got a basement?"

"They've got a tunnel and a bomb shelter. Follow it back a hundred yards or so and you'll wind up under that house behind the fence. It turned out my intruder didn't vanish, they slipped into a bedroom closet, climbed down a ladder, ran over, popped out here."

Then, thought Malort, they'd rigged it so he'd get a face full of propane tank shrapnel if he tried to follow.

The kid looked amazed. "Damn. Is this like a cartel operation? I have a buddy who said they busted a place that had tunnels running all through the neighborhood—"

"Sir!" shouted a new voice from behind the kid. "What's your business here?"

It was the older guy, coming to assert his authority. Malort tensed up. The dude was in his fifties or sixties but that only put him in the same range as himself. And you generally didn't want to tangle with a firefighter; they had muscles from hauling gear and bad attitudes from breathing toxic chemicals and remembering the screams of burning children.

"He's looking for a big box," said the kid. "He says the old guy who owns this land is dead over in that house behind the fence. And now he's found a secret tunnel under the Unabomber hut. And the house is radioactive, maybe."

"Who are you?" asked the older man, ignoring the kid completely.

Malort put his phone away. "I was just leavin'."

"No, you're not. I'm gonna need to see ID. Hey!"

Malort ignored him and made his way back to the Buick.

The senior fireman was talking into a radio now, hurrying to get himself between Malort and his car.

"You just wait right here."

He put a hand on Malort's chest. Malort stopped, looked slowly down at the gloved hand, then back up to meet the old guy's eyes. There he detected the same apprehension he'd seen on the faces of authority figures since his growth spurt in middle school. He decided that, if things continued to progress in this fashion, he would open with forearm blows to the head and then delegate the closing argument to his boots. No doubt the other firemen would try to jump in, but you can't waste your life worrying about stuff that's not gonna happen until thirty seconds from now.

"Everybody," announced Malort, "get out your phones and start recording, because if this old fuck doesn't get out of my way, what happens next should really be somethin' to see."

He balled his fists and his heart revved into another gear. As stimulants go, an early-morning ass-kicking was only a notch below speed. The old man gave him a perfunctory hard look and then backed down, allowing Malort to get behind the wheel of the Grand National unimpeded. The old man made a big show of photographing the license plate to save face.

As Malort backed up, he leaned out his window and said, "Never challenge a man in a Buick. He's got nothin' to lose."

As he headed back to the main road, he pulled up the pic of the shack's interior and zoomed in on the charred paranoia collage. Written on a handmade banner above the darkened scraps were three words:

THE FORBIDDEN NUMBERS

JASON PARGIN is the *New York Times* bestselling author of the John Dies at the End series as well as the award-winning *Zoey Ashe* novels. He previously published under the pseudonym David Wong. His essays at Cracked.com and other outlets have been enjoyed by tens of millions of readers around the world.